MW00830261

BOUND

BY

FATE

REALMS IN PERIL BOOK TWO

A. N. CAUDLE

Copyright © 2024 by A.N. Caudle

All rights reserved.

No portion of this publication may be reproduced, distributed, or transmitted in any form or by any means, including photocopying, recording, or other electronic or mechanical methods, without the prior written permission from the publisher or author, except as permitted by U.S. copyright law. For permission requests, contact ancaudle@ancaudle.com

The story, all names, characters, and incidents portrayed in this production are fictitious. No identification with actual persons (living or deceased), places, buildings, and products is intended or should be inferred.

Book Cover by Covers by Jules www.coversbyjules.crd.co

Maps by Cartographybird Maps & Eternal Geekery

Developmental and Line/Copy Edits by Noah Sky

Proofread by Jen at The Author Experience the-author-experience.com and Elyse at Phoenix Rising Literary

ISBN:

eBook: 979-8-9894445-3-3
Paperback: 979-8-9894445-4-0
Hardcover: 979-8-9894445-5-7

Content Information

Bound by Fate is a dark fantasy romance with some dark elements that may be triggering.
For a list of trigger warnings, please refer to my website at www.ancaudle.com/content-information
If you have any questions or concerns regarding this list, my DM's are always open or you can email me.

Your mental health matters.

THE
DRIFT
ISLANDS

JEHON

HELERIE

ULRIK

AHWEY
LAKE

TORX

NARH

GAOL

THE GREAT LANDS OF
TAERALIA

ORYN

VOARA

SAABHA

IHAB PASS

BORGARA

MIRREN

ATARA

RIYAH

BHARA

NAHALE
FOREST

ILREK

DUSAN

PLIYYA

THE DRIFT
ISLANDS

LUBLAD

SARAT ◉

KITALL ISLAND

S

THE GREAT LANDS OF
VANSERA

REFERENCE GUIDE

CHARACTERS

Kya: k-eye-uh
Malina: ma-leen-uh

Airo Drolvega: air-oh drol-vayg-uh
Aleksi: aal-lek-see
Arnesia: ar-neh-zee-uh
Asmen: as-men
Bavel: buh-vel
Brathir: bra-th-eer
Brynya: brin-ya
Cadoc: cad-ock
Coen: koh-in
Daciana: daa-she-aan-uh
Dainos: day-no's
Dego: day-go
Deres: dare-ess
Edmund: ed-muhnd
Enzo: ehn-zoh
Erix Samanya: ee-riks sah-maan-yuh
Fahmor: f-ah-more
Floria: floor-ee-uh
Hakoa: ha-koh-uh
Hanyo: haan-yo
Itham: ih-thaum
Jymar: juh-maar
Leysa: lay-suh

Ryker: riyk-er
Zalen: zay-lin

Alban: aal-bun
Alo: all-oh
Ander: ann-der
Arra: are-uh
Atrey: uh-tray
Belan Olad: be-lawn oh-lad
Brixey: bricks-ee
Cade: k-aid
Cazel: kaz-ill
Daegel: day-gull
Daxel: dax-ull
Delima Olad: dell-ee-muh oh-lad
Eamon: eh-mon
Ekatla: eh-kaat-la
Eraeya: e-ray-uh
Erryn: eh-rin
Fayeth: faith
Fyn: fin
Hamal: ha-maal
Hindella: hin-dell-uh
Jarna: jar-nuh
Kaiyana: k-eye-yon-uh
Kieran: k-ear-an

Lucar: loo-kar
Lyron Vika: lie-ron vic-uh
Makkor: maa-core
Moury: mawr-ee
Nascha: naash-uh
Niabi: nye-ah-bee
Njall: n-jaal
Odarum: oh-dar-um
Otoka: oh-toke-uh
Oya: oh-yaa
Paxtor: packs-tour
Penny: peh-nee
Qaala: kah-la
Rolim: row-lim
Sarn Taranth: sarn tare-anth
Seraye: sir-eye
Sora: sore-uh
Talum: tah-luum
Tarek: tar-eck
Theron: therr-un
Tsirra: t-seer-uh
Vicria: vik-ree-uh
Voron: voor-on
Zana: zaan-uh
Zeá: zay-uh

Lorotte: lore-aat
Luthon: looth-on
Maera Samanya: may-ruh sah-maan-yuh
Mavris: ma-vr-iss
Nephin: neh-feen
Nikan: ni-kaan
Nyla: nye-luh
Osar: oh-saar
Oveus: oh-vee-us
Paya: pie-yuh
Preya: pre-yuh
Rhona: row-nah
Riva: ree-vuh
Shalna: shal-nuh
Solana Samanya: sole-aan-uh sah-maan-yuh
Thane Taranth: thayn tare-anth
Trin: trinh
Umana: oo-mahn-uh
Von: v-on
Wayla: way-luh
Zareb: zair-ebb

WORTHY

KYA
Lady of Atara

RYKER
Lord of Oryn

DAINOS
Lord of Torx

ASMEN
Lady of Dusan

JYMAR
Lord of Gaol

VORON
Lord of Ulrik

TERMS

Beira: beer-uh
Dauði: d-auw-thee
Drehiri: dree-here-ee
Galadynia: gala-din-ee-uh
Heill: heel
Lurvinea: lure-vin-ee-uh
Nailu: nye-loo
Noavo: no-aav-oh
Raith: rayth
Skorn: s-corn
Tanganats: tang-uh-nats
Vord: v-ord

Braegia: bur-eh-gee-uh
Demid: dee-mid
Fylgjur: fil-g-yur
Glaev: g-lay-v
Horgor: horr-gore
Nagasai: naa-guh-sigh
Nex: necks
Onvera: on-ver-uh
Roav: rove
Tala: tall-uh
Vaavi: vaa-vee
Waalu: wah-loo

Places

Acalen: ah-kay-lin
Ahwey: ah-way
Bhara: baw-ruh
Damanthus: duh-man-thus
Dolta: dole-tah
Eckterre: ehk-tair
Halerie: ha-leer-ee
Igawa: e-gaa-wa
Ilrek: ill-rick
Ipara: e-par-uh
Kanth: can-thh
Liska: liss-kah
Mirren: meer-in
Myrrn: murn
Narh: naar
Pliyya: p-lee-uh
Riyah: ree-uh
Shara: shh-are-uh
Torx: torks
Ulrik: ole-rick
Vansera: van-sehr-uh
Voltaryn: vul-tar-in

Aedum: eh-dum
Atara: uh-tar-uh
Borgara: bore-gar-uh
Dichara: dic-are-uh
Dusan: due-saan
Gaol: gowl
Hylithria: hi-lith-ree-uh
Ihab: ee-haab
Innon: e-non
Jehon: jay-own
Kitall: kii-tall
Lublad: lub-lad
Morah: more-uh
Nahale: nah-ha-lay
Oryn: or-in
Rhaen: rayn
Saabha: sob-uh
Taeralia: terr-ay-lee-uh
Tyrnth: turn-th
Valle: vahl
Voara: voh-are-uh
Woltawa: wol-tah-wah

GODS

KLEIO (k-lee-oh)

GODDESS OF SILENCE
MOTHER OF ATARA

XAREUS (zarr-ee-us)

GOD OF CHAOS
FATHER OF ORYN

AYEN (eeh-yin)

GODDESS OF OBEDIENCE
MOTHER OF ULRIK

CETHAR (seth-are)

GOD OF NATURE
FATHER OF TORX

NOXELIA (nox-ee-lee-uh)

GODDESS OF DREAMS
MOTHER OF GAOL

UDON (oo-don)

GOD OF MISCHIEF
FATHER OF DUSAN

ODES (oh-dis)

GOD OF MERCY
THE FALLEN GOD

Prologue

Taeralia has suffered at our expense.

We did this.

The fighting may be done, but the peace is only temporary. Revenge has a fate of its own.

I will do what I must, no matter the sacrifice, because my silence has come to an end. I will not allow them to suffer any longer. It is our obligation to end the imbalance of her revenge.

Will you stand to wreak chaos with me? Or will you watch as I fall?

Chapter One

ZALEN

F ate was nothing to be feared. Not when it was something you made yourself. Not when you controlled it. Just like I controlled his.

The man dangling from the chains took his last strained breath. His blood pooled on the stone floor. As his body relaxed, a sickening crunch sounded as his shoulders snapped out of place from his contorted position—one specifically designed to inflict enough pain to keep him awake and alert. His arms twisted up behind him with a rattle of rusted chains.

In this room, I could release myself, the part I kept locked up inside me. When I brought my prey here to extract information from them, I shut out what little humanity I had left. And now that my last catch had finally given up what meager information he did have, I allowed him the mercy of death.

Shame it had to end so soon.

It was probably for the best. I had been here for hours, and I knew it had to be dark by now.

"Rydja." I cast the clearing spell with a wave of my hand—the pieces of skin, muscle, and blood on the floor and walls began to disappear. The body would remain. Someone else could deal with it—or let it rot in here for all I cared.

Spinning on my heel, I yanked the door of the Vord cell open and left the room. A waft of fresh air made me realize what a repugnant smell I had created in the chamber. Of all the events that happened in this room, the scent was the only part I detested.

There was only one scent I wanted. One so sweet and intoxicating it made a pleased shiver run down my spine just thinking about it.

My lips spread into a smile as I thought of my reward waiting for me. But that would come later. I would retire for the night—I would be nothing less than fully rested and prepared for the prey that awaited me tomorrow. I had one more hunt to complete. Then, I could have my reward.

My boot met with a face, one attached to the dark-haired man caught in the snare I had set this morning. And this annoying fuck wouldn't stop screaming.

I had tracked him through the woods from the south before catching up to him. It didn't take much more than a *svida* incantation before he was begging for the pain to stop and spilling that he was an informant from the Kingdom of Aedum, ordered to cross the Damanthus border to spy on us. But oddly, it took me more effort than it should have.

He held a palm against the eye I had kicked with my heel. "Please. I don't know what more you want, but I can get you money! King Erix will—"

I kicked him again.

King Erix Samanya of Aedum had a nasty habit of using defenseless humans as his pawns. He didn't care if they were caught and killed, and saw them as disposable. I despised his methods, despite how strategic they were. However, my job was to eliminate any threat to the Damanthus Kingdom, and this trespasser was just that.

"Kyrr," I hissed. But nothing happened. His annoying screams still pierced my ears. He should have been mute by now. My brows creased in confusion as I tried again, frustration pushing my magic harder. "Kyrr," I spat, and the sound of his choked cry finally came to a blissful stop as the spell took effect. I wasn't sure if it was my mind playing tricks on me—that my magic had seemed to struggle.

His eyes widened in disbelief as if I had cut off a limb. Which I would have no problem doing, but right now, I just needed him to be less problematic. I could finish him later.

I looked up to the sky, noting the position of the sun and re-alizing I was running short on time. I moved closer, crouching down in front of him as he scrambled back, then I reached out and grabbed his throat. Squeezing only hard enough to cut off *most* of his air supply.

I couldn't have him die on me just yet.

Leaning forward, I pressed my thumb to his head, just be-tween his eyes, being more forceful with the incantation, and muttered the sleeping spell, "Hvila."

His eyes closed, and he fell face down on the snow-covered ground.

That would keep him out until I reversed it.

Not hesitating, I released the snare, prying it from his bleed-ing leg, and deposited him on the back of my horse. I tied him to the saddle before climbing on and riding off through the trees, finally ready for my reward.

It had been several minutes of galloping through the forest before I had the unnatural urge to turn around and go back from where I came.

To ensure no one stumbled upon my little secret, I had cast a dissuasion spell around the perimeter of the clearing that deterred anyone from coming near. I circled around and placed the unconscious man behind one of the trees, hidden away, before turning to face the fabricated warning.

My horse hesitated but had been through this before and continued on.

Moving past the barrier, I came to what appeared to be a dense area of foliage, seemingly impassable. Another layer of artifice in order to protect what I valued most.

With an eager grin, I pushed through the conjured deception.

The quaint cottage came into view. It was also veiled with illusion, causing any persistent travelers to see a mass of impassable and treacherous vegetation. While the illusion was visible to me as well, all I had to do was simply walk through, and the clearing came into focus.

Just as I did, I caught a glimpse of a figure dashing through the forest. I quickly dismounted and pressed myself against the trunk of a tree.

Such a fool.

She was ignorant of my searching eyes. No sense of being watched by the very person who was deemed her enemy. This was the exact same situation that had gotten her into trouble in the first place.

Trouble with me.

I waited until she approached the cottage, glancing around before stepping inside. Then I smiled.

Finally.

This was my favorite part—the thrill swirling inside my gut as I quietly crossed the clearing to the structure and pushed open the wooden door. She spun on her heel, her blonde hair whipping behind her. That sweet scent I desired so much greeted me. Her breath caught as I came for her, and she squealed as I threw her over my shoulder.

Music to my ears.

I watched as Maera shuffled around the room, wearing nothing but my shirt. She was looking through the discarded clothes strewn across the floor from when we tore them off each other only hours before. Her luscious ass peeked out from below the hem every time she bent over, and I felt no shame in staring. I leaned back in the bed with my fingers laced behind my head and tracked her every movement with an insatiable hunger that would lead to the shirt finding its place on the floor again. The sheet pooling around my hips just barely covered my already returning erection.

If only we had more time.

"Are you going to help me or not?" Maera asked from over her shoulder. My eyes hadn't stopped roaming over her bare skin, wanting to feel it beneath my touch once more.

"I'd rather not. I quite like your current attire," I said. She turned to face me with a stern expression, yet her eyes flickered with enjoyment.

Maera bit her cheek in an unsuccessful attempt to hide her smile. She walked around the bed until she was beside me, looking down at the floor for her panties. I sat up, wrapped my arm around her waist, and pulled her on top of the bed. She gasped in delight, giggling as I climbed over her—the second-best sound ever to grace my ears. I'd get the first again in a few moments.

I pushed the shirt over her chest and kissed from her navel to between her breasts. I smiled against her skin at her half-assed attempt to wiggle out from under me.

If I could just get her to stay a little longer—

I grazed my lips across her nipple, flicking it with the tip of my tongue before languidly working my way to the other one. Her hands came up to my shoulders, and she dug her nails into the skin, letting out a quiet whimper of pleasure as I took her breast in my mouth while my fingers traveled down the curves of her body. I kneaded the soft flesh of her inner thighs, coaxing them to spread for me once again.

I could never get enough of her.

"Zalen…" she breathed. "I can't."

I released her breast from my mouth and looked up at her. My hands slid over her waist and up her arms to her wrists. Removing them from my shoulders, I pinned them above her head. She gasped when I pressed the tip of my cock to her wet cunt.

"Would you rather me hold you down so you don't have the choice?" I asked in a low voice.

Her eyes widened just a fraction, and I smirked. I knew exactly what excited her, having slowly learned over the years what she liked. I had helped her discover her true desires, without feeling ashamed of them. When we first met, she was embarrassed about exploring what she really wanted. It had taken time for her to reveal what little things made her insides flip with anticipation, to take her pleasure without hesitation.

My smirk quickly fell when that fiery thrill in her eyes dimmed, and she frowned. "I need to go. I don't want to, but I've already been here longer than I should have."

I closed my eyes and sighed. Releasing her wrists, I leaned down and rested my forehead on her chest. One day, we would have more time. One day, I would have more than a few hours to be in her presence, taking my time without worrying about each pained tick of the clock. One day. Soon...

"I know," I said quietly.

Maera brushed her nails through my hair before trailing them down toward my jaw. She lifted my head, encouraging me to look at her. And I did. I saw her. Every bit of her that no one else would.

I saw the anguish and sorrow, the guilt she held from being torn between what she truly desired and what her duty as an heiress demanded. I saw her beyond the crown she would one day wear. I saw through the facade she was forced to uphold, knowing she wanted more than the docile role she'd been bred into. To everyone else, she was quiet and reserved, just like she had been when I first met her in this clearing years ago. But deep down, hidden behind a lifetime of suppression, she had stolen moments of fiery passion.

I craved it. I wanted to unravel her—help her find more and more of that fierceness.

Lifting off her, I leaned forward and gave her a soft kiss on her full lips, swollen from our short time together. She smiled up at me, her eyes crinkling at the corners as I got off the bed.

Maera cleared her throat accusingly and held out her hand with a pointed look. "Hand it over."

I contemplated for a moment as I held the lacy undergarment in my hand. "I think I'll keep it."

9

"Is that so? And what would happen when the wind kicks up and the men back in Aedum get a show?" She crossed her arms and raised her brows.

My eyes narrowed. "I think we both know you would like that even less than I. Seeing as I would have to cut out their eyes for looking at you. Which would start a war between our Kingdoms. And isn't that what you've been trying to prevent these past few years?"

She rolled her eyes. "My father wouldn't go to war with Damanthus over a few dead men. He has more restraint than that."

I scoffed. "He'd go to war over an apple rolling to my side of the border. He's been looking for any excuse to wipe the Drolvega line from existence and take over the Damanthus Kingdom."

She huffed a sigh but didn't attempt to defend him. She knew I was right. That fucker has had it out for my Kingdom ever since he came into his crown.

But back to the matter at hand.

I reluctantly pulled her panties from beneath the sheets and handed them to her before standing at the side of the bed.

"Thank you," she said, grabbing them before I changed my mind, then hopped to the floor and slipped them on.

I rolled my eyes and growled with discontent, but began gathering my scattered, discarded clothing while I kept one eye on her, watching her for as long as I could. She tugged off my shirt and slipped into her sapphire-colored dress, bringing out the blue in her irises.

After we dressed, we tidied up the space so it would be ready when we returned. I took her hand in mine, placing a kiss to the almost imperceptible symbol I had scarred on her wrist. She put my matching scar to her lips before I led her from the bedroom and through the living space.

It was a small dwelling with only a single bedroom, a wash-room, a larger room with seating for the two of us, and a small kitchen area that was rarely used—most of our time spent here was in the bedroom. I had constructed the cottage three years ago once Maera and I had realized what we had between us was more than some simple attraction. So much more.

The wood of the porch creaked beneath my boots as we stepped out of our refuge. Glancing around for anything out of the ordinary, I took a deep breath, filling my lungs with the crisp air of the snow-covered forest surrounding us. The sun was descending over the treeline, casting deep shadows in the clearing.

Maera was right. It was time for her to leave. She would have to travel quickly over the border to avoid suspicion. Not to mention, I wouldn't have her going through the forest in the dark. Dangerous predators lurked within the trees and wouldn't think twice about snatching up a sweet little thing like her.

I would know.

I turned and pulled her against my chest. Her eyes turned up to mine, glistening as they always did when we were forced to part.

"I'll see you in three days, right?" she said softly, her hopeful smile betraying the heartbreaking sadness in her eyes.

I tried to hide my frown, wishing I didn't have to disappoint her. "I can't meet in three days." I flicked her nose playfully when her eyebrows pinched together. "But I can meet you in five."

"How come?"

"Because, love, sometimes I actually have to go hunting rather than just say I am." But I wished I could. If it were up to me, I'd never leave her side.

She pursed her lips. "Yeah," she drawled. "I'm betting by now everyone thinks you're a lousy hunter since you keep returning empty-handed. That, or they think you're going off to some brothel in a neighboring town since you smell like sex." She bit her bottom lip, and a blush crept across her cheeks.

I raised a brow. "You doubt my capabilities? I never return without a kill. I at least get something small on my way back but nothing like the bigger game that's expected of me. Big enough I actually need the time to track down." Whether or not she knew what I was truly hunting, I wasn't going to dampen the mood with the truth. "And just how close do you think I let others get? Certainly not close enough to smell me."

"You better not." She pinched my side, and I chuckled before kissing her forehead.

"Never. You're the only one I'll allow close enough to smell my sweaty, after-sex scent."

Maera giggled. At least I was able to get her to laugh, loosening the tension of the moment. She looked up to the sinking sun.

"You should go," I encouraged.

She nodded and lifted to her toes, kissing me one last time before her departure. The moment her sweet, soft lips touched mine, my hand came to the back of her head, tangling my fingers in her hair and deepening the kiss. My tongue swept out, and she opened her mouth, giving me one final taste. I desperately wanted to keep her there longer, but we both needed to return to our homes.

I broke away after the too-short moment and jutted my chin to the trees, a silent command for her to go. She gave a curt nod and squeezed my hand before turning to leave. I smacked her ass as she walked away, eliciting a crude gesture from her that had a grin pulling at my lips. My little witch grabbed her basket full of herbs from foraging—her own ruse for being here—before crossing the grass and disappearing into the trees.

"Soon, love. Soon, I won't have to watch you walk away. Soon, we'll never have to part again," I softly whispered, letting the wind carry my promise.

It was time for me to return as well, and with Maera gone, so was my gentle, loving demeanor.

My smile fell, and my eyes hardened as I went to the side of the cottage and retrieved my horse before riding west back to Kanth. Once I was past the barrier, I glanced behind me toward the cottage again, confirming everything still held in place.

Satisfied, I continued the trek through the forest, detouring slightly. It was only a few minutes' walk before I came upon the spot where I had left my spoils from my hunt on the way to the cottage a few hours ago. My captured prey remained unconscious and tied to the base of a tree. I pulled my horse to a stop and dismounted.

"Takaor," I said forcibly with a flourish of my hand, and the bindings vanished. I bent down to inspect closer.

The man looked to be around fifty of his short, human years. Magic users—comprised of male sorcerers and female witches—aged much more slowly. With only a few years between us, I looked half his age. The only identifiable difference between magic users and humans was our hair. Whether dark or nearly white, or even just a streak, magic users had some shade of blonde. All it took was one drop of human blood, and they were born with brown, black, or red hair—and no magical ability. Had he not trespassed into Damanthus, perhaps he could have continued into his old age. Unfortunately for him, he was found by a Vord, a hunter and guard of the Kingdom, and wouldn't see the next dawn.

I slung the man over the back of my horse and began trotting back to Kanth to complete my hunt.

An hour later, I had only just emerged from the forest when Thane and two other Vords rode up to meet me. I pulled my horse to a stop and eyed them suspiciously as they approached. No one came into this area. It was my assigned territory as a Vord to guard.

"Thane," I greeted. "Missed me so much you just couldn't wait for me to get back?"

He dismounted his horse and straightened with his arms crossed behind him, standing at attention. This wasn't an informal visit then. And the severe look on his face told me this wasn't a pleasant one, either.

"What's going on?" I pressed, keeping my tone firm and superior.

The other two, whose names I never cared to remember, glanced at each other warily. Thane took a heavy breath. "The King of Damanthus is dead."

Chapter Two

RYKER

"*Little gem?*" I reached for her through our bond. "*Kya?*"

Nothing. There was nothing there. The tether to her was fractured, broken. I had tried over and over and over again after she fell into the Rip, hoping she wasn't truly gone.

But she was.

The pain was unbearable. My soul felt as if it had been violently torn apart, and that feeling hadn't lessened. It was a constant ache in the depths of my very existence. It took everything in me not to scream while my heart tore itself apart from the weight of her absence.

I didn't know exactly what had happened at the time, but after Kya said goodbye, I felt our bond violently rupture, contorting into something unrecognizable. I had never known that kind of agony.

After flying non-stop from the moment I woke up in the cave, I had finally arrived at the small beach between the Rip and the sea to find Malina on her hands and knees at the edge of a small patch of Glaev. She looked almost dead, pale and weak, as she stared at an unconscious Nikan. Kya's magic continued to slowly eat the plagued land away toward the Rip's edge so Malina could get to her fellow Roav.

She barely glanced my way as I landed next to Nikan and lifted him from the small patch of cleared land. I flew him over the Glaev and laid him next to Malina, who scrambled along the ground to check him. His face was beaten and bruised, and didn't seem to be healing. He'd been here for two days, and small injuries like that should have healed by now.

He'd live. Malina would too. But my mate...

"Tell me what happened," I demanded in a voice dripping with lethality.

Malina didn't respond. With her unruly hair hanging around her face, she continued to stare down at Nikan, pointlessly fussing over his clothes. The distant look in her bloodshot, watery eyes told me she was in a state of shock. I didn't have time to push her past her grief so she could explain the events that occurred here.

Without hesitation, I entered her mind.

"Tell me what happened, Malina." I tried to sound more gentle rather than demanding, hoping that would entice her to answer me.

Still, she didn't respond. Her mind was filled with chaos and misery.

I went deeper, pushing further past the mayhem of her conscious thoughts. I rifled through her memories until I found what I was searching for.

Through her eyes, I watched as she awoke in the familiar room of Hakoa's barrack. I moved on, finding her arguing with him, Theron and Kya standing off behind her. Hakoa was angry and pleaded with her not to go, but she did anyway. Theron Traveled them to Dusan. Kya ordered him to leave and to ignore me.

She had orchestrated it...

I watched as Kya cleared the Glaev, creating a path for them between Atara and the Rip in order to get to the beach on the other side. As they hid behind boulders in search of Daegel. I watched as they fought against him. How Malina tried desperately to get to Nikan while simultaneously wielding her light—worrying over the Glaev eating its way to him. How Kya held Daegel off and used her energy in an attempt to create a path toward Nikan for Malina. Everything happened so fast, and Malina's mind was constantly torn between getting to Nikan and helping Kya. I watched as Daegel got his hands on Kya, holding her against him, as she pushed him back toward the Rip. Malina and Nikan shouted for Daegel to let her go. Kya screamed for Malina. The air left my lungs as Malina picked up the bow and a black-tipped arrow then drew it back. I watched through Malina's tear-blurred vision as Kya mouthed, "For them." I felt the shock as Malina begged Kya to reconsider, but she had to do it. The next second, the arrow pierced Kya's and Daegel's chests, and they fell into the Rip.

The last thing Kya had said to me was that she loved me. I hadn't even told her how much I loved her back. I was screaming, *pleading* with her, knowing she was choosing her fate, choosing to do what she thought was right—what she thought would save the realm. And I didn't tell her I loved her...

"I killed her," Malina whispered hoarsely. Her voice pulled me back from the dark, stained memories.

Movement made me reach up to my cheek, and I felt the wetness there. I pulled my fingers back to see tears clinging to them, not realizing they had fallen.

"I killed her," she said again, more sharply.

My eyes cut to her. Raw fury surged through me from the shattered bond. I had to hold myself back from tearing her to shreds for what she did. But it was Kya's fault—she told her to do it. Malina didn't want to do it. I had felt her heart breaking through her memory.

Malina was eerily still for a moment before her head snapped up to look at me.

"I killed her!"

I know. And I wish I didn't.

I stared at her for several moments, taking deep, steadying breaths and trying not to lash out. I knew she had to. I knew she didn't want to. But it took everything in me to not tear her apart where she stood for taking Kya away from me. I forced myself to hold back. Even with Kya gone, I knew she wouldn't have wanted me to harm her sister because of her choice.

"She asked you to," I said through gritted teeth.

Kya had left me. And that hurt worse than the splintering shards of our bond piercing my soul.

Malina held my stare but didn't say anything. I turned and walked away to the edge of the Rip, glaring down into the misty chasm that had consumed my wife. Glancing back at the Roav, I watched as Malina kept blankly staring at Nikan's unconscious body. I had learned all I needed to, and they didn't need to be here anymore.

"Will you answer me now?" I asked Theron with a calm I didn't feel.

He had ignored me for days—had left the realm and refused to answer my call, my pleas, as I begged him to take me to Kya. To save her.

The Spirit dragon appeared a moment later. His black scales, the same ones I shifted from him, shimmered in the dying light as he stood before me with his wings at his sides. At one point, I had feared his massive form, knowing I was but a mere speck in comparison, a single foot large enough to crush me completely. But that was a long time ago. Right now, *he* should fear me.

A cold rage flooded my veins, and I welcomed it. Bathing in the agony and fury that filled me, I unleashed it in the form of fire and shadows with a roar. The Spirit countered with his own fire, but only enough to keep the flames from his body. Not that I had expected to hurt him, but I was so angry I wanted to. I wanted to hurt anyone, *everyone*. I needed to inflict the pain I was feeling on others, no matter how wrong I knew it was. But I wouldn't.

I drew back my elements, still seething at my Guardian.

"Take them to Morah," I demanded, gesturing to Kya's brother and sister.

Theron didn't hesitate as he stepped over and touched Malina and Nikan with his nose, and they all disappeared. A few moments later, he returned alone.

I paced back and forth, glaring at him, fighting the urge to wreak havoc on the entire fucking world.

"Do you want to explain what the fuck your problem is?" I clipped.

"I did my duty," he snarled, making a show of his teeth.

"What duty? You led Kya to her demise—you brought her here. This is on you!" I made no attempt to hold back. I blamed him. This was just as much his fault as hers. If he hadn't brought her here in the first place—had consulted me or tried to warn me—none of this would have happened.

"Do not chastise me, Worthy." His jaws snapped with his words. *"My duty is to protect you, and I did so by keeping you away."*

"Fuck your protection. What about Kya?"

"I am not bound to her. I am bound to you. I am your Fylgjur," my Guardian growled.

"Exactly!" I screamed through our bond. *"You are bound to guard me from harm. What about my bond with her? It will drive me to the point of insanity. It will kill me. You allowed her, and our bond, to die. How is that protecting me?"* My hands balled into

fists, and I breathed heavily through my nose as I willed myself to remain in control.

"Did she?"

My eyes narrowed. *"Did she what?"*

"Did she die?" Theron articulated each word.

I froze. *"Are you saying she didn't?"*

He bent his horned head down, bringing his large, fire-filled eyes level with mine. *"You are her mate. You should know."*

After finding Malina and Nikan and sending them back to Morah, I spent days flying up and down the length of each side of the Rip, searching for Kya. I had gone to the towns nearby, desperately hopeful she had somehow emerged along the edge and was taken to a healer. Something. *Anything.*

I knew it was pointless. If she were here and unconscious, I would know. I would feel her, sense her. The bond would lead me to her. But I still couldn't help myself, and I needed to exhaust every possibility. Theron had to stop me from going into the Rip multiple times now. The bond, and beyond it, was driving me to madness to find her. To follow her.

Was she dead? How would I know? She was shot with a poisoned arrow—she should have died from that alone. Not to mention, the fact that she fell into the Rip, the grave of Odes—an endless, inescapable chasm.

Our bond was so maimed I hardly recognized it. And it didn't extend to her anymore. Rather than the continuous thread between us, it was frayed, spewing from the end like a river meeting the sea.

Yet, it *was* there. Which meant… She was alive. I gasped at a thought.

The Trial.

The Rip wasn't just a pit of death. During the last Trial, the Gods somehow Traveled the contestants to the Woltawa Forest. And if Kya hadn't died, then maybe she was somewhere else.

The scenario was too similar to ignore. Too familiar to the story I had heard so many times over and over no matter how unbelievable it seemed.

Perhaps he isn't crazy after all, and has been telling the truth all these years. All fifty of them.

"*Where do people go when they go into the Rip?*" I asked Theron.

"*Most die,*" he said.

"*But not all.*"

"*No. Not all.*"

"*Where do the rest go?*" I pressed with a tone of annoyance. Fucker just had to be less than helpful.

The dragon hesitated before responding. "*I do not know. The Rip is a void for Spirits, just as it is for mortals. What happens to them when they are there is unknown to Spirits, even to a Fylgjur such as myself.*"

I was stunned. Not just by the information, but also because I rarely heard him speak so much at one time. No one knew the Rip was anything other than a bottomless pit of death.

"*I can't feel her. Our bond… Where could she have gone that I can't sense her?*"

It wouldn't have been Hylithria. Though it was faint, I remember feeling our bond even when she was there during her Trial. It could have been the Woltawa Forest—I hadn't felt her there. Then again, her fate hadn't been sealed, and our bond wasn't enacted yet. Though some believe it's one of the Drift Islands, others think it isn't even in this realm. So it's possible.

"*Only the Gods know.*"

I didn't waste a moment as I lifted my head to the skies.

"Xareus," I called to the God who had chosen me. "I beg of you, come down. Interfere and take me to the mate you chose for me."

Nothing.

I tried again and again with each of the Gods: Udon, Cethar, Noxelia, and Ayen. All ignored my prayers. Even Kleio—silent as always.

Theron Traveled me back to the palace, which was almost fully restored by a team of terbis wielders when I returned. And it was empty. The refugees who used to fill the halls had been relocated to camps near the Noavo command station, and some were also placed in towns and villages throughout the Nation, distributing them where resources were available. I didn't know where the staff was, and I didn't care. I was in no position to speak to anyone in a civilized manner anyway.

I stormed down the corridor to my bedchamber, needing to rest before researching everything I could about broken mating bonds and the Rip. If that didn't work, I would leave for Dolta. If there was one person who could relate to this situation, it was my father.

I had barely slept since I woke up to find Kya missing, and I hadn't slept at all for the last few days. I stripped my filth-covered clothes and quickly bathed before returning to the bedchamber, where I found Mavris waiting for me.

I hadn't seen my brother since I abruptly left Oryn to rush to my mate.

"What?" I snapped, storming across the room to the wardrobe.

He flinched slightly but kept his face neutral. "Did you find Kya?"

"If I had found Kya, do you honestly think I'd be here without her?" I pulled out a set of clothes and put them on.

"Right." He pursed his lips and nodded warily. "Then what happened?"

I scoffed. I really didn't want to do this right now, but I knew he wouldn't leave me alone until I did. "Daegel took her."

His eyes widened. "Where?"

"I'm not in the fucking mood to play storyteller," I grumbled, turning my back on him to face the windows.

Memories of Kya's words and Malina's thoughts replayed over and over in my head. I didn't want to see them anymore. The constant nagging of 'what ifs' ate at me. What if I had woken up before she left? What if I went with her? What if I had stopped her? What if I had taken her place? What if...

The sensation of a hand on my shoulder snapped me out of my thoughts, but I was so on edge I startled when Mavris pressed again, asking what exactly happened.

Without warning, my overwhelming thoughts flooded into my brother's mind. The dam of my psyche burst, the overwhelming grief and confusion rushing through that connection to him. With nowhere else to go, the overpowering agony forcibly pushed into his mind, siphoning away from me to the nearest extension—my mind's way of keeping me sane.

My abilities grew to a level I had never consciously experienced before as I pressed Malina's memories into Mavris, showing him all I had learned. Never had I crossed the line of that kind of personal invasion before. Especially with someone I was close to.

My gift from Xareus was a curse I loathed and used as little as possible. At least I did when I used to care, however the only thing I cared about now was getting my mate back. I didn't bother trying to stop it.

Mavris stumbled back from the torrent of memories, gasping as his eyes darted unseeingly.

"Ryk…" He looked at me with horror and disbelief. "How are you even standing right now? They fell into the Rip. She's…"

In the blink of an eye, I had Mavris pinned to the wall with my shadows. I stalked my way over to him and stopped inches from his face.

"She's alive. And nobody will say otherwise." I released my hold on him, and he stepped away from the wall.

He could have used his blood-wielding to retaliate, but he didn't. As always, he was the more composed one. He didn't look at me with ire as I would have expected. Instead, it was sympathy and understanding. Pity.

I didn't need it, nor did I want it. I would have preferred he fought back so I could unleash some of my anger. Not that it would have helped. Nothing would. Not until I got Kya back.

I walked over to the restored floor-to-ceiling windows and gazed at the Eckterre mountains surrounding the Voara palace. Kya was supposed to be here with me.

But she left.

Not only did she leave me behind—going off alone rather than working with me—but she sacrificed herself, knowing what it would do to our bond. To me.

Had she known she'd go somewhere else? Or was she certain she was going to die? She had pushed herself into the Rip, ordered Malina to shoot her with the poisoned arrow. Seeing her tears through Malina's memories… She had been willing to die.

I braced a hand on the glass, resting my forehead against it, and closed my eyes.

She had had enough time to say goodbye. Enough time to think about her actions. She had known what she was doing.

"What happened to Nikan?" Mavris asked slowly. "And Malina?" he added.

I opened my eyes. "They're alive. I had Theron take them to Ilrek. Nikan is banged up, but he'll live, and Malina...I think her struggle is just beginning." When I turned around to face Mavris, he was shaking a perplexed look away, as if deciding not to voice whatever was on his mind.

"What are you going to do?" he asked.

I glanced over my shoulder at the darkening skies.

I would keep my promise. My little gem would not escape her shadow. No matter how damn hard she tried. Nothing would stop me.

"I'm going to tear the realms apart until I find her."

Chapter Three

MALINA

R yker's cranky lizard pet dumped us on Morah's doorstep without warning. I couldn't blame Ryker for sending us away and not coming with us to make sure we were alright. I wouldn't have even blamed him if he wanted to kill me.

He hated me. I saw it in his eyes when I told him. I hated me too. I had lost my sister, he had lost his mate. And I was responsible.

I killed her.

Yes, she had told me to. But that didn't stop the expanding hole of guilt. And when Ryker arrived, it all came crashing down on me like a violent wave in a storm. With each passing moment, I found myself drowning, sinking deeper and deeper until there was nothing left. I welcomed it, letting it consume me until I was nothing more than a hollow cavity.

I wanted to feel nothing—instead, I felt everything.

Nikan groaned as I leaned him against the dark, glass walls of Morah. I had already lost my sister, and I'd be damned if I let my brother die too. He was still injured and needed to be seen, but I couldn't lift his dense body. I rushed inside the Morah library and up to a couple of male Scholars sitting at a table close to the entrance.

"Von, Alban." Their heads snapped up, and their mouths widened into welcoming smiles. But I wasn't smiling, and their lips fell when they registered the seriousness on my face. "I need your help. Hurry," I clipped.

They bolted from their chairs, the wood scraping against the obsidian floor, and followed me outside to where Nikan's unconscious body lay.

"Malina, what happened?" Von, one of Morah's genealogists, said, running a worried hand through his auburn hair as he bent down to grab Nikan under his broad shoulders.

What happened… Two words that threatened to break me. I couldn't think about what happened. I couldn't let myself go there.

"Beaten." I gestured to Nikan. "He passed out last night and hasn't woken up since."

"You don't look too good yourself, Roav. When was the last time you slept?" Alban, one of the geneticists, said with a glint of concern in his brown eyes, grabbing Nikan's legs.

"I'm fine. Just help me get Nik to the healers."

I led the way to the second ring, and they followed while carrying my brother. My eyes were growing heavy. Blinking away the exhaustion, I focused solely on keeping my legs moving as we steadily made our way to the healers, stealing worried glances back at Nikan.

His injuries weren't recovering…

"So Mal, we think we discovered some…impurities in the Paya family line," Alban said.

I could tell he was just trying to strike up a conversation to distract me.

"Yeah! We're certain that three generations ago, when Trin married into the Paya family, she had some kind of affair and birthed someone else's child. We've got Brixey looking into those close to the family at the time. So risqué!" Von added.

It was baffling, really. Their excitement for something so mundane. Perspective mattered, I supposed. I never understood the importance of familial blood. I glanced back at Nikan as we approached the healers' ward. Anyone who saw us knew we shared no blood—his dark skin compared to my olive, and blue eyes to my brown. Nearly every visible characteristic was different, but we were still family. And so was Kya…

I blocked out the rest of their conversation. I knew I should be polite—they were helping me, helping Nikan—but I couldn't muster the energy to pay attention.

I opened the door to the ward and held it as Von and Alban came through and placed Nikan on one of the small beds. Two healers immediately came to tend to him. It was all I could muster to dismiss the Scholars with a nod of gratitude before I turned my attention back to the healers. They tended to him for several minutes, and my eyes glazed over while my mind started to involuntarily replay the events at the edge of the Rip.

"—miss?"

I blinked away my thoughts to find one of the healers standing in front of me with a concerned look on her face. I hadn't even noticed that she had approached me.

"What is it?"

"I'm Wayla. Can you tell me who the male is and how he was injured?" she asked, likely for the second time.

"His name is Nikan. I'm his sister, Malina. And I don't know exactly what happened. He lost consciousness last night after dusk." I wrapped my arms around myself and leaned my head to peer around her shoulder at Nikan.

She nodded. "Well, he's dehydrated. And from the looks of it, he's been assaulted."

"Will he be okay? Can you tell why he isn't healing properly?" I asked, trying to concentrate on her words and absorb what she was telling me.

"He'll be fine. The wounds *are* healing, just at a much slower rate than would be considered normal. I don't know why, but I'll find out soon. In the meantime, we're giving him nourishment and medicine to speed up his recovery." She gave a gentle smile. "He'll need to stay here for a day or two. You look like you could use some assistance as well. Do you want me to take a look?"

"No," I bit out. I didn't intend for that to come out so harshly, but I also couldn't be bothered to add anything else. I didn't deserve to be healed, not when my sister was—

"Alright," she agreed, sounding reluctant. "If you want to tell me where you're staying, I'll send word once he's awake or when we find some answers. Whichever comes first. Are you sure you don't want to rest here? If you're having trouble sleeping, I have some—"

"No," I said quickly. "I'll be at the Morah library. You can find me there." I turned to leave but stopped myself and went back to Nikan. Brushing my fingers through his tangle of curls that I always needed to comb out for him, I bent down and whispered, "I'll be back to check on you in the morning. Don't do anything stupid while I'm gone, alright?" I didn't know if he could hear me or not, but I wanted him to know I was there for him anyway—that he wasn't alone. Perhaps it was partly for me as well.

I kissed him on the head and left quickly, before I broke down entirely. It was dark when I emerged on the street and made my way back to Morah. Eamon wasn't waiting for me, so he likely hadn't heard of our return yet. If he had, I would have expected him to be standing just within the library's doors, or he wouldn't have been waiting at all and would have gone to the healers' ward himself.

But thank the Gods, he wasn't here. It was the only small mercy they gave me. I couldn't stomach seeing him. I couldn't have that conversation… Let him have one last night before I shattered his peace.

***

There was this moment between sleeping and waking where none of life's problems existed, and you were suspended in bliss. But it was only for a moment.

The thing I hated most about living in a giant piece of glass was that from dawn until dusk, the light was everywhere. And while the glass was tinted, it was still fucking bright when you were utterly exhausted and hadn't had enough sleep. I probably could have slept for days, if it wasn't for the stupid sun. Pair that with the incessant banging on my door, and my mood instantly soured.

If it were a few days before, I would have put in the effort to be bright and energetic—a mask I had mastered. As the weight of recent events threatened to swallow me whole, I didn't have the energy—or the desire—to keep it up. I was too concerned with keeping myself afloat.

I made my way out of the bedchamber and through the sitting room before opening the door just enough to peer through the crack.

Eamon stood on the other side with his fist raised, relief washing over his features upon seeing me.

"Malina, you're alright," he sighed, lowering his hand.

I couldn't look at him, instead averting my eyes to the door frame. "In a manner of speaking, sure."

"A healer from the ward came early this morning, before dawn. She informed me Nikan was injured and had been taken there last night, and he's awake. She was looking for you—"

"Is he okay? Has he healed?" I interrupted the High Scholar, snapping my head up to finally look at him and letting the door swing open farther. "Why didn't you come tell me sooner?"

"I came immediately, but you didn't answer. May I come in?" Eamon gestured to my sitting room.

I nodded and stepped aside, allowing him to enter before following and sitting across from him in one of the cushioned chairs with a wooden table between us.

"After you didn't answer, I went to see Nikan. He's...healing. Faster than he had been apparently, but still not as fast as normal," he said in his usual, gentle manner.

"That's... That's good," I mumbled, staring at the floor.

Eamon didn't say anything, but I could feel his eyes on me.

"Did they figure out why?" I asked after a minute or so. I didn't register how much time had passed, too lost in the cavernous hollow of myself, focused wholly on the deep void that choked the breath from my body, leaving me numb.

He hesitated for a moment. "Yes. But we need to speak with Nikan. He wants to discuss this with us both."

I gave a curt nod. "Just give me a minute to dress, and we can go." I stood, attempting to keep myself together for this, and began to walk back to my room.

"Malina, wait."

"I'll be right back—"

"He told me about Kya."

I froze in the doorway. A swell of debilitating emotions rippled through me, pinning me in place. Guilt, shame, fear, sorrow. My ears hummed as if I were underwater.

I was back at the Rip, the wood of the bow digging into the palm of my hand. The string thumping with the release of the arrow as the feather brushed against my cheek. Daegel's eyes wide with horror, Kya's lifted to the stars. Both of them falling.

I killed her.

31

"Malina." Eamon was standing in front of me with his hands on my shoulders. A single tear fell down his cheek. "You are not alright."

No, I wasn't alright. How could I be? It all crashed into me like a wave breaking against jagged cliffs. My heart had become vacant, pushing out all that would destroy me and shutting it away so I could function—barely. I wished I could have gone back to that feeling.

My chin trembled. "I ki—killed her." My voice broke. "I'm sorry. Eamon, I'm so sorry."

I collapsed against his chest with my hands cupped over my face. He wrapped his arms around me, stroking a hand down my loose hair. I sobbed as he held me, barely managing to gasp for breath.

"Child, you did no such thing. You saved her from what would have likely been a terrible end. She didn't have to suffer. You gave her the ability to choose to leave this world on her own terms, of her own volition. And," he pulled back, taking my face in his hands, "you allowed her to save you and Nikan and everyone else the Dark Wielder would have harmed."

But at what cost?

There was a ringing in my ears, muffling the world around me and trying to dim what little light I had left inside.

Was the sacrifice truly worth it for the greater good? Was there some other way Daegel could have been killed that didn't result in the loss of Kya as well? I couldn't help but think of all the ways things could have been different. Was that the only option at the time, or was it just what was easiest at that moment? I had replayed the events over and over again in my head, trying to think what could have been done differently—in what ways didn't result in her end.

The more I thought, the darker everything seemed.

I wiped away my tears and stepped back from him, gathering myself again. I didn't want to think about this anymore. I didn't want to feel it. No matter Eamon's words, the facts were still the same. Pushing away my internal torment, I turned my back on him and went into my room.

"We need to see Nik," I said flatly before shutting the door.

Chapter Four

KYA

This wasn't what I thought would happen. I thought I would die when I fell—when I took Daegel with me into the Rip and away from those I loved and cared about, those I vowed to protect.

When I went into the Rip, I thought I had died, assuming I was transitioning into the After. For a long while, I couldn't see anything, I couldn't feel anything.

And then I could.

My lids lifted as consciousness returned. I was lying face down in the dirt, my body still pierced by the poisoned arrow. Daegel's bellows of pain above me faintly registered through the fog in my head. Pressed against the ground, my lungs struggled for air, unable to expand fully with the weight of the dark wielder's body atop mine. Then the pain started.

The intensity was paralyzing. There was nothing I could do other than think that I would spend my last moments face down while my enemy howled in agony. At least he would die with me.

That was the only peace I had.

My vision wavered, and the next thing I knew, people were standing over me. I was flipped onto my back, and I could see the feathers from the arrow in my chest from the corner of my eye. Several people were attending to Daegel, and I saw wisps of color and light as they spoke, but I couldn't make out what they were doing or saying. I could feel the Onyx Kiss corrupting my veins toward my heart. I knew it wouldn't be long before it consumed me entirely.

I tried to move my arms—instinct driving me to pull out the arrow despite knowing that it was a pointless task—but I struggled to lift them, feeling as if they were weighted down. Perhaps I was weaker than I thought, most likely from using too much of my magic at the Rip while fighting and trying to save Nikan.

A female fell to her knees next to me and held my arms down, the additional pressure too heavy for me to fight against. Her eyes held a cold, malicious hatred as she stared down at me. I tried to speak, to tell her to kill Daegel and help me. But my lungs felt crushed, and I only managed a pathetic gasp in place of words.

I failed. I hadn't killed him. I hadn't saved anyone.

"Ryker. I messed up."

Silence.

"Ryker?"

Still, there was nothing.

"Gods, please, let Ryker be okay," I prayed.

A commotion occurred where Daegel was. I couldn't focus on what was being said over the pain and desperation to take a full breath. The female's head snapped in the direction of the dark wielder, who was screaming and pointing at me. When she turned her head back to me, her face was twisted into a sneer.

What did he say? Did he tell her to kill me? No. She doesn't understand, I was trying to stop him from destroying our realm—I was trying to save her, save everyone.

Where is Mal? She'll explain. He's the cause of the Glaev. I was only trying to stop him.

But I couldn't speak. I couldn't tell her any of my thoughts as she raised her hand and wrapped it around my throat. I couldn't warn her of the monster next to them as she poured something down my throat. My eyes locked with hers, pleading the words I couldn't speak.

"...let her die..." were the last words I heard before everything went dark.

I was certain I was dead this time. There was no pain.

As the fog cleared from my head, my senses started coming back. I cracked my eyes open to find nothing but darkness.

I'm definitely dead.

Or so I thought, until I felt the hard cushion I was lying on. I moved my hand, reaching out across the scratchy fabric until the tips of my fingers touched rough stone.

There was no light. No sounds. And...no terbis.

Pressing my hand down firmly against the stone floor, I willed my ability to feel vibrations. But I couldn't feel anything. I couldn't *do* anything.

My other gifts from Kleio, the ones she granted me after deeming me Worthy, held no value right now. Invisibility would be of no use and neither would my aligist magic to understand languages.

Waalu. I could use my energy magic from Odarum.

Though weak, I reached inside myself for that electrified orb of jade. I grasped it and felt nothing. It wasn't humming like it had been. It wasn't energized and glowing. It felt...dead. Even with Odarum's death, it wasn't tied to him. It was mine, a part of me. But it seemed as lifeless as my Spirit Guardian as I wrapped around it and felt nothing at all.

I searched for my other magic and found the same thing. The translucent orb of my invisibility and the orb with whispering tendrils were both lifeless, as if they were encased by something that blocked my access.

No tethers. No magic.

There was a buzzing in my head, and I instantly realized why. Just like those on the Drift Islands, my magic had been suppressed. And when a fae couldn't use their magic, their body—and their spirit—suffered.

All I could feel was the burning in my chest—the bond driving me to return to Ryker.

"What's happening?" My voice was a hoarse whisper, echoing off the stone surrounding me.

Sitting up used more exertion than usual. I ran my hands down my body. They had taken my weapons, my clothes, my shoes, and even the tie that held my braid, leaving my hair loose. Tracing along my bare chest, right over my heart, I felt some small scarring where the arrow had once been. They had to have healed me. Likely used a blood wielder to remove the poison, as Mavris once had. I was surprised they had enough time.

I continued feeling along my body. My hand reached down to my left wrist. A slight sense of relief filled me when I felt the metal of the marriage band.

"At least they couldn't take that from me." Still unbreakable and impenetrable.

I continued roaming my hands over my body up to my neck. Some kind of unexplainable ring curved around my throat. I only felt a whispering over the tender skin of my neck until

37

I touched it with my hand. It wasn't solid—not that I could tell at least—and felt somewhat pliant. It consisted of lines—lines moving in all directions as if they were alive—creating some kind of intricate design, like a necklace that hovered just above the skin from the bottom of my jaw to the base of my throat.

I reached for the bottom of it, curling my fingers through the small gap between it and my neck to pull it off. I winced as the underside seared my fingertips, and I quickly pulled my hand away.

The air rushed from my lungs. I had grasped it just long enough to feel what was wrapped around my throat. It wasn't a necklace.

"It's a collar…" I rasped into the darkness.

I snaked my hand up the wall until I was standing and the tips of my fingers brushed the ceiling. I walked along the walls, using my hand as a guide in the darkness until I reached the small cushion again. I felt walls all around me; it was some kind of small room, three strides wide from end to end. There was no door, no window. The floor, walls, and ceiling were all made of the same rocky material. I felt every inch, every nook and corners until my hands were raw from rubbing over the coarse stone, searching for any opening at all. Nothing. They—whoever they were—had thrown me in a fucking box with no way out.

I'm locked away, naked and collared, like an animal. But what's the point? Why did they leave me here to die when they had every opportunity to kill me before?

My entire body began to tremble. Sweat licked down my clammy skin, and my lungs heaved in short, rapid contractions. Stumbling back against the rough rock of the wall, I pressed my hand to my chest, feeling the erratic beat of my heart. And even though I couldn't see, it felt as if everything around me was closing in.

I was panicking.

I need to figure this out. I need to get out of here. I need to get back to Ryker.

But I couldn't breathe. I couldn't think. All rational, controlled thoughts evaded me as my mind spiraled into chaos.

Five minutes. I'll give myself five minutes to break down. Five minutes to lose control. I think the present circumstances warrant five minutes of panic, right?

As my chest heaved, I fully took stock of my situation. I was some kind of prisoner with no way out. No access to my magic or abilities. No connection to Ryker. Bound with a collar like a fucking pet. No food. No water—which would have been nice because it was so Godsdamn hot. No light. Nothing but my own thoughts.

I let the emotions run their course, spilling tears down my hot cheeks as I cradled my face in my hands, and my gasping sobs filled the silence of my prison. I counted in the dark, giving me something to concentrate on, something to ground me. And after five minutes, I stopped.

I refused to cower in the darkness for the rest of my life, no matter how long or short it may be. Attempting to calm my panic, I filled my lungs with deep, even breaths.

Slow down. Work it out. I've got to pull myself together.

Once my heart had slowed, I lowered to the floor—with a new-found resolve—sitting with my legs folded and placing my hands on the stone beneath me. I tried to use my terbis again to feel the rock surrounding me, searching for the smallest of vibrations in hopes I still had the ability I had been born with.

Nothing.

I still couldn't feel anything. I couldn't see anything and without my terbis, I felt blind in every way. There were no sounds except my own breaths.

Someone had put me here—likely Daegel or those with him.

"They don't want me dead," I whispered to myself.

Otherwise, they would have killed me or left me to die from the Onyx Kiss. They took the effort to heal me. But why? What do they want? And who are they? How do I get out of here?

I took a few more calming breaths.

What can I do? Okay, I don't have my terbis. I can't access my magic. Did they do that? What's the collar for? Maybe that has something to do with it?

I gasped when an idea came to me. Turning my back away from the wall, I faced it, wanting enough room. With a thought, I shifted my wings, feeling them protrude from my back. I instantly wished for the wind beneath them to carry me back to my husband. The familiar strain of my muscles was a welcome sensation as the weight of my wings hung in the darkness.

I could shift. Not the best idea in such a small space, and it wasn't particularly helpful to me at the moment, but perhaps it would come of use later.

I shifted them away. If someone came in here, I didn't want them to know I had that ability. If I could just get outside, I could shift them and fly back. But how would I get out?

They put me in here somehow, which meant that there was a way, and I would find it. I would dig my way out with my fingers until nothing was left but bone if I had to. I would get back to my mate. I thought of nothing else—only getting out of here and returning to Ryker. I just had to survive long enough to do so.

They could take my magic, my light, my basic needs. They could even try to take my sanity, but I refused to let them take my life.

I refused to be contained.

Chapter Five

ZALEN

Now I understood why my magic felt so difficult to use. With the King dead, the magic of his Kingdom—and subjects—had weakened. Magic users drew their power from their King—the more powerful the King, the more powerful the people. And when a King died, much of that power did too, leaving the Kingdom vulnerable until the next in line took the throne. Which was really inconvenient for me right now.

Slamming the doors open, I stormed my way into the Damanthus castle in Kanth. Thane and the two Vords that escorted me remained outside. The moment I crossed the threshold, guards flanked my sides. Sarn was standing in the foyer with his hands resting behind his back and a cold stare. As the counselor of the now-dead King during his entire reign, he was closer to him than anyone. Even myself.

"Take me to him," I demanded coldly.

He bowed at the waist then turned to lead the way as I followed. I expected him to take me up the stairs to the royal chambers, but instead, he headed in the direction of the throne room. He stopped in front of the wide double doors. I waved off the guards to leave us, and they moved to line up along the corridor.

"*You* found him?" I asked Sarn. My eyes were trained on the doors before me.

"Yes. It's a…gruesome sight, Zalen. Are you sure you want to see?"

I huffed. Of course, I did. I needed to see for myself what happened. I wasn't just going to take his word for it. Without a response, I pushed open the doors.

I sucked in a breath when I saw my father on his back, strewn across the steps in front of the throne. His skin was in ribbons—his lifeless body shredded, lying in a pool of blood that trickled down the marble steps. Crossing the room to get a closer look, I had to stop myself from gagging at the stench. Although Thane had said he'd only been dead for hours, he smelled of rot. I'd seen bodies decay—I knew how fast the process happened.

I knelt down to examine him, bracing my arms on my bent knees. I had never seen something like this. Sarn was right; it was gruesome.

"What happened?" I asked, feeling Sarn lingering in the doorway.

I wasn't sure if his apprehension was due to his dead King or my presence. We had never gotten along. In fact, I had hated him since I was a boy. For all the times he had falsely blamed me for things to get me punished, and his own cruel punishments for his son. I wanted to wring the fucker's neck with my bare hands. And now, there was little stopping me—and he knew it.

Sarn's shoes clacked against the marble floor as he approached. "I don't know. I found him like this and tried to identify the cause, but we've never seen anything like it before. This is something unknown."

"Hmm." I waved my hand over his body, mumbling the spell to reveal any incantations. But just as it was for Sarn, nothing came of it for me either.

"Zalen."

I looked up from the corpse.

"You'll need to make an announcement to the people. They're likely already aware if they have tried to use their magic," he said with a serious expression. "And preparations need to be made. You're going to—"

"I know what needs to be done, and it will be in sufficient time. Right now, we need to figure out who did this. The King didn't do this to himself. He was murdered, and I want to know by whom."

Damnit, this fucks up everything.

I snarled and abruptly stood, straightening my spine and raising my chin. I needed to get Sarn out of here. I needed to be alone and fast.

"Go assemble the Elders. They will handle the pyre while you oversee the preparations. We'll keep to tradition and have the funeral in seven days. A preservation spell won't last longer than that."

"Understood," he said with a stiff bow of his head. Regardless of his thoughts about my position, at least he still had the good sense to respect it. He'd be a fool to do otherwise. "And I would also suggest—"

"As counselor to a dead King, your words are as useful as his lifeless body." I stepped closer to him.

His lips pursed, holding back whatever remark rested on his tongue.

"I'm granting you the courtesy of being involved with King Airo's pyre, but only as a reward for your loyalty to him. Don't mistake my kindness as a lapse of judgment for your fate here. You knew this was coming. You made sure of it."

He averted his eyes with a sneer on his face.

I leaned in close. "Finish your duty, then get the fuck out of my Kingdom."

I wanted him gone, but it would look better if he were present for the funeral. Not that I cared for appearances, but I needed the Elders on my side, and they *did* care for appearances. Out of respect for my father, I'd let him live.

Sarn spun on his heel and quickly left the throne room, shutting the double doors behind him. Now that I was alone, I could do what needed to be done.

Finally.

I went back to the body, kneeling down beside King Airo, and trailed my eyes over him. King or not, I had little respect for him. Externally, I had been the epitome of a devoted subject. But in truth, he was a bastard, and I wasn't upset that he was dead. Not even a little. I was just disappointed that it happened sooner than I had planned, and that I wasn't the one to do it. Whoever had killed him had done me a favor, and I wanted to know why. And who. If they had the capability to do this to Makkor, then they were a threat.

Makkor—King Airo's magical title, and ultimately his power—was granted the magic of the Damanthus Kingdom after completing the ritual of Kings, the Drehiri. But even dead, his magic remained. I wasn't about to let it burn away with his body.

Just remember what you learned from the texts, I told myself as I lifted my hand.

Holding my palm just over his chest, I closed my eyes and recalled the dark spell needed to forcibly absorb his power. "Stela."

I didn't know if it would work. It was a dark spell I had learned from an ancient book—a book that went missing after I told my father, likely hidden or destroyed to prevent me from using it against him. Which *was* my intention.

Bastard.

I hissed as my hand began to sting, and opened my eyes. I could see his power stretching out from his body, being drawn into my palm and forging itself with my blood. It wouldn't be much, seeing as he's been dead for some time, and from what I studied about this process, the power would be much weaker for me than it was for him. But it was still more than I had before. Had things gone the way I planned, I would have had even more if I were present at his death. I supposed that meant I had to adjust my strategy a bit.

I would be stronger than him—I would make damn sure of it.

It only took a minute for what remained of Makkor's power to transfer to me. He had never deserved the title, and now it didn't mean anything. Now, he was just a dead King. About fucking time. He never deserved it.

As the heir to Damanthus, I now possessed enough magic to strengthen the Kingdom, so we weren't so damn vulnerable until my ritual. Or until I gained even *more* power.

Standing and turning on my heel, I shoved my red and irritated hand into my pocket, not wanting anyone to see, and left the throne room without looking back. Thane was waiting just outside the doors. I closed them behind me and approached him.

"Zalen," he said with a slight bow of his head. With a tight expression, he looked me up and down.

"Thane." I didn't return the bow. "Follow me."

I led the way to the eastern wing of the castle and up to my private study. The entire eastern wing belonged to me, while the western wing was for the late King—my late father. My mother died when I was young. My father had told everyone that she passed from an illness too virulent to be cured, even with the best potions the witches could brew. But the truth was that he killed her himself in a fit of rage, only to find out that the adultery he had believed her guilty of was a false accusation. Just another reason I had wanted the fucker dead.

I walked over and sat behind my desk. Thane sat in the chair across from me.

"Close the door," I commanded, testing to see if the magic had been restored to others and not just myself.

He rolled his eyes and flicked his hand toward the door. "Luka." The door slammed shut and the side of my mouth briefly twitched up as his spell worked, confirming the power transfer was successful. "Feeling bossy already?"

"Just keeping up appearances in case anyone overhears," I muttered, keeping the information about the magic to myself. I'd tell him later. I told him just about everything.

Thane and I grew up together. With his father, Sarn, being the counselor to King Airo, we have been near each other nearly our entire lives. It was inevitable that we became friends, but we quickly bonded over our shared hatred for our fathers.

"What happened?" he asked, leaning back in his chair.

"You didn't see him?"

Thane shook his head. "No. Sarn told me, but I never actually saw Makkor." Thane detested his father so much that he only ever referred to him by his name, never verbally acknowledging their relationship.

I blew out a breath. "I don't know. It was some kind of spell I've never seen, and neither Sarn nor I were able to determine what it was."

I wondered if it was the same form of magic I had used to steal his power, but even that should have been revealed.

"Do you want me to cast one on his body? You aren't exactly the best with them." It wasn't an insult, just the truth.

"I can read a detection spell just fine. Nothing came of it. As if it wasn't even magic that did it, but those weren't injuries that could have been caused by any weapon." I ran a hand down my face.

Thane leaned closer, his elbows resting on his knees. "And you didn't do it?" he whispered.

"If I had killed him, it wouldn't have been such a statement. I would have done it more discreetly. This felt like a message."

"Yeah, but if you didn't do it, then who did? No one in the Kingdom is powerful enough to kill Makkor."

He was right. Makkor was the most powerful sorcerer in Damanthus. But that didn't mean he was the most powerful one in the world. There were still a few who could have killed him. But very few.

I went ahead and told Thane about the dark spell I had used on my father's body, explaining that was why his magic wasn't as weak anymore. He didn't seem all that surprised, which wasn't unexpected with his nonchalant personality.

"I need to speak with Osar," I began after my explanation. "The borders need to be maintained. No one in or out."

Thane's eyebrows creased. "Are you afraid the killer is still here or that they will come back? You know who is the most likely suspect. He's had it out for Damanthus since the beginning of his reign."

It was possible. Even the most probable…

"I don't know. And I need to speak with the Elders after."

Then I needed to find a way to talk to Maera. If the Elders came to the same conclusion we had, then my response would put her in harm's way. If King Erix was really responsible—if he truly was that powerful—then I had it in for myself. There were only two possible outcomes: either I succeeded and gained even more power as I intended, or I failed. And that wasn't a fucking option.

I crossed my arms over my chest and leaned my head back, looking up at the stone ceiling. "Are you ready for this?" I asked quietly.

"To have my life turned upside down or to change the fate of the entire Kingdom?" I glanced over at him. He shrugged his shoulders. "A bit sooner than expected, but yeah, I'm ready."

I raised my head and nodded. "Good. Because I have a feeling it's about to be much bigger than we anticipated."

"Zalen, you're about to be King and whatever other title you gain from the Drehiri. How much bigger can it get?"

A malicious smile crossed my lips. "Use your imagination."

After strategizing with Thane about possible upcoming scenarios, we left and went to the Vord headquarters to speak with the Head of the Vord, Osar. Regardless of my position as Prince, Osar outranked me as a Vord, and he had no problem flaunting it every chance he could.

He was about to regret every time he took advantage of his superiority.

"How are we playing this?" Thane asked as we approached.

"I'm done playing. It's time he learned his place." Osar was standing on the balcony, watching over the Vord training. "Osar," I greeted.

Osar turned around and rolled his eyes upon seeing me. "What do you want?"

"I'm glad you asked," I said smugly. "In light of recent events, I need you to deploy as many Vord to the borders, effective immediately."

"Nice try, Zalen. Take your dog and get your ass back down there and do your job with the rest of them." He pointed to Thane and nodded his head to the barracks below.

Thane snorted a laugh.

"Oh, I *am* doing my job, Osar," I smirked. "Now, I'll ask nicely one more time: get the Vord to the border by morning. And for being a prick, you will be joining them."

"I'd watch your tongue if I were you. Regardless of your blood, I'm still Head of the Vord, and you answer to me."

So he doesn't know the King is dead yet.

"And if I were you, I'd reconsider my words." I walked over to the railing and looked down at the training. So many times I had watched him watching me, forcing the other soldiers to go harder on me just because he hoped to break me before I became his ruler.

"And why is that? Because you're a pompous brat?"

The side of my mouth curved up. "Because," I leaned closer and lowered my voice, "soon, I'll be going through the royal ritual and be sworn in as your King."

Osar sucked in a breath, and I could see the color drain from his face. "King Airo—"

"Is dead." I turned to face him fully and tilted my head up to look down my nose. He wasn't so cocky now. And just to make sure he knew it, I flicked my hand at him. "Kyrr," I muttered.

Osar's eyes widened, and he opened his mouth to speak—but nothing came out. It took little effort to cast the spell. I hid my amazement at my enhanced power but internally relished the feeling.

"Makkor was murdered last night. Likely by someone outside our borders, but they could still be within Damanthus. So you will get the Vord to stop all traffic from entering or leaving the Kingdom, or you will forfeit your title. Or your life." I shrugged. "Personally, I prefer the latter, but I don't have a replacement, so I won't kill you just yet."

With a sneer he spun on his heel to leave but stopped himself and turned back around, pointing to his throat.

"He can't exactly order his men with no voice," Thane said pointedly.

"Shame. I like him better this way." I released the spell, and Osar growled with discontent before leaving.

I watched after him. He would become a problem, but it was something I'd deal with later. For now, I had more pressing matters.

"I'm thinking Makkor's funeral should be memorable. An event that no one will ever forget," I said as I turned to Thane, now leaning against the railing with his arms crossed over his chest.

He raised his eyebrows. "Risky. Given that it's already going to be a busy night."

The side of my mouth twitched up but not quite into a smile. "Exactly. If you're going to make a show of force, make it so everyone can see."

Chapter Six

KYA

I think I was mistaken. They did want me dead. They were starving me and depriving me of water.

After what I had assumed was the second day, I began to seriously worry. I yelled and screamed so much my voice scraped across my tongue, then I slammed my fists into the walls over and over until they were bloody and raw. Sweat clung to my skin from the high temperature, and I was quickly becoming dehydrated. By the fourth day, I had become so desperate for water that I drank my own urine, gagging down only as much as necessary and trying to keep myself from vomiting all over the hot floor.

I counted as much as I could in an attempt to measure the days that passed. I knew I could last three or four days without food from missions as a Roav before I became weak from hunger. My best guess was it had been at least five days now, and I made slices along my calf to keep track. Running my fingers over the faint scars, I took a rock that had chipped off the floor and made another cut.

Six.

I had barely slept, fearful someone would return and I'd be at an even greater disadvantage. Not to mention, I didn't want to see what waited behind my eyes. But I was so damn tired.

"Ryker..." I whispered in the darkness.

I wished for his presence, even for the feel of him through the bond. It was tearing me apart and worse than starvation or thirst.

I wanted to remain strong. I wanted to be ready for whenever someone would come so I could fight my way out of here. But I doubted they would. And even if they did, I was too weak to do anything. I couldn't even summon the strength to sit up.

Maybe I should just sleep. Maybe I should just stop counting. Maybe I should just...stop.

It would have been easier.

At the sound of a loud clank, my eyes snapped open. It was the first sound I had heard, besides myself, since I was put in here. In the next second I was weightless, floating in the air above the floor for just a moment, before slamming into the ceiling face first.

"Shit!" I didn't even have time to raise my hand to my face before I fell back down and crashed against the hard, unforgiving floor.

The impact knocked the wind out of my lungs, and I couldn't breathe. Something was trickling down my throbbing face. I gasped, only to suck down the blood that had pooled in my mouth, causing me to choke.

I rolled to my side, spitting and hacking onto the stone until I could finally take a breath. Raising a shaky hand to my face, I whimpered, feeling the blood there but unsure where it was coming from. I didn't know what the fuck had just happened, and my mind was too disoriented to think about it. Curling my legs to my chest, I held my face in my hands and tried to calm my heaving breaths.

After what was likely only a few minutes, I heard what sounded like stone cracking in front of me. Perhaps whatever had happened had broken the cell. A flame of hope ignited in my gut.

I scrambled to my hands and knees, crawling through the darkness to the wall. But, before I could reach it, the wall split, and blinding light flooded my prison.

I screamed as it found my eyes, having not been exposed to light for days. Or at least, I tried to scream. It was more of a garbled moan as I shrunk back from the light, throwing my arms over my face. I never thought I'd wish to have darkness again. I collapsed against the other wall, no matter how much I told myself not to, and faced away from the opening, cowering in the corner.

I wished for Ryker and his shadows to smother me in its soothing darkness.

My ears were ringing. Between slamming my head on the stone, the deafening crack of the walls, and the piercing light, my senses were completely overwhelmed.

Footsteps sounded behind me and I knew someone else had entered the cell. I barely had time to register the large hands wrapping around my ankles before I was being yanked backward from my confinement. I let out an animalistic cry as my body was dragged across the jagged rock.

I tried to kick, but the grip was unyielding. The moment I removed my arms from my face to reach forward to grab the hands, I immediately regretted it. The light hurt too fucking much. I covered my face again.

For the first time, I was grateful my stone enclosure was small, because it meant a shorter distance that my body was scraped against rough stone. The texture of the ground changed, becoming smooth and cool. A welcome feeling from the coarse, hot box I had been trapped in for days.

I could feel tears leaking from my eyes against my palms. I wanted to scream. To fight. To do anything other than just let it happen, but my body didn't belong to me anymore. I was barely managing to keep my head off the ground, nevermind fighting off whoever was dragging me.

I felt the chill of wind against my bare skin. I hadn't felt wind in days, and it brought a lungful of fresh air. I took it in deep, feeling as if my life was being restored. I felt soft grass beneath me, and I could smell wild vegetation all around. Everything was so different and welcoming compared to the environment I had been cooped up in for days. I relished in it even as I was being dragged away.

Eventually, we came to an abrupt stop, and my legs were released, dropping to the ground. From the grumbling voice at my feet, I assumed whoever had dragged me here was male. I tensed, not knowing what he wanted, but aware I was naked and practically defenseless. I only felt a small sense of relief when I heard the sound of footsteps retreating. I curled into myself, pulling my knees up and hunching over to try to hide my body and keep my eyes away from the brightness of the outside world.

With my face buried between the blades of grass, the scent of soil filled my nostrils. I removed my hands from my face, slowly lifting my eyelids until they were fully open.

Subtly turning my head, I saw two figures out of the corner of my eye. I assumed one was the male that brought me out here. He was broad, wearing dark clothes and boots, with long blond hair tied behind his head. He was talking with someone shrouded in strange red robes with only a small gap for their eyes.

They were standing off to the side, and I couldn't make out what they were saying. By the sound of his tone, the male seemed to be getting frustrated, and they both turned to face something he was gesturing to.

They're distracted.

I didn't know where I was. I didn't know what I would do. But I knew that this was my only chance to try to run as far as I could. Find a way back.

My mate.

It was all I could think about.

Taking quick note of the landscape, I spotted trees in the distance, deciding that was my mark. The patch of forest looked large enough that I could find a way to conceal myself long enough to lose anyone who followed. If I could make it to the trees, I could hide until I figured out what to do.

I felt my stomach twist, knowing this was a stupid idea but not willing to miss the opportunity to get far, far away. I took a deep breath and jumped to my feet.

Then I ran.

My feet slapped against the ground as I thrust myself across the field. I stumbled, my legs feeling heavy and tired from lack of use, but I pushed through it. I pleaded with my body to cooperate—I could rest and recover later. I just had to get to the trees which seemed so far away. My lungs burned from the exertion even after just a few moments, and the chill of the wind against my bare body reminded me of how utterly exposed I was.

Then I heard a shout from behind me, and I knew I had been noticed. I could hear his heavy steps coming toward me. And fast.

No no no.

I was still far from the treeline, and he was gaining on me quicker than I was getting away. I wasn't going to make it. Fear coursed through me.

It has to be now.

Afraid of the repercussions of being caught, I exerted more strength than I knew I had, and I tried to shift my wings. I felt them make an attempt to emerge, but they didn't.

Come on. Come on!

But it wasn't enough. I was too weak.

A voice roared behind me, and the next thing I knew, a body crashed against me and slammed me to the ground.

"No!" I screamed, and once I started, once I finally found my voice, I couldn't stop. I was so close, so close to freedom, I couldn't lose it now—

I kicked and thrashed, my body being crushed under the weight of the male. I clawed at the dirt, trying to get away, but his leg was pinning my calves. I threw my elbow back, trying to catch him in the face, but he caught it in his hand.

"Get off of me!"

He grunted something I didn't understand. I kicked harder and kept trying to free my arm and hit him. My struggling was futile, but I managed to scratch his face, causing him to hiss as his blood leaked from beneath my nails.

He grabbed a fistful of my hair and shoved my face down on the ground, hard. My screams were muffled as he held my head firm against the dirt and lifted off of me. Then, he yanked me up after him, and I cried out.

My hands went straight to his as I tried to pry his fingers apart, desperate to free myself from his grasp and the pain on my scalp.

He shouted in my ear, and it was the first time I got a look at him, but I was too concerned with being dangled by my hair—my feet no longer touching the ground.

I didn't care what he was saying—even if I had been able to understand it. He could go fuck himself. I spit in his face, which angered him further, and I regretted it the moment he pulled his free arm back and drove his fist into my face.

Over and over.

The most I could summon of a scream were garbled moans that sounded unnatural.

My body went limp, and if it wasn't for his tight grip on my hair, my head would have lolled back. I tasted the blood in my mouth, and I was certain my teeth were cracked. My jaw felt like it might have been broken. Everything hurt, but he wasn't done. My ears were ringing, and I still couldn't make out the words he spat at me just before he drove his knee into my stomach.

My legs buckled and I gasped for air, aspirating my own blood and praying to Kleio that it would end.

Mercifully, he stopped.

Perhaps my Goddess was listening.

He jerked my head back, forcing me to look up at him. He had a cold expression, like beating a weakened and naked female didn't phase him at all. I took in his face—every line, every curve. Etching it into my memory. The face of a despicable creature with a voice that grated my ears. Eyes the color of a horrendous and noxious river, eager to swallow me in its depths.

I would never forget who I was coming back for later.

But for now, he had me.

He let go of my hair, and I slumped to the ground, unable to muster up the strength to stand. Then he hoisted me up and slung me over his shoulder. From the short walk back, I knew I hadn't made it far, and it only confirmed just how idiotic my attempt was in this state.

Without warning or care, he dropped me face first onto the hard, unforgiving ground, and I grunted from the impact.

I didn't even know who he was or even *where* I was.

I lifted my head slightly, getting a better view of my surroundings. Everything was bathed in warm, dim light. It was like nothing I had ever seen.

I was in a field of luscious green grass, with a small body of water in front of me and mountains off in the distance. But it wasn't the field, or the water, or the mountains that took my breath and dropped my jaw. It was the moon behind it.

Encompassing the entirety of the sky before me, a moon—a magnificent blend of every shade of blue and purple curling across its breathtaking surface—filled my vision and momentarily captivated me. I glanced from left to right, taking in its massive size, and could just see the edges of the circumference, craning my neck up to see the top of the curve.

After seeing nothing for days, gazing at the greatest wonder I had ever seen was overwhelming. It was so unlike anything I had ever known, so different from the two moons I was accustomed to—a singular celestial sphere without a story of two Spirits who became the moons of my world.

The thought of those moons brought me back to reality.

This isn't Taeralia.

Chapter Seven

MALINA

I was in a daze as I walked from Morah to the healers' ward. I hardly had any recollection of getting there until Eamon and I stepped into a private room, and I saw Nikan. I had never seen someone bandaged like that before. We generally healed fast enough that it wasn't required unless the wounds were severe and life-threatening.

It was the look he gave me that threatened to topple me over the edge again. A look of understanding. I wondered if he would ever look at me like he did before...

"Eamon," Nikan greeted.

Eamon lowered his head in return.

"Mal," Nikan said softly as I sat on the edge of the small bed and took his hand in mine. "You're alright?"

I gave a shallow nod. "I should be asking you."

His lips flattened, and he had a solemn look in his eyes. "I'll be fine. I'm...healing."

I looked to Eamon who gave me a nod, confirmation to discuss what we came here for. "But why is it so slow, Nik?"

He stared at me for a moment. "Close the door."

Eamon walked over and did so, giving us privacy from the bustling in the main room of the ward, then sat in a chair against the cream-colored wall.

"The reason may have to do with Daegel," Nikan started.

I stiffened at his name.

"On my way here from when we captured Vicria in Bhara, he took me. When he had me, he threatened your and Kya's life." He started removing the bandages around his torso, and I could see the dark color of the bruising beneath the fabric. "My attacks were pointless—he overpowered me easily. So, I began pleading. And ultimately, I… I made a deal with him."

I felt the blood drain from my face at the same time he finished removing the wrappings across his chest, revealing a black spot in the center.

Just like Vicria's.

My lips parted in a silent gasp.

It looked like an ink blot that spanned from one side of his chest to the other and from his collarbone to the top of his abdomen—a ghastly mark upon his dark skin. All of it was outlined in red, which was different from what I had seen before.

"What is that?" I asked with abhorrence, though I already knew.

"The deal," he said plainly.

"He did this to you?" Eamon asked, rising from his chair and coming closer to inspect it.

Nikan blew out a breath. "Partly him. Partly me. It's some kind of dark, magical bargain."

"Nik… Vicria had this same mark. She made a deal with Daegel too. It killed her when she broke it. Do you know what that means?"

"I—" he started, but I didn't let him finish.

"It means that whatever bargain you made your life depends on it now. If you break it, you'll die. It's not just a *deal*, it's a curse." My voice was growing louder, fear and anger taking over. All I could think about was if I lost him too, I'd truly be alone. "What was the deal?"

He held my stare—his eyes expressionless.

I stood abruptly, stepping closer to him and shouting, "What was the deal?

"The deal was that he spared your lives, and in return, I would help him find a diamond. Once he got it, I'd be released from the deal, and he wouldn't kill either of you."

"*The* Diamond," I corrected. I closed my eyes and sighed.

"Whatever. Either way, it doesn't matter now. The—"

"It doesn't matter?!" I couldn't fathom that he was now bound to that fucking bastard and had done so willingly. "The Diamond was Kya. It's what he called her. It's what Vicria warned her about right before the curse killed her for breaking the deal. The same curse you have. You think it doesn't matter? Of course it fucking matters."

"If you would let me finish, I can explain why it doesn't," he said sternly, and I shut my mouth, crossing my arms over my chest. "See this line around the black?" He pointed to the red marking encircling the curse. "The healers didn't know what it was and thought it was some kind of infection. They took red ink and marked the perimeter. But do you see how there's a gap between it? It's receding. And when it first appeared, it extended to my shoulders. The deal is disappearing. I'm guessing it has to do with his death, but I don't exactly know how his magic works. Either way, from the rate it's shrinking, the healers estimate it will be completely gone in a few days. We'll just have to wait and see."

"Why did you agree to help him in the first place?" I shook my head.

"Because, it was worth it to save you and Kya. I didn't know she was the Diamond."

"Except she died anyway…" I muttered, sitting back down on the bed.

We all remained silent. Neither of us had had time to grieve her death. And I didn't want to. I didn't want to feel it.

"Nikan," Eamon broke the silence. I twisted the sheets between my fingers, staring down at the material. "Who is Daegel?"

Nikan explained to Eamon how it was discovered that Daegel was a dark wielder and the one responsible for the Glaev that had plagued the lands, finally confirming it was indeed not a disease but dark magic.

"He's from another realm. He wanted Kya because of the power she possessed," I said, recalling Vicria's final words as she tried to warn Kya of her demise.

"Whatever that jade-colored magic was that she wielded, that's the power he wanted? It ate away at the Glaev." Nikan sat up more in the bed.

"I think so. Doesn't matter now," I sighed.

I met his eyes. "What happened to him?" Eamon asked.

"I killed him when I killed Kya."

The room fell silent once again.

I stared down at my hands and resumed twisting the sheets. They conversed a bit more but I wasn't paying attention. It was taking everything in me not to break. My throat was growing tight, and tears pricked at the back of my eyes.

Daegel.

That piece of shit… If it wasn't for him, none of this would have happened. Not the loss of Kya, not the loss of my Nation, none of it. I was glad he was dead and I was glad I was the one to do it. That was the only good thing to come out of this entire fucked up situation. But Gods damn me if everything else didn't tear me apart at my already fragile seams.

"So you'll be okay?" I asked Nikan as I stood up.

"Yeah. I'll be fine. They said I can go back to Morah tomorrow night." His eyebrows pinched together.

"See you then," I said shortly, then spun on my heel and quickly left, weaving my way through the people in the ward.

Not yet. Not here.

I needed to get out. I needed to breathe. But the moment I stepped outside, where I expected relief, people surrounded me and I felt even more unease. I didn't want to be near anyone. I just wanted the pain to stop. I wanted to forget, just for a little while.

Fuck this, I need a drink.

I threw on my hood and shoved my way through the morning rush of residents and went to the nearest place that had something strong enough to give me what I wanted.

Erryn's Lounge was a quiet place in the secondary ring usually frequented by residents of Ilrek—and not me. You could get a drink there, but it was more of a refined establishment than a bar. I generally preferred going to the taverns in the outer ring—the ones that were rowdy and filled with patrons from out of town only looking to loosen up and have a good time.

But those places weren't open at this hour, and Erryn's was closer.

I pressed the door open and quickly shut it behind me, resting my back against it to quiet the ringing in my ears. The oak tables were a rich brown, and the dark green walls created a welcoming and sophisticated atmosphere. There were only a few people inside near the front—a couple seated near the window talking over coffee, and some others standing at the counter ordering.

I made my way to the bar near the back. There was only one person there and he was near the end with a shoulder against the wall and a drink in his hand. I pulled out the chair and sat on the opposite end.

I only had to wait for a few minutes before I was greeted.

"Good morning."

I looked over to see Erryn making his way over to me behind the counter. He recognized me once he got closer.

"Oh," he stiffened slightly and looked me up and down. "What can I do for you, Roav?"

"I'm not a Roav today. I just need a drink. Strongest one you have," I said quietly, fishing out coins from my pocket and handing them over. At least my status as a Roav would guarantee he wouldn't deny me.

His lips thinned into a tight smile. "Rough night?" he asked nervously as he slid a drink to me a minute later.

I sighed heavily. "You could say that."

I lowered my hood and stared blankly at the drink in my hands. He took the hint that I wasn't interested in elaborating and walked away.

I stared at the gently moving liquid, praying what was in this cup would save me from my memories. I brought the rim to my lips, scenting the bitterness of the amber substance.

"I don't want to remember."

Well, I got what I asked for because I sure as shit didn't remember a damn thing when I woke up to someone poking me in the shoulder.

"What?" I snapped. Or I tried to, but it came out more sluggish than I intended.

Fuck, I'm tired. And why is it so dark in here?

I lifted my head, peeling my face from where it was buried in the crook of my elbow.

Oh. That's why.

Another poke.

This asshole has a death wish.

Prying my eyelids open, I squinted into the daylight.

Wait. Daylight? What in the After am I doing outside? And how is it the next day?

My vision was distorted. I blinked rapidly, clearing away the blur of the world. The sun's early light was too bright for my liking, so I lifted a hand and shielded my eyes, wishing I could wield away the light of the sun. Nikan's frame came into view.

"Shouldn't you be healing in bed somewhere?" My words were slurred.

"Yes. But seeing as I heard you never made it back to your room, I had to come find you. Thankfully, I didn't have to go far."

I slowly sat up, wiping the drool off my chin and lifting my chest off the cold obsidian steps beneath me. I knew those steps. The entrance to Morah.

"When did I get here?" I asked, not necessarily to anyone.

"I don't know. I just found you. Are you drunk?" He sounded somewhere between concerned and astonished.

"I was at one point," I grumbled. "What time is it?"

Nikan extended a hand to help me stand. My legs wobbled, and everything began to spin. He grabbed my elbow, preventing me from toppling straight into the wall.

"It's a little past dawn. Where have you been, Mal?"

I tried to think, but I honestly couldn't remember anything past my second drink at Erryn's. *Yesterday.* I must have had more than that, which was odd since he has a two-drink-per-day limit. He doesn't like it when his patrons get sloppy. Perhaps he made an exception to the rule for once.

"I was at Erryn's. I must have come here when he closed a few hours ago."

Nikan started walking me back inside, holding me upright the entire time while I leaned on him.

Great. I'm the bitch using her injured brother as a crutch.

As we ascended the stairs, Nikan whispered, "What were you thinking drinking that much? I've seen you drunk before but never like this."

And the overbearing attitude is back.

"I preferred you when you were unconscious. At least you didn't nag me," I said lazily.

"Mal—"

"Back off, Nik. I drank too much. So what? Just leave it. At least until I've slept it off," I said with a snap as he guided me through my bedroom door.

Nikan sighed, "I just thought, with everything that's happened…"

He steered me to my bed, and I flopped down on it, not bothering to remove my clothes or shoes. I was too tired. My eyes closed the moment my head hit the pillow.

"Just…be more careful next time. Okay? It's just us now."

"Mhm," I hummed.

He said something else, but I was exhausted and didn't catch it. Then I heard the soft click of the door just before sleep took me.

When I woke, I kept my eyes shut as I lay in bed. I could sense the afternoon light streaming in from the glass walls. I didn't want to wake up. I wanted to remain in my dreamless—and for once, nightmare-less—sleep, where I didn't think about what

I had done or have to worry about dealing with the reality of Kya's death. I didn't want to wake up in a world without her in it.

I didn't want to wake up and remember.

But I did. I remembered Kya's last words to me. I remembered fighting to save Nikan, struggling for days as the Glaev between us slowly retreated. I remembered the look of acceptance in Kya's eyes when she understood her fate.

I remembered everything. Well, almost everything. Just not most of yesterday. Whatever I had done worked exactly as I wanted—I forgot. I was numb.

I wanted that back.

Chapter Eight

RYKER

R *yker…*

I dreamed of Kya. Her voice rang through my mind like the sweetest song, and it was so fucking clear, like she was right next to me. If it wasn't for the ache in my soul, I would have thought she was.

I wasn't ready to face reality, grasping those moments where I could feel the whisper of her memory beside me.

Opening my eyes, I turned my head to find I was still alone—her side of the bed vacant.

No matter that the majority of my life spent in this room was without her, the only memories I had were the precious few we shared. And that only made me even more bitter—more motivated.

She thinks she can just leave me? I won't stand for it. She's mine, and I will have her.

But at the same time, my anger was blended with concern—terror of the unknown piercing my heart and knocking the breath from my lungs.

Is she alright? How is she feeling? Are the shreds of our bond biting into her soul the same as mine? Has she healed from her wound? Is she safe? Is she afraid?

I didn't hesitate jumping out of bed and storming my way down to the library on the lower level of the palace. It wasn't as big as Morah, but it was the largest library in Oryn and had many titles that even Morah didn't—several of them being ones Eamon had been trying to obtain from me for decades. Kya had spent a considerable amount of time here translating and deciphering the dark book.

Just another place imbued with her memory.

While the palace had been restored, the books were still in numerous piles on the floor, not yet shelved. Looking around at the disarray, I made a promise to myself I would have it all back in order before I got Kya back. And I *would* get her back.

Working my way through the titles, I found anything that was related to the mating bond or the Rip. I had them all in small stacks set off to the side, and I was deciding which one to look at first when Mavris came in.

"Ayen's ass, Ryk. You scared the shit out of me," Mavris said as he crossed the room.

"I didn't do anything." I didn't look up from the books.

"You slept for two days and then disappeared from your room. I thought you had left again."

"I will. But first, I need to find out more about the mating bond and the Rip."

He sighed. "Look, I know you're concentrating on finding Kya, and you should. I can take care of things here, but there's something you need to see."

"Not now. Whatever it is, it can wait," I clipped.

"It'll only take five minutes, and it's something you *need* to see." Mavris rarely raised his voice to me, and his tone had my attention.

"What?" I huffed.

"Just…come on."

I followed Mavris out of the library and up to the balcony on the top level of the palace. He braced his hands on the railing and jutted his chin out toward the city.

"Look."

I followed his line of sight out over the city of Voara below. It was still there. Or at least what was left of it from what had been destroyed by Daegel.

"What about it?" I gritted through my teeth.

"The Glaev," he said quietly. "It's gone."

Now that he had mentioned it, I noticed the once black, decimated land was green with a thin covering of snow.

"Kya's energy magic…it didn't stop. It kept restoring the land even after she cut off her magic. The buildings are still gone, but…"

"But the city can live again," I breathed.

With Voara having been mended by Kya, I left Mavris to oversee the reconstruction of the buildings and returning the citizens back to their homes where they belonged. My duty as Lord was pushed behind my duty as mate. While it riddled me with guilt, I needed to concentrate on finding her.

I spent the next several days locked away in the palace library, pouring over every piece of information I could find about another realm. It was the only thing I could think of, where she would be if not here or dead.

The information about the Rip was less helpful. While Scholars had tried to study it for millennia, not much was known. Anything that entered the Rip never came out, whether that be people or elements. Once you touched the mists, it took you.

I had seen it happen more than once. Most recently at the last Trial when a particularly arrogant contestant decided to wield her fire into the Rip—despite my warning. It latched onto her fire and drew her in after it, dragging her to her death.

The most we had learned about the Rip was from the Sages, but even then, it was very little. It wasn't until the most recent Trial that we learned not everyone died when they went in there. Apparently, if the Gods so chose, they could spare them.

But where did they take my mate?

I felt even more driven to find her, and I wasn't wasting another minute. I left the library and went back to my bedchamber to bathe before getting dressed, taking note of the colder temperatures I'd be facing up north. I reached out to Theron just as I was lacing up my boots.

"I need to go to Dolta. Meet me on the roof."

His only response was a short growl.

Once I was ready, I grabbed a jacket and flung the door of the bedchamber open to head up to the roof of the palace. I stopped short when I noticed Hakoa leaning against the wall, arms crossed over his chest.

"What do you want? I'm leaving," I bit out.

He looked me up and down with a blank expression before meeting my eyes. "I can see that. Mav told me you found Malina. He told me what happened at the Rip."

"And?" I started to put on my jacket.

"Well, is Malina okay?"

I shrugged. "Physically, she was fine when I left her."

He nodded slowly and looked at the floor. "You could have brought her *here*, you know."

I huffed a breath. I cared little for conversing with him at the moment. "Nikan needed to be seen by a healer, and she wasn't exactly in the best state to come here. Besides, I...I don't want to see them right now."

His eyes widened, his face beginning to twist into anger. "You can't blame her for what happened, Ryk. She was told to do it. And from the sounds of it, she didn't want to. Kya—"

"I know, Hakoa," I snapped. "I didn't say I blamed her, but I still don't want to see her right now. I don't have time to deal with her grief and mine. And honestly, I don't really give a shit. I need to concentrate on finding Kya."

"Right. Mav mentioned you don't believe Kya's dead."

My eyes narrowed. "She's not."

"I'm not questioning it," he said, his voice softening just a bit. "If you say she's alive, then she is. But..." He paused.

"Out with it. I don't have all damn day."

He ran a hand down his face. "It just sounds...eerily familiar. Don't you think?"

"Where do you think I'm going?" I gestured to the corridor leading to the balcony.

"You think the two of you can figure out where she is? Where *they* are?"

"That's what I'm going to find out." I started walking away. "I'll be back when I'm back."

I only made it a few steps before he caught up to me.

"I still think we should bring Malina here. Maybe she could help. Perhaps she heard something. Or even Nikan. He was with Daegel for a while." He stopped walking, but I continued.

He had a point about Nikan, but this was likely just a ploy for him to get his bed warmed, and I just wanted him to shut up so I could leave—so I could find answers.

"Do what you want, Hakoa. I'm going to find my mate."

And with that, I left him in the corridor and made my way up to the roof where Theron was waiting. Even after all these years of being with my Spirit Guardian, I struggled to determine his mood. But today, he seemed more solemn and quiet. And definitely less hostile. Perhaps it was guilt. Guilt at knowing he could have prevented all of this by not betraying me, and taking my mate away. Not to mention, ignoring me when I had needed him most.

Whether he agreed or not, he deserved his shame.

"Let's go," I said as I approached him and placed my hand on his scaled leg.

He blinked slowly and growled, but didn't protest as we Traveled away.

Chapter Nine

RYKER

Dolta was a small village on the northern end of the Eck-terre Mountains. The temperatures were much cooler than back in Voara. I had constructed a home—an estate, really—for my father and mother just on the outskirts of the village, hidden behind dense trees. Which proved beneficial, giving my father the privacy he needed since my mother had disappeared.

Theron and I appeared on the front lawn. With winter in full force, the ground was covered in a thick blanket of snow that crunched beneath my boots as I walked up the stone steps.

I didn't bother knocking, opening the wooden door and stepping into the foyer. All was quiet for the most part, and I glanced around the space. The foyer was mostly empty, with the exception of a bare table against the wall, and the open sitting room to the left was furnished but looked unused with dust collecting on the surfaces. Which wasn't surprising.

While Mavris and I arranged for healers to attend to my father regularly, no one else came here. I wondered many times if a place this big was too much for a single person to reside in. Perhaps it'd be more manageable if he had a smaller home. But he held hope my mother would come back and insisted she would want her home when she did.

"Hello?" I announced, my voice echoing off the walls.

A moment later, footsteps sounded from upstairs, and I looked up to the landing.

Althea came around the corner and descended the stairs, greeting me with a bow. "Lord Ryker."

"Althea." I nodded in return. "How is Cadoc?"

"I've been giving him an elixir over the past several days to keep him calm. He's been more agitated than usual lately. You were wise to request we tend to him full-time. Something about his recent trip to see you has him more…unsettled than before," she said softly.

"Yes, I know." I didn't want to offer up any more details. I had assumed that since he had met Kya, knowing she had once gone into the Rip and returned, that he would be more erratic than usual.

She craned her neck, looking behind me.

I gave her a questioning look with a quirked brow.

"Cadoc mentioned something about your mate. And I heard rumors of her as well—a Worthy. I thought she might be with you," she said sheepishly, lowering her head.

I inhaled sharply. She hadn't heard of what happened. I doubted many had. It wasn't exactly something I had announced, and while word had likely gotten around in Voara, it hadn't reached here yet. And I wasn't going to be the one to mention it—not yet.

"No, she's not with me," I said stiffly.

"Oh. Well, maybe next time."

I can only hope.

"I'll go see him now. He's in his room?"

Althea nodded, and I went up the stairs to my father's bedchamber. I reached with my mind, listening for his, and could hear his chaotic thoughts. His mind gripped me instantly, thrusting me into a cavernous space, pulsing with a frenzied energy.

"She's out there..."

"Trapped."

He couldn't fixate on a single idea, bouncing around without a grasp on reality.

"...wouldn't leave me. Something happened. I have to find her. I'm not crazy."

"...she's not dead..."

"My mate."

The anguish of the words in his head...it wasn't so different from mine.

I knocked softly, then entered when I didn't get a response. My father was bent over his desk, papers scattered across it. His thoughts may have been frantic, but he was so still I would have assumed he was sleeping while sitting up. That elixir Althea gave him calmed his body, but did nothing for his mind.

I couldn't help but wonder if this is what would happen to me if I didn't get Kya back in my arms—going completely mad and needing healers to make me seem sane. I couldn't lead a Nation like that. I couldn't live like that. No, I had to find her. I needed her.

"Father," I greeted.

He slowly lifted his head to look at me. There was nothing in his distant brown eyes. There hadn't been in nearly fifty years. Not since my mother fell.

"What are you doing here, son?" he asked almost sluggishly. He wouldn't meet my eye, and I wasn't sure if it was because he was upset with me or if he just couldn't.

After observing him for another moment, I grabbed a chair from the corner of the room and pulled it up next to him. I sat and rested my elbows on my knees, running a hand through my unkempt hair.

"I need you to tell me everything you know about what happened to Mother."

His eyes narrowed. "I have told you everything. You failed to listen. For years, I've told you and your brother. Either you didn't care, or you thought I was crazy!"

"I'm listening now!" I yelled, smacking my hand on the desk. My temper heated faster than I anticipated. "Yes, we all thought you were crazy, but trust me when I say, I believe you now. So tell me what the fuck happened!"

He remained silent, holding my cold, demanding stare. "You believe me?" he asked carefully.

"I don't know anything about Mother, which is why I'm asking you. You would know." I repeated the same words Theron had said to me. "So tell me everything."

He hesitated for a moment. "Why now?"

"For the love of Xareus… Will you just tell me already?" My patience was wearing thin.

"Why now, Ryker?" he articulated each word. "Is there something you know?" The question sounded more accusatory than curious.

"Because I think the same thing may have happened to Kya. Now tell me what happened to Mother before I find out for myself," I warned, lowering my voice. I had never threatened my father, but when it came to Kya, I would do just about anything.

Father tsked and glanced out the window for several moments before finally speaking. "The Glaev had been around for half a century, showing up at random all across the continent. While it was concerning, it hadn't been a pressing issue at the time, only appearing in small, deserted, and desolate areas of land."

I leaned back in my chair, wondering where this was all going.

"But then it started to show up near towns. Inside of towns. And people died."

"I don't need a history lesson. I was there," I snapped, but he ignored me and continued.

"Your mother had a friend whose family was killed by the Glaev, a Scholar. She was determined from then on to find out what it was, how to stop it, and how to cure it."

"She left to find some of the Scholars who were working on it at Morah. She and Vicria followed a lead, then she fell into the Rip. I know the chain of events. I'm asking what else happened." My temper was holding on by a thread. I understood how the last fifty years had driven him mad.

"I wasn't there," he said coldly.

"You're her mate. Didn't you speak to her? Through the bond? How did she fall?"

"She didn't fall!" He stood abruptly. "It wasn't some accident. She wouldn't have been that careless. Someone sent her over the edge—to somewhere else."

"And you think it was Vicria?" I asked.

That had been the running theory for years, seeing as she was the last person to be with her and only offered up that she fell in by accident while researching the Glaev's origin. It was the main reason I despised her so much. She had been my mother's friend, yet couldn't bother to be transparent about how she died. But I suppose she never did die.

He shook his head, looking back down at the papers. "I don't know. That's what I've been trying to figure out."

His unusually calm demeanor made it easier to talk to him than it had been for decades. Perhaps just finally giving him the validation he was right all along settled something in him.

"Why do you think she's alive?" I asked. This was the entire reason I was here.

He gave me a look as if I was the one who had lost their mind. "I've told you before. I know she's not dead."

"But how?" I pressed.

"The bond," he said pointedly. "It lives. And so does she. I can't reach her, but I know she's there. She's just…lost. Everyone thinks I'm crazy, and I wish I could somehow show you our bond—that it's still there, no matter how faint. " He looked me directly in the eyes before they narrowed slightly, and his face softened. "But you know this, don't you?"

I said nothing.

"Your mate. The Worthy I met—Kya."

I stiffened at her name.

"What happened to her exactly?"

Do I tell him?

If I did, he could think I knew more than I did and lash out, and that was the last thing I needed right now. On the other hand, he knew this connection—this loss, this drive—better than anyone else.

"She fell into the Rip."

I explained everything that I knew to my father—what happened to Kya at the Rip, what I felt. His confirmation of the bond was all I needed to know Kya truly was alive and his theory of my mother being somewhere else was likely correct, but that posed a greater problem.

Where the fuck is she?

"You've been bonded much longer than I have. What do you know about it? What have you learned over the years? We now personally know what the bond feels like when they're…gone. But would we know if they truly died or not?" I needed to understand more than just the basics of the mating bond.

I knew bonds had been forged by the Gods since the beginning of time. They were a gift, giving the fae one true companion to live their lives beside with a divine fusion of their souls. Everyone was born with half of their soul resting in another, but it wasn't guaranteed their other half would be born within their lifetime. That connection, that drive, encouraged breeding which ensured the species to survive and thrive. It wasn't until the fae were bestowed abilities by the Gods that those with the bond realized their powers grew along with their connection.

Males felt the bond stronger than females. It forced them to an almost primal state, causing them to be possessive and even violent. The females only felt that same compulsion to protect the bond after their mating.

"I don't know what it's like when a mate dies. I just know Leysa hasn't. But like you, after she disappeared, I became obsessed with finding her and learning everything I could about the bond to see if there was any way I could use it to find her. Like when she was here, it would always lead me to her," Cadoc started.

It was the same for me. The tug of the bond, was irresistible and unrelenting. Fighting against it was pointless.

"What I discovered is also why I know she's alive." He twisted his hands together, like an anxious tick I had seen so many times. "When the mating bond is broken, half of the soul is lost. The majority of those who lost a mate couldn't bear to live without them and would ultimately follow them into the After to rejoin their souls once again. And it's been more commonly seen when the female passed first."

I assumed it was because the bond was more controlling of males.

"I don't think… I couldn't live like that." My father shook his head. "I barely can now."

He had been suffering from this for decades. I felt bad for never having believed him before. I wished I hadn't had to have experienced it for myself before I took his word, even though there was no way for anyone to fully understand it without that experience.

"And nothing in all your years of research mentioned anything about mates being separated?" I asked. Surely someone in the past few millennia had to have some experience with this.

"Nothing other than simple distance, like being in another Nation. I even searched for anything I could find on anyone whose mate could have been on the Drift Islands or gone to the Trials. Still, nothing like this has happened before." I could sense his anger rising. "And why would it? Mates are rare. The fact you and I found them at all is an anomaly. The Gods, damn them all, only want some of us to experience this kind of connection—and the pain that comes with it."

He wasn't wrong. They gave us this bond and then made it unbearable whenever it was broken or fractured. But even with all of this pain, I would have always chosen to be mated to Kya. No matter where she was, no matter that she left me behind, I wouldn't have spared myself from this. Even if all I had had with her was a few months, it was worth it. But I refused to allow us to be separated forever.

"We need to find out where they are." I stood and began pacing, speaking more to myself than my father. "Another realm. Obviously there's more than one. There's Hylithria—the Spirit realm—but when she was there before I still felt her, even before we sealed our mating."

"I don't know, son," Cadoc said, following me back and forth with his eyes.

I paused for a moment. I needed to know more about the Rip. I needed to know more about what else was out there.

How many realms are there? How can they be found? How do I get there? How did Daegel?

"I'm going back to Voara," I stated, facing my father. It was an open-ended invitation for him to come along.

He stared at me for a moment, contemplating. I resisted rolling my eyes. What did he have to hesitate about?

"Ryker, I've been looking for answers for years. Decades..." He sighed.

That made little difference to me. I wouldn't stop. "Well, you're welcome to join me. Two of us is better than one. And like you said, you were all alone before."

He made no attempt to move, and I was growing frustrated with him. I really thought we were making some headway.

"Fine. You know where to find me." I didn't waste another moment before I walked out of the house and had Theron Travel me back to Voara to meet with Mavris.

While he was my brother, Mavris was also my advisor and for good reason. He was incredibly smart and resourceful.

I tracked Mavris down, finding him in his study a few doors down from mine. When I entered through the open door, he was standing next to someone, deep in discussion. They both looked at me. My eyes darted to Mavris, then the male he was with.

"Leave," I commanded.

The male's eyes widened just before he gave a curt bow and fled from the room, leaving Mavris and me alone.

"Not exactly the most polite greeting," Mavris mumbled, crossing his arms over his chest.

"He'll be fine."

"I get you're in a pissy mood, but you're still the Lord of Oryn. You owe people respect."

"I didn't come here to get berated, Mav," I snapped.

"Fake it if you have to. Just be nicer." He rolled his eyes. "You went to Dolta?"

"Yes. And I think Father has been correct all this time. If he feels like I do, then Mother is alive. I think she and Kya are in another realm. Could be the same one or not. I have no idea. I need you to tell me what you know about the other realms."

Mavris wasn't moving. He didn't respond, and I swore he wasn't even breathing for a moment.

"What?" I barked.

His mouth gaped slightly as if he couldn't find the words. "Ryk…that's kind of a big announcement to make to someone who has believed their mother dead for the last fifty years."

I had been so consumed with the thought of Kya that even I hadn't truly taken in the fact that my mother was likely still alive. It was my father who told us something had happened. He felt it. We had tracked Vicria down, and all that bitch said was that she was 'gone.'

Her death broke me. Even after I became a Lord, she still mothered me as if I was an adolescent. I missed her love and care, her sweet, gentle demeanor. Being there, supporting me, no matter what.

But she hadn't died. And neither did Kya.

I exhaled sharply, kicking myself internally for being so careless. "I'm sorry. I should have been more considerate. But, yes, Mother is alive, and I need you to tell me what you know about the other realms so I can find them both."

He shook his head slightly, attempting to clear away the shock. "The only other one I know about is Hylithria. Are you sure there are others?"

"Yes."

"Well," he shrugged. "There's one place that would have that information if it exists."

Morah.

I didn't want to go back to the library in Riyah. Just another place with a memory of Kya. And her family was there. But now that Kya and I had wed, they were my family too, I supposed.

Fuck.

And Mavris was right. What better place to find information about other realms than the most extensive collection of information and Scholars?

"Fine. We leave immediately," I snipped. I turned to leave and was just about to tell Theron where we were going.

"Wait," Mavris said.

I stopped and looked at him over my shoulder.

"The male that was here—that was Atrey."

"And his significance to this conversation is..." I drawled.

"He's a messenger," he paused. "From Bhara."

My breathing stopped. I had completely forgotten with everything going on. The Sages, the Worthy... They didn't know. No one had informed them. *I* hadn't informed them.

I turned to face him fully, noting the paper he picked up from his desk and read from. An unnatural wave of rage, mixed with a deep sadness, pulsed through my veins.

"You're due to appear in front of the panel of Sages and Worthy in accordance with the law or be subjected to the Raith." He looked up from the paper and met my stare. "Your mating trial starts in three days."

Chapter Ten

KYA

"Holy Cethar... Where am I?"

To be honest, Cethar and the other Gods could kiss my ass for all I cared if they had sent me to another fucking realm, another world... One with a moon so big, it took up half the sky.

Was it the Rip? If it was the Rip, and it worked like it did for the Trial to get to the Woltawa Forest, then the Gods were certainly the ones who sent me here. And they could definitely kiss my ass for that.

I wouldn't even know where to start to get back. If I even could. It wasn't like there was a giant chasm around that I saw to repeat the process.

The bond ached to be repaired, to be back with Ryker. But I didn't know how to even fathom passing between realms without a Spirit or a God.

That would have to be an issue for another time. Right now, I needed to concentrate my concerns on the present, specifically the male gripping both my arms and yanking me up to my feet.

I didn't want his grotty hands on me. I didn't want anyone to touch me except Ryker.

My legs were so weak they were shaking just from holding up my weight.

Behind me, the male's voice spat something I didn't understand before he turned me around to face the strangely robed figure. The same one from before, who was now standing in the water.

Except it didn't look like water at all.

It had a dark sheen to it, almost like molten metal, reflecting the light from the large moon on the surface. It was so dark you couldn't see the bottom.

Memories of the Nagasai from the Trial flashed through my mind—dragging me under the water of the river... The water-wielding assassin in Voara...

The figure stretched a hand toward me.

Oh, Gods.

"No..." I whispered, but the male shoved me forward.

I started kicking and trying to free my arms. "No, please. Don't make me go in there," I pleaded. But it wasn't as if I expected him to listen to me. I wasn't even sure he could understand me.

I continued to struggle, trying to fight back. I was able to swing my arm around and hit him in the face. He said something I assumed was vulgar, and he threw me into the pool of liquid.

It was thick and cool, feeling like silk all around my body as it began to encase me. The robed figure wrapped their gloved hands around my throat and pushed my head under the surface.

I clawed at their hands and arms, but it wasn't long before the liquid invaded my mouth, crawling its way down my throat and filling my burning lungs.

When I woke—

Wait. I'm alive?

My eyes sprang open, eager to prove I still lived.

I was in a room of sorts. Bare plaster walls surrounded me with a small, single barred window near the ceiling. Craning my neck to look behind me, I blessedly spotted a solid, wooden door. I thanked the Gods I wasn't thrown back into that dark box from before.

Taking it slow, I sat up in a small, hard bed. The single sheet provided slid down my chest and pooled at my waist.

What the fuck was all that about? And for the love of Xareus, why am I still naked?

I didn't understand their purpose in drowning me only to keep me alive. I didn't know who they were. I didn't know what they wanted. But, clearly, they had no intention of killing me. They'd certainly had every Godsdamn opportunity to do so.

I examined my body. There was slight bruising on my stomach where the male had kneed me, and I could feel tenderness on my temple. But beyond that, I was fine—

Ha!

I was far from fine. I was naked and alone in a strange place—another fucking realm—with suppressed magic and a broken mating bond that was likely about to start driving me insane.

I twisted and placed my feet on the floor, momentarily forgetting I couldn't feel any vibrations. The disappointment of being without my terbis hit me once again.

But I could hear others. I wasn't alone this time. It was then I realized I wasn't just in a room. I was in a prison.

I leapt to my feet, racing across the room to the door. I twisted and pulled the handle but it didn't budge—which was to be expected.

"Damn it," I mumbled under my breath.

I turned and pressed my back against the door, then slid down until I felt the cold floor on my bare ass and rested my arms on my knees. I groaned as I ran my hands through my tangled hair.

I was trapped again and still starving. And I still had this stupid thing around my neck. I just wanted to go home.

"*Ryker?*"

Silence.

I knew it was pointless, but I refused to stop trying. Closing my eyes, I let my head fall back against the door with a thud.

After a few minutes, I heard a soft *whoosh*. I opened my eyes to find a set of clothes folded up on the floor in front of me.

I looked around. The door was still closed, and the window was sealed.

Maybe I'm going crazy faster than I thought.

I stretched my foot out and nudged it with my toe. I didn't know what I expected to happen but nothing did, and it was, indeed, clothing. Deciding not to take it for granted, I put on the clothes. A loose pair of gray pants, a shirt, and thankfully, underwear and cloth binding for my breasts.

I sighed with relief, finally having the comfort of fabric covering my body. I hadn't felt this relaxed since before I went to hunt Daegel with Malina. I closed my eyes, basking in the momentary peace.

Peace quickly disrupted by the sound of a scream echoing outside the door. I froze in place as a chill ran down my spine.

A moment later, a door closed and steps came closer down what sounded like a long corridor.

My breathing grew heavier as they drew near. My chest rose and fell rapidly, and the hair on the back of my neck stood when those steps stopped just outside my door, the shadow of the figure was visible beneath the door. I quickly stood and pressed myself into the corner of the room, between the foot of the bed and the wall.

I held my breath. All the blood drained from my face with dread when I heard a click, then the door opened.

Black boots stepped into the room. My eyes followed them upwards. Black pants were tucked into the boots. A long-sleeved shirt hugged a muscular frame with broad shoulders, and tattoos snaked around the neck. A head of blond hair and a trimmed beard around the mouth and…rounded ears. Cobalt eyes stared into mine. Eyes I could never forget.

Daegel came into my cell.

"Hello, Diamond." His deep voice filled the space, causing cold trepidation to run through my veins. That was the voice that filled my nightmares.

I didn't respond. Whether from shock or disbelief he had survived, I couldn't find any words.

He came closer, crossing the room in three long strides until he was directly in front of me, and leaned down until our faces were nearly touching. I braced myself. His cruel eyes made a calculated account of my body with a maliciousness that had me frozen in place before they met mine once more, holding the promise of something I didn't want to find out.

"Welcome to Vansera."

I breathed heavily as Daegel backed away until he was leaning against the wall and crossed his arms over his chest.

"Vansera?" I whispered.

"My realm," he answered.

My eyes darted to the door, which was slightly ajar.

Could I get past him fast enough to get out?

"Don't try it," he warned, and I looked back at him. The look on his face was hard and unforgiving. "I'm going to get straight to it, so listen closely."

I stiffened, not knowing what to expect.

"It's clear you don't understand our language. Not after you were instructed to comply with the cleansing Paxtor forced you to…endure." He rolled his eyes.

At least I knew that fucker's name.

"Cleansing?"

"I'm not going to bother answering your questions, so shut the fuck up and listen," he snapped.

My jaw clenched. I wanted to beat him until his face caved in but there was no way I could take him in this state.

"My request is simple: submit yourself and obey. *Willingly.*"

"Over my dead body." I narrowed my eyes in challenge. I refused to bow down to his demands, no matter what they were.

Daegel smirked for a brief moment before it became a sneer, and he was across the room and his hands were lifting me from the ground by my collar. I could hear the sizzling from the collar burning the flesh of his fingers, but he didn't react.

"You'll be begging to be dead if you don't. Unfortunately for the both of us, I need you alive. So you will be, but just barely."

Daegel let go and I collapsed to the floor. I looked back up, adamant to keep my eyes on him at all times. His fingers were singed from the collar, but he didn't seem to care as he turned to face the door.

He said something in his language, and I glanced at the door to find the same male—Paxtor—who had dragged me outside. The same one who beat me nearly unconscious. I glared at him, ready to keep my promise and strangle the life out of him.

Daegel turned back around and bent down. "He's going to give you food and water. Take this as a gracious offering..." Daegel muttered something with a flick of his hand and chains appeared, piled on the floor. "...and learn to behave."

Paxtor looked at me and winked. My lips curled, and I bared my teeth. I didn't like the look in his eyes. It made an uneasy shiver run down my spine.

Daegel stood and walked out the door. Paxtor gave me a once over and closed the door as he left as well, leaving me alone once again.

Chapter Eleven

KYA

P axtor took his sweet time bringing me something to eat or drink. It had been hours of waiting. During that time, I stared out the window, watching the small piece of the sky I could see. Daylight was fading, and I could just see the top curve of their moon. I had nothing to do but sit there and wonder. At least it gave me time to think.

I couldn't get Ryker out of my head. I missed him desperately. I missed his patience, his gentle demeanor. I missed his stories about the moons and the way he made me laugh. I stared at the sky-encompassing moon outside and wondered if there was a love story behind it too—or if it was alone like I was.

Like Ryker was.

I wondered if he was in just as much pain, with the same burning in his soul that threatened to consume him. I wondered if it would have been better if I had died rather than how I was feeling now—ripped from my world with a shattered bond.

The sound of the lock clicking brought me out of my thoughts. I wanted to feel relieved when Paxtor came into the room with a cup and a tray of food, but the look in his eyes, the way they hungrily trailed over my body, had me tensing with trepidation. He slowly shut the door, locking me in here with him.

I stiffened when he approached and relaxed only slightly when he set the tray on the other end of the bed and handed me the cup. I took it without hesitation and brought it to my lips. Foolish or not, I was so thirsty I didn't care what it was and gulped it down while watching him over the rim of the cup.

Thank the Gods it was only water.

"Can I have more?" I asked, gesturing to the cup.

He said something in his language, shaking his head.

How inconvenient it was that I just happened to be trapped in another realm with people who spoke another language and didn't speak mine when I was gifted magic that would have solved that issue, only for it to be taken away. The fucking irony.

Paxtor jutted his chin toward the tray of food, and once again, I didn't hesitate. I ate the bread, some kind of meat, and a mashing of something I assumed to be like a strange vegetable. I chewed and swallowed so fast I didn't even taste it, but it was such an amazing feeling to have a little weight on my stomach.

He watched me the entire time as if it was the most interesting thing in the world to him. Just as I was finishing, he slowly sat on the bed next to me. I eyed him warily.

He began to speak, and the only word I caught was 'Diamond', as he enunciated each syllable slowly like he was learning to pronounce it. I just stared at him. I didn't know what he wanted from me.

I grabbed the tray and tried to hand it back to him. He smiled and pushed it aside before placing a hand mid-way up my thigh. I didn't have to understand his language to know what that gesture, mixed with the heavy look in his eyes, meant.

Fuck this shit.

I slapped his hand away and bolted to the door. I nearly reached it before he grabbed the back of my shirt and threw me on the bed.

"No!"

He held me down with a victorious grin on his disgusting face. "Binda."

The chains piled on the floor suddenly lifted and moved, crossing the room and wrapping around my wrists and ankles before securing me to the bed. I was completely bound, unable to move aside from thrashing in place—which I did with all my strength.

I tried to buck him off as he climbed over me, but he only seemed to enjoy that more. He pushed up my shirt, and aggressively fondled my breast.

"Get off of me! Stop!"

The first thought that came to mind was to shift my wings, but with me bound on my back I could possibly break them.

His other hand began roaming over my body—my chest, my stomach, my waist. I thrashed harder once his hands reached down for the top of my pants.

He paused momentarily. He said something, pointed to the scratches on his face I had inflicted on him last night, and then pointed down to me with a cruel smile.

I spat at him. He flinched slightly before his lip curled into a sneer and reached up to wipe it off his face.

He looked at my spit on his hand then slapped me across the face with it, the sound bouncing off the walls. My head snapped to the side from the impact. The wet sting lingered on my skin as he roughly pulled down my pants and underwear to my ankles, exposing me completely.

I wouldn't let this repulsive male have his way with me, be inside me. The thought alone threatened to waste the food I had just consumed.

He can't have me. He can't. I belong to Ryker.

I began screaming at the top of my lungs.

Paxtor punched me in the stomach so hard it knocked the breath out of me. I grunted, gasping for air. I couldn't stop the tears as he spoke to me in a lust-filled tone, pulling out a length of fabric and fastening it over my mouth.

This can't be happening.

My kicking and thrashing only seemed to excite him more…

Memories of girls I had saved from this exact situation in the past flashed through my mind. This was what they went through. And while I knew fighting wasn't going to stop him, I tried anyway. Just like they did. And no one was going to come to save me…

"Please! Please, stop! Don't do this!" I said, but my words were muffled through the cloth.

Paxtor ran his grubby finger up my slit. It was sickening. I could feel the bile creeping up from my stomach to my throat. I hoped he felt how fucking dry I was because he wasn't getting a drop of arousal from me.

He said something without looking at me before he started fumbling with the fastenings to his pants. Thrashing harder, I looked away. I couldn't watch. I didn't want that image in my head. If I ever got back to Ryker and he saw…

Gods, please, please don't let this happen.

I felt his hard cock rub against the inside of my thigh. His head came next to my ear as I faced the wall. Close enough to my arms, the chains used to hold me down…

I knew no one was going to save me like I had all those girls over the years. There wasn't going to be a Roav bursting in and rescuing me from this horrid circumstance. But there was already one in this room right now. And I didn't need rescuing.

I would save myself.

With Paxtor concentrated on angling himself, I stopped fighting, making him think I had given in. But just as he relaxed slightly, I bucked my hips hard and jolted him forward, making him slam the top of his head on the wall. I twisted my arm, using what little slack I had in the chain to wrap around the underside of his neck, and then used the chain on my other arm to constrict him from behind.

Then I pulled.

I turned my head to look at him, wanting to see the life leave his eyes as I strangled him with the very bindings he had used to hold me down. His mouth opened and closed, gasping for breath. The chains dug painfully into my skin, but I didn't care. I'd lose my hands before I lost my dignity to this repulsive bastard. His fist came up and started striking my face over and over while his other hand tried to pry the chains from his throat.

My initial instinct was to let go and protect my face, but if I could hold out, if I could just take the searing pain, then I knew it would all stop soon.

I can take it. I can take it. Just a little longer.

A blue tint began to spread across his face, and I knew I was close. I tasted blood in my mouth, felt it trickling across my skin, and my jaw rattled under the constant battering.

Then a sound came from the door, and the weight of the male was torn from my murderous grip.

Daegel threw Paxtor against the wall, holding him by his throat. His voice was low and lethal, making a shiver run down my spine along with an instant flood of relief.

"Do *not* defile the Diamond!" Those words I understood. He pulled a knife from his waistband and twisted it between his fingers, leaning in close to Paxtor's face. Paxtor gasped, sucking down air with his hand around his bruised throat. "And don't even think about using a healing spell."

Paxtor's eyes went so wide, they bulged out of their sockets.

Daegel didn't hesitate, severing Paxtor's dick with a vicious swipe. He dropped him to the floor before wiping the knife clean on Paxtor's sleeve.

I sucked in a sharp breath, shocked by the violent act.

Paxtor screamed through his gasps of pain, blood gushing from between his legs and pooling on the floor. He jerked violently, frantically grappling to stop the blood from pouring out of him.

"Silence," Daegel boomed. "She was not to be harmed and you will suffer for what you did."

Paxtor's mouth closed as his screams turned into whimpers through his nose, and his entire body shook.

Still chained to the bed, all I could do was gape. But Paxtor's compliance to Daegel's orders—in my language—made me realize he was able to understand me the entire fucking time.

Daegel slowly turned on his heel to face me with a cold look on his face. He waved his hand, and the chains disappeared. "Did he fuck you?"

I shook my head, scrambling to pull my clothes back on with trembling hands and curling around myself.

"You'll be fine then," he said with a look of disgust.

With that, he turned back around and ordered Paxtor to leave—which he did despite his injury, trailing blood along the way as his severed appendage remained on the floor. Daegel followed and slammed the door shut. A grunt and the sound of something falling to the floor made me flinch. The lock of the door clicked into place, and I heard the sound of steps retreating. Just one set.

I couldn't hold it in any longer as I bent over the side of the bed and hurled.

Chapter Twelve

KYA

It was stupid of me to vomit on the floor of the cell. The smell, mixed with the putrid odor of Paxtor's decaying dick on the floor, was an assault on my nostrils. I'd taken the only sheet I had and tried to gather the vomit as best I could, depositing the entire thing in the bucket they left for my waste after tearing off a piece to cover the penis. I wasn't touching it.

I felt revolting and dirty. I could still feel Paxtor's hands on me, the detestable echo of his body on mine. I craved to scrub it away, wishing more than anything I could wash despite my aversion to water. It didn't help that I could still see his shadow as he sat against the door.

I wanted out. I wanted to be back in Ryker's arms, feel the familiar vibrations through the ground beneath me, hear the sound of Malina's laugh, Nikan's grumbling tone, and Eamon's soft words. I wanted to go home.

Tears welled up in my eyes as I pulled my legs to my chest, sitting on the bed with my back against the wall. I tried to blink them away. I wouldn't break because of some fucked up male.

Daegel had threatened that my experience here would be unpleasant, that I would wish for death, unless I complied. If that was some sort of sick attempt to get me to submit, he'd have to try harder.

But then why did he stop it? Why did he tell Paxtor not to defile me if his goal was to break me?

It was all making my head spin.

I'm in another realm with beings that have rounded ears and magic. I'm a prisoner, collared and isolated, with no access to my magic. What do I do now?

I pondered this for some time, getting lost in my thoughts. Glancing at the door, I noticed blood seeping into the room from underneath. I guessed it was from Paxtor's body on the other side.

Good.

I could only stare as it crawled its way across the floor for several minutes until it stopped and began to pool.

It had been a few hours, and I lay back on the bed, staring out the small window. The only thing I could think of was Ryker. Every moment of every day, the drive to be back in his arms grew achingly desperate. Even in such a short amount of time as his mate, having his presence, knowing his thoughts, feeling his emotions as if they were my own, had become a comfort—the completion of my soul. The fractured bond cut like glass every time I caressed it.

And it hurt even more that I had lost so much of what had become a part of me. It wasn't just the bond. I had lost Odarum, the tether to him having gone dark. The magic from him, as well as every gift I was given by Kleio, was locked away—inaccessible as the orbs lingered like lifeless bodies floating in water. I lost my terbis, leaving me feeling blind.

It pained me that I didn't know if Malina and Nikan had made it. But I was hopeful, since I took Daegel from Taeralia, they at least had a better chance than before and they could live in a world without that monster to haunt them.

My mind reeled endlessly as the hours passed, and my eyes grew heavy as night fell. I tried to stay awake, the memory of Paxtor's touch keeping me on edge, but I still had little energy and the events of earlier were taxing.

My eyes flung open when I heard steps approaching. I sat up straight. Two sets. One sounded heavy—perhaps Daegel's. The other was lighter, likely a small male or a female. They stopped in front of the door. A moment later, Paxtor's shadow and all the blood beneath the door disappeared as well as the small lump under the sheet on the floor.

The door opened, and Daegel stepped into the room with a female—one with *pointed* ears. Daegel pushed her farther in, while he remained in the doorway.

"Don't forget," he told her. His tone was ominous.

She looked to the ground and nodded. She seemed fully submissive, and it filled me with rage. No one should have that amount of control over another.

Daegel didn't even glance at me before he left the room, closing the door behind him.

The female continued to stare at the floor, her body still facing the door, and I watched her awkwardly. She had long, wavy brown hair loose down to the middle of her back, covering the side of her face. The color was bold against her golden skin. The dull clothes she wore—a long-sleeved shirt that was too big and pants that were slightly too short—hung off her tall, slender frame.

I remained wary, not knowing the purpose of her presence. But I couldn't stop looking at her ears. The only people I had seen here so far had rounded ears. And knowing I was in a different realm, I wondered if none of their ears were pointed, or...

She took a deep breath, and I thought perhaps she would finally turn to face me and say something, but after another couple of minutes, she remained still and quiet.

Tired of the anticipation, I broke the silence, "Who are you?"

She didn't respond. She didn't even move, and I wondered if she could understand me.

"Why are you here?" I tried again after a few more moments.

She sucked in a sharp breath and raised her head, revealing the side of her face. Then she turned to face me fully.

I nearly stopped breathing. A set of bright, silver eyes met mine, eyes I knew in the depths of my soul. The same eyes passed down to the one who had followed me across the continent.

"Hello." Her voice was low.

"Oh Gods…" I breathed.

"My name is—"

"Leysa?" I asked in disbelief. The eyes. The pointed ears peeked out from her long brown hair. She was from my realm, and she was the mother of my mate.

Standing before me was the one who had been believed dead for half a century—by all but her mate, Cadoc.

Her eyebrows creased, giving me a look of suspicion. "Yes," she said slowly. "Daegel has assigned me to you."

"What?"

"You asked why I'm here." She gestured to the room. "It's because Daegel assigned me to you."

I gaped at her for a moment, wondering if she knew who I was—who I was *to her*.

"You're alive." It was a statement and not a question.

Leysa looked at me strangely. "Good of you to notice."

She wasn't understanding. Clearly, Daegel hadn't told her who I was.

I reached up and tucked my hair, revealing my pointed ears. Her eyes flicked to them, and her face softened slightly, but she offered no recognition.

"You're from Taeralia," she said nonchalantly. "A shame you have to be here."

Anger began to rise in my chest. I didn't know much about her, but seeing as she was Ryker's mother, I had a hard time understanding how she could be so callous. "He didn't tell you?"

"No." She shook her head.

I stood up and held her eyes with an intensity that made her waver. I pushed up my sleeve, revealing my Trial mark and the bruising of the chains around my wrist.

She tilted her head. "A contestant. Interesting."

"I *was* a contestant. The Trial already happened." I pulled down the collar of my shirt, revealing my Worthy mark. "My name is Kya, terbis wielder and Roav of Morah, deemed Worthy of Kleio—the Silent Goddess and Mother of Atara, which has been decimated by the Glaev."

Leysa's eyebrows rose, and she crossed her arms.

"And," I pulled up my other sleeve, showing my mating mark and the marriage band around my wrist. I met her eyes. "The mate to your son…"

Her mouth fell open.

"…Ryker."

She stared at me with wide eyes, and I swore she wasn't breathing. "Ryker," she whispered, her fingers covering her mouth as her bottom lip trembled.

"Yes."

"But you're a Worthy." It sounded more like a question than a statement.

"I am," I said firmly. "And I need to get back to him. Now. Do you—"

"But that's impossible. Two Worthy can't be mated. Can they?"

I raised my eyebrows and gestured to my arm. "Apparently."

She snatched my arm and pushed up the sleeve just enough to see the marriage band. She studied it for a moment before a smile crossed her face, and a light laugh escaped her lips. "And you're married?"

Her eyes lifted to meet mine. They were filled with unshed tears. My shoulders relaxed. I hadn't even realized I was so tense, but meeting my mate's mother for the first time—one I thought was dead—was unexpected, and significant.

I nodded. "It only just happened a— Well, I don't actually know how long I've been here, but it wasn't very long ago."

Her face fell, and she squeezed my arm. "You're here. That means that your bond…" Her tears began to fall. "He's suffering so much right now. And so are you."

I dropped my head. "Yes. As are you and your husband."

"I'm sorry you know…"

We stayed like that for a few moments in complete silence.

I couldn't help but reach for the bond, trying to speak down that once swirling tether.

"Ryker. Your mother lives! I'm with her! I wish I could tell you. I wish I could feel your joy."

Nothing. Nothing but the burning pain in my soul, urging me to get back to him. I rubbed at my chest, wishing I could relieve the ache.

A sniffle returned my attention to Leysa. She brushed a finger across her cheek, swiping away a tear. "I would love to be able to give you some comfort and say it gets better, but it doesn't. You never get used to the constant ache. It only gets more intense, so prepare yourself."

She had had to find out all on her own. I felt a wave of pity.

"You've been fighting this for fifty years." My chest tightened. I couldn't imagine... Tears welled in my eyes, blurring my vision.

Ryker...

"But there's nothing that can be done. So, I suppose congratulations are in order." She smiled softly, and I was taken aback at how unaffected she seemed. But then I remembered, this was something she had already learned.

"Congratulations?" I said thickly.

She grinned, but there was a sadness to it. "You're my daughter now." She took my hand and led me to sit next to her on the bed. "Tell me everything."

Sitting cross-legged on the bed across from each other, Leysa and I spent hours talking about Ryker, and Mavris too when she asked, though I didn't know too much about his life. It was mostly me doing all the talking, but she would ask questions, veering us off topic onto something else. She was so personable and kind. I had very few memories of my mother and it was refreshing to talk to the female who had raised the male I fell in love with.

"And...have you met Cadoc? My mate." She perked up with a hopeful look in her eyes.

"Once," I said, trying to keep any sadness from my voice. But she had the right to know his current state. I would want to know about Ryker's, even if it hurt me. "But he's...different now, from what I understand. He's—"

My voice was cut off when the door to my cell slammed open and Daegel walked in. "Time's up. Let's go," his voice boomed in the small room.

Leysa didn't even look at me before immediately obeying his demand. She hopped off the bed and rushed out of the room. I hadn't even considered the fact that our time was limited, and I internally kicked myself for not asking more about where we were and how she got here. My thoughts had been consumed by the bond and our mates.

Daegel looked at me with hard eyes. "Do you see how easy it can be, Diamond?" He jutted his chin in Leysa's direction. "It doesn't have to be painful."

A flood of defiance coursed through me even though I didn't fully understand what it meant. He swiftly left, locking the door behind him. I could hear them walking away until I heard another door open and the sound of...wind?

She's not a prisoner? Does her compliance allow her to leave this place? If it does, why hasn't she escaped? Why hasn't she found a way back? Why hasn't she gone home?

Chapter Thirteen

RYKER

I had only ever been to the Temple of the Sages once in my life. It was over a hundred years ago when the last full panel was held. Standing before it now, I was reminded of the intricacy of the structure. Just as most temples took architectural inspiration from the Temple of Odes, it too was crafted of white marble with excessively large pillars holding up the rectangular building and its dome ceiling.

I commended the Sages and their sacrifice to gain spiritual enhancement. But meddling in my mating had killed any shred of respect I previously held.

In light of everything, this mating trial seemed so trivial. Something that was once so important to my and Kya's mating was now meaningless. All I had to do was tell the panel—the council of Sages, Lords, and Ladies—it was now irrelevant, and I could move on. I didn't want matters to be worse once Kya returned. I would have this settled to absolve her of this burden.

I entered the temple and was immediately hit with a wave of spiritual presence. It was a feeling I wasn't sure I'd ever get used to. Once I made it to the large panel room, everyone was already seated at a long table along the opposite wall to the entrance doors. Five places for the Sages and the remaining four for the other Worthy. Each seat was occupied, alternating between Sage and Worthy—to keep them separated—with one chair on the end left empty for a Sage. I knew that seat was meant for Vicria, but what they didn't know was that she wouldn't be attending this panel she had been so adamant about. Or any other, for that matter.

A small, stone table sat across from them. As I approached the table, I noted the *two* chairs. One intended for me, the other for Kya. A deep sadness filled me as I moved the chair away from the table. It wasn't that I had wanted her to have to endure this with me, but the fact that it wasn't a choice stung. I didn't get to argue against her attending, only for her stubbornness and strong-willed nature to push back until I would begrudgingly relent.

Gods, I missed her…

But then I remembered this was her own doing. She willingly sacrificed herself to the dark wielder. My hands balled into fists as I continued to think about it, festering in my anger.

The clearing of a throat brought my attention to the panel before me. All eyes were on me but it was Zareb, sitting between Lady Asmen of Dusan and Lord Voron of Ulrik—the two newest Worthy—who leaned forward.

"Lord Ryker," Zareb began. "You came alone?"

"Worthy Kya was to attend as well. This is not just about you," Eldrick, one of the Sages and an arrogant prick, added.

"I am aware," I said through gritted teeth.

"Then why has she failed to appear? Where is she?" Jymar, Lord of Gaol, interjected and was only stoking the fire of my temper. He had a knack for getting under my skin the few times we encountered each other.

Pompous ass.

"I don't know," I answered honestly.

"Interesting," Jymar said with a smirk. "As her mate, I would think that you'd keep better track of her. Unless, perhaps, she finally realized you simply aren't worth the trouble—"

That was all it took. I stood abruptly with a snarl, knocking over the chair. The Sages gasped at my outburst. Fuck them and their trial. They, along with Daegel, were contributors to my and Kya's delayed mating.

I blasted out my shadows, aiming to suffocate the words from Jymar's throat. But in my fit of rage, I had forgotten his magic nullified elements within a certain proximity. My shadows surrounded him, but with his hand raised, they never touched him. I didn't let up, heating the shadows with my fire to singe any part of that bastard I could.

"Enough!" Zareb demanded.

I stopped and pulled back my shadows but continued to glare at Jymar, who displayed an amused smirk.

"Lord Ryker," Zareb stood with his palms planted on the table, "you will remain civilized and diplomatic during this panel in accordance with Spiritual Law or be subjected to temporary restraint of your abilities."

His eyes flicked to the corner of the room and I followed them. Standing in the corner was a male with a cold, calculated expression—waiting for a command to perform the Raith or the Nex. A blood wielder. One of the only ones left alive and under the strict control of the Sages.

Having grown up with a blood wielder for a brother, I knew what they were capable of and why they were so dangerous. I bit back my retort about where Zareb could put his Spiritual Law.

Zareb turned his attention to Jymar. "And you, Lord Jymar, are to comply with the conditions of your participation in this panel and refrain yourself from accusatory comments during this trial."

I, personally, would have used far fewer words and told him to keep his fucking mouth shut, but Zareb got the point across well enough because Jymar shrugged and leaned back in his seat. I used my shadows to pull the chair back upright and sat with my arms crossed, keeping my eye trained on Jymar.

That sleazy bastard... It was no wonder his Nation was the scum of the continent, somehow allowed to go about its heinous ways without punishment. He could rot in a Voltaryn cell for all I cared. Maybe Gaol would be better for it.

"Now, let's resume this panel, and the issue of the mating between the two Worthy, Lord Ryker of Oryn and Worthy Kya of Atara." Zareb lowered into his seat.

"Lord Ryker, please roll up the sleeve on your left arm," Eldrick requested.

Without breaking eye contact, I did.

Disapproving gasps escaped their lips as I held up my mating mark and the metal marriage band around my wrist.

"So it *was* you we felt." Eldrick gave me a look of disdain.

I didn't care. I had no regrets, and I would display my mark proudly for the realm to see.

"You were to wait until *after* this panel was convened before you mated," Eldrick chided.

"I'm certain he's aware of that," Zareb sighed, pinching the bridge of his nose, "Moving on..."

"Lord Ryker," Fayeth, the only remaining female Sage on the panel, spoke. "If you do not know of Worthy Kya's whereabouts, do you at least know *why* she is not in attendance? This is a serious matter and her failure to appear will result in an equally serious consequence."

What should I tell them? Should I hide the truth about her being in another realm? Should I lie and say she's dead? Maybe the truth was just what was needed to resolve all of this...

"She fell into the Rip."

Everyone stiffened. Except for Jymar.

"Please describe the events of what happened," Fayeth requested.

So I did. Sort of. I only provided the information I knew could be verified should they go investigating it. None of it was a lie. She did go after the dark wielder and she did fall into the Rip, taking him with her.

Let them decide what to think.

"And you can't feel her at all?" Fayeth asked.

I shook my head and her face, along with the other Sages, turned to a look of pity. But it was Lord Jymar's attempt at hiding a triumphant grin that had my suspicions raised. My eyes narrowed on him. What did he have to be so Godsdamn happy about—thinking my mate was dead?

Needing to know, I entered his mind. I had no qualms about doing so. Not when it came to Kya. And not when he was such an asshole.

"How convenient...quite the opportunity..." was all I could skim from this distance as his magic prevented anything more.

Convenient? What the fuck was convenient about Kya's disappearance? I would turn his mind inside out if not for his ability.

"Then this mating trial is no longer required," Dainos, Lord of Torx, stated. I didn't miss the brief glance he and Lord Jymar shared.

I entered his mind as well, but all he was thinking was that he and Jymar shared similar interests—which didn't make a bit of sense seeing as they had been bordered enemies for decades.

Zareb nodded slowly, though the look he gave Dainos was skeptical. "But a decision still has to be made. Seeing as they have already mated, and their combined power is no longer a threat since Worthy Kya has been claimed by Odes' grave, this matter seems settled. Any opposition?"

The other Worthy shook their heads, some more eagerly than others.

"Then your mating has been approved, and you do not have to undergo the Raith. This panel is now concluded," Zareb faced me. "Lord Ryker, you are free to go."

That's it?

I wasn't going to wait around for them to change their minds. Standing to leave, I noticed Zareb eyeing the Worthy, all seeming relieved with the exception of Asmen who appeared tense and apprehensive of them. But I'd had enough. I wasn't going to question the ruling even if it was mostly on a technicality with them *assuming* Kya was dead.

I still pondered Jymar's thought about her death, but it didn't matter. She was gone, and he couldn't hurt her. Besides, I had bigger concerns.

I had a realm to find.

Chapter Fourteen

ZALEN

The five days I had promised Maera turned into seven, and I was itching to see her again. I hated every moment we were forced to be apart, but with the death of the King, things changed.

I had met with the Elders, as well as Sarn, on several occasions regarding who was suspected in the King's murder. The only leads we had were several trespassers from Aedum who were caught and killed. The theory remained that he was killed by someone from another Kingdom, and Aedum was the likely perpetrator—but nothing was certain. Our centuries-long feud was assumed as the motivator.

Thane and I had spent the last week making all the necessary arrangements. Makkor's funeral was planned for tonight at dusk which left me several hours to race back to the cottage in hopes that Maera would be there.

I had so much to tell her, but I honestly didn't know how she would react when she found out I'd be King of Damanthus so soon. She understood what it meant.

Being heirs to our respective Kingdoms, Maera and I connected in a way we couldn't with anyone else. We each understood the hardships and pressure the other had to endure. I hated to admit it at first, but it was nice for someone to know what it was like and how cruel of a life it was. And it didn't hurt that she was incredibly smart and adorably quirky, which had captured my attention from the beginning.

Pushing through the illusory barrier, I immediately knew she wasn't there. With disappointment rising in my chest, I dismounted my horse and went inside.

Nothing was particularly out of place but I could tell from a few moved items that she had been here. For quite a bit of time, too. She had tidied up the living space and small kitchen.

She waited for me...but I never showed.

It angered me to let down the one person I cared for in this godforsaken world. I wasn't a man who broke his word. And once I took my place on the throne, it would be even harder, if not impossible, to see her again.

The side of my mouth curved up.

I wouldn't have that.

I made my way into the bedroom. Floating just inside the door was a tala thread—like a small lightning bolt suspended in time. My eyebrows raised.

Conjuring a tala thread was something that would have been difficult for Maera, seeing as her specialities were herbs and potions—as with most witches—while sorcerers had an affinity for casting. But she was bright, and perhaps she had found some sort of brew that allowed her to do so.

A tala thread was a way for a message to be left by someone, capturing their voice for someone specific to hear. While it was meant to only be heard by the person of your choosing, there were some powerful sorcerers who were able to access any of them if they chose to—myself included. It was risky for her to leave this here.

But I didn't have to worry about that now. No one had discovered this place.

I ran a finger down the length of the thread. Recognizing my touch, it activated, releasing Maera's voice. Just hearing that sweet sound settled something inside me, my soul—a peace I couldn't find anywhere else. I watched the tala thread as it glowed its light blue sheen, pulsing with her words.

"Minn astir," her voice greeted.

My love.

"Meet me at our old place on the night of the Raven migration, at the darkest hour. I can't risk coming here anymore. Something has happened and..." she paused.

What? What is it? I wanted to ask. The Raven migration was tonight.

"...my father fears for my safety. He's making me take a tracing potion tonight." She sniffled, and my fists clenched. "He wants to secure my position as heir. My mother agreed and suggested a suitor..." her voice broke. "They've promised me to the captain of the royal guard. They think it will guarantee my safety from whatever it is they're scared of."

That bastard wants to control her—keep her under his watchful eye and marry her off to some low-life. And I questioned why he was in such a hurry...

"I'm sorry, minn astir."

With nothing more, the tala thread flickered before vanishing. I closed my eyes and took a deep breath. This made things even more complicated, hindering my plans.

No matter. I would just have to move up the timeline even more.

Maera was something akin to a forbidden fruit, which only made me want her more. Regardless of our Kingdoms' rivalry, we couldn't stay away from each other. She was now promised to marry someone chosen from her Kingdom. Heiress to the throne, she would one day become Queen of Aedum. And a Queen needed a King, according to the fucked up old laws.

Just as I was heir to Damanthus, I was intended to be King and married to a *suitable* woman before I took the throne upon my father's death—not that I found that manipulative woman suitable by any means. Jarna—my betrothed—may have been chosen for me by my father, but he was dead now, and I would choose whom *I* wanted.

And I wanted Maera.

I didn't care that our Kingdoms had warred for centuries. The Aedum heiress had my heart.

Three years ago, Maera went traipsing through the forest having some sort of breakdown, and stumbled across the border into my Kingdom. It was my job as a Vord to hunt down trespassers and send back their heads. But when I saw her...I couldn't. Even knowing I should have, even recognizing her as the Aedum heir, something stopped me.

She was crying and I didn't know why at the time—only found out later it had to do with her mother putting unrealistic expectations for her as the future Queen, driving her further into her obedience. Servitude. She was nothing more than a slave to their personal agenda.

I had watched her from afar, hiding within the forest while she gathered plants and herbs. She went there almost daily, and so did I. I was fascinated by her, but I didn't know why.

One day, I tired of watching her from the shadows and stepped into the light. Her bright blue eyes drank me in, and though I thought she would be fearful and run away, she saw right into me—as if she could see my very soul—and didn't back down.

It was foolish on both of our accounts, but from then on out, our journey together began.

Over the course of months, she would come back to the same remote place and I would always find her. Eventually, it turned into something more than just two heirs venting out our frustrations to someone who understood. So much more.

After a year, I constructed the cottage for us.

My father—and everyone else—believed I was off hunting, while her father believed she was off gathering rare herbs for potions. We never got more than a few hours a week together if we were lucky. We couldn't risk any more than that, otherwise we could be discovered.

We'd be killed. And it would have been done publicly and torturously. Not that I would have ever allowed that to happen to her.

I had a plan. One that would ensure we could be together for the rest of our lives. I needed to act quickly before they forced her to marry someone who would become the new King following her father's death.

But her parents were becoming a bigger issue, threatening to ruin what Maera and I had.

I wouldn't have that.

"I'm coming, love."

A knock came at the door to my room just as I was buttoning my formal jacket.

"Come in," I called.

I faced the long mirror in the corner, giving my attire a once-over and ensuring I looked the part of the perfect heir—black pressed pants tucked into boots, and a dark shirt beneath a vest decorated with adornments and finery. All for a facade. I was far from what the Elders expected for their future King. I was simply playing into the guise they wanted to see.

Thane's reflection in the mirror came into view behind me. He met my eye. "They're waiting."

"Did the Vord gather the information on the captain?"

"They did. The rumors are true," he confirmed.

Fucking piece of shit. I'm not waiting any longer than I absolutely have to.

I nodded once and spun on my heel. "Everything's ready?"

He smirked and nodded.

"Let's not keep them waiting then," I said with a devilish grin.

The Rhaen River sat at the bottom of the hill at the Castle of Kanth. It was the widest river in Damanthus, coming down from the Kingdom of Innon from the north, and flowing into the Tyrnth Sea. Being so far north in the Kingdom, it was frozen over for the majority of the year. But since winter had only just begun, the river was still flowing gently.

A crowd of spectators had gathered at the bank of the river. From an outsider's perspective, you would only see citizens of Damanthus coming together to mourn the loss of Makkor and see off his soul. But for those who knew where to look, there was a clear division amongst the people.

I knew where to look and so did Thane.

Under Makkor's tyrannical rule, he had made many silent enemies. I made that my advantage, hoarding their allegiance until almost the entirety of the Kingdom was behind me. They were my armory.

The crowd parted, and I met the eyes of those who gave a subtle bow of their heads. I glanced at Thane by my side. His nod communicated that all was going according to plan.

I approached the edge of the water where the Elders and Sarn waited by the vessel holding my father's body, surrounded with trinkets and flowers from the people. Several other boats lined the bank and would be occupied after the King's pyre was set.

Laying on a bed of straw, Makkor's sword rested on his chest with his hands clasped around the hilt. He failed to look regal, like a King should be. He was anything but, and now his mangled and deformed body finally reflected his worthless, ugly soul.

The Elders bowed at the waist when I approached, Thane remaining just behind me. I nodded for them to begin.

I couldn't help but roll my eyes as one of Makkor's loyal subjects—and my betrothed—Jarna, began to sing with her hands raised to the heavens. Her voice carried across the water in a prayer to God—who had abandoned our realm—to return and take the King's soul with him. I had refused to interact with Jarna since our arrangement was announced. She and her parents had deceived their way into my father's good graces to affix her position as future Queen.

Not fucking likely.

After several *charitable* words from the Elders, it was time to commence the pyre.

About goddamn time.

Night was in full force and I only had a couple more hours until I needed to meet with Maera.

"Zalen," Oveus addressed, his voice rising over the congregation, "as heir to the Kingdom of Damanthus, it is your honor to send off King Airo's soul through the flame."

Oveus held my stare for a moment with a knowing look. He took my hand in his and put our heads together—a cultural gesture of respect—and whispered so no one else could hear, "We don't get to choose our King, but we can choose true loyalty."

He knew... Yet, he did nothing to stop me.

He pulled back and stepped aside, outstretching his hand for me to step toward the table, draped with a white cloth, and fire drum.

Sarn took the honor of pushing the funeral boat into the water, allowing the current to take it down river, with a final deep and solemn bow.

I grabbed the wooden bow and arrow laid out on a table, nocking the arrow. Sarn stood straight and glared at me from the corner of his glistening eye.

"Don't worry," I said quietly, so only he could hear as I dipped the oil-covered tip into the drum of fire. "You'll see him again."

Sooner than you think.

With the end of the arrow lit, I walked into the water, soaking my formal pants and boots.

With no one in front of me to see, I smiled in exhilaration at finally getting to fulfill something I had dreamt of doing for years. I felt the direction of the wind before aiming the arrow high into the sky.

There was a pause in the world, as if everyone had held their breath for a moment. I released the arrow, watching its trajectory as it hit its target down the river. Catching fire, the vessel carrying Makkor lit up the night.

It's time.

I spun on my heel, squared my shoulders, and raised my chin. "It gives me great pride to see King Airo leave this world with his most loyal subjects present. In honor and respect for his reign, let us flow down the river with him until the bend so our God can truly witness the virtue we all know he deserves."

Keeping with tradition, anyone who wished could board the boats and be part of this transcendent moment, but only those who were most loyal to him—and least loyal to me—would join.

I stepped forward to guide people to the boats. Only the Elders remained while Sarn, Jarna, and many others climbed into the small ships. They filled quickly, and—just as I had hoped—they hadn't noticed their few numbers or the fact I wasn't joining them.

Thane came up to my side. We shared a glance, and he looked back behind him then snapped his fingers. Men emerged from the crowd and pushed the boats into the water. Two of the men stayed beside us, holding three bows and four arrows. Thane handed one to me.

Someone in the crowd snickered, and it caught Sarn's attention. It was then he realized I wasn't on any of the boats. He glanced around before he finally saw me on the shore.

Then his eyes widened when he saw Thane, his son, and the two others holding flaming arrows, aimed at the boats that had been doused in oil the night before. They wouldn't have time to counter the fire with how hot and fast it would burn.

Even from here, I could see Sarn's face twist in rage.

How he hadn't seen this coming was beyond me. Sarn was just as vile as the King, corrupt to his core with greed of power, and it reflected in how he treated his son. He had once even plotted Thane's murder, but failed when Thane's mother protected him. Sarn then killed her out of sheer spite.

"Burn, you bastard," Thane said, locking eyes with his father and pulling back the string.

We released the arrows all at once, and when they struck, the screaming started. I had originally planned to stick around and watch them be consumed, but time was of the essence. I spun around and handed my bow to Thane, who wouldn't take his eyes off his father with a pleased grin.

"You wanted revenge," I roared to those before me over the screams from the water. "You wanted a new reign," I glanced at the Elders who, except for Oveus, had a look of horror on their faces. "Now, you have one."

"King Zalen!" someone shouted with a raised fist.

"King Zalen!" the crowd echoed.

They began to cheer and I turned to face the Elders.

"But I can't be King without a wife, can I?" I asked with a cold stare.

Being married was a requirement in order to take the throne—at least until there was an heir—and I just burned my betrothed alive.

Enora, one of the Elders, swallowed before she spoke, "In accordance with the old laws, yes. Otherwise, the next in line will assume the throne."

"Then I better find myself one," I said with a sinister grin. "Thane!"

Thane stepped up next to me.

"There's been a change of plans," I said, as if the revelation had just come to me.

Thane raised his eyebrows. Not even he knew my plan.

My blood began to race in anticipation. "We're going to Aedum."

Chapter Fifteen

MALINA

*T**his is a bad idea.*

I knew that. I did. But my logic was put aside because all I could think about was chasing that feeling of emotional paralysis. For the past few days, I had gone out every night, alternating between different places to avoid anyone noticing a pattern. Not to mention, I didn't want Nikan finding me. At least the last time I saw him, I couldn't see the black of the curse peaking over his collar anymore.

Each morning when I woke up, I was in my bed with no recollection of how I got there. And each time, there was a tonic for headaches and a glass of water at my bedside. I knew it was Nikan. I wasn't sure if he had carried me back to my rooms, or if he brought them for me after I got back, but I knew he was aware of what was happening. A couple of nights ago, I had woken up to find him in the chair across the room with his elbows on his knees and his head in his hands.

I had been avoiding him since he insisted we needed to talk, because that was *not* happening.

But no matter where I went, how many males and females I fucked, or how much I drank—trying to chase that numbness—it was never enough. Nothing compared.

Tonight, I was at The Whispering Axe—a small but bustling tavern frequented by travelers located in the outer ring. With the dim lighting and smoke-filled air, it provided an atmosphere of liberation from day-to-day responsibilities. It was one of the places I preferred to go to since the patrons didn't know who I was, and I could be anyone I wanted for a few hours. I didn't have to be a Roav or a lost child of Atara, didn't have to be a mourning sister. Here, I could just be Malina. Kya had her books, I had my bars. It was my place of escape.

Except, right then, I wanted to escape *from* here.

I had somehow found myself in an alley with an inexperienced, slender hand down my pants and two fingers in my pussy, groping the breast of a beautiful female from… Well, I forgot where she had said she was from. She had been much more appealing paying for my drinks than she was with her tongue down my throat in the alley outside. As pretty as she was, as much as I wanted her body to make me forget everything, she had no idea what she was doing, and I definitely wasn't drunk enough for this.

Ever since that night at Erryn's Lounge, I had been disappointingly unsuccessful. All I could remember from that night was the male from the bar. At one point, we were sitting next to each other, and sometime later, we were outside, and he was handing me something. Then, nothing. Blissfully nothing. That's what I wanted most.

I'm in the wrong place and with the wrong person.

I let go of the female's breast and started to push her off me, trying to pry my lips away from hers.

"Mmm," I tried to speak, but her mouth was consuming my words.

She must have assumed that was some sort of drunken, pleased moan because she squeezed my ass, and her fingers plunged in and out faster. With a grunt, I pushed her away, pulling her hand out of my pants with her fingers covered in my arousal. She stumbled back. Wiping her saliva from my lips, she gave me a confused look.

"What's the matter?" she asked before giving a knowing smirk. "Do you want to take this someplace more...private?" She licked her wet fingers suggestively.

"No, thanks," I said nonchalantly, retying my pants before running my hands down my shirt to straighten out the fabric. "I'm done here."

While I'm sure she was nice enough, I wasn't going to waste my time with someone who couldn't give me what I needed.

I waved my hand in her direction as if I was shooing a cat away. "Thanks for the drinks."

Her mouth gaped open as I turned around to walk away, down the dark alley, toward the inner ring. I didn't have much time before Erryn's closed for the night, so I moved as quickly as I could, despite my slight inebriation. The heels of my boots rhythmically clicked against the cobblestone, and it made my head pound in the quiet street.

Once I made it, I stumbled my way inside and glanced over each face, hopeful he would be here. A wave of disappointment washed over me when none of them resembled the male I was searching for. But since I was already here, I figured I might as well make it worth my while, and I sat myself at the counter.

Erryn approached from the other side of the bar.

"Roav," he greeted quietly, with a polite smile. "Could I get you something to eat? The kitchens are closed, but there are still a few things back there that I could grab for you."

"Just a drink. I'll have whatever is strongest." I leaned back in the seat after tossing some coins on the counter.

Erryn's lips flattened into a thin line, but thankfully he didn't argue with me. "Coming right up," he said, then turned away to make the drink.

I closed my eyes for a moment, soaking in the calm commotion of the tavern. But it still wasn't enough to distract me from the image of my arrow in Kya's chest replaying over and over.

"Back again, huh?"

I opened my eyes and realized I must have dozed off, because my drink was placed on the counter in front of me. I turned my head toward the voice, noticing Erryn on the other side of the room wiping down tables.

The male I had come here searching for was lowering himself in the seat next to me. My memory of him was a little fuzzy, but I knew it was him. His dark, shoulder length hair was pulled back this time. He looked cleaner and more sober tonight, wearing nice clothes. He was much more attractive than I remembered, and he had this charismatic way about him that made it difficult to peel my eyes away.

"Yes, actually. I was looking for you," I said as I sat up straighter and gripped the glass in my hand.

His eyes flickered with amusement. "I thought you might be. And if I'm being honest, I thought you would have sooner."

My eyebrows pulled together. "So you know *why* I'm looking for you?"

He nodded. "If you want to finish that up," he gestured to my drink, "we can take this outside."

Without hesitation, I lifted the glass to my lips and threw it back, wincing from the burn in my throat as I gulped the entire thing down. I set it down with a thump. The male flashed me a charming smile before rising and holding his hand out for me.

I didn't take it, hopping off the seat on my own. His smile widened, displaying a set of dimples that somehow made him even more appealing. He held out his arm, gesturing toward the door, and followed me outside.

The fresh, cool breeze felt good against my skin as I emerged from the tavern.

"This way," the male whispered as he led us down the street.

It was quiet and peaceful, but I decided to break that silence and get some answers.

"What's your name?" I asked.

"You first," he chuckled.

I rolled my eyes. "It's Mal."

I didn't want to give out my full name until I learned who he was. Funny how I didn't trust him with my name, even as I willingly followed him in the middle of the night, but I didn't really care. I just wanted the images of Kya out of my head.

Did that make me a monster? That I didn't want to think about her? It felt like I was dishonoring her memory and that was only building up the guilt I was carrying inside of me.

All the more reason to just forget all together.

"A pleasure to formally meet you, Mal," he said. "I'm Daxel, but you can call me Dax."

"Well, *Dax*, where are we going?"

"My home. You've been there before." He shrugged. "But I'm guessing you don't remember that, do you?"

I shook my head. "No."

"And I bet that's exactly what you're hoping will happen again." He winked at me.

I didn't say anything, not wanting to admit he was right. I almost hesitated and second-guessed going with him, but when I saw the image of Kya with a tear rolling down her cheek and Daegel's arm around her body as they slipped over the edge, that hesitation died along with her.

Gods, I have issues.

We walked in silence until we came to a single home built of different stones, giving it a unique aesthetic. Now that I had seen it again, I vaguely remembered it. Dax held open the door for me as I entered and gestured for me to sit in a plush chair.

"Wait here," he said as he walked down a hallway toward the back of the home.

I took the moment to take in the space. The ornate furniture and lavish paintings on the walls gave off a sophisticated atmosphere, but the sparseness of it felt as if it wasn't really occupied. It was exceptionally clean, and made me wonder if he actually lived here.

After a minute or two, Dax came back with a small marble box in his hands. There was nothing special about the box, but it looked...familiar. He sat down across from me and placed the box on the small table between us. He opened the box with his terbis and pulled out a small glass vial, no bigger than a finger, with a cork stopper. He extended his hand, offering it to me.

It was cool in my palm as I studied it. The vial was nearly filled to the top with a clear liquid that glimmered as it shifted in the glass. My lips parted when I finally understood what it was that I was holding—when I realized what it was that had made me forget so efficiently.

"Is this what I think it is?" I asked softly, still studying it.

"If you think it's a demid elixir, then yes."

Shit.

I nodded slowly. I expected to feel shame, but I didn't.

Demid had been created by healers to counteract a disease that caused memory loss, and it worked. But anything good can always be twisted. Black market chemists had altered it somehow so it would incite a state of artificial euphoria. One of the side effects was temporary memory loss. It was an atrocious concoction—and highly addictive.

And now I understand why.

"This is what you gave me that night." It wasn't a question.

"Sure is." Dax leaned back in his chair, and his fingers lazily traced circles on the arms. "Do you still want it?"

Did I want it? No.

Did I feel like I needed it? Like I needed the air in my tightening lungs as my reality threatened to strangle the life out of me.

"Yes," I whispered. I knew I should have been appalled by the mere sight of the elixir, but at that moment, it looked like the Gods' grace.

I reached to unstopper the vial, but Dax plucked it from my fingertips.

"Ah ah," he said, shaking his head with a sly grin. "Last time was complimentary. You're going to have to pay for it this time."

I sighed, "How much coin do you want?"

I never had to worry about how much money I had before, rarely spending my earnings as a Roav on anything but food and a good time in taverns, but I hadn't been taking on jobs since I got back. And I hadn't worked since before Ryker came and retrieved Nikan and me and took us to Oryn. My funds were running dangerously low.

Dax leaned forward, resting his arms on his knees and twirling the vial in front of him while looking me in the eye with a devilish smile that would make anyone melt. "I never said anything about *coin*."

His low, lust-filled tone and the sinful look in his eyes told me exactly what he was wanting as payment.

And I was willing to give it for the peace in that elixir. Not to mention, I had fucked worse people for far less. At least this time was guaranteed to be beneficial for me by the end of it—unlike my recent encounters.

My only hesitation was the unexpected thought of Hakoa. I didn't know what we had, but it ended the moment I left Voara to go to the Rip with Kya. And he wasn't here. Dax was, and he had something I needed.

I stood slowly, let down my hair, and began to undress piece by piece, holding his gaze the entire time. His breathing quickened, and he reached down to adjust the growing erection in his pants.

After removing everything except for my lacy panties, he looked me up and down, pausing to stare at my bare breasts. He nodded approvingly, then stood.

"Follow me."

It felt awkward walking through his home in nothing but a small piece of fabric to cover my sex. I followed him into a room with a large, luxurious bed with posts and sheer curtains draped loosely over the top of them. Dax went to the side of the bed and turned to face me as I stepped through the doorway.

I took in the immaculate room, matching the same level of finery as the rest of what I had seen. He continued to stare, and I took that as him wanting me to take the initiative. I went to the bed, about to climb onto it, when he stopped me with a raised hand.

"Wait there."

I held back a scoff. Wasn't that what he brought me back here for? "What do you want me to do?"

Dax's lips curved into that same charming smile from before. Still holding the vial, he took off his shirt and—thank the Gods—revealed a toned body. At least he was just as attractive underneath his clothes. It made this whole thing much easier. Then he proceeded to take off his pants, his hard cock springing out of its confines. I tried not to glance at it too long, only enough to get a look at its slightly above-average size.

My body reacted, and I felt myself getting wet.

Naked, he lay on the bed with his head propped up on a pillow. "Ride my cock."

It's just one time. It's worth it. I told myself as I removed my last article of clothing then crawled on the bed and over his body, straddling his hips. His pleased look made me want to roll my eyes. But we were both getting what we wanted, so I refrained.

I lifted up and grabbed his dick at the base, giving it a single pump. Dax released a shaky, excited exhale. I swirled the tip around my entrance, lubricating him—mostly for my benefit. I pushed his tip just inside of me but didn't go any farther. Dax grabbed my hips, trying to pull me down as he thrust. But I rose higher, refusing him. His face pinched in confusion.

I held out my hand.

"All business with you," he chuckled. He handed the demid to me, and I grasped it in my palm.

I looked him in the eyes, and I saw them roll to the back of his head as I slowly sat down, filling myself with him. I released a soft gasp and my eyes fluttered closed.

I certainly didn't mind this form of payment. It felt good. In fact, it helped me forget about everything. But, like with everyone else, it was only for a moment. I unstoppered the vial and tossed the cork aside. I should have been humiliated, but I was too focused on obtaining the oblivion the demid was about to give me.

As I brought the glass up to my lips, I promised myself I wouldn't let it get out of control. I convinced myself I was stronger than the others—the ones that had fallen to the addiction. This was just a temporary fix until I could stop feeling the weight of what I had done.

Dax moaned when I started riding him just as he requested. His grip on my hips tightened, and he kneaded the flesh there soothingly before he started slamming me down on top of him.

"Don't worry," he said between grunts. "I'll make this feel good for you too."

But that wasn't what I was here for.

"I don't want to feel anything," I whispered. Then I tilted up the vial and swallowed my damnation.

Chapter Sixteen

KYA

I t had been another two days, and no one had come down the corridor outside my cell. No one brought me anything to eat or drink. And if I wasn't going to starve to death, I was surely going to die of pure boredom—I had nothing to do but think to the point of insanity. But I did everything I could think of to keep myself occupied, hoping to distract myself from my thoughts and the burning bond inside me.

The constant ache of my unused magic was slowly driving me crazy. I wanted to tear myself free of my own skin at the unnatural feeling buzzing inside me. I wondered if this was what it was like on the Drift Islands, if this was what my family had been going through for over twenty years.

I started exercising in the small space, doing various stretches and activities—I wasn't going to let myself get any weaker. To keep my mind busy, I hoisted myself up to the window to observe the landscape as far as I could see outside of the prison. This proved to be beneficial in more ways than one—not only was I able to keep my thoughts focused elsewhere, but I was also making mental notes for when I could escape. I would need to know where the best places were to hide, such as behind other structures, or in the trees. I learned that the mountain was barren and while it was a good vantage point for higher ground, it provided no cover, and I would need to steer clear of it. I replayed the fantastical stories of books I had read, trying to recall all I knew about other magics or realms and wondering if those were all actually real or myth as I had believed before.

But most of my time was spent lying on the bed, staring up at the ceiling and replaying my memories—namely the ones of Daegel. I needed to learn about him the most. However, from the few interactions I'd had with the dark wielder, I knew very little besides that my Waalu had a negative effect on him, and he was remarkably fast and powerful.

Over and over in my head, I thought of what Vicria had said.

She had served under him after they struck a deal together. She helped him find where to attack with the Glaev based on his reserves. And reserves meant he had limits. He was searching for the dark book, but from everything I had learned from the translations, I couldn't think of what was in there that he needed so badly.

Not that I could remember everything it said. I didn't consider myself stupid but I sure-as-shit wasn't *that* smart. And did he even need it?

He had been looking for me, the *diamond*. I closed my eyes to recall Vicria's exact words.

"A diamond, found within the darkness of fate—a female, one of the last daughters. A Worthy with no Nation."

Yep. That was me.

But that didn't give me any indication as to why he had been looking for me. I knew he wanted me to submit to his will, but for what?

"What do you want with me, Daegel?" I whispered into the empty room.

Then there was Leysa. She and I were both taken from Taeralia, and we both wanted to return to our mates. My lips stretched into a smile.

We can work together.

She had been here for fifty years. She knew this place, at least better than I did. She had to have some kind of information that would prove to be useful. If not against Daegel, then at the very least on how to get back home.

Leysa clearly wasn't a prisoner like I was. She wasn't confined to a cell—at least not in here. And she didn't have a collar. Perhaps she had gained Daegel's trust. That could be used to our advantage.

I heard footsteps approaching my door. I sat up and waited with my legs crossed beneath me. It was nerve-wracking, wondering who would come through that door next. I just hoped it was someone with food and water.

And thank the Gods it was.

The lock clicked, and Leysa entered, holding a tray of the same food as last time with a large jug of water. I couldn't restrain myself as I leapt off the bed and met her halfway, taking the items from her hands. I didn't even sit down or greet her before I began shoving the food in my mouth and chugging the water.

Leysa didn't say a word as she sat down next to me and watched while I ate. When I was finished, having eaten everything and drunk over half of the water, I finally looked up at her.

She was freshly bathed, with clean clothes, and the top half of her hair was twisted into two braids behind her head. What I would have done for a bath, clean clothes, and a brush to get the tangles out of my hair. Except for compliance.

"Thanks for that," I said, nodding my head toward the empty tray and water jug.

"Don't thank me just yet. I'm not here for a social visit." She offered a tight-lipped smile. "Daegel wants you to begin."

My eyebrows creased. "Begin what?"

"I don't know." She shrugged. "But I doubt it's anything good."

"And it's happening...here?" I asked skeptically.

"No, he's taking us somewhere else. And before you ask, I don't know where. He didn't tell me."

I glanced down at my clothes and eyed the fact I still didn't have shoes. "In this?" I gestured to myself.

Leysa nodded. "You're suffering enough already. Take my advice and the lessons I've had to learn the hard way. Do what he asks. It's not a fight you can win."

A few minutes later, I was stepping through the door to my cell. I entered a long, seemingly endless corridor lined with doors that looked identical to mine. I assumed they each held a prisoner. Leysa stood with another male I hadn't seen before. He had a tightly trimmed beard that matched his long, light blond hair pulled half up to reveal his rounded ears, and eyes so dark they almost looked black. He was tall, slightly taller than Daegel but not quite as tall as Ryker. His broad, muscular frame was clothed in a short-sleeved, leather shirt lined with fur, and I noted strange tattoos with designs I had never seen before peeking out from beneath the sleeves.

"Diamond," the male greeted in an accent with a stone-cold expression.

"My name is Kya," I snapped.

I hated the name Daegel gave me, and I didn't care if that's what Kya meant. I was also caught off guard that he spoke my language.

He held my stare. "A name is nothing more than a word to differentiate you from every other ant in this world. A title is what sets you apart and establishes your power here. Titles are what define you."

Not where I come from.

I narrowed my eyes. "And what is your *title*? Daegel's bitch?" I sneered.

The male huffed a humorless laugh and glanced at Leysa. "She's got quite a mouth on her."

Leysa didn't say anything, and her face remained expressionless.

He looked back at me. "It's Talum. And I'd keep that mouth shut if you know what's good for you." He began to walk away.

Leysa gently nudged me to follow, and I only did at her urging. I fell into step next to her, and we walked behind Talum down the corridor until we came to a set of stairs leading up to a metal door. He pushed the door open, and I squinted against the sunlight as we stepped through.

Leysa shut the door behind us, and I turned to face her. My lips parted when I saw the building I had been held prisoner in. I thought it would have been an intimidating sight but it was shockingly underwhelming. The roof was just below my eyeline, mostly buried underground, and it was no bigger than an average home with a flat roof littered with guards.

"*That's* the prison? How is it so small?" It seemed so large from the inside.

Leysa shrugged. "Magic? One of the many mysteries I haven't figured out yet."

"Their magic is very different," I mumbled quietly as my eyes roamed the surrounding landscape.

"Indeed," Talum said.

I turned back around to look at him, and he led us toward the patch of trees I saw from the window in my cell. Everyone remained quiet as we walked. Out of the corner of my eye,

I noticed Leysa looked unbothered. Perhaps she was just used to being here, but I was on edge, keeping my eyes trained everywhere, looking for any dangers and learning all I could. I hated that I couldn't feel anything with my terbis—its absence made me feel blind.

"It'll be okay," Leysa said, offering me a sad, understanding smile. "Remember what I said. If you do what he asks, it won't be as bad."

We breached the treeline, and I felt something inside of me settle. The familiar scent of the damp forest floor and the bark of the trees was welcoming to my senses and my eyelids fluttered closed for a moment as I inhaled deeply.

When I opened my eyes again, Talum was looking at me with his head cocked to the side. I glared back at him.

"What?" I snapped.

He exhaled. "Look, I get that I seem like an enemy, but I promise I'm not."

I rolled my eyes. "Right. We're just the best of friends."

Leysa cleared her throat, her eyes asking a silent question to Talum, and he nodded his head.

"Kya, he's not so bad." Her voice was soft, but her eyes bored into me with a warning, a plea. I understood her message: Behave.

We walked in silence for the rest of the journey through the forest. The vegetation was becoming more and more dense the deeper we went. I wondered where we were going, but I wasn't about to ask. Following a narrow path, we emerged into a small clearing. There was nothing significant about it aside from a perfectly circular stone set into the ground.

We approached it, and it was then I noticed the stone was engraved with symbols.

"Wait…" I whispered under my breath. I pushed up my sleeve to reveal my Trial mark.

The symbols marked upon my skin by the Gods were the same symbols on the stone. My lips parted in awe, and I whipped my head around to Leysa.

"What is this?" I asked.

"It is Horgor," Talum offered, saying the strange term in a thick accent.

I looked at him with a quirked eyebrow, not understanding what that was supposed to mean. I glanced at Leysa, but she just shrugged, clearly not knowing what it was either.

He sighed, "It's a… How do I explain in your words? It is a sacred stone of…foot."

"A stepstone?" Leysa asked.

"Sure." Talum shrugged. "It's a sacred stepstone of God."

Both of my eyebrows raised. "God? As in singular?"

"Yes," Talum said flatly.

Leysa cleared her throat. "There is only one God in this realm."

My mouth fell open as I stared at them.

Only one? Is that even possible? Can the Gods have their own realms? Do they all have different realms or is this the only one?

My mind reeled with question after question.

"Well…which one is it?" I asked Leysa.

She shook her head and opened her mouth to speak but stopped when the symbols on the stone glowed with a soft white light.

Daegel materialized out of thin air upon the stone—his eyes already locked on mine. He held out his hand to me with a hard look in his eyes.

"Come, Diamond. It's time to see if you're truly worthy."

Chapter Seventeen

RYKER

After the mating trial, I needed to clear my head. I had to follow that drive within me to get to Kya, and the closest I could get to her was the last place she was before leaving this world.

Theron Traveled me to the Rip, right where Kya had fallen. He remained away from the edge but kept his eyes on me the entire time, like he was concerned I'd do something stupid.

"Will you stop staring? I'm not going to jump in," I snapped. I could feel his gaze on my back as I stood at the edge, looking down into the endless depth of Odes' grave.

"You have tried before," he growled.

True. But because I couldn't help but wonder what would happen if I went in. Would I be taken where she is? Or would I simply fall to my death?

"Little gem... Where are you?" I reached for the bond but, just like every other time I had tried, there was nothing.

It was only pissing me off more, so I decided to back-track everywhere she went before she fell, studying the land with a trained eye. I followed the now-sparse trail of the Glaev, tracking it along the beach which was quickly being washed away with the rising tide. Careful of my steps, I continued to follow it north, toward the Atara border at the end of the Rip. But once I got to the very edge of it, there was grass.

Interesting.

"Theron, where did you leave Kya when you brought her here?"

"On the other side of the Rip, in a clearing."

"On the other side?" I echoed.

"Yes, that is what I just told you."

"But then you left." I bent down to inspect the ground.

"We have been over this. Yes," he said harshly.

"So she had to get her and Malina to this side, right?" I asked.

"I assume. But again, I was not present for the events that occurred here."

"Damnit, Theron. I know that. I'm just…talking it out, so for five minutes, stop being such a fucking ass."

He didn't say anything else, and I resumed studying the once Glaev-infested land.

"Kya did this. She cleared the way from one side of the Rip to the other. And her energy continuously restores, even after she's left. Just like Voara." I stood up straight and gazed at the expanse of clear land before me.

"That is how Waalu works. Once it is given form, it will not stop until something just as equally—or more—powerful stops it," Theron offered. And less harshly this time, though I could hear the annoyance in his voice.

"Atara is healing," I whispered. I could see the Glaev in the distance and just at the edge of it was a soft, almost indiscernible glow of jade.

My jaw fell open in awe of what Kya was capable of.

My strong and powerful mate.

I nearly smiled to myself, pride filling me and making me stand tall. I could be angry with Kya all I wanted, but it didn't mean I wasn't proud of her.

Without thought, my feet carried me forward as I walked, landing lightly on the freshly formed grass. My breath caught, and I swallowed back the ache in my throat. A bittersweet smile tugged at my lips—I was the first person to stand here since its destruction. The Atara Nation, my mate's Nation, was renewed. And I was going to make sure Kya would see it.

Theron Traveled me straight to Ilrek just outside the city right before dusk. I didn't waste any time getting to Morah, shifting my wings and flying over the city's rings to the library. The gravel crunched beneath my boots as I landed, then I bounded up the steps, two at a time, and pushed open the large double doors into the library.

I tried not to think about it, but I couldn't help the pang of longing for Kya when I entered. My eyes gazed up to the residential level that held her rooms. The memory of staying with her that night almost made me smile, but it quickly fell.

I shook my head, clearing my thoughts. I didn't want to lose myself and wallow in my grief. I needed to stay on task and motivated.

I made my way up the stairs to the High Scholar's study. The door was ajar, and I heard voices, but they were too quiet for me to make out the words. I stopped just outside the door and listened.

"...would have done so by now. It's not your decision to make, and you can't force it."

"Maybe this is for the best, Nikan. He's here to help. We can get her out of this—"

At the mention of "her", I burst through the doors. Hakoa was standing there with his arms crossed, glaring at Eamon. Eamon and Nikan startled and spun to face me—the latter instinctively wielding a fragment of the stone floor into the air, and aiming it at me.

"Lord Ryker," Eamon gasped with wide eyes and a hand over his chest. "What are you—"

"*Who* are you talking about?" I stomped my way across the room. If they had any information about Kya and had been keeping it from me...

"Wha— Erm, Malina," Eamon said with a confused look.

I relaxed slightly. "Not Kya?"

"No." Nikan guided the stone back into its place in the floor with his terbis. "Not Kya."

My eyes cut to Hakoa.

"Nikan and Eamon were just telling me about the *unsettling* situation with Malina," Hakoa explained with a sneer aimed toward Nikan.

Nikan crossed his arms and looked at Hakoa with narrowed eyes. "She's...going through something. But I've got it handled."

Hakoa opened his mouth to speak, but I stopped him with a whisper into his mind, *"Later, Hakoa. This is important."*

"So is this. You're here for your female, I'm here for mine."

Nikan lifted his head and glanced behind me. "You didn't bring your brother?" he asked.

"He's dealing with things back in Oryn. Some of which I need to discuss with Eamon," I said, giving Eamon a pointed look.

Nikan nodded with understanding, but his eyes flickered with something else. Whatever it was, it wasn't my concern.

"What can I do for you?" Eamon asked, and gestured for us to sit down.

"I'll be going," Nikan excused himself and bowed his head to Eamon then to me, and briefly glared at Hakoa before leaving the study.

Hakoa cleared his throat as I sat down and subtly jutted his head toward the door.

I nodded, conveying we would talk later.

He rushed out of the study to catch up with Nikan.

Eamon sat across from me with his hands clasped in his lap, patiently waiting for me to speak. There was a lot to catch him up on and I didn't know what Malina or Nikan had told him.

"There are several things I need to inform you of, and I will also need a favor. First, and most importantly, Kya is alive."

Eamon's neutral expression became one of pity. "Lord Ryker, I know you hold out hope but...Kya fell. She's gone. What you're feeling—"

"Stop." My cold voice boomed in the room. "She *is* alive. I know it. I haven't gone mad and I don't have the time to explain my bond. This isn't a false hope, it's a *fact*."

The look in his wary eyes told me he still didn't believe me. Fine. He didn't have to.

"I need to show you something. Come with me."

Eamon didn't hesitate to follow me up the stairs to the top of Morah, until eventually we were on the ledge that Kya had shown me.

"What... I didn't even know this was here," Eamon breathed.

"And you still don't." I gave him a firm look as we stepped to the edge.

"But how did it get here?" he asked with astonishment.

"It's not my story to tell."

"Then why did you show me?"

"This isn't what I wanted to show you. It's just the easiest place for him to meet us."

Eamon tilted his head to the side. "Who?"

"Theron," I called.

Theron appeared in the air directly in front of us, his massive body moving up and down with each beat of his leathery wings, my cloak lifting from the chilled gusts of air. His chest rumbled and he lowered his head until the slits in his red eyes were level with mine.

I could smell fear pouring from Eamon, but I ignored it and placed my hand on his shoulder as I touched Theron's snout just above his protruding teeth. Then we left and appeared in a field. I closed my eyes and took a deep breath, scenting the fresh grass that filled my senses.

Eamon coughed back a gag, covering his mouth and clenching his stomach through his beige shirt.

"In all my years, I never thought I'd ever transport with a Spirit." He finished his coughing fit and stood fully. His eyes widened when he spotted the Rip behind me. "Where are we?"

The side of my mouth lifted.

"Atara," I said quietly. I raised my head slightly, gesturing to the soft jade glow at the edge of the Glaev behind him.

"Atara? That's imposs—" He stopped when he turned around and saw the Glaev being eaten away.

His jaw dropped as he gazed at the plague that had terrorized the continent for decades transforming into life once again. He stepped forward, and I followed until he stopped at the edge and bent down to inspect the wondrous magic.

"That's Waalu—Kya's energy magic from her Spirit. It counteracts the dark magic, wielded by Daegel, that makes the Glaev," I said.

"Worthy in so many ways..." he whispered to himself as he continued to marvel.

Indeed.

"Eamon." He looked up at me. "I need your help."

He stood and faced me, giving me his full attention.

"Our mating trial was conducted in Bhara today, and the panel granted approval of our mating—but only because they think she's dead. If the other Worthy find out Atara is healing—"

"They'll want to claim it," he finished.

"Exactly."

Eamon nodded slowly. "So, what do you need me to do? I certainly can't stop them. We're a neutral Nation run by councils," he huffed a humorous chuckle and shrugged.

"And *you* are the High Scholar."

His brows bunched in confusion.

"You're part of the Council of Scholars, which means you hold the highest influence over the laws and how information is distributed among the Nations." He nodded as I continued, "I need you to stifle any rumors about Atara and help me keep people away from it until Kya comes back to defend it. No one rational will touch a Nation that has a Worthy to protect it. Especially one mated with another Worthy of a bordering Nation."

He sighed and ran his hand through his graying hair. "Let's say Kya is alive."

She is.

"I can withhold information for as long as possible but I can't do it indefinitely. They will discover it eventually, and there's no proof, aside from your claim, that she isn't dead—let alone that she will come back. And this," he gestured to the land, "doesn't prove it either. You can't protect it forever."

I won't need to.

"I know you're a male of facts and evidence of truth. But just this once, I need you to have faith. Kya *is* alive. She's lost in another realm, and I *will* get her back." I stepped closer to him. "I'm not asking the High Scholar of Morah. I'm asking the male

145

who is like a father to my wife." I pulled up my sleeve to reveal the marriage band around my wrist.

His eyes softened, and his shoulders lowered. "For Kya."

"Yes. For Kya."

Eamon nodded. "I'll do what I can to divert any information about Atara. And I can issue a prohibition from the area—say it's unstable or something."

If Eamon could control the flow of information, we could keep any rumors at bay for the time being. Hopefully. I planned to go back to Voara and give the order to keep away from the Ataran border. And any who did go near it would be strictly instructed to hold their tongue about anything they saw.

There wasn't anything I could do about Dusan. Thankfully, most Dusanian citizens had moved away from the border since the destruction of Atara, and it had remained mostly uninhabited with the exception of travelers making their way north through Riyah.

And again, Eamon was the High Scholar—one of the most influential fae on the continent. And he just so happened to be the closest thing to a father Kya has had. He would help her. He'd want to do everything he could to keep a war from ensuing between the Nations.

"What else do you need from me?" he asked.

"I just need time."

Chapter Eighteen

ZALEN

The problem with morality was it was subjective. Nothing was ever inherently right or wrong.

And I had my own definition.

Thane and I stood with a select group of loyal sorcerers at the edge of the treeline just inside the Aedum border. We wore all black, and masks covered our faces. We could see the castle in Myrrn from where we hid, but the difficult part was getting across the open plain between here and there. I had a plan for that, but planning took time and that was the reason for our arrival at the early morning hour.

I hated to do it, but I had to miss my window to see Maera earlier. It took time to gather what I needed for tonight. It was a choice between one more stolen moment or solving my problems all at once. I preferred efficiency.

Thane and I spent the entire night coordinating this moment. We continued to wait, watching the castle's first line of defense—human guards. While humans had no magic, they were great in numbers. But numbers weren't enough.

Finally, it was time for the guards' shift change. The new set of guards emerged to take their place, and this was the moment we were waiting for—when their defenses were only stationed at the entrances.

Thane and I exchanged a look. With a nod of my head, he gave the hand signal to launch the first attack. We all stood, getting into position and holding out the spears in our hands.

"Leggja," we uttered in unison, and the spears lifted from our palms and flew across the landscape.

I could hear the spears whistling through the air just before the thumps that followed. Apart from the singing of the spears, it was a silent attack. More thumps sounded as bodies fell to the ground with grunts, and that was our signal to jump out from behind the trees and race across the plain to the castle walls.

We ran as fast and as quietly as we could. I pumped my arms and legs harder as one of the guards on the ground groaned loudly.

"Kyrr," I cast a silencing spell when I was in close enough proximity. His pleading eyes went wide as I bent down and slit his throat with the large knife I drew from my hip.

Thane rushed past me, continuing on as ordered, and leapt up the stairs to the doors of the castle while everyone else rushed to the other guards and finished off those that still breathed. I stood and followed after Thane, who had his ear pressed to the door.

He looked at me and held his finger up. I glanced over to see the rest of the group gathered behind me.

"Take over Aedum. Bring me the Elders. Kill all in the castle but the King—he belongs to me. And anyone who so much as touches the Samanya daughter will be my next guest in a Vord cell," I ordered. I needed the King, and I needed him *alone*. After that, the Kingdom was as good as mine.

With blood-hungry grins, they began dispersing around the perimeter of the castle, going to their designated breaching points. After a couple of seconds, Thane nodded and stepped back.

"Gatt," I whispered the opening spell and twisted my hand. The large metal door lock clicked softly.

Thane pulled on the handle, opening it just enough for me to pass through and followed in behind me. The antechamber to the Aedum castle was a large space with long corridors splitting off in all directions like the spikes of a star. The largest one, in the center, would lead to King Erix's throne room. The left held the barracks, the ones on the right would lead to the eastern wings and the residences.

That was my target.

I jutted my head toward the western wings. "Find the captain of the guard. I want him in a cell."

The side of Thane's mouth lifted into a malicious smile. "Gladly." He set off around the corner, and a few moments later I heard the whispers of spells being cast.

I spun and stealthily made my way to the eastern wing, navigating through corridor after corridor, killing every guard in sight until I came upon a set of wooden doors carved with the symbol of the Aedum Kingdom. I pushed open the door, leaving a bloody handprint on the smooth grain, and crossed the room to the side of the bed where King Erix lay asleep next to his wife, Queen Solana.

I tilted my head to the side as I studied them. They looked so peaceful in their sleep—peace they didn't deserve. I didn't have to convince myself they needed to die, I had always known. From years of hearing Maera recount stories of the torment they had inflicted upon her, I had long fantasized about putting them in one of the Vord cells and spending days listening to the delicious sounds of their screams.

But I didn't have time for that. Not when their Kingdom's magic was still enhanced by a King.

I removed the rope from my belt.

"Binda," I said with a wave of my hand. I was pleased at how easily the spell flowed from my fingers, and I couldn't wait for the day when I didn't need words at all and only required the simple movements of my hand—something only the most powerful sorcerers could achieve.

The rope wrapped around Erix's wrists and ankles, binding him such that he wouldn't be able to use magic. He started to move, jostling beneath the sheets. His movements stirred Solana and she woke first, turning to face her husband.

She gasped, instinctively reaching for the defensive potion bottles on her nightstand, and screamed when she saw me looming over Erix.

That would certainly wake the rest of the castle.

"Slitna." I conjured the spell to snap Solana's neck, killing her quickly and efficiently before she had the chance to unleash whatever concoction she held—most witches lacked spells, but their potions were just as deadly. Even sorcerers had little defense against them.

She had agreed to marry off her daughter to someone who wasn't even worth walking on the same ground as Maera. She deserved to die, but she didn't need to suffer. Not like Erix would. He was the greatest threat to my existence.

I knew that Maera would feel conflicted. She still loved her mother for some fucking reason, but she had also confessed how much better her life would be if her mother would just peacefully die to release her from her wretched clutches. I was only giving her what she truly desired.

"No!" Erix screamed. "No! Lana, no! What have you done?" He was scrambling against his bindings, trying to get to her. "Fjoturr!"

I dove, leaping out of the way as hidden shackles burst from the walls toward me. I fucked up and underestimated how powerful he was. A mistake I wouldn't make again.

Erix kicked and thrashed, falling to the floor with a crash as he tried to get up. "Guar—"

"Shut up." I punched him square in the jaw, his head snapping to the side.

"You fucking bastard," he yelled, showcasing the blood crawling across his teeth. "I will hang you by your useless balls and laugh as you fill my throne room with your screams. Ta—"

"Kyrr," I said quickly, cutting off his words and rendering him mute. I should have done that initially. Lesson learned.

I sat down on the floor beside him. His pulse raced, each breath coming sharper and quicker as I placed the tip of my knife at his throat.

"A tempting proposition. But you're not the one I'm here for," I said with a sinister grin.

His eyes widened, and he shook his head rapidly. I savored the fear in his eyes.

Leaning in close, I pressed on the blade, puncturing the skin. Curling my lip, I pushed harder until the knife hit the back of his throat. His mouth gaped open as he choked, blood trickling from the sides of his mouth as he began to aspirate his own fluids.

"Don't worry. I'll take good care of your daughter. And I fully intend to fill your throne room with *her* screams."

With a snarl, I ripped the knife to the side, severing half of his neck and spraying the crimson liquid on the walls. I watched the life leave his eyes. I wasn't moving from that spot until I knew for certain he was dead.

I hoped this fucking worked. It was one thing to take power that shared my blood, but it was completely unknown if this would work for someone I wasn't related to.

The moment his heart stopped beating, I held my hand over his chest, repeating the same spell I had used with Makkor. "Stela."

I grunted, gritting my teeth as Erix's fresh power stretched out from his lifeless body and into my palm as his magic was drawn into my blood. With the majority of his magic still present, the sensation was much more intense than it had been with Makkor. And it took considerably longer.

While my father's power took only a minute, Erix's took several. Sweat beaded along my brow and I willed myself to remain, absorbing every last bit of his power no matter how unnatural it felt. For a moment, I second-guessed myself and wondered if this was a mistake, but then I shoved that thought aside. It wasn't a mistake. It was necessary.

The transfer of power from one King to another would have been fast enough his people likely wouldn't notice. But the moment they learned that I held the power of the Aedum Kingdom, they would fall in line. They couldn't kill me. Not when I was now the pillar of their strength.

A soft gasp came from the doorway behind me, bringing me out of my thoughts, and I snapped my head toward the sound.

Maera stood just outside the room, braced on the door frame with trembling fingers over her lips, staring in horror at the gruesome sight of me standing over her dead father. Even in a state of terror, she looked beautiful. Her hair was down, cascading across her shoulder over her silky, knee-high nightgown.

I stood slowly. I couldn't resist the urge to touch her, and I made to step forward but stopped. She pulled something from her pocket I recognized as a potion vial. Her eyes blazed, glistening with tears, but I wasn't sure if it was from sadness or relief—maybe rage.

My fiery little witch.

I remembered then that I was still masked, and she didn't know who I was. I smiled under the fabric, my eyes crinkling at the sides.

This will be fun.

The sounds of shouting and fighting came from somewhere within the castle, and Maera flinched. I took a step toward her, raising my hand to remove the mask. Her eyes widened, and she threw the potion on the ground. She fled down the corridor as the glass shattered. Red smoke billowed from the concoction—lightning brew.

Shit!

I dove to the side of the bed, hoping it would provide enough cover, just before the potion erupted with streaks of lightning bursting from it. Chips of stone from the walls, glass from the window, and debris from the furniture were zipping across the room. I covered my head.

The potion didn't last long—about five seconds—but it was a *very* long five seconds. Once the lightning stopped, I jumped to my feet and rushed out the door. Maera now had a head start on me. But I was faster, and the hunt was my specialty.

I couldn't help the thrill tingling in my veins as I bolted down the corridor, sensing which direction Maera had gone.

There.

A flash of blonde hair darted around the corner.

I didn't even need to run. There was nowhere for her to go. I knew my men had all the exits blocked, and the rest of them were taking care of those left in the castle. I continued to prowl down the corridor, listening for her hurried steps.

Someone burst through a door next to me, a castle guard that had been missed. He lunged for me with a maiming spell that I interrupted with a knife to the stomach. I pulled out the blade and stabbed him in the chest just as I heard Maera scream. The next thing I heard was the shattering of glass and the yelling of men—probably mine—coming from the antechamber. Then the sound of those light footsteps against the stone floor coming down the corridor toward me.

Maera stopped in her tracks when she turned the corner and saw me dropping the dead guard. She spun around and ran in another direction. This time I did run. She was headed in the wrong direction.

It didn't take long for me to catch up to her, and I could hear the fear in her erratic breaths as I wrapped my arm around her stomach and covered her mouth with my other hand. Maera kicked and thrashed and fought, trying to get away from me. She screamed against my hand and even tried to bite me.

Such a wicked little thing.

I loved seeing her break free from the delicate, subservient role she had been forced into.

Chasing her down had me hard and ready, but having her fight me like this just made me want to press her against the wall and have my way with her. And I would, in time.

She reached back and tried to scratch my face only to be met with the fabric of my mask before I pinned her to the wall, face against the stone. I trailed my nose along the column of her neck, up to the soft spot behind her ear.

"You remember what to do if you want me to stop?" I said in a low voice against her ear.

She stopped moving and relaxed slightly, her shoulders dropping in recognition of my voice—but still tense.

"I need an answer," I said firmly, and she shivered before she nodded.

Good.

Releasing my hold on her arms, I reached underneath her skirt and trailed my fingers up her inner thigh. Her soft skin pebbled at my touch. It had been too long since I felt her against me and I vowed right then and there I wouldn't let it happen again.

She slapped my hands, prying off the one over her mouth and fighting against me. "Zalen, what is the matter with you? You just *killed* them!"

I kicked her legs apart and my fingers moved up farther until I touched her undergarment.

It was damp, just as I suspected.

I ran my finger across her wet cunt, and her breath hitched. I pushed two fingers inside, curling them forward just how she liked it.

"And I'll kill anyone else who gets in my way of having you," I said in a lethal voice that left no room for question.

"You're a monster," she said breathlessly.

"I'm *your* monster."

I grabbed her arm and spun her around, pushing her against the wall and pinning it above her with one hand. Her pupils were wide with excitement, high on the pleasure I was providing her, but the blue in her eyes sparkled with deep desire. Her life had been dull and mundane. I had changed that for her. I had shown her that she didn't need to be ashamed of what she craved.

She willingly raised her other arm and I snatched her wrist in my grasp. She leaned forward and gripped the fabric of my mask between her teeth and pulled it down to my neck, revealing my face.

My mouth crashed into hers, greedy for her taste—devouring her lips, her jaw, her neck, as the palm of my hand rubbed against her. Her lips parted for me, and my tongue roamed in her mouth, tasting and consuming her.

There was nothing to stop me. Nothing to get in my way any longer. This was what all of this was for—her.

It pained me almost as much as it pained her when I peeled my mouth off her and removed my hand.

Maera whimpered in protest, but I softly kissed it away.

"Shh," I said, pulling back. "Not yet."

Still holding her wrists, I bent down and curled her over my shoulder before releasing them as I stood, then carried her away down the corridor.

"Zalen!" she squealed. "Put me down, I'm too heavy."

I smacked her ass, the sharp slap echoing off the walls, and she yelped.

I chuckled, "You insult my strength, love."

She scoffed. "So where are you taking me now that you've successfully seduced me and killed my family?"

"I made your father a promise."

We approached the throne room. Thane and two others stood outside the doors with their brows raised as they eyed the Samanya daughter hanging over my shoulder.

"Close the doors behind me and let no one enter," I commanded.

They bowed their heads as we passed, and closed the doors behind us.

My boots clicked against the floor, creating an echo that punctured the silence of the large space as I approached the throne.

I turned and set Maera down facing the throne, to see it in all its glory one last time.

Her expression was neutral as she looked at it, but I could see every emotion swirling in her eyes. All warring with each other. And she had every right to feel it all. While her parents had been callous and selfish, they were still her parents, and the man she loved just killed them in their bed. But I knew she had silently hoped for this. She wanted to be rescued from this hell of a life she had no control over, even if she never said it out loud.

"What kind of person am I, upset my family is dead but also happy they're finally gone?" she asked in a low whisper, more to herself than to me. A tear fell, and she tried to blink more away—trying to be brave in the face of it all.

I hooked a finger underneath her chin and lifted her head to look at me. I brushed my thumb across her cheek, drying her eyes.

"It's alright to be upset. But they have never earned your tears."

"What about you? You did this," she said with that same boldness that had made me fall for her, the one that few had the honor of seeing in her monotonous life.

I gripped her chin hard and pulled her closer, our lips nearly touching.

"I have earned your tears and more."

"I don't know if they deserved death. Others have gone through worse. What makes me so special?" she asked bitterly. She could try to be mad at me all she wanted, but I knew her better than she knew herself.

"Because, love, I don't give a shit about anyone else but you." I released her chin and stepped back, seating myself on the Aedum throne. It was a statement more than anything, but really, it was just a chair.

"Come here, Maera." I curled my index finger toward her.

She hesitated, looking at me warily, but did as I requested and stood in front of me.

I reached underneath her nightgown and tore away her thin undergarment, stuffing it in my pocket. Her mouth gaped as she made a sound of protest I ignored. It wasn't the word that would stop it all, so I continued. She could end this at any moment, but she chose not to speak the word. I twisted her around and pulled her down on top of me, making her straddle my legs with her back against my chest.

She didn't know it yet, but she needed this. She needed to spit in the face of her past, and rise above every demand placed on her since birth. This was how she would begin to take control of her life and make it into what she truly desired—what she deserved.

I shifted her hair over one shoulder, kissing the delicate flesh at the base of her neck. Trailing my fingers over her skin, I pulled the straps of her nightgown down each arm and the silky fabric pooled at her waist, exposing her breasts—the chill of the air peaking her nipples.

"What are you doing?" She sounded nervous, eyeing the doors where my men were stationed just outside.

I grazed my lips up her neck, leaving a hot trail that made her shiver. "Ensuring the world knows who you belong to."

I shifted my knees, spreading her legs further apart. I rubbed my hands along her thighs, up and up and up, lightly grazing my fingers over her clit with a whisper of touch—a tease.

She pressed herself against me, and I worked her harder, circling my palm against her clit. Her breaths grew heavy, and her head fell back on my chest. I leaned my head down and licked up the column of her throat, eliciting a moan from her.

She was opening up to me, the worries of her life falling away with every stroke of my fingers. She started riding my hand and I couldn't help but grind myself against her perfect ass. Her palms slapped against the arms of the throne as she used it for leverage to push against my hand harder and faster, and I continued to fuck her with dripping fingers. She was ready for me, greedy for me.

I pushed her forward, balancing her on my knees, and un-buckled my belt—the clanking of the metal was deafening in the quiet room. There was no hiding my intentions, but then again, I wasn't planning on discretion.

Her eyes flared as she nervously looked across the room, then to her father's blood drying on my chest.

I was sitting on his throne, in his Kingdom I'd just over-thrown. And goddamn, I wanted her. Needed her. Needed to claim her, just like I had this Kingdom.

I knew this was different for her. For both of us really. We weren't in the safety of our cottage. This was a statement, and fuck it, I'd never wanted her so badly.

"Zalen, I don't think—"

"I want you, Maera. And I finally get to have you." I pulled her back, angling her so she rested against the length of my cock.

"What if someone comes in?"

"They won't," I assured her.

I moved my hips against her sweet cunt, grinning as I felt the slickness of her, threatening to make me lose all control.

I knew she wanted me. She didn't *want* to want me at this moment, but she did. She always did.

She leaned back against my chest. I moved back and forth, rubbing my cock against her and feeling how utterly soaked she was.

Languidly roaming my hands over her body, I took my time—coaxing her sadness and anger to fall away until there was nothing left but us. The breathy sounds that came from her lips had me grabbing her hips and lifting, holding her in place to position myself at her entrance.

I cupped her cheek and turned her to face me. I wanted to see the look in her eyes.

Our mouths crashed together just before I thrust into her, burying myself to the hilt. I groaned at the tightness of her hot, wet pussy.

She gasped as she stretched around me.

"Zalen," she moaned softly against my lips. "This is wrong and fucked up in so many ways."

I chuckled and slowly pulled out of her, just to the tip, then slammed back in.

"When I'm done fucking you on your father's throne, I'll take you back to Kanth and fuck you on mine." I pulled out and slammed back in. "Then I'll have you begging me to fuck you on yours." My hand moved to her clit, rubbing in circles, and her breaths came quicker. "I'll conquer every Kingdom and claim you on every single one of them. I don't care how wrong it seems."

I felt her pulse racing with anticipation. Her body was tensing, and she was breathing so hard she couldn't respond.

I lifted her slightly, gripping her soft hips tightly enough to bruise—I would lick them away later.

She touched herself, swirling her fingers over her clit while meeting me with each thrust. Seeing her enjoying her own body, it did something to me.

"That's it. Just like that," I praised. Seeing her bring herself pleasure while I was inside her was irresistibly sexy. "Fuck, Maera. Look at how powerful you are—touching yourself while fucking your enemy on the throne."

I could feel her body tensing, her pleasure building. Her head fell back as she panted, her lust-filled eyes rolling back with a moan that filled the room.

I groaned, my own pleasure threatening to spill into her. But I wasn't done just yet. I needed more from her.

"Hold on tight," I said in a husky tone and nipped at her throat.

Maera braced her hands on the arms of the throne. With her holding herself up, my hands hungrily roamed her body as I leaned back farther and continued to thrust. At this angle,

I could see my soaking wet cock sliding in and out of her, stretching her pussy around me.

I grasped her breast in one hand, pinching her nipple to the point of pain before brushing over it soothingly with my thumb. My other hand snaked down to her clit, picking up where she left off.

She cried out as I slammed into her hard and fast, and *fuck* did she feel good. I grabbed a fistful of her hair, pulling her head back and pounding into her relentlessly.

"Zalen… Zalen… Zalen!" she screamed my name, her voice piercing every corner of the throne room as she came on my cock, pulsing around me with her climax.

Her release was my undoing and I groaned, filling her with my cum.

I had kept my promise.

Chapter Nineteen

KYA

*T*ime to see if you're truly Worthy...

Daegel's words repeated in my head over and over as he held out his hand toward me. I didn't care if he saw me as Worthy or not. I knew my value, and a male's opinion wouldn't change that. I *was* Worthy. Of those closest to me, of the God that chose me, of the Nation I was deemed to protect, and of my mate.

"I am Worthy. I don't need to prove that to you," I said sternly. "And I'm not going anywhere with you until you tell me where."

"I dictate your entire life now. You're either coming willingly or by force. It's your choice." He dropped his hand.

"The only thing you can dictate is whether I shove my foot up your ass or not."

Talum's lips pursed as he tried to restrain his laugh.

Daegel gave him a scornful glare before returning his gaze to me and sighed. "Do you always make things more complicated than they need to be?"

"Nope. This is just for you. Feel special?"

"I'm growing impatient. Let's go." He extended his hand toward me again.

I crossed my arms and planted my feet firmly on the ground.

Leysa looked at me with wide, worried eyes, begging for me to comply.

Daegel's hand remained outstretched between us in an unquestionable demand to take it and go with him. To where, I had no idea, and I didn't care. But what if it was back to Taeralia? Or anywhere I could feel Ryker again and talk to him? Daegel clearly had a way of passing between the realms, so it was possible.

Except, I couldn't trust him.

"This is your last chance, Diamond," he said through clenched teeth.

I remained still, locking eyes with him in a war of wills. I hoped he could see the ire burning inside them.

He dropped his hand again and closed his eyes, inhaling deeply as if to calm himself. I kept my face hard, expressing a false confidence, and swallowed the nervousness creeping up my throat. With a curl of his lip, his eyes snapped open, and my stomach dropped.

"You had a choice. Remember that." The lethality in his voice promised regret, and a cold chill ran up my spine.

Leysa gasped.

He came at me like a lightning strike, and I dove. I rolled over quickly, and he was already there, reaching for me when I kicked him in the face as hard as I could. His hand shot to his nose, and he stumbled back. I took the opportunity to scramble to my feet.

This is my only chance.

A small twinge of guilt hit me for leaving Leysa behind, but I knew I could help her more if I was able to get away, get this stupid collar off, then come back for her later. I shifted my wings, ripping them through my shirt. They snapped out, extending fully, and I couldn't help the smile that crossed my lips. I ignored the gasps behind me. Two quick thrusts, and I was rising into the air, feeling my feet leave the ground as the wind grazed beneath my wings.

Faster than I could process, Daegel jumped and struck me across the head with a snarl, and the next thing I knew I hit the dirt with a sickening crack and searing pain. My eyes flashed with spots of black as I fought to stay conscious.

Daegel stood to his full height with a split lip. "Stodva," he said with a casual wave of his hand.

I think I tried to swing at him, but I was disoriented, and unsure what was happening.

I blinked.

Except it wasn't a blink. I had blacked out, and when my eyes opened he was dragging me back the way we came across the forest floor by the front of my collar. My heels bumped over the ground, my tender wings hung limply as they scraped against the rocks and dirt.

Shift them away. Shift them away!

My mind was screaming at my body to cooperate. I couldn't shift them. I couldn't move at all, aside from moving my eyes. But I could feel everything. I whimpered, the weight of my body on the fragile, broken wings was one of the worst sensations I had ever felt.

I noticed Leysa and Talum briskly following. Leysa's face was pale, while Talum seemed completely unbothered. The smell of burning flesh kept me conscious for a few more moments, giving me the chance to note the feel of Daegel's knuckles against my throat with the flesh of his hand smoking around the collar.

Darkness claimed me again.

Chapter Twenty

KYA

In what seemed like only a moment, my legs were smacking down the steps of the prison, and I was tossed back into my cell.

An icy sensation jolted me fully awake, and my lips parted with a sharp gasp. I was facing the small window, where I could see night had fallen on the moon-filled sky. I was resting on my hip with my legs bent to my side. My arms were above my head uncomfortably. I tried pulling on them, but the most I could manage was a twitch followed by the soft sound of chains rattling.

Shit. This is bad.

I didn't need to turn my head to know that Daegel was still in the room. His sinister presence was palpable in the air as I inhaled through my nose, scenting Daegel, Leysa and Talum.

Daegel stepped into view from behind me, instantly making adrenaline rush through my veins. He looked at me with an unreadable expression.

"It seems you have a unique capability. One that poses a problem for your compliance and gives you the hope you actually stand a chance of getting away," Daegel said, glancing behind me.

My wings.

It was stupid of me to shift them in front of him earlier. I thought I could have gotten away—that it was the only chance I would get—but instead I had thrown away my last advantage.

I tried to speak but only managed a weak whimper.

Daegel's face remained neutral. "I don't need your cooperation for this part." He turned his head and nodded to someone. "And I certainly don't need to waste my energy in the future by keeping you paralyzed in case you try to use them again."

The chains were pulled, lifting me until my feet dangled with only my toes grazing the floor. My eyes darted around frantically, and my breaths came quickly as uncontrollable dread washed over me.

A hand gripped the collar of my shirt behind me, and I felt the cold spine of a blade slide along my back as my shirt was cut down the middle, along with my breast binding. I heard as the cloth was torn from around my wings, the fabric hanging loosely at my shoulders. I continued to stare at Daegel while he watched.

He yanked a large knife with a slightly curved blade from its sheath at his hip and flipped it in his hand so the handle was facing outward. He held it out, offering it to whomever was standing behind me.

"Take it," he ordered in an authoritative tone.

Nothing happened for a moment. I could smell the tension in the air between them, but I had no idea if it was Leysa or Talum.

"This is your doing. You're the one who failed," Daegel said.

Daegel pulled his hand back, and when I noticed the missing blade from his hand I began willing my body to move, to shift, to fight, to scream, anything. All I could manage was one small jerk that was barely anything. I heard Leysa sniffle behind me.

"She doesn't need them to live," Daegel sounded annoyed as he reassured whoever had the blade.

No!

"Will they come back when she…transforms again?" Talum said from behind me. But I still didn't know which one was holding the blade intended to destroy the gift given to me.

Daegel studied me with cold eyes and tilted his head. "I guess we'll find out."

He stepped back and leaned against the wall beneath the window with his arms crossed over his chest. He looked behind me and nodded.

Not my wings! Please, Gods—anyone—don't let them take my wings! No. No!

I screamed internally when I felt the tip of the blade on my back at the top of my wing.

Don't do this! Please, don't do this!

But I couldn't scream. I couldn't beg. I couldn't move no matter how hard I tried. I couldn't do anything… The blade dug deep into the flesh around the base of my wings.

They weren't just cutting them off—they were *carving* them out.

My mind and body were crying out from the unbearable pain with each excruciatingly deep slice. My body shook uncontrollably, and I felt the blood rushing down my back, soaking into my clothes. It felt like an eternity as I suffered through it all, praying I would pass out.

Daegel continued to watch with nothing but indifference etched across his face.

I heard a heavy thud, and the weight of my wings lessened on one side. Tears streamed down my face.

Every memory of flying with Odarum flashed before my eyes. The memory of pride and elation from Ryker when he saw them for the first time. And the future memories Daegel stole of soaring through the sky with the wind beneath me...

Then the blade moved to my other wing.

Why are you doing this? You bastard! I will kill you. I will make you pay!

A fiery rage erupted in my chest. Through tears and sweat, my eyes bored holes into Daegel's with the promise of a wrathful vengeance.

He leaned in close—close enough I could see the cascade of color that crafted the blue in his eyes reflecting his dark, cold soul.

"I need you to be broken so I can fix you."

After my second wing fell, Daegel waved his hand, releasing me from my chains and restoring my ability to move. Two sets of hands helped me to the bed. I lay face down, with the tatters of my shirt still clinging to my arms and soaked with my blood. I could feel the gaping holes in my back, and each soft brush of air felt like scorching flames.

"He'll come for me," I whispered, and I wasn't sure if it was to myself or to Daegel. "He'll tear the realms apart to find me."

My shadow will come for me.

My eyes dragged to Daegel's, who turned to look at me. I hoped he could see the promise that rested in my glare. To my surprise, his icy, empty eyes softened.

"I know he will." He stated it plainly, not with anger but…understanding.

Daegel, Talum, and Leysa left, leaving me alone with my discarded wings. I stared at them, lifeless on the blood-covered floor. They were close enough to touch, and I reached out, brushing the soft, black feathers with my fingertips. I removed a few of them, then pulled them to my chest. I didn't know what would happen to my wings, and if they were going to be taken away, I wanted at least a little piece of them to stay with me.

I closed my eyes and fresh tears fell, trailing down my sweat-crusted cheeks. I sobbed into the thin pillow.

The weight of everything threatened to bury me, and I didn't know what to do. There was nothing I could do…

Sometime later, the door to my cell opened. I didn't look to see who it was. I didn't want to see anyone, and I was hoping they would just leave.

My body tensed when I saw a pair of male's boots step in front of me.

Please don't be Daegel. I can't handle anything more right now.

Talum bent down, placing a wooden bowl and a clean washcloth draped over the side on the floor next to him. He looked at me with sympathetic eyes. The bowl was filled with a thick liquid that had a silvery sheen—the same liquid I was dunked into for my "cleansing," as Daegel called it. I wished he had explained what the fuck it was.

I eyed the liquid warily.

"It's not going to hurt you. This is heill." He gestured to the bowl. "It's a… I don't know how to say it in your language. But it cleans you."

"It cleans me?" I croaked out. My voice was hoarse.

"In a sense. More than just a bath though. I don't know how to say it. It keeps you healthy." Talum picked up the cloth and soaked it before wringing it out and placing it on my back.

I didn't fight him. I didn't even say no. I didn't have the energy or the will.

But he was right, it didn't hurt. At least the liquid didn't. The cloth felt like sandpaper on my sensitive skin making me hiss. He eased the pressure but didn't say anything as he continued. The wounds were already starting to feel better.

"Who did it?" My voice was thick at the thought of Leysa, my mate's *mother*, taking my wings away.

Talum met my eyes for a moment before looking away again. "Does it matter?"

It didn't. Not really. If it was Leysa, maybe I didn't want to know. They were gone, and knowing wasn't going to bring them back. And maybe it was better for me to believe that if it was her, she would have fought for me. But Talum wouldn't.

"I don't understand why he's making you clean me."

"Daegel has never *made* me do anything," Talum said.

Leysa could say he wasn't so bad, but anyone who willingly aligned with that fucker was diabolical in my eyes.

"Why are you helping me?" I whispered. Wouldn't they want me weak and suffering? Wasn't Daegel's purpose to make me suffer as much as possible?

I supposed he was already. The collar prevented me from using my magic, making me crawl in my own skin.

He destroyed my home. He had taken my Spirit Guardian from me. My mating bond was fractured. And now, my wings. He had taken everything but my life.

"Because," Talum sighed and dipped the cloth back into the liquid then resumed, "while we don't have mates like you, I know the pain of being kept from the one you love." He leaned over so I was forced to look at him and he spoke softly. "He knows what your mate will do to him. And trust me, he's being merciful to you because of it."

"Why does Daegel need my compliance? For what?" I asked.

Talum finished and draped the cloth over the side of the bowl, then leaned back on his heels. "I honestly don't know. But even if I did, I wouldn't tell you."

He didn't say it in a snarky way. It was just the truth—words filled with blind loyalty.

I nodded. I didn't like it, but I understood.

"Can you at least tell me why he wants *me* specifically? What do I have to do with anything?" I pleaded with my eyes.

He chewed on the inside of his cheek for a moment, contemplating, then gave a single, shallow nod. "He was told to find the Diamond—you. You're the one who can give him the power he needs. For what, I'm not sure."

"Yeah, I know that part. But who told him?" My brows furrowed.

"God," he said, like it was obvious.

"And you only have one?" It was still a wild concept to me that this realm was only ruled by one of the Gods.

Talum nodded. I hissed as he ran the cloth over my wounds again. The conversation was providing a welcoming distraction.

"What's your God's name?" If it was Kleio—or even Xareus—perhaps there was a way for me to talk to them. This world was different, so maybe the rules were different too.

"Odes," Talum said, and my eyes widened. I wasn't expecting that. "But he abandoned this world long ago. Long before our ancestors were even born."

Odes, the Fallen God, and the one whose death ended the War of the Gods. The very reason why none of the Gods or Spirits could interfere in my realm.

I pushed up to my elbows, cringing at the pain in my back. "He didn't abandon it. He died in *my* world thousands of years ago."

Talum's brows flattened. "A God can't die."

"Well, this one did. He fell, and it nearly tore our realm apart, causing the Rip. It caused such an imbalance that the rest of the Gods can't interfere with us at all outside of the Trial. Not even when Daegel came to our realm and started destroying entire Nations—and *lives*—with the Glaev."

"Not everything is as it seems." My head snapped to the doorway to find Daegel leaning against the frame with his hands in his pockets. His eyes met Talum's, and he said something to him in their language.

Talum stood up, taking the bowl with him and left the room.

Daegel stared at me for a moment with a cold, unfeeling expression. And just before he left, he warned, "Just remember I could have killed more. And I still can."

Chapter Twenty-One

—◆—

MALINA

Days turned to weeks, and time blurred together as I concentrated solely on chasing that numbness. All I could think about, all I wanted, was to become completely empty inside.

"Just so you know, I'm happy to come to you for payment and delivery," Dax said, bringing me back to the room, as he was putting his pants back on. "You don't always have to come here."

Not a chance.

"No. I prefer it this way." My hands brushed down my black hair that I really needed to get trimmed, flattening the mess before gathering it and tying it back high on my head.

Dax shrugged. "Fine by me. Just offering."

I finished slipping into my boots and fastened my cloak. Dax stood, leaning over a desk and jotting something down. I walked over and stood next to him, holding out my empty hand with a pointed look.

He didn't look up as his lips curved into a smirk. "Always business with you," he chuckled.

I rolled my eyes. "Just give it to me," I sighed.

He used his terbis to unseal the marble box then opened it and pulled out the vial, placing it in my hands. "For the record, I enjoy doing business with you."

I gave him a tight smile, then left briskly without another word. I was eager to get back to my rooms at Morah and take the demid. After the last time Nikan found me passed out on the street, I decided it was better to wait until I was back in my rooms. And it had been working out well. Locking myself away, body and mind, was the most I could manage.

I watched my feet as I weaved my way through the inner ring, and I was nearly back to Morah when I heard a familiar voice that stopped me in my tracks as I rounded the corner.

Hakoa.

It had been so long since I'd seen him—when I left with Kya to get Nikan back. He had begged me not to go or to take him with me. And the look on his face when I walked away, when Theron stopped him from following…

But I knew then, just as I did now, while what we had was great at the time, it was always inevitable to come to an end. He didn't know how much of a mess I was—and I didn't want him to.

He was the Chief of the Noavo. The last thing he needed was me in his life fucking everything up.

Hakoa was standing outside Morah talking with Nikan, and he had his arms crossed over his chest with his eyebrows drawn together. Damn, he looked good. His dark hair was unstyled, and he wasn't in his usual Noavo attire. As much as I liked his warrior gear, it was twice as attractive to see him in common clothing.

What is wrong with you, Mal? You just got done fucking another male for demid. Stop undressing Hakoa with your eyes.

I started to back away, but before I could, Hakoa's eyes flicked to me. His face softened with what looked like relief, and I stiffened. His lips lifted, and his eyes brightened. But they quickly fell as I turned and fled.

"Malina, wait!" he shouted. The desperation in his voice made my breath hitch.

I wanted to wait. I wanted to be able to be happy to see him and not feel ashamed for what I had done. But I couldn't, and I couldn't face him like this.

Maybe someday. When I'm better.

I hoisted myself up a drainage pipe to the roof of one of the houses and pressed against the chimney—every bit the elusive Roav.

Craning my neck, I peered around the stone structure to the street to see Hakoa as he ran around the corner and came to a stop. He was a capable warrior, but he didn't have my training in stealth. I thanked the Gods that he didn't have any Vaavi training. He spun, looking in all directions with hopeful eyes that quickly grew dull with the realization I had escaped him.

The sight tore a hole in a piece of my heart I hadn't realized belonged to him.

He continued to search for me, and I watched as he wandered away to the secondary ring. My shoulders slumped—not with relief but with disappointment in myself. There was only one thing that was going to make me stop feeling this way, and it rested in my pocket.

I threw my hood up and jumped down from the roof, startling a couple passing by. I kept my head down and went back to Morah, keeping an eye out for Hakoa. And Nikan.

Shit... Nik.

I'd been avoiding him, despite the fact he was making every effort to talk to me. But I couldn't avoid him this time when he was standing at the doors to the library waiting. He was leaning back against them, blocking any way to go around him and get inside, while he wielded a rock around his hand, playing with it with distant eyes.

I drew my shoulders back and raised my chin before making my way up the steps.

Nikan noticed me and gently glided the rock to the ground, pushing off the door to meet me. "Mal—"

"Look, it's been a long day. I'm just heading up to my rooms. I'll talk to you later, okay?" I interrupted and tried to push past him, but he stood firm. I couldn't look him in the eye. I didn't want to see the disappointment I knew would mirror my own.

"Malina. What's going on? Talk to me. Please." He tilted his head to the side so I would look at him.

My heart cracked a little more when it wasn't disappointment but rather genuine concern in his expression. Words rose in my throat, itching to tell him everything. But I couldn't put that on him.

"There's nothing to talk about." I shook my head and stepped around him. He let me but followed me inside Morah.

"I don't know what you've been up to lately but... If you don't want to talk to me about it, then we don't have to." His voice was hushed as we walked past the Scholars and up the stairs. "I just..." he sighed.

I just wanted to get back to my rooms. I groaned internally.

"I'm worried about you. It's been weeks since you've trained or accepted any missions. And I barely see you eat."

I opened my mouth to argue with him about being over-bearing, but he didn't give me the chance.

"I'm not trying to berate you. But you've been through a lot, and you're not talking to me. You're constantly showing up either here or in the street unconscious," he said with concern. "It's just me and you now. Except you're not *here*. We always used to talk to each other, no matter what."

We ascended the last flight of stairs to the residential level. Memories of late nights out on the ledge laughing and sharing stories rushed to the forefront of my mind.

"I know you're hurting, Mal. I am too."

My eyes pricked with unshed tears, and the back of my throat tightened.

"Remember I'm still here, and I'm here for you."

I blew out a breath and blinked back tears while my hand rested on the door handle. "I know, Nik. But *I* can't be here right now. I need to be somewhere else."

I pushed open the door and stepped inside. Nikan followed, despite my lack of invitation.

"But you *are* here. Whether you like it or not." He closed the door behind him, and I walked over to the obsidian wall that overlooked the north side of the city. "You don't have to tell me what's going on, but whatever you're doing to deal with it *isn't* dealing with it. You can't run away from this."

"I'm not running away. I just need time. I need to be alone." I spun to face him. "Can you leave? Please."

Nikan looked into the distance with pursed lips for a moment, then looked back at me and crossed his arms. "No."

I scoffed. "Excuse me?" I was itching for the vial in my pocket, my hand twitching to grab it, but I stopped myself.

"No," he said firmly. "Let me help you."

"I don't need your help," I snapped. "You've helped enough. If you hadn't gotten caught, none of this would have happened in the first place."

Nikan flinched.

I regretted the words the moment they crossed my lips. I didn't even know where they came from. I truly didn't blame him for Kya's death. I blamed myself.

"Nik—" I started.

"It's fine." He held up his hand. "I'll leave you be for now, but I'm not giving up on this. I'll be on the ledge tonight if you want to join me. No talking. I promise."

With a tight smile, he turned and walked out, softly shutting the door behind him.

I closed my eyes and sighed, relieved to be alone. I wasn't waiting another minute. I didn't want to go out on the ledge with him and be pummeled with more guilt that it would only be two of us out there when it should be three.

I went to the door and locked it before going into the bathing room to run the water. Pulling out the vial, I held it up to see the contents I had become so reliant on. As much as I wanted it, I was beginning to hate it. I knew I needed to stop and deal with all the shit in my head. I told myself I could stop whenever I wanted to—whenever I was ready. I just wasn't ready yet.

A few more days. I'll give it a few more days.

I waited until the bathing room was filled with steam from the hot water and I stripped, hissing at the luxurious stinging heat as I sunk down in the tub. Resting my head on the edge, I unstopped the demid and brought it to my lips.

Chapter Twenty-Two

MALINA

"*Malina.*"

A distant voice sounded in my dreams—a deep melody that soothed the roughest edges of my mind.

"Malina. Gods, sunshine, what happened to you?"

Wait. That's not in my dreams.

My eyes opened to find the silhouette of Hakoa. He came into view as I blinked away the sleep from my eyes. He held my face in his hands with worry etched across his face. I was on a cold surface, and I had no memory of how I got there—the last thing I remembered was lying in the tub.

"What are you doing here?" I asked groggily as I sat up.

Hakoa leaned back but didn't take his eyes off me. I was on the floor in my bathing room. I twisted my fingers to wield light into the room. I looked down at my body…

"Udon's balls. Why am I naked?"

"The water was freezing, and your lips were blue. You were unconscious so I pulled you out of the tub," Hakoa said roughly.

"Naked?" I asked again.

His brows flattened. "I've seen you naked before."

I scrambled to cover myself, but there wasn't anything around. "Where's the towel?" I felt my body and my hair, noting I wasn't wet anymore. "How am I dry?"

"I'm a water wielder, remember?" He reached up and grabbed a towel from the cupboard then handed it to me, and our fingers brushed against each other. "Shit," he exasperated. "You're still as cold as ice. You scared the shit out of me."

The side of my mouth curved up. "It's okay. I don't feel anything." That was all I wanted.

I draped the towel over me, covering my breasts to mid-way down my thigh.

"Come on." He got to his feet and grabbed my hand. "Let's get you some clothes."

I used my arm to hold the towel in place while he helped me up. I stumbled a bit and nearly fell over, but Hakoa caught me with his arm around my waist. My hand instinctively braced against his broad chest to keep from falling into him. His hand came up to mine, resting over it while my fingers grasped his shirt.

Time seemed to stop when I looked up at him, finding his amber eyes gazing into mine. Still dazed from the effects of the demid, I smiled.

Gods, he was handsome. And strong. And sexy. I had missed him.

Our particular situation was appealing in so many ways. We were alone in the dark, and I was already naked.

Fuck it. I could use a good time, and I know he can give me one.

I walked backward out of the bathing room, leading him toward my bed before letting go of his hand. He immediately went to the wardrobe and pulled out a loose pair of pants and a shirt, then handed them to me.

I didn't take them.

I dropped my towel and slowly stepped closer to him until we were nearly touching.

He didn't take his eyes off my face the entire time. I rose to my toes to kiss him, but stopped. His eyebrows creased as he looked more closely at my face.

"Malina. Your pupils…" His face fell.

Oh no.

He didn't say anything more, just bent down to retrieve my clothes and help me dress. He didn't look at my body once, despite my nakedness. He led me to the bed and pulled back the covers, encouraging me to lay down.

I crawled under the blankets, and the moment my head hit the pillow my eyes grew heavy.

"Stay right here. I'll be back soon," he said.

"Don't bother…" I said as I began to drift off to sleep. It would be better if he didn't come back.

I felt his weight lift off the bed then his lips lightly brushed against my forehead.

My eyes cracked open sometime later to the sound of grunts and clamoring in the distance. Drowsily, I got out of bed. I wrapped my arms around myself and padded out of my rooms. The sounds were coming from Nikan's rooms down the corridor.

His door was ajar, and I could see light spilling out onto the floor. Scholars peered out their doors, curious about the commotion. I quickly tiptoed over and peered through the crack, wondering what he could possibly be doing at this hour making all that ruckus. My mouth fell open, and I felt adrenaline wash the remnants of demid from my system.

I shoved the door open and burst into the room.

Hakoa and Nikan were fighting. The floor rumbled as they threw their bodies around, slamming into the walls and furniture. Nikan had a busted lip, and Hakoa's skin had split above his eye.

All I could do was balk at the sight. I didn't know what to do, and I certainly wasn't getting in the middle of two strong males who were clearly out for blood. But they weren't using their elements, which told me no one had intentions of killing.

I flinched when Nikan pulled his fist back before squaring Hakoa in the jaw. Hakoa lunged for Nikan and tackled him to the ground.

"Why didn't you tell me she's on demid? Why didn't you come to me?" Hakoa roared in Nikans face, punching the side of his head.

"What the fuck are you talking about?" Nikan shouted and twisted his leg up and over Hakoa's torso, slamming Hakoa's large frame to the floor and flipping over him. Hakoa shielded his face with his arms as Nikan pummeled him.

"I know what it looks like! I've had to dismiss warriors because of it." Hakoa elbowed Nikan in the side of the head and flipped them over again, pinning my brother beneath him.

"Stop!" I yelled. "He didn't know, Hakoa."

Both of them stopped and looked up at me in surprise. I rushed over and shoved Hakoa.

"Get off him, you brute!"

Hakoa fell on his ass, relieving Nikan of his weight. They looked at me as if I were a stranger.

"Why?" Hakoa asked.

I blew out a breath. There was no use in holding it in anymore. I couldn't even deny it if I tried. I closed my eyes and willed myself to finally speak of my torment.

"Because I can't handle the fact Kya made me kill her. I can't handle that I did it, and I can't look at myself. I don't know how to keep going, knowing what I did. Or that Nik made a deal with that *bastard* to spare our lives. I don't want to feel like this. I just want to forget everything."

"Mal…" Nikan whispered and rose to a stand. "Her death is not on you."

"Yeah, yeah. I know. She told me to. But I'm the one who put an arrow in her chest. I'm the one who took her life, and I can't live with that."

Hakoa stared at us, horror dawning on his face. "You haven't talked to Ryker?"

Nikan and I glanced at each other briefly before looking back at Hakoa and shaking our heads. He held my gaze as he stood.

Hakoa approached me and took my hand. His voice was gentle. "Kya's alive."

I held back a scoff.

"What do you mean Kya's alive? How?" Nikan asked warily.

"I don't know. But Ryker is certain." Hakoa shrugged.

"Can he talk to her? Feel her?" Nikan pressed for information.

"I don't think so. But he's adamant about it. Something about their bond."

"The bond is driving him crazy. Of course he claims she's alive. If she weren't, then he would be driven to death by insanity," I stated. It wasn't that I didn't want it to be true—there was just no way she had survived the Rip or the Onyx Kiss.

"I know it sounds unlikely, but I believe him. And you should too." Hakoa stepped into me and placed a hand on my cheek, tilting my gaze to his. "It means you didn't kill her."

"Get out," I whispered.

This was too much to handle right now. I didn't want false hope only to be crushed all over again. I wouldn't survive it. And Hakoa was threatening to cut what little shred of myself I had left.

"What?" he asked with bewilderment, his eyes searching mine. Whatever he was looking for, he wasn't going to find.

"Get. Out." My voice nearly broke.

A.N. CAUDLE

"She told you to leave, so leave. I'll find you later, and we can talk, but right now, you need to go." Nikan stepped forward and pressed on Hakoa's shoulder, trying to push him away from me.

Hakoa's eyes slid to Nikan with a glare that would make any normal male tremble. I started to pull away but Hakoa gripped my arm. I really didn't want to fight him and make this situation worse.

Hakoa swirled his hand, and I heard the crackling sound of ice. Nikan jerked back and looked at his feet. I glanced down and saw Hakoa had frozen water over Nikan's shoes, securing him to the floor.

"Let him—Hey!" I shouted.

Hakoa threw me over his shoulder and quickly walked out of Nikan's rooms. The Scholars with their heads poked out of their doors quickly shut them as we emerged.

"Put me down, and let Nik go," I demanded, pounding on his back with my fist, but all he did was hold me tighter. I could hear Nikan grumbling from the room.

Hakoa took me down to one of the lower levels of the library. It was dark, and with the tinted glass walls of Morah, the moonslight didn't provide much help.

He stumbled slightly. "Sunshine?"

With a frustrated sigh, I threw up my hand and wielded a small ball of light above us, intentionally smacking the back of his head at the same time.

He gave my leg a grateful squeeze and weaved through the maze of floor-to-ceiling shelves, filled with books of all kinds, until we came to an area with several tables.

I knew the library like the back of my hand, having lived here for most of my life. I knew without looking at the titles we were in the theological section of the third level.

Hakoa carefully placed me on my feet and gave a small smile. I wanted to hit him, but I refrained. I turned around to see Ryker's familiar frame sitting at one of the tables on the far end.

I stiffened.

I didn't want to see that asshole. I didn't want to talk to him. I didn't want to feel the blame in his glare like I did during our last encounter.

But something was off about him. He was muttering to himself, and his head twitched as he flipped the pages of the books haphazardly strewn about the table with a small flame-lit lantern in the center.

He looked crazy to me already.

I glanced at Hakoa with a look that conveyed my earlier skepticism about Ryker's sanity. He just placed a hand at the small of my back and led me over to the Lord of Oryn.

"Ryker," Hakoa greeted.

Ryker looked up from the pages, and my heart sank. It wasn't blame that I saw in those silver eyes, but unimaginable pain and anguish—a desperation so potent I could taste it.

He glanced at me for a short moment before turning his attention to Hakoa. "What do you need?"

"I need you to explain to Malina that Kya is alive. Maybe she'll believe you."

Ryker's face was blank as he looked at me. "I don't care if you believe me or not, but she isn't dead. Our bond is fractured, but it's still there. She's in another realm, and I'm going to find her. If you're not going to help, then get out of my sight."

I flinched. I would always help her. He still had no idea what kind of bond Kya and I had. If he did, he wouldn't have made it sound like I didn't care. I knew Kya still hadn't told him the three of us were from Atara. That we were bound on a different level by our mutual trauma over losing our homeland to the Glaev and our families to the Drift Islands.

I contemplated telling him just that but decided against it. Kya didn't want to tell him until she was inducted as Lady of Oryn and could ensure she was able to bring back our people safely and give them a home. Personally, I didn't think it mattered anymore. She was the Worthy of Atara anyway. But it was her choice, and I wasn't going to go against her wishes.

Could she really be alive?

I allowed myself to consider the possibility.

If she was alive then that also meant...

"What about Daegel?" I blurted.

Ryker's entire demeanor changed right before my eyes, and I could see the Bloodlust Lord of Oryn.

"If she survived, he could have too," I clarified.

"I don't know," he growled through clenched teeth. "As far as I'm aware, he hasn't returned here—but that doesn't mean he's dead."

"So I may have sent her into another realm wounded for no reason?"

"Yes," he clipped.

I looked at the books on the table. All of them were related to the Rip and myths. I glanced back up to my sister's husband. "And how are you going to find her?"

Ryker continued to hold my stare as he pushed one of the books over for me to see and pointed to a passage. Hakoa and I bent down to read it. Both of our jaws dropped.

Hakoa stood straight up and tensed. "No. Absolutely not."

"But..." I stumbled. "What if it doesn't work? What if you die?" I turned my head to face him.

Ryker leaned forward. "What if I don't?"

Chapter Twenty-Three

KYA

I was given a day to heal before Talum and Leysa retrieved me, and took me back to the stepstone. Daegel was there waiting.

"Leysa," he said, cutting his eyes to her.

Leysa went to him with her head down and stood next to him on the round stone. I wished she would fight back, show some struggle against him, but after what he had done to me, I understood. After being here for fifty years, she had probably suffered worse.

"As a little incentive, we'll be bringing Leysa along," he said with a cold expression. It felt like a threat.

Swallowing the pang of intimidation, I couldn't help but glance around. It was habitual for me to always look for a way out, planning for an escape.

"Attempt to flee again, and I will not hesitate to hunt you down," he rumbled.

"I hear she likes to be chased," Talum smirked.

I narrowed my eyes. "Not by you."

While running had crossed my mind, I was exhausted, and I feared the consequences. They already took my wings. I didn't want to find out what would happen for my next punishment.

I released a resigned sigh. "What do you want me to do?" I asked Daegel.

"I'll show you." He held out his hand toward me.

I hesitated for a moment before taking it and stepping onto the carved stone. I had no idea why he needed me to go willingly rather than just force me. He didn't seem to have a problem forcing me to do just about everything else.

"Fara." Daegel waved his hand in a swirling motion above his head, and the symbols in the stone glowed, getting brighter until I had to shield my eyes with my arm.

It dimmed just as quickly, and I put my arm down. My eyes widened when I saw that we were now in a field of gently rolling hills. The sound of crashing waves had me spinning around to see the edge of a cliff. Beyond that was nothing but water as far as I could see. I stumbled back as the intrusive thoughts of falling over the cliff's edge and being dragged beneath the surface rippled to the forefront of my mind. With the moon engulfing half of the afternoon sky, it looked like it was swallowing the sea before me.

The paralyzing moment was cut short when my skin started to feel painfully tight. I whimpered as the sensation quickly became overwhelming, and I thought I was going to burst through my own skin.

My knees buckled, hitting a circular stone that was just like the one we had been standing on before. Leysa sighed heavily but didn't act like she was in pain—she wasn't having the same sensation as I was. Daegel inhaled deeply, and his mouth stretched into an exhilarated smile.

"What…is happening?" I struggled to get the words out as my chest tightened, and my breath faltered. My body shook. I could feel my magic thrash violently, demanding to be released.

"We're on Kitall—an ancient island, and the birthplace of Vansera. This is where Odes stood when he made this realm."

Daegel gazed out over the landscape. I tried to concentrate on his words but the buzzing in my head became a deafening roar that made me want to tear at my skull. "The sacred land here is imbued with his magic, and simply stepping foot on it enhances our reserves." He looked down at me. "And it's why you're experiencing such an intense reaction."

My hand went to the collar around my throat, and I grimaced.

"Yes. The band around your neck still prevents you from accessing your magic. What do you think will happen if you stay here and you can't release it?" he asked.

I already knew the answer. It wouldn't kill me, but the pain would continue to worsen until I could release it. With the fresh magic flowing into me, this was exponentially worse than what I had been experiencing before.

"Take it off. Please. I won't attack you," I begged.

"Your promise is empty. But I'll remove it on one condition." He bent down and held out his hand.

I bit my tongue. I couldn't take it. I knew I wouldn't die from this, but death would have been more merciful.

"Do what I ask, and I'll not only take it off, I'll consider letting you go back to your dying world when I'm done with you. Both of you. Do we have a deal?"

"Make a deal? With *you?*"

How stupid does he think I am?

I clenched my teeth and looked at his hand like it was covered in the same shit that spilled from his mouth.

"I'm waiting, Diamond," he clipped with a curled lip.

I spit in his face.

"There's your answer." I knew the kind of havoc his deal could cause, and I refused to take any part in it.

I can take it. I can take it.

Daegel sighed and stood. "So be it."

I watched as he strode over to Leysa. She stiffened at his approach but didn't balk as he pulled out another collar and placed it around her neck.

"Fjoturr," he uttered under his breath, and the collar around her throat came to life. The designs of the collar began to shift, like chains moving in opposite directions.

"Don't!" I tried to yell, but it came out more as a grunt.

The moment it was sealed around her throat, her hands went straight to her head, and she fell to her knees groaning.

Daegel turned to face me. "Since you refuse to make a deal, and your own suffering doesn't seem to bother you, let's see what you do when the consequences of your actions cause *her* to suffer." He grabbed Leysa and pulled her to a stand. She stumbled as he led her over to me.

"You haven't told me what you want," I sneered.

"I want you to comply," he said.

Leysa started crying. Her eyes pleaded with me and it tore a hole in my gut. I didn't want to be the cause of her pain. She was my mate's mother, and she had already been through more than I could imagine.

"Okay, okay. I'll do what you want, just let her go."

"I will. But first, I need to make sure you understand what happens if you don't." Daegel spun his hands around each other and muttered under his breath.

Some kind of strange light rose from the ground around Leysa, encircling her. It crawled up in the air, like liquid spilling across the floor, until it encased her entirely in a dome structure.

Leysa's eyes darted around frantically, and she tried to push her hand through, but it was like a wall. Her eyes widened, and her chest rose rapidly. It was some kind of magical barrier with a pearlescent sheen. She beat her fists against it over and over, screaming to be let out. She moved her hands and body in the way a water wielder would. Except she had the collar on, and she couldn't wield anymore.

Daegel grabbed my arm and yanked me to my feet then pushed me in front of him and away from Leysa, walking farther inland.

"Daegel. Daegel!" Leysa pleaded. "Please! I didn't do anything wrong! Don't leave me here!"

I looked at her over my shoulder and tried to push against Daegel to get to her, but he shoved me forward.

"She'll be fine so long as you behave," he said in a cold tone.

"What is wrong with you? Why are you doing this to us? I already said I would do as you asked." With all the strength I could muster, I pulled my free arm back and drove my fist toward his face, then shoved my knee between his legs.

He snatched my hand before it made contact and then grunted, bending over from where I kneed his groin. His eyes snapped to me with malice. He held my arms out to my side as far as they could go, and holding my stare, he twisted the wrist of the hand that nearly struck him until I heard a pop. Immediately I felt a shooting pain up my arm.

I cried out through clenched teeth, and tears welled in my eyes.

"Do you want me to leave her here? Keep up this rebelliousness and I will," he barked in my face.

Shit. I'm just making things worse.

I shook my head, and my bottom lip trembled despite my efforts to put on a bold face. But, fuck, my wrist hurt, and I *needed* to use my magic. I needed to let it out. It felt like I would combust if I didn't.

"Do not move," he demanded.

Resentfully and shamefully, I nodded.

He released me and took a step back. I whimpered and brought my now-broken wrist up to my chest to cradle it in my other hand.

Daegel created the same barrier over me, but this one was bigger—about the size of my cell. I glanced over to Leysa and saw the agony in her eyes. She had been enduring Daegel's unhinged wrath for decades and was powerless to do anything about it.

Right then, I decided I would fight for the both of us. We would both get out of here. I didn't know how, but I would make it happen. And I would make sure that Daegel died by my hand.

I sniffled as I pushed down my pride, reminding myself it was still better than making a deal. "What do you want me to do?"

"Lauss," he uttered.

The collar around my neck fell onto the ground and all of my magic, those lifeless orbs, came flooding back. My eyes fluttered closed, and I sighed deeply with relief as my body relaxed. I could feel vibrations with my terbis again. I felt the entire landscape of the island, even things I couldn't feel before—the gentle sway of the grass, the breaking of the waves at the bottom of the cliff, the shifting of the sand in the wind on the other side of the island.

My eyes snapped open when I felt Daegel step toward me—the magical barrier the only thing separating us.

The side of his mouth lifted. "I want you to create the Glaev."

Chapter Twenty-Four

KYA

"You want me to *create* the Glaev?" Holding my broken wrist, I took a step back from the pearlescent shield.

"Yes," he said flatly.

My brows furrowed. "Why?"

Not that I understood his diabolical reasoning, but I could make sense of him wanting to destroy the land on Taeralia. What I couldn't fathom was why he would want sacred land, touched by Odes, to be ruined. On his own world at that.

"Does it matter?" He tilted his head to the side just a bit.

"Yes," I bit out. I wanted to know, damnit. I was sick and tired of not knowing a fucking thing.

He shrugged. "Too bad."

Loathsome bastard...

I glanced to the ground, curling my bare toes into the soft green grass and feeling the soil beneath me. I couldn't help but reach out and feel everything with my terbis. I missed it too much. I wanted to use everything at once. I wanted to use my invisibility, I wanted to use my Waalu.

Magic is energy.

My eyes snapped up, and I looked around at the dome shield he had erected over me.

I wonder if my energy could break the barrier. I bet if I could get him distracted—

"It won't work, Diamond," Daegel said, clearly knowing where my thoughts were as I continued to observe the dome structure.

"You're sure about that?"

I let go of my wrist, reaching for the jade orb inside me and wrapping around it, releasing streams of Waalu down my arm in a soft glow. The feeling of releasing my magic was intoxicating, filling me with hope and confidence. Without the collar and absorbing magic from the island, I was stronger than when I fought him at the Rip.

I could kill him this time.

Daegel's expression remained cold and closed. "Yes. I'm much more powerful than you. Especially here."

He's bluffing.

"If you're so powerful, you wouldn't need me caged. You wouldn't need me at all, would you?" I asked.

His nostrils flared, and he bared his teeth in frustration. I could feel his heart rate increase through the ground.

I kept my lips tight, preventing myself from smirking.

That's it! He needs me. He doesn't have a choice.

Though I didn't know what he needed me for exactly, it still gave me an advantage I hadn't realized I'd had. It was something I could use against him.

"Why don't you just do it? You can create the Glaev. I've seen you do it." I raised my chin.

"I'm not going to ask you again." Daegel raised his hand, and the collar levitated off the ground coming up to me.

My eyes widened. I didn't want it back on. I didn't want to have my magic suppressed again. "Okay, okay."

Of course he wasn't going to tell me...

He dropped his hand, and the collar fell back to the ground with a light thump.

"Fjold," he said as he flicked his hand at me. I assumed it meant he wanted me to start.

The more I thought of it, the more I realized this wasn't such a horrid thing. At least it wasn't Taeralia. Not to mention, this would give me the time to figure out a plan without the collar on.

I took a deep breath and backed up, still facing Daegel—I wasn't letting him out of my sight—leaving about ten paces between us. Taking a deep breath, I reached my hand out toward the ground tentatively. Then, I was stuck, not knowing how to do what he was asking. I knew how to cure it, not how to create it. I dropped my arm to my side.

"I can't make the Glaev." I shook my head and looked up at him. "I don't have dark magic."

"Yes, you do," he said, and I tensed defensively. I didn't want that abhorrent ability. "You have Waalu right?" he asked with a raised brow.

What the fuck? How does he know what it is? How does he know the Spirits' name for it?

My mouth gaped, silently answering his question.

Daegel crossed his arms and nodded. "Energy can be used in almost any way imaginable. You've used it to counteract the Glaev, but you can reverse that. Instead of restoring the land, you can destroy it."

"Why would I ever want to do that?" I asked, completely perplexed.

Daegel pointed a thumb over his shoulder. "Because I will leave her here if you don't. Remember? And if you do what I ask, I'll take off her collar."

I glanced over at Leysa, rocking back and forth on her knees with her fingers pulling at her hair. I hated that she was being punished for something that wasn't her fault.

"I'll be sure to let her know you're the reason for her prolonged suffering," Daegel stated pointedly.

Fucking prick.

"Fine," I whispered and blew out a breath.

I had no idea how to change what my energy did. I had never had the time to truly explore its capabilities. I supposed now I was about to learn. I extended my hand once again. Calling to the orb inside me, I pushed the streams of energy to the ground and continued to hold it for a minute before letting it go to see its effect.

No Glaev. No spots of decimated land. I only made a small patch of grass in front of me grow taller.

I looked at Daegel and threw up my hands. He stared at the patch of grass for a few moments, and I hoped he would see I couldn't do it and realize I wasn't able to give him what he wanted and let me go.

"Try again."

Hours. I spent hours trying and failing, pouring out as much energy as I could to do as Daegel asked. Hours of listening to the wails of Leysa as she was filled with more and more unreleased magic.

At one point, I had tried hitting the shield, but all it did was absorb the impact and make it thrum. From the scowl on his face, I knew Daegel wasn't happy about it, and he likely had some kind of punishment planned for later.

But I continued to pour the energy into the ground over and over until it was nearly dark. I *was* trying. I really was.

I bent over panting and rested my hands on my knees. While Kitall Island continued to replenish my reserves as fast as I was depleting them, it was still taxing, and I was completely exhausted. The only good thing about it was that I healed incredibly fast. My broken wrist was slightly sore after only a few hours. But I kept pushing and pushing, keeping the thought of Ryker and Leysa on my mind for motivation.

It was useless.

"My standards are not being met, Diamond," Daegel scalded.

"Yeah, well, maybe you should lower them," I quipped irritably.

Daegel sighed, and I raised my head to look at him. He pinched the bridge of his nose. "We will continue this tomorrow."

I groaned. I wasn't looking forward to going back to my cell, or coming back here and doing this again.

"And the next day," he added, now glaring at me. "As well as every day after until you do what I ask. And Leysa will be joining us each and every time. So, unless you want to keep coming back here and forcing Leysa to endure this torture, you better figure out a way to give me what I want."

That's it!

I was sick of being here. I was sick of him constantly berating and threatening me. I was exhausted, tired, and hungry. I wanted to go back to my mate. Fuck him and his power.

In a fit of rage, I spun around and released a large flare of my energy, slamming it against the barrier. Magic was energy and the barrier was magic. So, in theory, my energy should have done something.

Except it didn't.

Daegel crooked a brow. "Are you done?"

Gods, I want to kill him. How can someone be so cruel?

But I nodded. Too physically and mentally drained to argue.

"Good." He waved his hand, and the collar lifted from the ground up to my neck then clasped around my throat.

"Lauss," I whispered, hoping his same words to free me would work.

He chuckled. "Our magics are different. But nice try. Fjoturr."

The collar came to life, and I felt the designs moving. The intensity of my magic being suppressed again was just as crippling as before. It was a brutal reminder of what Leysa had been enduring all day. But I remained on my feet, fighting against it.

Daegel released both my and Leysa's shields, then he released her from her collar.

I looked at her with pleading eyes, desperately wanting her to use her ability to fight against him and get out of this wretched place. She refused to look at me, keeping her head down and wiping her tears as she obediently went over to stand behind Daegel.

Before, I *never* understood how she could give up and stop fighting to get back to her mate. Now I did. I didn't know what she had gone through, but if I had suffered this for fifty years, I wasn't sure that I wouldn't do the same.

"Are you okay?" Leysa whispered, finally looking at me.

"Not while I'm here," I said. "Sorry you have to be part of this too."

Her lips tightened, and her eyes flicked to Daegel. "It's not your fault."

Daegel gripped my arm, tight enough I couldn't get away, and led me to the stepstone while Leysa followed. We all stepped up on it and Daegel didn't hesitate to speak, "Fara," taking us away.

I closed my eyes, remembering the blinding light from last time. When I opened them again, we were back in the forest where Talum was waiting. The relief of being off the island was immediate, and while my unused magic still clawed to get out, I was grateful more wasn't pouring in.

Daegel shoved me off the stepstone, and Leysa stepped off as well. "Do better," he said from behind me.

When I turned around to tell him to fuck off, he was gone.

"Let's go," Talum said.

I followed without dispute. I wasn't eager to get back to my cell, but I wanted to lay down and sleep. The walk back was short, and I was pleased to see food and a pitcher of water, but I was confused when I approached the bed and noted there were two trays and a small bucket of water on the floor. I turned around at the sound of the door shutting.

Leysa stood by the wall. "I'm to stay with you until you're convinced to submit." She shrugged.

"I'm already convinced, but I'm happy for the company," I said politely, hoping she didn't blame me for her suffering on Kitall. Despite her saying it wasn't my fault, I still felt bad about it.

"I've also been permitted to clean you," she said with a small smile.

I looked at her with a confused expression.

She moved her arms together in a motion that I recognized. The water from the bucket lifted as she wielded the element over to me.

I was right. She is a water wielder.

Happily, I extended my arms out to my sides as she ran the water over every inch of my body. It wasn't really a cleaning since there wasn't soap, but it felt amazing to have the sweat and grim washed away from my clothes and body. I really wished I had something to remove the grease from my hair but I wasn't about to complain.

Once she was done, she twisted her arms in a swirling motion, pulling all the water from me, leaving me dry and free from the filth I had been covered in for days.

I released a sigh and smiled. "Thanks, Leysa."

We ate in silence, sitting on the edge of the bed and sharing the pitcher. They only ever gave me enough to keep me fed, never enough to fill my stomach. It was better than starving to death, I supposed. Leysa had tried to offer some of her food, but I declined. I knew she had to be hungry too. We both needed our strength if we were going back on that island.

Once we were finished, we rested with our backs against the wall. My mind wandered with so many questions. I wanted to take this opportunity to learn as much as I could from Leysa while I had the chance.

"Why can some of them speak our language?" I broke the silence with the first question that popped into my head.

"I'm not sure. At least I don't know where Daegel learned it, but Talum learned from him, and I helped. I think the others just started picking it up from us, but most don't bother."

"You helped Talum learn?" I asked. "Why would you help *him*?"

"I didn't want to at first. I was a lot more stubborn and hard-headed back then—like you. But it was more beneficial to have someone who could understand me, other than Daegel."

That made sense.

"Do you understand their language?" I asked.

"Some. Mainly just a few words and phrases. Most of them don't talk around me, so it's been difficult to learn." She shrugged.

"Talum didn't return the courtesy of teaching you his language?"

"No," she shook her head.

I picked another topic.

She gladly answered each of my questions to the best of her knowledge, seeming happy to have someone from her world to talk to, especially one mated and married to her son. I learned the stone cell I was in when I first arrived was far away and remote. Its intended purpose was to isolate me while I acclimated to the new realm. At least that's what Leysa gathered.

She opened up after a while, and told me about some of her horrid experiences. How she had a collar on for over thirty years until she had proven herself trustworthy with good behavior, and then continued to behave so she didn't have to suffer quite as much. She told me how, for over ten years, she had tried to escape over and over, but every time she tried, they caught her and punished her again.

"Tell me about Daegel. What do you know about him?" I needed her to tell me everything she knew. The more I could learn, the more I could use against him.

"Not much I'm afraid," she sighed. "Though I wish I did."

"Well, you have to know some things about him. You've been his captive for half a century. What... What *is* he? Is he a Lord?" I asked.

"No," she huffed. "They don't have Lords here. They have Kings."

"What are those?" It was an odd term, one I had never heard before.

"I think they're similar to Lords. They rule over their respective Kingdoms of magic users and humans."

My brows creased, utterly confused. "What?"

"Kingdoms are like Nations. I think. Witches and sorcerers are the magical people here—they all share similar character-istics—and I guess humans aren't. I don't actually know about humans, though. I've never seen one."

"Hmm." I bit my cheek taking in all this information. "So these keens—"

"Kin*gs*," she corrected my pronunciation.

"Oh. These *Kings*, rulers, who are they?"

Leysa inhaled through her nose, and I could tell she was getting tired. Learning the social structure of another realm was fascinating to me. I wished I had something to write this all down with. I tried to keep the rest of my questions to a minimum, sticking only to what I needed to know.

"Daegel is one of them, I know that. And I've heard a King Zalen mentioned a couple of times. I think they're enemies."

I perked up. *That* was something I could use. The enemy of Daegel could be my salvation.

"You *think* they're enemies?" I needed to be sure.

"There was mention of some kind of fight or something, I'm not certain, but a King was killed. Then I heard talk from some of the guards about King Zalen and how ruthless and feared he is. I could only understand parts of what they were talking about, picking up a few words here and there. But my theory is that Daegel started whatever is going on out there." She nodded her head toward the window.

"What makes you say that?"

"Because I'm pretty sure Daegel killed a King."

So if we could get to King Zalen...

We didn't talk for some time as I thought of how I could use this information to my advantage.

"What are you thinking about?" Leysa interrupted my thoughts.

"Oh, uh, nothing." I didn't want to tell her my ideas just yet.
I wanted a plan in place before I said anything.

"I can practically feel your mind working. So let's hear it," she
sounded so motherly and I was tempted to answer, but instead
I diverted.

"What happened…when you were taken?" Leysa and I had
migrated to lying down on the bed.

"Vicria never told anyone…" she said. I couldn't tell if she
was pleased with that or disappointed.

I shook my head. "No. No one knows. Everyone thinks
you're dead. Except Cadoc."

"He can feel it too…" she whispered.

The bond. The fractured tether that made our souls ache for
our mates.

"I shouldn't be surprised she never told anyone. We were best
friends. I can't say I wouldn't have done the same for her." Leysa
blew out a sharp breath. "Vicria and I had been working on
discovering the cause of the Glaev for years, but we could never
figure it out. One day, after an entire town had been wiped
out, we decided to meet up with a friend—Rolim. He had been
obsessing over the Glaev and was the most knowledgeable on
the subject. Anyway, Vicria and I went to an area near the Rip.
We were supposed to meet with him there about something he
had found, but he wasn't there."

Because he was dead…

I wondered if she ever found out about that.

"Instead, we found Daegel. There was a skirmish, then he had
me in his grasp and was about to kill me when Vicria pleaded
for my life. She made a deal with him and became cursed."

"What were the conditions of the deal?" I turned on my side
to look at her.

"He agreed he wouldn't let me die so long as she never spoke
of him and did as he asked, telling him where the Spirits of the

land were. I begged her not to. It wasn't worth it. One life wasn't worth it. But she took his hand anyway…"

She remained silent for a moment, staring up into the darkness.

"I'll never forget the look on her face when he threw me into the Rip, bellowing to the skies. I thought for sure I was going to die, but I wound up here. He's kept his end of the bargain, keeping me alive yet still 'out of his way.'"

Gods, he needs to die.

"That's why Vicria couldn't say anything…"

Leysa turned her head toward me. "Because she knew I was alive. The deal hasn't been broken."

At least not until she spoke of him, and the curse killed her. But I didn't tell Leysa that.

"How is she? Vicria." Leysa asked.

"Oh, erm. She's fine." I didn't particularly like lying to her, but the air was heavy enough with misery, I didn't want to add to it by telling her that her friend was dead.

Leysa turned to me fully and propped herself on her elbow. "I want to go home, Kya. Please," her voice broke. "Just do what he wants." She rolled over and faced away from me.

I wanted to go home too. And now, I had a plan. His name was King Zalen.

Chapter Twenty-Five

RYKER

"Kleio's tits, Ryk. The mating bond *has* driven you insane. You can't just jump into the Rip." Hakoa was standing over me with a look of outrage.

"I think the Rip is a way Gods can send people to other realms. Like with the contestants of the last Trial. The Gods are the only ones who know what happens there. I don't really know what else to do," I said, standing up from the chair and leaning against the table with my arms crossed over my chest.

"How about not going in the Godsdamn Rip?" he asked pointedly.

Malina remained quiet, her eyes darting back and forth between us as we spoke.

"I'm a Worthy of Xareus. If I go in there, he could send me to Kya. I've been loyal to him for centuries. His task for me is to reveal the darkness. What if that's what this is? What if it's my fate to discover first-hand what the Rip is and return to unveil its true nature?" I had thought of it over and over. It made sense.

I had spent three hundred years trying to decipher Xareus' task for me, and while I did my duty of protecting Oryn, I had always felt as if I was failing him in that aspect. This had to be his ultimate purpose for me. And in the meantime, I could find Kya and bring her back.

"You're just guessing," Hakoa argued.

"Of course I'm guessing." I pushed off the table. "But it's worth the risk. *She's* worth the risk."

"What if you're wrong?" Malina asked.

"What?" I snapped my eyes to her. She was already skeptical, I didn't need her encouraging Hakoa against me even more.

"Hakoa is right. What if it doesn't work like you think it does? What if it's only because it was Daegel who took Kya that it worked like that? He's a dark wielder. It could be that his magic works differently, and he has that power."

I didn't respond.

She had a point. I didn't know how it worked. As Theron said, only the Gods knew. And possibly Daegel. But I wasn't even sure they had gone back to *his* realm—just that it wasn't ours.

I stared off distantly.

What if Daegel can go back and forth? Could he return here? Would he? He was after Kya, but he was also searching for the book. Which is still in my possession. He could try to come find it again. There's something in there he needs, otherwise he wouldn't have been searching for it in the first place. I need to find out what it is.

Hakoa sighed. "What do the books say about other known mates who fell in?"

His voice brought me out of my thoughts.

"That their bond was severed entirely. Their tether was gone. Not even a shred was left." I traced my fingers along the pages of the book in front of me. "Which is why I know this is different. Our bond is still there. I know she's on the other side of it."

"And what about the Rip?" Malina asked. "What do the books say about that? Or what about your Spirit? Have you asked him?"

"The books don't say anything we don't already know." I glowered. "Just about how it was formed by the fall of Odes and it's an endless chasm. And of course I asked Theron. He's the one who told me that only the Gods know."

"Then maybe you're not meant to," Hakoa said with a hard expression.

"I—" I began but he cut me off.

"What if she's trying to get back?" he asked.

"I know she is." She would be doing everything she could to come back to me, like I was doing everything I could to find her.

"Exactly. What if she does get back and you're dead? Who does that help? If you die, it'll only hurt her more."

I hadn't wanted to hit Hakoa this bad since our last squabble. He was my oldest and closest friend, but he didn't understand.

"I'm done arguing for the night," I stated, and walked away into the darkness of the library.

I couldn't just sit here and hope Kya would find her way back to me. *I* needed to find her. But I didn't know how. I didn't know what more to do. They were right, jumping into the Rip was a terrible idea and it wasn't as if I wanted to—I wasn't even sure I'd be able to. But I was driven so intensely by the need to have her back it was the only thing I could think of.

I hated not knowing anything. I felt helpless. I didn't know if she was okay. I didn't know how to find her. I didn't know what to fucking do, just that I had to do something, any-thing—everything.

With only a sliver of moonslight to guide me, I continued to aimlessly walk through the rows and rows of books of Morah. A twinge of sorrow hit me as I thought of Kya running through the towering aisles of the library she had called home, of how much time she spent here growing up, and how ironic it was I was here and she wasn't.

It felt wrong being here without her. Not just Morah, but this whole realm. I was meant to be at her side no matter what. She made her choice to sacrifice herself, but Gods be damned, I wasn't going to let that happen.

I found myself walking over the bridge that overlooked the lower levels. I stopped in the middle and rested my arms on the side that looked out through the obsidian wall. Something didn't seem right, and it took me a moment to realize it was because the crack that once extended along the entire length was repaired. Knowing what I knew now, I made the assumption Daegel was the one who was responsible for it. When he was either looking for the dark book or for Kya.

I admired the seamless restoration for a few moments before I heard quiet steps approaching behind me. I didn't even have to turn my head to know who it was.

"When did you fix it?" I asked Nikan without looking at him.

"I didn't do it alone," he said as he came up next to me and leaned his hip on the railing with his head turned toward the glass. "The restoration started before you came to get me and Malina, but it wasn't completed until about a week ago."

I nodded absently. "How'd you do it?"

I had no idea what made me decide to talk with Nikan about such a mundane thing. Perhaps I just needed to think about anything else at that moment.

"A lot of trial and error. Ultimately, we figured out it requires the collaboration of each of the common elemental wielders at the same time." He shrugged and I glanced at him from the corner of my eye.

"Yeah? How's that?" I asked, only half paying attention.

"Fire wielders melted the damaged area while terbis wielders re-formed it. Air wielders had to create pressure while the water wielders cooled it quickly." He blew out a breath. "Thousands of years and the threat of its destruction later, and the world finally figured out how Morah was created."

I hummed in response.

"Have you seen Eamon? I got a message that he wanted to see me but I had been tracking down a source and when I got back, he was gone. I guess he went to Bhara," Nikan said.

"I haven't seen him," I lied. At my prompting, he had gone to Bhara to meet with the Sages—probably to warn them of possible disturbances between the Nations.

Nikan and I remained silent for several minutes as we stared out into the night, absorbing the peace while it lasted.

"Did you talk to Mal?" he asked.

I nodded. "Yeah. Hakoa brought her down to see me. I told her Kya's alive, but I'm not sure she believed me."

"She's taken it really hard and she blames herself. She's been on demid, I don't know for how long. I just found out tonight." He ran a hand down his face. "I don't know how to help her out of this. But I'm guessing she was on it to avoid dealing with Kya's death. And now that she knows Kya's not dead, maybe she'll stop."

"Or you could *make* her stop." I shrugged one shoulder. "If she's getting it on her Roav missions, just stop her from taking any jobs for a while. I've heard you don't have a problem being authoritative over your sister's lives."

"I don't control them," he hissed. "I push them to make the right and *smart* decisions but I never force them to do anything. And Malina hasn't been on any missions. I've been taking her and Kya's jobs so she can have the time to get better. I've also been putting money aside for her so she doesn't find herself starving one day with nothing." He closed his eyes and let out a deep exhale. "I'm just trying to protect her. That's all I've ever done for them."

I turned to face him fully.

He looked utterly spent but held himself as if he wasn't. It was the weariness in his eyes that gave him away. He had taken on the load of three Roav since Kya was gone and Malina had her own shit she was going through.

I had never taken the time to truly appreciate Nikan's role in Kya's life. He had raised and guided her just as much as Eamon had. He was also responsible for her Roav training and teaching her how to defend herself. If it wasn't for that, she may not have survived the Trial. He watched over her, protected her. He had helped shape who Kya was.

I owed him more respect than I had given him.

I nodded and swallowed back any previous discontent I'd had for him. I didn't want Kya to come back to find her family fucked up and broken. The least I could do was appreciate the people my wife loved.

"If either of you ever need anything, just…let me know. And take it easy on Hakoa. You're *brutal* to the males your sisters are with," I huffed. "He'll be good to her. Let him help."

He pursed his lips. "Alright," he grumbled, then gestured toward the floor below. "Are you headed back down?"

"No, I'm done for the night. I'll pick back up in the morning when the Scholars are awake."

Nikan pushed off the railing. "Well, if *you* ever need anything, let me know. I'll do whatever I can to help Kya."

"I appreciate that." I nodded.

With that, we parted ways.

Seeing as it was the most convenient place to sleep, I made my way to Kya's rooms. Everything was exactly the same as the last time we were here. I inhaled deeply. Her scent of lavender and eucalyptus flooded my senses, and it only made me long for her even more. That was the real reason I wanted to stay in her rooms. I wanted to feel closer to her, smell her, feel the essence of her past within the walls. Her clothes still hung in the wardrobe, her soaps still sat on the edge of the tub. The memory of her was still present from her years spent here.

One look at the bed had me aching to lay next to her. So much so I decided to sleep on the couch in her sitting area again. I removed my shirt and grabbed a blanket, draping it over me as I stared at the ceiling thinking of my mate and trying not to let the anxiety of the unknown tear me apart. Exhaustion settled in the moment I lay back, and the soothing moonslight streaming in through the glass walls was the last thing I saw before I closed my eyes and held onto the fractured bond to my mate.

"*I love you, Kya,*" I said down the remnants of our tether. "*Beyond the bond. Beyond the realms between us. Beyond your choice. Beyond whatever it takes to get you back. We're bound by fate, and I will find you. No matter what forces try to keep us apart.*"

Chapter Twenty-Six

MALINA

All I wanted was to be left alone. I hadn't wanted to be taken to Ryker and hear his nonsensical spiel about how he believed Kya was still alive. He was crazy, and I couldn't understand how everyone else didn't see it. I chalked it up to them either wanting it to be true or lying to appease him and trying to make me feel better.

I wasn't falling for it. I didn't want to deal with this shit.

There was no way she had survived. And Hakoa, standing here trying to tell me Kya miraculously survived not only the Rip but also the Onyx Kiss, it just pissed me off.

She was dead.

Ryker was insane.

And it was my fault.

The moment Ryker stormed off, I spun and headed in the opposite direction, wanting to get away to my rooms where I could find a sliver of peace.

"Malina," Hakoa called out, following me as I darted through the dark rows of books. "Stop."

Part of me desperately wanted to crawl into his arms and pretend like everything was right in the world. But it wasn't. I didn't know what I wanted. I wanted to forget. I wanted him again. When I was with him, it felt right. But how could I let things feel right after all the horrible shit I'd done? Kya, Dax, the demid... I was in a dark hole, and I didn't want to drag him down with me.

He didn't deserve that. I just needed to get away from him. So, I made my choice.

I knew it was useless trying to run. It wasn't as if he couldn't find me back in my rooms later but at least there was a locked door and a stashed demid elixir tucked away in a cabinet. All I had to do was take it, and I could drift off into nothingness.

Hakoa was much faster than I was and caught up to me quickly, grabbing my upper arm and pulling me to a stop.

"Damnit, sunshine. Stop running from me."

"No," I said firmly. "And don't call me *sunshine*." There wasn't any light left in me.

"Why are you fighting against me?"

"Because you're already fucking everything up." I ripped my arm from his grasp and walked off, but he continued to follow. *Persistent, stubborn-ass brute...*

"How?" he asked incredulously. "I haven't done anything except save you from freezing to death because you passed out from demid. And try to show you Kya is still alive."

"Stop! You can't take the word of a male who lost his mate. He's deranged and desperate. Of course he wants to believe she's alive, but there is *no way* she survived," I clipped as I opened my door and walked in.

I tried to throw it shut behind me but Hakoa caught it and entered anyway, closing it softly.

"You don't know that for sure—"

"I do!" I shouted as I spun and got in his face. "You weren't there. Ryker wasn't there. *I* was. The arrow pierced her in the heart. I wanted her death to be quick. I didn't want her to suffer the fall. It would have taken only *minutes* for her to die, if that.

Not even a blood wielder could have saved her or Daegel. She made me part of her sacrifice, and now she's *dead*. They both are."

My chest heaved, and my heart was racing. I was so angry. With Hakoa for pushing this so damn hard. With Ryker for leading people on with his delusion. With Nikan for getting caught.

With myself.

With her...

"Malina—"

"I can't do this right now, Hakoa. I need you to go. I need to— You need to leave." My body was buzzing, and my head began to throb.

"Why? So you can take another vial?" He looked around. "Is there another one here?"

"No," I lied defensively.

But my dumb-ass quickly glanced at the cabinet, as if to reassure myself I still did have it. I kicked myself inwardly and hoped he hadn't noticed.

He had.

Hakoa followed my eyes. Then he looked back at me with realization etched across his face, with disappointment.

Shit.

He took a step toward the cabinet, and I maneuvered around him, trying to stop him from finding the elixir.

Fear took over.

I kneed him in the stomach, grabbed his wrist when he bent over and twisted it behind him. Then I planted my foot in the middle of his back, knocking him down. I knew he wasn't fighting back, but I took the win regardless and jumped toward the cabinet.

Hakoa was up in a second, and he wrapped his arm around my waist, pinning my arms to my sides.

"Let go," I demanded.

"No," he boomed. He had never taken such a harsh tone with me before, and I nearly flinched.

Desperate, I wielded bright light from my hands—not bright enough to blind him, but uncomfortable enough he had to turn his head away. Light didn't bother me, and I could see through the luminescence as Hakoa reached for the high cabinet and fumbled through it, pushing the clutter around until he pulled out that blissful vial.

I let my light fade, staring intently at the liquid while wishing it was draining down my throat.

He held up the demid, looking at it as if it was a venomous serpent. "*This* is what you want?"

I didn't respond—too concerned with how I was going to get that vial out of his hands and into mine.

"Malina, look at me."

I couldn't. I couldn't pry my eyes away from the elixir as my mind reeled.

What is he going to do? Will he take it away? Will he dump it down the drain? If he gets rid of it, I won't be able to get another one until tomorrow. I can't wait that long...

Hakoa sighed, shaking his head. "I can't let you do this to yourself. Even if you hate me for it now."

I barely had time to react before he raised his hand and threw the vial down onto the floor, shattering the glass and splattering the demid.

"What have you done?!" I screeched.

Panicking, I ripped myself from his grasp and threw myself to the floor on my hands and knees. The broken glass cut into my skin as I tried gathering the demid in my palms, licking up as much as I could get before the liquid could seep between my fingers. I wasn't fast enough, and fear coursed through me at the thought of the elixir going to waste after all I had gone through to get it—at the shameful price I had had to pay.

Not knowing what else to do, I brought my lips to the floor. In desperation, I began lapping it up from the stone, not stopping even as splinters of glass found my tongue.

"Gods above..." Hakoa whispered. He yanked me up from the floor, and I kicked at him.

"Hold on, there's still more!" I snarled, clawing at the floor, at his arms, as he carried me away.

"Malina," he said, setting me down. My eyes were glued to the liquid as I watched the last of it slip through the cracks. "Malina!"

My eyes snapped to him, mortified by his actions. "What is wrong with you? I'm not hurting anyone."

"Sunshine..." His features were contorted with something mixed between sympathy and bafflement. "You need help," he whispered.

"*You* need to leave," I said with a lethality I rarely used.

He shook his head. "Let me help you. Please."

He still didn't get it. I didn't want his help. This was exactly what I didn't want him to see.

I can get him to leave...

Hakoa's eyes were pleading for me to stop this. But I couldn't stop. I didn't want to. He was a good male, and he didn't deserve to be put through this. I was hurting him for his own sake.

I sighed with resignation. It was better to wound him now, rather than making him suffer longer by concerning himself with me. I was nothing more than an anchor destined for the depths of my own demise.

My stomach twisted as the words crawled out of my mouth, tasting as repulsive as they sounded.

"Do you know what I had to do to get that?" I said with heartbreaking calm, and Hakoa stilled. "I fucked my supplier. Each and every time. Over and over, for weeks."

A hole opened in the pit of my stomach when his deep, golden face paled, and whatever light he had in his amber eyes faded into pained despair.

"Do you know what I'm going to do to get more? I'm going to fuck him again." My vision distorted as tears formed. "I don't want your help. I don't want you here. Now *leave* so I can replace that vial."

It was the look of betrayal that punctured a piece of my heart and nearly knocked the breath from my lungs. I regretted it the moment I said it, but it was too late. I couldn't take it back now. Whether it was due to my pride or the fixation I craved, I didn't even try to retract my words.

It's better this way.

He backed away, eyes filled with devastation and rage.

"I thought... I just wanted..." he stumbled on his words as his gaze burrowed into mine, searching.

Whatever he was looking for, he didn't find it. I made sure of it, keeping my stare empty.

I didn't know what he thought or what he wanted. Whatever he was thinking, whatever it was he hoped for, I had tarnished it. I had run away from him. I had told him to leave. I had fought against him. It didn't matter what he wanted. He wasn't getting it.

And he knew it.

After a moment and without another word, he backed away. There was the slightest hesitation, as if he was waiting for me to take back what I said, before his face glowered with fury, making my heart twist painfully. Then, he turned and left, slamming the door behind him.

I released a shaky breath, relieving the tension in my body. I backed up, sat in one of the cushioned chairs, and hung my head.

As the air settled, the reality of what just occurred hit me. I replayed the event in my head and realized just how low I had sunk—realized how I had broken my own promise to myself, how the demid was ruining me when I thought it would save me.

"What have I done…"

Chapter Twenty-Seven

ZALEN

Sated and utterly exhausted from our time on the throne, Maera slumped against me as I praised her and ran soothing hands down her arms. I kissed her neck softly, my chest filled with the honor of having this beautiful and strong woman all to myself.

"Sofna," I whispered quietly enough she couldn't hear, and the spell made her fall fast asleep. It wasn't one she couldn't wake up from on her own, but it would last longer. A revolting sensation swirled in my stomach at the act, but she needed to rest. We had a long journey ahead of us.

Carefully, I dressed her back in her nightgown and then covered her with my cloak. While I didn't mind if everyone in the Kingdom heard her pleasure, I wouldn't allow anyone else to see what was mine alone.

With one arm beneath her knees and the other around her back, I held her to me and left the Aedum throne room. She didn't know it yet, but riding my cock was the last she would ever see of this place.

After today, it would burn to the ground.

Opening the doors with a whisper, I found Thane and several of my men waiting outside. They had surrounded the thirteen

Elders of Aedum—the only ones they were instructed to keep alive in the castle. Many of them gasped when they saw Maera unconscious in my arms.

A cruel grin spread across my lips. I could only imagine what they assumed I had done to their precious Samanya heir.

I lowered my head to Maera's so my lips brushed her forehead.

"Daufr," I whispered, temporarily taking her hearing. I didn't want to wake her while I threatened the Aedum people.

"I am Zalen Drolvega, heir to Damanthus and soon-to-be King, ever since one of your people killed Makkor, King Airo." I raised my head with a cold expression, looking down on the cowering group. "Aedum is no more. King Erix died by my blade, and I claim the Kingdom and its heir for my own. Through forbidden magic, his power now resides within me. *Your* power now resides within me." The look of dread on their faces had me holding back a triumphant grin. "You vowed your lives and loyalty to the Samanya line. That will *not* change. You will protect and follow Maera Samanya until your death. She will still be your Queen, but *I* will be your King."

Their expressions of apprehension and outrage were enough to relay they got the message. It looked as if I was stealing away their future Queen, as if she was an unwilling participant, unconscious and limp in my arms.

I turned and walked away, leaving them with the Vord. Thane followed behind as I descended the castle steps.

"Hlyda," I muttered under my breath, restoring Maera's hearing, and kissed her head softly. My boots crunched against the gravel as I stepped off the last stair.

"So, that was very…kingly of you. No grand threats?" Thane said loudly, coming up to my side as we walked toward the treeline where our horses had remained.

"Keep your voice down," I scolded, glancing at Maera to make sure she didn't wake. "I don't need to scare them. They already think I'm the vicious beast who killed their King and stole his daughter."

"Which you are…" he said carefully.

"I am. But they will continue to hold fealty for their stolen heir—and therefore me. Especially since their magic now rests in my hands. Have the rest of the Vord arrived?"

"Yes. Along with the rest of those loyal to you." He jutted his chin toward the other end of town, and I saw my men surrounding the city, prepared to stop anyone who tried to leave or retaliate, and informing them of their new sovereign.

"Good. Everything is going according to plan, despite the timeline having been moved up so quickly. With all of the major cities being invaded at the same time, the Kingdom will be under control. I want these people to know who killed their King and who now has become their new one. Let them see what happens when someone attacks the Drolvega line."

We approached the treeline and Thane ran a hand through his long hair. "What makes you think they won't start some kind of rebellion? What makes you think they'll be loyal to you after fucking and kidnapping the Samanya heir?"

Even my life-long friend had no idea Maera wasn't being taken against her will—not that she was actually aware of it.

I turned to face him with a smirk. "Because I absorbed Erix's power, the power of Aedum. And after I fully take over this Kingdom, I'm going to make her Queen of Damanthus."

***

My horse gracefully galloped through the trees on the way back to the Damanthus castle. Dawn was breaking as the first rays of the morning's light trickled across the sky, painting the clouds above in a spectrum of purple. I had imagined this day for years—the day I would take Maera with me to Kanth without having to hide my true intentions.

I relished the feel of her warm, soft body in my arms.

Maera stirred slightly, nuzzling against my chest. She looked up at me with tired eyes, still half asleep. "Zalen?"

"It's me, love."

She looked around without moving her head. "Hmm. Where are we going?" she asked sleepily, her eyelids already fluttering shut.

"Home," I said.

I didn't know if she heard me before she fell back asleep. Thane wasn't far behind me, and we were quickly approaching Kanth. I was eager to return with my prize and show her what it truly meant to be mine—beside me.

When we arrived, I dismounted with Maera still in my arms. She startled awake when I hit the ground and Thane took my horse, taking it with his to the stables around the side of the castle.

At first her face lit up with elation when she looked up at me, but then her eyes widened when reality reasserted itself.

"Oh my—" She struggled out of my hold, and I placed her on her feet.

She gaped at the sight of the castle, her eyes traveling up and up to the top of the stone towers, taking in the Damanthus castle for the first time.

"Zalen! I thought that was a messed-up dream!" She spun on me, her hair whipping around her shoulder. "Did you really… Dear God," she gasped. "You really killed my father in the middle of the night, then fucked me on the throne and brought me to Kanth?!"

I nodded.

She smacked my arm with that adorable fiery look in her eyes then attempted to shove me when I smirked. I couldn't help it. Her passion was endearing. It was one of the things I loved about her.

I had expected her to react this way. I grabbed her wrist when she went to hit me again, pulling her against my chest. Grabbing the back of her head, I kissed her roughly, ravaging her mouth with my tongue and taking her breath away. She didn't resist me, and after only a second her tongue met mine with a flaring intensity as she gripped my shirt and pulled me closer to deepen the kiss.

She backed away abruptly. "Zalen," she said breathlessly, her lips red and swollen. "We have to talk about this. I…" She glanced around, conflict washing over her face. "I can't be here. Your father—"

"Is dead," I finished.

Her eyes snapped to mine, and her lips parted. "How—"

I swallowed her words when my lips crashed into hers again.

It felt so good, so freeing to be able to claim her mouth whenever I wanted. I pulled back and took her hands in mine.

"Come with me. I promise to tell you everything."

I trailed a finger down her jaw then gripped her chin, pulling her face up to mine to kiss her softly once more. I needed her willing to accept me for what I'd done—what I was willing to do for her.

"Okay," she whispered. I knew she was still apprehensive, many questions probably spinning in her mind. She never thought we'd get to be together. She never knew I'd been planning this since the day I fell in love with her. I had never wanted to tell her—couldn't stand the idea of letting her down—so I kept it hidden until everything was in place. Allowed her to believe we'd never have more than a few stolen hours in our cottage.

I nodded and led her into the castle.

With both of us having lived in a castle all our lives, it wasn't surprising she didn't feel the same awe others did. She didn't gasp in wonder or marvel at the size. To her, it was just another structure. But her eyes wandered, learning the complicated layout as I guided her with my arm around her waist down hallways, stairs, and around corners. She gave a nervous nod to each of the guards we passed, and politely smiled at the keepers going about their duties. We reached a single wooden door, and I opened it and gestured for her to enter as she released a relieved sigh to be away from others.

Even after my father was killed, I remained in my same bedchambers. It was nearly as spacious as the King's, and it had a better view from the balcony—one I wanted for Maera, to be able to watch the sunrise over the orchard. She always loved sunrise.

Maera strolled around the room with her hands fidgeting behind her back, observing the large four-poster bed, two wardrobes, a desk, and two sitting chairs by a large arched window overlooking the orchard. I leaned against the wall with my hands in my pockets and my ankles crossed, wondering what she was thinking as she stared out the window hugging herself.

She would need time to adjust. I knew that. But I didn't want her to feel as if she was here against her will. This was her home now, even if she didn't know it yet.

After several moments, she took a deep breath then turned to face me. Even sleep deprived and still in her nightgown, I could see the regal Queen she had been trained to be. It was in the way she held herself. It was in her blood, her eyes, her stride. The voice she had been forced to lock away.

How I wished to hear her finally roar.

"It's a lovely room," she said, but I could tell her thoughts were far away from these four walls.

"I'm glad you like it." I stepped toward her then stopped when she raised her chin. I could see the fire in her eyes, and I couldn't help but be drawn to them. "Do you like the orchard?" She glanced back at it briefly. "Yeah. It's nice."

"Just on the other side is an entire garden. It's filled with plants and herbs of every kind that are tended to around the clock. It's new, but thriving. I've made sure of it." I smirked, hoping it would pique her interest. She wouldn't have to forage anymore.

Her eyes widened. "Do you really? We never had anything like that at the castle. Father thought all herbs needed to be monitored so witches wouldn't have access to anything threatening," she said irritatedly, rolling her eyes. "Can I see it someday? I won't disturb it."

"You can disturb it all you want. It's yours."

"Mine?" she repeated the word like she couldn't believe it. "Well...what about the other witches? Won't they need it too?"

I shrugged. "They have their own. This one was made just for you."

She started to smile before it finally hit her. Her eyes glazed over in thought, and I could see her working things out—that her presence had been expected for a long time now.

"You planned this?" she whispered, but it was more of an accusation than a question.

"Yes." I gently wrapped my fingers around her arm and guided her to sit down in one of the chairs.

"All of it? My father and yours? The invasion of Aedum?" she asked.

I nodded, proud she had figured it out even when no one else had.

"How long were you planning it?"

"Around two years," I said impassively and sat down in the opposite chair. "But I didn't kill my father; someone beat me to it, and I don't know who. That poses its own issue, but we'll get to that later. I was going to wait until I was King and went through the Drehiri ritual to inherit my royal magic before I invaded Aedum, but when you left the tala thread…" I shrugged. "Everything was already in place. I only had to move up the timeline. I took over my father's magic, then I killed yours and did the same thing."

She looked at me like I had horns growing out of my ears. "Why?"

"Because," I stood from the chair and placed my hands on the arms of her chair, leaning over her and making her look me in the eye to understand the truth in my words, "I made a promise we would be together. Neither of our Kings would have allowed it, so they had to be removed. And I refused to give you anything less than you deserved. One Kingdom wasn't enough, so I gave you two. And I'll give you the rest. I'll give you the world."

There was nothing I wouldn't give her.

"Zalen, I didn't ask for this. I didn't want this." She shook her head sadly.

"Didn't? Or *don't*?" It was our fate whether she realized it or not. "You *do* want it. You just think you're not supposed to."

"I—"

"You what?" I cut her off. "You didn't want me to kill that spineless bastard you called father? You didn't want me to kill your bitch of a mother? The one who *sold* you to the captain of the royal guard," I sneered. Thinking about it now, I wondered if I had been too merciful with their deaths.

Maera's eyes narrowed. "At least my father didn't kill people in their sleep," she clipped. "And my mother didn't sell me. The captain—"

"Only wanted to fuck you and get you pregnant, to secure his place as successor to the throne. Then what do you think he would have done, after he bred you like a prized horse and had what he wanted? He beat his two other wives to death, you know. Your father and mother knew. They're the ones who kept it buried." My anger rose thinking about him even touching Maera. At the fact that her parents would have allowed it. They definitely hadn't suffered enough.

Maera's eyes were wide, and her breaths quickened as I continued.

"I knew about *every* single person who was anywhere near you, Maera. Do you really think I wouldn't?"

"You've done all this for *me*?" she asked doubtingly.

And I would do it all again.

"Of course."

"Why?" she breathed.

I reached up and held her face in my hand. "Because my life has been yours since the moment I loved you."

Her eyes searched mine, though I didn't know what she was looking for. "Is this really happening?"

"It already has, love." I had promised I would take care of her, and I always would.

Her body eased as I moved closer.

"Do you want me, Maera?" I said, my lips so close I felt her breath. I already knew her answer.

She looked into my eyes and whispered after a moment, "Yes."

Chapter Twenty-Eight

ZALEN

For the next day, Maera kept to herself. She was angry yet relieved at the same time. I gave her time, leaving her with her thoughts but staying nearby. She spent quite a bit of time on the balcony, gazing over the orchard until the sun rose the next morning, challenging the glow of the sky-spanning moon.

I was just about to go out there when she stormed in through the double glass-paned doors.

"You said you took each of our father's powers."

I nodded from my seat in the room. "I did."

"How? Their power returns to the land when they die, and only the Drehiri ritual can pass the King's magic to the heir." She crossed her arms.

"That's not entirely true." I rose, walking across the room to meet her. "Yes, the magic of Kings returns to the land when they die. But the Drehiri doesn't *give* you their power. It enhances what you already possess with the magic of the Kingdom itself. What I did was different."

"But *how* did you do it?" she demanded.

I took a breath before responding. I wasn't sure she actually wanted to know it all. She needed to though.

"Many years ago, when I was young and foolish, I went exploring in the lower levels of the castle. One of the rooms I stumbled upon was filled with books—forbidden texts that had been locked away for their contents and rightfully so." Maera tilted her head in curiosity as I continued. "The books were magically bound to that room, and couldn't be removed no matter how hard I tried. Instead, I went down there occasionally to read them. I wasn't particularly interested in reading, but I knew my father wouldn't have allowed it—I mainly did it out of spite. I hated the bastard enough that defying him, even in that small way, was satisfying. Little did I know what I had actually discovered."

She leaned back apprehensively.

"One of those books was about a type of magic that had been lost to our kind."

Her breath caught. "Dark magic…"

My brows raised. "You've heard of it?"

"Yes. I've heard about how the Elders of every Kingdom came together and forbid its use thousands of years ago, even destroying all written evidence. It twisted and corrupted the souls of those who used it."

"I didn't know that part. Well, too late now." I shrugged.

"So you did use it?" Her eyes widened.

"It's how I was able to siphon the magic from the Kings once they died. The Kingdom's powers now rest within me. And until I have an heir, it will die with me."

"Unless someone else does the same thing to *you*," she said pointedly, but her eyes reflected the fear behind her words.

"That won't be happening. Once my father found out about the book, it disappeared with the rest. I don't know if he had them destroyed or hidden. If he hid them, he's done a damn good job because I can't find it. So now I'm the only one who knows about that spell, otherwise the other Kings would have done that a long time ago."

She looked at me as if she was truly seeing me for the first time. "You used dark magic. *Twice.* Is this why you're so fucked up?"

I threw my head back and laughed.

"No. It's probably not helping, but this is just who I am, minn astir. Who I've always been." I reached up and brushed her hair behind her ear. "And you still love me, so a little more corruption won't do any harm."

She leaned into my touch as I grazed my finger down her jaw, closing her eyes. She accepted me long before all of this. And she still accepted me now. It made my heart open for her even more.

She squealed when I lifted her from the chair, and I couldn't help my devilish grin. She instinctively wrapped her legs around my waist, her nightgown riding up to her hips.

"What are you doing?" she asked breathlessly.

I leaned in and licked the column of her throat. "I'm about to watch as you stuff that pretty little mouth of yours."

The flat, unamused look on Maera's face when I had *food* brought in was priceless. I had to bite my cheek to keep from laughing. And she made me pay for it by making little moaning sounds with every bite. But I leaned back in my chair and made sure she got plenty to eat, keeping my hands to myself.

Not that I didn't want to crawl over the table and ravage her. I was hard the entire time, desiring to worship at the altar of the woman who held my heart.

I took my time eating, observing her expressions with each bite to learn what she preferred and what she didn't. How she savored the juicy pieces of fruit and pushed away the greasy meats.

From the dark circles under her eyes and the sluggishness of her movements, I knew she was exhausted. She needed sleep more than anything.

While she insisted she wasn't tired, I was able to convince her to lay down with me. She could argue with me all she wanted, but I knew she needed it. It was more than just being deprived of sleep, her spiraling mind keeping her awake on the balcony. Her entire life had just been uprooted, and I understood the toll it must have taken on her.

Not that I regretted it.

It took less than a few minutes for her to fall asleep on my chest. Of all the time we had spent together over the years, never once was I able to see her sleep—both of us were too concerned with spending every precious moment with each other and making the most of it.

Her long hair ran down the length of her back. Unbraided, it reached to her hips. She snored ever so softly with each deep breath. I wanted to keep watching her, learning all of the little things I still didn't know.

The quiet knock at the door, interrupting my peaceful admiration, nearly made me snarl.

Easing my way out from underneath her. I pulled the blankets over her before going to the door.

I yanked it open and stepped outside, closing the door behind me.

"What?" I snapped at Thane. "I explicitly told you not to disturb me."

"You're going to want me to for this," he said in a low, grim tone.

"Did you find the captain?"

Somehow Lyron Vika, captain of the Aedum royal guard, had eluded us. He couldn't have known we were coming, so his absence was intriguing if not suspicious. As captain, he should have been in his quarters in the castle.

"No. We never found him. And he's the only one. The rest of the guard are dead."

"Did you assess their power?"

While the main purpose of the invasion was to secure Maera, we were also trying to find Makkor's murderer. It had to be someone extremely powerful and capable. We could measure the potential with just one drop of their blood in a simple potion.

"We did, and no one met that level of magic. But then again, Lyron is the only one missing," Thane said. "And his absence is particularly interesting given recent events."

"Which are?" I asked impatiently.

"King Belan Olad of Innon was found dead in his throne room. Torn to shreds…"

I froze.

"…as was Queen Delima."

Someone was hunting Kings and Queens.

Chapter Twenty-Nine

MALINA

"*Mal, come on. Stop showing off. You're supposed to help me,*" *Kya whined with her hands on her hips.*

I giggled at her glaring up at me from the floor, while I balanced on top of the ceiling's rafter. I had just learned how to wield my own light, and I was proud of it even though it wasn't a lot.

"Malina, we're here before daybreak so we can be in the dark. It kind of defeats the purpose if you're making it bright," Nikan chided from the other room.

I huffed and let my light go out, allowing the darkness of the abandoned building to wash over us once again. Nikan was having us work with Kya on her terbis abilities. She wasn't able to wield like Nikan or the other terbis wielders.

I thought her ability was even better though. She could do something most others couldn't. Like me. Which made training a little more difficult, but at least we could figure out our abilities together.

But Kya was marked for the Trial of the Gods. That was part of the reason we were here training. Every spare moment Nikan had away from his missions, he would spend training us. I think most of it was for Kya, to prepare her for the Trial, but it was also for both of us so we could have the skill we needed to one day be a Roav. Once we hit our staying age in a few years, we'd be going on missions of our own.

I pulled the dull practice dagger from its sheath and fumbled with it as I tried to spin it in my hand like I had seen Nikan do. Clearly, I needed more practice.

The goal for today was for me to learn to stay hidden and for Kya to find me and Nikan in the dark using her ability. Whoever hit the other with one of the practice daggers first got to go to Penny's bakery at dawn.

I heard Kya's breathing below me as she navigated her way around the large rocks Nikan had placed randomly in the space. It made my blood race. I enjoyed the thrill of these training sessions. The stealthier I became, the more I looked forward to when I could go on a practice mission with Nikan and prove myself. He said I still wasn't ready, but I knew it would be soon.

I heard Kya gasp below me just before the sound of her dagger clattering on the stone floor. Nikan's laughter had me smiling, and I lit up the room once again.

He had snuck up above her and startled her with his practice dagger pressed against her shoulder while he crouched atop one of the rocks.

"And you're dead," he sang. "You really need to work on your breathing. You're too loud."

"Hey, that's not fair, Nik. You were supposed to stay still, and I was supposed to find you." Kya smacked away his dagger.

I smiled and jumped down from my spot on the rafter.

"Not everyone you'll be looking for will be still. They'll be moving around, and that's what you need to feel for. And you need to feel the vibrations through different kinds of rocks. So long as they're touching, you can sense those right?" Nikan slid down to his feet to stand in front of her, and I came up next to them.

"Yeah. But it's not easy. I really have to concentrate on each one. It's not as difficult when it's through something continuous," she huffed and leaned back against the rock.

"Then you'll have to just work harder," he said.

"Okay, but can she concentrate on her vibrating pebbles later? I'm starving, and I want to get that new pastry from Penny's while it's still hot," I interrupted. Training was important, but food was my priority right now.

"Mal, you didn't win. You don't get a pastry." Nikan raised his brows in a knowing look.

But I knew better. Regardless of who won, he always got us all pastries. "But we both worked so hard today."

Nikan shook his head, pursing his lips to keep from smiling. Kya and I exchanged a glance, knowing exactly what would convince him.

"Please," we both said at the same time, giving him our saddest looking gaze.

He rolled his eyes and couldn't hold back his smile. "Fine. But I get first pick since I actually won."

"Yes!" Kya and I quietly cheered.

I hadn't dreamt of that moment in a long time. Everything was so much simpler back then. It was a welcome respite from the usual nightmares, replaying Kya's final moments over and over. I wished I could have stayed asleep, but I was shaken awake from the peaceful dream.

"Get up." Nikan ripped the blanket off me and dropped clothes on my chest.

I sat up with a groan.

"Fuck off, Nik," I grumbled and shoved the clothes off me.

"Not today. We're going on a job," he commanded.

I scoffed, throwing up a small ball of light to illuminate my bedroom since it was still dark. "Seriously? I don't—"

"Malina, I'm not going to let you sit here and rot. You're a Roav, and you have a job to do. Now, I've been more than patient by giving you time. I've taken every job to give you a break. I've tried helping you, but you won't let me—or anyone else, apparently. Are you ready to talk now, or are you going to get off your ass and get to work?" His determined stare bored into me.

That wasn't happening.

I jumped out of bed, grabbed my clothes, and headed to the bathing room to change.

"That's what I thought," I heard him say before I closed the door behind me.

Once I was dressed and armed with daggers, I met him out in the sitting area. He looked me up and down then turned and led the way out of my rooms. I obediently, yet begrudgingly, followed.

Thankfully, I didn't see any sign of Hakoa. It was for the best. Besides, all I could think about was how I didn't have any demid, and that I needed to get another vial. Hakoa had destroyed the last one I had, and the little I shamefully licked off the floor was only enough to sustain me for that day. Jobs could be days or weeks. I couldn't go that long without it. I didn't want to.

Nikan led me to the outer ring of Ilrek to the stables. I couldn't help but glance in the direction of Daxel's house, wondering if I could somehow sneak over there to see if he was awake and able to give me another vial. But I knew I didn't have the time. Payment took awhile.

"Where's the job?" I asked Nikan as we approached the stables. If it was a city, I bet I could find a dealer somewhere. It couldn't be that hard. Not to mention, I already knew of several in various places.

"Ipara," he said as he went to grab two already tacked horses, clearly having planned this little journey.

Ipara would work. It wasn't a large city, but it was big enough I knew I could find something. And it was in Gaol. That Nation was crawling with dealers and every kind of criminal you could think of. And the best part was I wouldn't have to fuck anyone; I could pay with coin.

I had a plan. Get to Ipara, find a way to get away from Nikan for a little while, get a vial of demid, finish the job, and head back to Morah. Simple. Easy.

With more enthusiasm than I had before, I hopped on the horse and Nikan and I rode off to Gaol.

"Where are you going?" Nikan asked, as I tried to rush off around the corner of the building we were staking out.

Thankfully we had made it to Ipara within less than a day, partly due to the fact I rushed to get here. However, I hadn't been able to get away from Nikan. He had kept a close eye on me the entire time, even as we stalked our target for an entire day, entered the store through the high windows after dark, and took the tome from the locked desk inside. It was a smooth mission, and one that didn't take long at all. But it was still too long.

It had been thirty-four hours since I'd had demid. I knew it was affecting me, but I didn't want to admit it to myself. While I did debate on how complicated it was making things for me and others, I wasn't ready to face what withdrawal might come without it. I still wanted it for now.

Just remember your excuse. He'll think it's legitimate.

"I wanted to see one of my contacts about some information on the Paya family."

Nikan's brows scrunched. "The Paya family? Why?"

"To learn about their true lineage. Alban and Von talked about it, and I figured since I was here, I'd see what information I could find for them. They're certain that the family has some false records, and they want accurate accounts of who actually bore one of the children." I shrugged, my stomach tingling with nerves.

I had never lied to him like that before. Not that most of what I said was a lie. I vaguely remembered Alban and Von talking about the Paya family when they were helping me take Nikan to the healers. But I had never deceived Nikan before, and I certainly had never used the Scholars for my excuse. I was getting desperate, and I convinced myself it wouldn't do anyone any harm. I would just say that I didn't find out anything.

He eyed me for a moment, readjusting the book under his arm. I thought he would call me out but, to my surprise, he didn't.

"I did hear them go on about some kind of familial scandal they were looking into. And that works out anyway. I need to check in on one of my own informants. Let's meet up at the forest where we left the horses in an hour. That should be enough time for the both of us."

Thank the Gods.

"Yep. Will do." I didn't hesitate, taking off down the alley.

I had mentally mapped out the path I planned to take while Nikan and I had been watching the store all day, obsessing over which dealer I thought would be the best prospect. Having been fully aware I would only be able to visit one, I needed to be selective.

Rhona was the most likely. She was also the only one who didn't move around, having enough resources at her disposal to bribe the Gaol Watch. She had to have demid.

Eager to get there, I quickened my pace to the other side of the city. Just as dusk was falling, I approached the compound where Rhona handled most of her exchanges. But as I reached for the door, a hand gripped my upper arm and yanked me back, spinning me around and pulling me to the side of the building.

"I knew it…" Nikan seethed, dragging me away.

I pulled against him. "You followed me? Let me go!"

"And let you walk in there just to get more demid? Why do you think I took you away from Ilrek? To hopefully get you away from this shit for a few days and let you see that you don't fucking need it," he scolded through gritted teeth.

I groaned. He didn't understand. I didn't need it. I wanted it. I wasn't hurting anyone else, so what did it matter anyway.

"Is Rhona your regular dealer?" Nikan demanded, getting in my face.

If I said no, he'd know it was someone else and probably try to find Dax. He could ruin my access to demid. But if I told him yes, I'd be lying to him again.

I nodded.

Nikan just looked at me like he was disappointed, and it hurt more than I thought it would. I'd rather have his scolding.

"You wait right here. Don't move," he commanded, and just to make sure I couldn't move, he wielded stone around my feet to trap me.

"Ugh, you ass!" I shouted at him as he ran off around the corner.

Shit, shit, shit.

I had no idea what he was going to do. I wasn't leaving here with a vial, I knew that. Now, all I wanted was to go back to Ilrek so I could meet up with Dax as soon as possible. My skin had already begun to twitch from not having demid after only a little more than a day.

After only a couple of minutes waiting with my feet engulfed by the immovable ground, I felt a rumble just before the entire building came crashing down. Nikan killed Rhona. But more than that, he killed her entire operation. He destroyed her compound.

The sound was the loudest thing I had ever heard, painfully piercing my already sensitive head. The stone of the building collapsed, taking with it any hope I had of finding a vial inside. My imagination spiraled, picturing the demid being wasted.

I could have strangled Nikan. And seeing him come around the corner, emerging from the dust with a glare, I wanted to.

"Happy now?"

"No." He released my feet. "You'll just find it somewhere else. But at least I could make it a little more difficult for you."

"Fuck you too," I snapped.

I turned and darted back to the horses tied to the trees just inside the forest outside the city. Nikan kept up. He wouldn't let me out of his sight all the way back to Ilrek.

I had to lose him.

Chapter Thirty

RYKER

For days, I pored over every book the Scholars could find about the Rip and other realms. I would growl at them, and they would bring me more.

One book in particular seemed interesting, but it was mainly all myths. Myths often took inspiration from the world around us though. So perhaps there was some merit to it. It was a story about an adventure of passing through forgotten gates into other realms and discovering new creatures, people, and cultures. But none mentioned dark wielders. None mentioned what these forgotten gates were. I spent all that time researching for absolutely fucking nothing.

I was out of alternative solutions.

Hakoa had had some sort of fight with Malina and went back to Oryn. And thank the Gods because I didn't need him getting in my way. Nikan and Malina had been away for the last couple of days on a Roav job. There was no one to talk me out of it. I would fly there instead of Traveling with Theron, who would just stop me.

I shut the heavy book in my hands with a deep thunk that echoed through the shelves. Glancing to the nearest wall, I noted the position of the sun. It was nearly dusk.

If I leave now, I can make it to the Rip by morning.

I took a deep breath, taking in the calming scent of the great library before I stood and made my way down the stairs of Morah with firm determination. I patted myself down, ensuring I had my knives as I hit the bottom level and headed straight out the large doors.

I'm coming, little gem.

Just as I cleared the last step onto the street, Nikan came galloping around the corner on a sweat covered horse and pulled to a halt directly in front of me then leapt off.

"Ryker," Nikan panted. "You're still here."

"I was just leaving," I said as I made to move around him.

"Wait," he said hurriedly, holding up his hands.

"I'm done waiting," I said in a low voice. I turned around and began removing my shirt to shift my wings.

"He's back," Nikan blurted.

My entire body froze before I slowly turned around to face him. From the concerned look on his face, I knew Nikan wasn't lying. And I knew who *he* was before I even asked.

"Daegel."

Chapter Thirty-One

MALINA

I had left Nikan in the wind and ran my horse as hard as I could all the way back to Ilrek. I didn't let up. I didn't stop. But Nikan had. He gave up, knowing full-well there was nothing he could do to stop me. I had arrived hours before him, which gave me plenty of time.

After what had happened with Hakoa, I wanted a larger cache of the elixir to keep on hand and in multiple places. I had become a little paranoid that Hakoa would return and look for more vials to smash so I made sure to find better hiding spots. I also feared Nikan would follow me here, so I made a mental note to ensure I was never followed.

As disgusted with myself as I was, I went back to Dax. I gave him his payment, he gave me more demid.

Dax and I were finishing cleaning up when I turned to face him. "What do I need to do to get more demid?"

"Well, you have two options: find another dealer who will take your coin, or pay me…more." He winked.

"What more can I pay you with?" I asked. Even with the amount of coin I would get from the mission, it wouldn't be enough unless I skipped most meals.

"If you want to get more, you have to give *more*." He leaned back on his arms.

I rolled my eyes. "I only have one pussy, and your dick doesn't look like it's going to rise again any time soon."

"Our little sessions have been pretty mild. They're good, don't get me wrong, but they're basic. Only worth one vial at a time." He shrugged. "What are you willing to do for more than one?"

Almost anything.

I swallowed. "Do you have anything specific in mind?"

Dax smirked with that charming look in his eyes. "While you only have one—glorious, might I add—pussy, you do have two other holes. I'd like to explore them."

"Alright," I agreed. That didn't seem so bad. It wasn't my favorite, but it wouldn't be my first time.

"And I like to get a little...rough." He tilted his head.

"Hmm. Rough how?"

"Tying you up. Gagging you. Choking. Hitting. Those kinds of things."

I had done some wild things for a good time, but what he wanted was on a different level. "You want to choke and hit me? That gets you off?" I wasn't judging, I was genuinely curious.

Dax sat up and leaned forward. "It's not as bad as you think. And you'd be surprised at how pleasurable it can be for you," he said reassuringly.

I had to hand it to him. For someone society considered despicable, at least he was bluntly honest. But it still didn't sound like something I wanted to do.

"What other options do I have?" I asked as I gathered my hair to tie it back.

Dax pursed his lips, contemplating for a moment. "I have a few friends I owe favors to. They'd be happy to do business with you, if you're willing to pay them the same way you pay me."

I sighed. I felt enough shame fucking one male for demid, I preferred not to do it with several. Not to mention, I had come to trust Dax a little more. "Alright. I'll give the 'rough' option a try."

Dax smiled widely and stood then practically pranced across the room to open the door for me. "Looking forward to it. Same time tomorrow then?"

"Yeah," I mumbled and left with a vial in my hand. At least one good thing came out of today. And I couldn't wait to swallow it.

I went to see Dax almost daily. He did everything he'd said he wanted. Some of it I didn't mind and even found a little enjoyable, but most of it wasn't satisfying or even pleasant for me. And since it wasn't giving me the escape I was searching for, I relied on the demid even more than I used to. I needed to obtain more, and therefore pay more. I fucked two of his friends.

As degrading as it was to my body, it was more degrading to my dignity.

I didn't enjoy it, and I was sore and sensitive from the amount of stimulation.

It doesn't matter. It's just a body. It'll heal.

I told myself that as I sank into the hot, soothing water of my bath with a vial in my hand. My body would heal. My soul wouldn't, and *that* was why I needed the demid.

The only good thing to come out of so much rough sex was the exhaustion. It was almost as good as the demid, making me so tired that I slept dreamlessly.

It didn't help that I would get drunk before each visit to Dax or one of his friends. It was the only way to make it more bearable, and I had the hope that if I was drunk enough, then I wouldn't remember as much of it.

My life had been reduced to drinking, fucking, and sleeping. And that was just fine by me.

I got back to my rooms about midday and was planning to sleep off the alcohol after my bath, when someone banged on my door. I groaned and hopped out, throwing my clothes on.

Maybe if I don't answer, they'll go away.

It wasn't Hakoa. I knew that. He left Ilrek after our fight, and I assumed he went back to Oryn. I was too stubborn to go down and ask Ryker about him, not to mention, I didn't want to see him. After what I had said to him, I had no right. Eamon had tried talking to me a few times, but every time I came up with some excuse as to why I couldn't, and I would dismiss him until I ultimately just avoided him altogether.

Content to ignore whoever it was, I lay in bed and pulled the blanket over my head. Then I heard my door burst open and feet quickly approaching.

"Mal. Mal." Nikan shook my shoulder. "Wake up."

I threw the blanket off. "I am awake, thanks to you." I rolled over and glared at him.

He was filthy. His clothes were covered in dirt, and his dark face was crusted with dried sweat. But his eyes were alight with excitement.

"Get your dirt-covered ass off my bed," I chided.

"Oh, sorry," he mumbled and stood. "But I had to tell you Daegel is back."

That sobered me up, and I suddenly found myself no longer tired.

"Your deal…"

"It's completely gone." He lowered the collar of his shirt so I could see nothing but his skin, free from the curse.

"I thought it faded because he died," I questioned.

"I have no idea. I don't exactly have a manual for how deals with dark wielders work. Maybe he was weakened enough the magic failed. But regardless, he didn't die."

I sat up. "Why are you telling me? Shouldn't you go tell Ryker?"

"I did. And he left immediately after." Nikan nodded.

"Where did he go?" He couldn't seriously try to go after him.

"I have no idea, he wouldn't tell me. And for good reason," he said.

"And that would be…?"

"Daegel tried to force me into another deal, for me to find the dark book. I didn't do it. I didn't give him the chance to tell me what I would get, but I know it wouldn't be worth it. I managed to slip away before he could try another method. Ryker left to hide the book and didn't tell me where in case Daegel comes for me again. We don't know all he's capable of," he explained. "I'm going to be joining Ryker after the book is hidden. If Daegel shows up again, Ryker will be there."

It was a lot of information to take in, and I was still coming off my last dose of demid

"Well… What's Ryker planning to do about Daegel?" I asked.

"Fight him? Subdue him somehow? I don't know, but he'll come up with something." He was smiling, and *that* was very concerning.

"You need to go back to the healer. Your face is broken."

Nikan's face twisted with confusion. "What?"

"Why are you smiling? This is kind of an unfortunate situation," I said pointedly.

Nikan's features softened, and his smile returned. "Because Daegel is *alive*. He survived the Rip. If what Ryker says about the bond is true, then that proves even further that *Kya* is alive."

"Ayen's ass," I muttered under my breath and rubbed my temples. "Daegel is a dark wielder. Who knows what kind of shit his magic can do. It doesn't mean Kya survived."

Nikan shook his head. "You're being unreasonable, Mal. And I'm blaming the demid. You're ignoring the evidence that's being presented to you."

I wasn't being irrational. I was being realistic. Demid or not. "I'll believe it when I see her."

Chapter Thirty-Two

―――•◦•―――

RYKER

My plan to go to the Rip was extinguished by the return of Daegel. If Nikan hadn't told me he disappeared after Nikan turned him down and ran, I would have gone after him.

I wanted to kill that motherfucker with my bare hands. I wanted to burn him alive. But I knew I couldn't just yet. If I were able to capture him, I could force him to take me to Kya. I had to catch him first.

And sometimes a hunter needed bait.

Daegel was still looking for his book, which was back at the cave. After Nikan informed me of his encounter, I called for Theron, and he Traveled me back to Oryn.

The bite of the winter air was welcoming when we arrived on the roof of the palace in Voara. I inhaled deeply, filling my lungs with the familiar scent of home. Except it was stale without the presence of a certain green-eyed female. It wasn't home without her.

My soul burned for her.

Making my way into the palace, I reached out to Mavris.

"Mav, where are you?"

"Such a pleasant greeting…" he grumbled. *"Good to know you didn't have to go through the Raith. I'm in my study."*

I made my way down to his study and let myself in. Mavris was sitting behind his desk with his hands folded on top of a stack of papers, waiting for me.

"Welcome back," he said as I took a seat across from him. "What was the verdict of the mating trial?"

The panel regarding our mating seemed like ages ago, and it made me realize how long I had gone without speaking to Mavris.

"Our mating was approved since they think she's dead," I said flatly.

His eyebrows raised. "You didn't correct them?"

"No. It's better they think she's gone for now. Especially now that Atara is currently being restored."

Mavris's jaw fell. "How—"

"Kya's energy has continued to spread just like with Voara. Atara will be whole again—and soon. Which poses a problem of its own."

"Like the fact the other Worthy think she's dead, and now an entire Nation's worth of land will be up for grabs? Yeah, I'd say that'll be a problem if it isn't already. Gods above," he sighed.

"Exactly. I need you to write letters to our representatives in the other Nations. We're going to need to know if they get wind of this information so we can prepare." I nodded toward his desk.

Mavris immediately pulled out a fresh piece of parchment and started drafting the letters.

"Prepare for what?" he asked with his head down.

"I don't know yet." I ran my hand through my hair. "Oh, and another thing."

"Hmm?" Mavris hummed over the scratching of the quill.

"Daegel came back."

Mavris's head snapped up. "You saw him?"

I shook my head. "Nikan did. Which is why I'm here."

Mavris stiffened. "Is he alright?"

"He's fine. For now. Daegel wanted to make a deal with him to find the dark book. He denied it and escaped. But I'm going to hide it so Nikan *can't* know where it is in the event Daegel has some ability to find out through him." I didn't know what Daegel needed the book for, but I wasn't letting that fucker get anywhere near it.

"You're helping Nik?" He raised a brow.

I leaned back in the chair. "Yes."

"But you hate him," Mavris stated.

"He's an asshole, but I don't *hate* him."

"Could have fooled me." He shrugged.

I sighed. "He's Kya's brother. I can't let anything happen to him."

Mavris nodded, but I could tell his thoughts were elsewhere.

"What about your research on the other realms? Did you learn anything?" he asked after a few moments.

"Nothing useful."

"So…what are you going to do now?" He tilted his head to the side.

"I'm going to lure Daegel to me."

Mavris blinked. "Why?"

"Because I need him to take me to Kya," I said.

"Ryk, you might be one of the smartest people I know, but this is the dumbest thing I've ever heard." Mavris crossed his arms.

"Excuse me?" I balked.

"Oh, come on." Mavris shook his head. "You really think you can take the dark wielder on your own? Be practical. Last time there were two Worthy, two highly trained wielders, and two Spirits—one of which he killed. He nearly killed Kya too. What makes you think you can defeat him and convince him to take you to your mate?"

"I know that, Mav," I snapped, my temper rising at the mere mention of Daegel hurting Kya. "I wasn't intending to do it alone." Taking a calming breath, I pulled my chair closer. "I'm going to hide the dark book, and I won't tell anyone where it is. Not even you. I'm going to send a few of the Vaavi to look for any indications on his whereabouts. Nikan will stay near me so if Daegel tries to interact with him again, I'll be there, and he'll lead him to a false location where an ambush will be waiting for him."

I wasn't ignorant enough to believe I could defeat Daegel on my own. It was insane, I was fully aware of that. But I needed Kya. I needed her to be here, to be safe. I was willing to do anything.

"And who will be a part of this ambush?" He eyed me curiously.

"The most powerful wielders in the realm. The Worthy."

Mavris pursed his lips. "I take it back. *This* is the dumbest thing I've ever heard."

"It'll work," I argued.

"*If* the other Worthy agree." He gave me a knowing look.

"Do you have any better ideas?" I challenged.

"No. But that doesn't mean this is a good one," he mumbled under his breath then sighed. "How exactly do you plan on convincing the other Worthy to cooperate with you and risk their lives? On *your* land, might I add."

I shrugged. "I haven't gotten that far yet. But thankfully, I have a wise advisor for times like this." I smirked, and Mavris rolled his eyes.

"I'd rather scrub Theron's ass with a thorn bush on his crankiest day."

"As much as I'd love to see that, I can't have you killed by my Guardian," I chuckled for the first time since before Kya fell. I stood to leave, patting his shoulder. "Write up those letters to the representatives. I'll draft up a request to meet with the Worthy."

I turned to leave with a wave, but Mavris' voice stopped me just as I was stepping out the door.

"For the record, Ryk." I glanced over my shoulder to look at him standing with his hands in his pockets and slumped shoulders. "I don't like the idea of leaving Nikan vulnerable like that, using him. If Daegel does get his hands on him, he could get caught on the wrong side of the fight."

I eyed him. This wasn't the first time he had shown his concern for Nikan's well being.

"I can't protect everyone at the same time, Mav." With that, I left.

I went to my own study and spent the rest of the day sorting through papers. Much that required my attention had built up from my prolonged absence. I promised myself I would catch up on everything once Kya was back and everything settled.

After that, I swallowed my pride and drafted up the letter to send to the Council of Sages in Bhara, requesting for them to host an urgent meeting with the Worthy, one that was imperative to the balance of the realm. I hoped it would be convincing enough. Unless invited, Worthy weren't welcome in each other's Nations, and they certainly wouldn't all meet anywhere except a neutral location. The Council of Sages was a mediator between the Lords and Ladies.

The last thing I did was send a message to Arra, summoning her to my study first thing in the morning.

Finally, I went to my bedchamber. As I lay there in bed staring up at the ceiling after eating and bathing, the unoccupied space next to me weighed heavily on my heart.

I tossed and turned all night, bothered by the knowledge that Daegel had returned and constantly wondering what was happening with Kya. He hadn't brought her with him. I would have felt her.

Did he leave her? Did he have her at all? Was she hurt or scared? Was she trying to get to me just as much as I was trying to get to her?

And Daegel… Why did he need the book so badly that, even after getting Kya, he still had come back for it? What was he planning?

The questions on top of the worries of the other Nations discovering Atara, kept me up almost the entire night. I couldn't close my eyes without seeing an enemy or replaying Malina's memories of Kya falling.

Just before dawn, I sat up in bed and scrubbed my hands down my face. There was no point in trying to sleep anymore, so I decided to get up and get dressed to go to the cave. I put on my thicker shirt with slits in the back and pants. After tying my boots, I went out to the balcony.

It was a particularly calm day with little wind, but the sky was blanketed in dark clouds. I felt a harsh winter storm coming, and I knew I needed to fly fast to get to the cave and back, then hopefully have time to get to where I needed to go after the storm. I probably could have had Theron just Travel me there, but I wanted to feel the air beneath me.

Without wasting another moment, I shifted my wings and lifted into the sky.

I hadn't been back to the cave since I left to chase Kya to the Rip. Landing at the mouth of the cave, I walked down the dark tunnel and flicked my hand, lighting the lanterns lining the length of the tunnel. Remembering Kya had stored the book on the chair in the alcove with the bed, I made my way through the main chamber, the walls embedded with gemstones that reflected the light of the flames.

What was once my place of tranquility had become a tomb for aching memories. The alcove was exactly as I had left it. The sheets were still thrown across the bed from when I rushed out, clothes still strewn across the floor. And something I hadn't noticed before...

I walked over to the bedside table where a black feather—small enough I knew it belonged to Kya—and a gemstone rested. I picked them up, cradling them in my palm as a wave of fury crashed inside me.

This had been her farewell.

I roared and threw the gem hard enough to crack the wall.

I didn't have time to sit here and sulk. I needed to use this pain to keep myself fueled. I tucked her feather into my pocket, careful not to bend it.

The dark book was on the chair where Kya had left it. I wanted nothing more than to burn it, if only to spite the dark wielder. But I knew if it was valuable to him, then it held value to me. It was the only bargaining chip I had...

That's it.

My lips pulled into a malicious smile.

I could use the book as leverage—a trade. The book in exchange for Kya.

Vicria mentioned he had been searching for the book for years, and it was only recently he diverted his attention to Kya instead. And he was still looking for it, even after he had her.

I grabbed the book, wrapping it up and tucking it under my arm, then left the cave with more confidence that I was one step closer to getting my wife back.

Landing on the balcony of the palace, I noted the storm building. I still had enough time to meet with Arra. I also needed to check with Hakoa before I left to see if there were enough water wielders in Voara to stave off the snowfall, and fire wielders to heat the air. People were still displaced, and the last thing they needed was to be buried in snow and freezing. This was going to be a nasty blizzard. I could sense it.

I made it to my study and busied myself with more papers, while also mentally plotting out how I would coordinate the ambush against Daegel as I waited for Arra to arrive.

A few minutes later, she hastily entered the study.

"Ryker, I didn't know you were back until I got your message," she said in greeting.

"I only just returned last night, but I'm leaving right after this." I stood and tucked my hands in my pockets.

"You might have to delay your departure. Since I didn't know you were coming back, I sent one of the Vaavi to Riyah to give you an urgent message." Her eyes were like stone, filled with calm concern.

"Well, I'm here now. What's going on?"

"It's... You haven't found Kya have you?" she said, rushed.

I stiffened slightly. "No. Not yet."

"Shit." Arra ran her hand through the loose strands of her red hair. "It's about Atara."

I stilled. "What about it?" I asked stiffly.

"It's...coming back."

For the love of Xar. Only Eamon and I knew, which meant...

"A couple of Vaavi reported they heard whispers that Atara is healing. Just like Voara, after Kya touched it with her magic. And you know we don't take rumors at face value. They took the initiative to travel to Atara and see for themselves. Sure enough..." She shook her head with a look of astonishment.

"I see," I said much more calmly than I was feeling. I nodded absently as my plan to keep Atara's recovery concealed went up in flames. "I appreciate the Vaavi being so thorough."

Arra's brow creased. "Why aren't you more concerned? I honestly expected more of a...reaction."

I sighed, "Because I already know." I dragged a hand down my face.

"So it's true?"

"Yes. And I'd hoped I could keep it a secret a little longer. That's actually why I wanted to meet with you. We need to keep this contained. You know as well as I how this could play out with the other Nations."

Arra nodded once and stood up straighter, every bit the leader of the Vaavi. "What are your orders?"

"To make sure these rumors don't spread. I've already worked things out at Morah. I need you to track down anyone who is spreading the information and make sure they're no longer a problem. And while you're at it," I added, "Hakoa also needs to be informed. Have him put warriors around the border at Atara to keep any citizens or travelers from discovering it."

"He won't take official orders from me when it comes to the Noavo, you know that. You're going to have to do it yourself," she stated.

"Yeah, I'll do that." I paused. "Where were the Vaavi when they heard about Atara?"

"Gaol."

I stood, tucked the book under my arm, and began walking out. "Get this done, Arra. Before we have a war on our hands."

A full-on war between the Nations would be devastating. We'd had small battles before, and those were cataclysmic enough. But a war? It would disrupt the balance even further. It would result in the loss of so many lives, displacing and harming even more. It was the last thing our fragile world needed.

She nodded and left ahead of me.

I went out to the balcony, ready to fly to Hakoa, and paced along the railing. We needed to get this under control. Quickly. It was only a matter of time before the rumor spread and Lord Jymal confirmed it himself. Then there wouldn't be any way to keep it from the other Worthy.

Chapter Thirty-Three

ZALEN

"**H**ow the fuck did this happen?" I whispered through gritted teeth.

"I have no idea, but three Kings killed all around the same time? This isn't good." Thane leaned against the window frame in the hallway.

Two Kings killed in separate Kingdoms within weeks of each other was concerning. It wasn't a secret I killed King Erix—I had practically shouted it from the rooftop. And it could easily have been assumed I killed Makkor. Without anyone claiming his death or the death of King Belan of Innon, their assumptions would likely lead to me being the killer of all three.

My head tilted to the side as I thought of the possibilities.

"What if it is?" I asked quietly.

"What if *what* is?" Thane's brows creased.

"What if this is good?"

"That someone is murdering all the Kings? How is that a good thing? It seems like we should be concerned for your life—and Maera's—and that's definitely *not* good." Thane crossed his arms.

"Only two Kings were killed by someone else. Have you heard anything about the Shara King?"

Shara was the Kingdom south of Damanthus, and while we'd had our skirmishes with each other in the past, we hadn't had much issue with them in a while. They mostly kept to themselves as of late.

"No, but I can send someone down there to check on things," he offered.

"Make sure they don't make a fuss," I clarified.

Thane nodded. "So, again, why is the death of so many Kings a good thing?"

"Because this presents an opportunity. One we can use to our advantage." The side of my mouth lifted. "I can add the power of Innon to my collection."

Thane's brows raised with intrigue. "But if Shara is without a King..."

"Then I could give them one."

He blinked. "I don't understand. The only way you could be King of Innon is to go through the Drehiri in their lands. And your intention is to become King of Damanthus, which now encompasses Aedum. You can't go through the Drehiri twice."

"No. I can't. I could have absorbed the power if I had been there when Innon's King died. But that doesn't mean someone can't go through the Drehiri in my place." I gave him a know-ing look.

It wasn't the best plan, but it was something. Innon was weak. It was best to take advantage of the situation by using the chaos to invade. Without an Innon heir, the Kingdom's power was up for grabs, leaving me the opportunity to select the new sovereign.

He grinned at that. "I'll send someone *else* to Shara right away."

"Good. In the meantime, have the northern forces assembled. I want the Innon castle razed to the ground. And I want you to continue searching for whoever was strong enough to kill both Kings." I opened the door to my rooms then glanced over my shoulder at Thane. "Come get me when it's done."

I closed the door softly then went back to the bed, crawling in behind Maera as she still slept. Brushing her hair behind her ear, I placed a kiss on her cheek. As much as I would have enjoyed watching her sleep for the rest of the day, there were things we needed to discuss.

"Wake up, love," my lips whispered against the soft skin below her ear.

"Mmm," she hummed with pinched brows, trying to pull away from me.

"Come on. I want to bathe you."

"I can bathe myself," she said stubbornly, but she sat up and stretched her arms over her head.

"I have spent years only having mere moments with you, and I've never had the pleasure of washing you. I get to take my time with you now, and I intend on doing everything I've imagined doing with you for the past three years." I removed my shirt, and I didn't miss the small gasp from her parted lips.

I wanted to personally wash away the scent of Aedum from her skin.

"I suppose I could be convinced," she said, biting her lip.

She grabbed my hand as I stood to help her out of bed and led her to the bathing room. I released her hand and ran the bath as she waited patiently for the tub to fill.

While the water was running, I turned back around and stepped closer to her. Those remarkable eyes of hers looked up at me as I towered over her.

"Lift up your arms."

Without breaking eye contact, she did as she was told.

I grabbed the hem of her nightgown and pulled it over her head, tossing it to the corner and making a note to have it cleaned for her later. My hands grazed down her sides, brushing over the curve of her breasts as I reached her undergarment.

Trailing my hand between her legs, I pushed her panties to the side and pressed two fingers inside her, feeling how wet she was for me.

Not enough.

Pulling in and out, I fucked her with my fingers, curling them inside before pulling them out and circling her clit, then back in again until she was writhing beneath my touch, utterly soaked.

"Zalen...I thought...we were...going to bathe... Oh!"

The little noise of protest that came from her lips as I pulled my fingers from her had my mouth spreading in a pleased smile.

"We will." I grabbed her undergarment and pulled it down to her ankles, lifting one foot at a time to remove it. I stood up and began removing my pants, admiring her luscious body.

Maera's eyes glazed when my already hardened length sprung free.

I wrapped her hands around my neck then lifted her by her thighs, carrying her to the overly large tub. With her legs around my waist, I sat down in the steaming water, slowly lowering her onto my cock. She felt so tight with the way we were angled, stretching around me as I eased her down.

Her head fell back with a gasp when I filled her completely.

Gripping her hips, I guided her up and down until she started fucking me on her own.

"Right there," I said huskily. "Keep going."

I grabbed the soap and a cloth from the small table next to the tub and began washing her—taking my time as I lathered her with torturous slowness. I paid extra attention to her breasts, alternating between sharp flicks at her nipples and soothing rubs.

Maera's breathing came faster, and my body was beginning to tense. I couldn't wait any longer. I tossed the soap and leaned over her so I was on top, her back against the tub. She held onto the edge as I pounded into her, water sloshing onto the floor.

As our mouths crashed together, our tongues clashed seeking a desperate deepness within each other as if we couldn't get enough.

"More," she moaned into my mouth, and the sound alone had my balls tightening.

"Touch yourself," I growled against her lips.

She didn't hesitate to snake her hand down her body.

I tilted my head and watched as she played with her swollen clit. The tips of her fingers brushed over the base of my cock as she rubbed herself in short little circles, heightening the sensation even more.

"Fuck, that's sexy," I said breathlessly, slamming into her. She bit her lip, and I could tell she was holding back. "Let me hear you. We both know that pretty little mouth of yours can be louder."

Her lips parted, releasing her unrestrained moans.

The sound of her cries mixed with the slapping of wet skin as she began to tense. I claimed her mouth again, wanting to taste her scream. I thrust with a grunt as I spilled myself into her just as she came hard, pulsing around my cock.

We were panting as we rode out our release, until we came down from our state of euphoria. I pulled her forward and held her against me.

"You did so good," I whispered to her, running my hands soothingly down her back and kissing her neck softly.

Her lips turned up into a smile that wars could be fought over. And I would for her, only for her.

Maera had the ability to settle my soul with a simple look, taming the violence below the surface. She made me feel as if I could breathe freely. But most of all, she gave me purpose.

After a couple of minutes, I pulled out and began properly washing her—running the cloth over her body, massaging the soap into her scalp, and tipping her back into the water to rinse it. Then she washed me.

It was a different level of intimacy, taking care of each other in this way without the need for words. The silence between us was filled with comfort and serenity.

I stepped out of the tub.

She took my offered hand as she stood and got out after me.

"So," she began. "What's next?"

"Well," I said as I handed her a thick towel then grabbed one for myself. "We'll dry off, and I'll have my way with you in bed."

She huffed a laugh. "Do you ever think about anything other than sex?" She lightly smacked my arm, and I chuckled.

"Not when you're *naked*."

She wrapped the towel around her body, grinning widely with a light giggle.

"*Next* is the Drehiri in two weeks," I finally answered her question, folding the towel around my waist.

She stiffened. "The ritual for Kings."

I placed my hand on the small of her back and encouraged her to go back into the room. "Yes. As well as anyone else I grant," I added. "But usually, Kings don't want to share."

"Oh," she said quietly. "Are you nervous about it? I heard it's...intense."

I smirked. "Not at all." I leaned against the bedpost and crossed my arms. "Are you?"

"Am I nervous?" she asked with a tilt of her head.

"Yes."

"About your ritual?"

"No," I said slowly. "About yours."

"You want *me* to go through the Drehiri ritual?!" she squeaked out.

"Of course." I nodded.

"But… Has a woman ever done it? *Can* a woman do it?" she asked incredulously.

I shrugged. "As far as I'm aware, you'll be the first. There's nothing saying you can't. Nowhere has it ever stated a woman isn't able to, just that no King has ever permitted it."

I loved the idea of watching her rise above all others, becoming the most powerful Queen in history by my side.

"Will I now? Right," she drawled sarcastically. "So long as I'm strong enough to survive it."

I pushed off the bedpost and walked toward her, grabbing the side of her face. "You are. And I don't want to hear you doubting yourself again. Understand?"

I took a step back, and she sighed with a small smile then nodded. "Good."

She glanced around the room. "What about in the meantime? What do I do to keep myself busy?"

"Today, you're resting. Tomorrow, I'll show you some of the things I want you to do before the Drehiri."

"What am I supposed to wear?" She looked down at her damp towel.

"I'm perfectly fine with you wearing nothing for the foreseeable future."

Maera rolled her eyes but failed to hide the blush crawling up her neck. It satisfied something in me that I could still get that kind of physical reaction from her.

I walked over to the wardrobe and pulled out one of my shirts then tossed it to her.

"All of your clothes and belongings are being brought here. You should have all that you need by morning."

I grabbed a pair of pants for myself and pulled them on. I watched as Maera put on the shirt, her damp hair falling down her back, then she glanced out the glass doors to the balcony.

"Do you want to come sit with me?" She held out her delicate hand toward me.

Always.

In answer, I took her hand as I led her outside. She made to sit, but I pulled her down on my lap as I sat down in the other chair. I wanted to be able to touch her as much as I could, making up for lost time.

We sat in blissful peace and watched the last rays of the sunset dance over the glistening water of the Rhaen River. I took in the appreciation of the moment without having the urgency we had become so accustomed to.

"I still can't believe I'm here." She absentmindedly traced circles on my arm. I could tell her thoughts were trying to organize themselves.

Sitting there allowed for my mind to wander, and I was reminded of my discussion with Thane about the elusive Captain Lyron Vika.

"Maera," I said. She flinched slightly as I pulled her focus back to me. "I need you to tell me if you ever heard anything about the captain planning to kill Kings. Or maybe your father ordered him to?" I knew it was a long shot, but perhaps he had confided in his future wife.

She turned to the side and shook her head. "I barely knew him."

My brows flattened. "He's been the captain of the guard for decades. Surely you know something about him."

"No." She shrugged. "He's new. Captain Lyron got drunk one night, a few weeks ago, and got in a fight with a group of disgruntled humans. Apparently, he was so wasted he couldn't utter spells correctly, and they managed to kill him. The next thing I know, someone new took his place."

My nostrils flared, and my hands balled into fists. I was going to kill the Vord assigned to tracking down the information about the captain. They should have fucking known he was dead. I shouldn't have been focused on someone who was killed weeks ago, rather than searching for someone else—someone she didn't even know.

"And your parents were going to marry you off to a complete stranger? Someone you didn't even know?"

She nodded, her eyes trained on the floor.

I lifted her chin. I would not have her feel shame for anything those fuckers had force her to do.

"Do you know who he is?" I asked.

"I never met him. I don't even know his name. All they told me was that he was originally from Shara and quickly rose in the ranks of the guard, and would provide good seed for breeding. When my mother told me I'd be marrying him, she said the wedding would be after he returned. And before you ask, I don't know where from. I didn't care to ask."

I gave a tight smile. "That's fine. It's over now," I reassured, and she smiled in return.

I kissed her forehead as she rested her head on my shoulder. *Shara...*

Chapter Thirty-Four

RYKER

With the book still tucked under my arm, I landed in the middle of the Noavo station just outside Hakoa's barracks. He should have made it back by now, after the way he stormed out of Morah. And from the grueling drills he was having the warriors run, I guessed he was in a particularly foul mood.

I found him standing outside one of the rings with four warriors, all sparring with different elements—paired in twos and facing each other. It was harder to team up with someone who didn't share your element, having to work with them in tandem rather than joining their wielding for a stronger attack. A male fire wielder and male air wielder were paired against a female water wielder and a female terbis wielder. Water and terbis were clearly the stronger set.

Thunder rumbled through the dark, looming clouds above, promising a fierce downpour.

"Chief," I greeted Hakoa, approaching him as he stood just outside the ring with his hands behind his back. He was the epitome of the hardened leader of the Noavo warriors.

"Lord Ryker," he returned without so much as glancing at me as I came up by his side.

I hated when he called me that, but the formality was necessary when amongst citizens. I noticed his eyes were squinted and red, which was odd since the storm clouds rolling in made it somewhat dark outside.

"We have some things that need to be discussed." He turned to look at me then. I nodded to his barracks. "Best done privately."

He gave a sharp nod then shouted at the warriors to break until he returned. He turned and headed to his barracks without a word as I followed. He opened the door and entered, heading straight to a sitting chair but continued to stand in front of it.

"Warriors giving you trouble?" I asked as I sat and gestured for him to do the same, placing the book in my lap.

"No," he said shortly with his hands tensed on the arms of the chair.

"You're working them pretty hard."

"I have to ensure they're trained for any situation."

"One of which is now," I said with a nod.

Hakoa's face remained neutral. Malina must have really upset him. While it was standard for him to keep the stoic mask in front of others, it was unusual for him to keep it up while we were alone.

Deciding not to drag this on any longer, I got right to the point. "I need you to station warriors along the Ataran border."

Hakoa's brow creased. "And what will they be doing there?"

"Keeping anyone and everyone away from the border within a visible distance," I stated.

"Right away," he agreed without question—one of the reasons I chose him to be the chief. "Is there a danger I should be aware of so we may better prepare?"

"There's no immediate threat, but it's possible we may have to defend Atara. And soon," I sighed, rubbing my temples.

"Defend it? Why? From what?" he asked.

I blew out a breath. "From the other Nations that will want to claim it now that the Glaev is vanishing due to Kya's magic."

Hakoa opened his mouth to speak but then closed it. He stood and roughly ran a hand down his face, pacing back and forth before spinning on his heel to face me with a glare.

"Why didn't you tell me this back in Morah?"

I leaned back in the chair, remaining calm. "You were a bit preoccupied with Malina."

"And I'm still the leader of your forces. That doesn't stop just because I was off-duty," he defended.

"Hakoa, you were on leave. Not an official Noavo assignment." I lowered my voice. "Your head was in the wrong place. I get it. It wasn't something you needed to know right away. But I've since been informed by Arra that the recovery of Atara has been discovered, and now we need to try to contain it."

His jaw clenched, but he sat back down, collecting himself. "Discovered where?"

"Gaol."

"Shit." He tilted his head back against the chair. "And they believe Kya is dead."

"Exactly. It's only a matter of time before word gets to the rest of the Worthy, and I'm trying to buy us more of it. But eventually, it's likely we will have to defend Atara against the other Nations' claims."

Hakoa shook his head. I could see his mind already strategizing on how we would approach this.

"So we're going to go to war? Possibly against *four* other Nations?" he asked.

I gave a slow nod.

"Have you thought about just…talking to them?"

"Of course I have, Hakoa," I clipped. It's not like I wanted a war, but I knew it was going to happen. "I'm working on a diplomatic angle, but I doubt they will believe me about Kya having survived. All they're going to see is an entire Nation's worth of land without a Worthy to protect it. More resources, space for citizens, better trade opportunities. I might be able to negotiate something, and that's what I'm going to attempt. Perhaps even find a way to come to a truce. I'm hoping I might be able to convince them to mine some of the mountains for jewels. They've wanted that for centuries."

Hakoa blew out a breath, and his shoulders sagged. "You're right. If you can convince them Kya's alive, maybe they'll back off."

"I never even told them she was dead. That was their assumption, and one that worked out in our favor at the time in order for them to approve our mating. But now it's coming back to bite me in the ass. I think the only thing that will convince them she's alive is... *her*." Everything was getting so complicated. I just needed to find her so I could fix it all.

"Isn't her magic proof enough? I mean, wouldn't it stop if she were dead?" he asked.

I didn't know how else to explain it, but I could show it. I spat on the floor between us and gestured at the saliva.

"If I died, would that disappear? No. Her magic is energy. Once she's released it, it works on its own. Just like my fire. I could ignite a forest, and if I died, the flames would still continue to consume. I can't prove she's alive. The Nations will still come for Atara until I get her back. And there's more..." I sighed.

"Kleio's tits... What more could there be?"

I told Hakoa about Daegel returning and that he was searching for the book as well as my plan to ambush him, using Nikan as a lure. As expected, he argued with me but ultimately conceded. There weren't any other options.

"Now," I started, standing and tucking the book back under my arm. "I need you to get those warriors to the border. I'll be back in a couple of days before I head to Bhara to meet with the Worthy."

I turned to leave but stopped when he spoke.

"You're going to have to convince your people to die for an empty Nation."

"I know." I glanced. "Do I need to convince *you*?"

He snorted a laugh. "Nope. We're overdue for a proper fight as it is."

I nodded. Leave it to him to find the light in a dark situation.

"Ryk." I turned around to face him fully. "You have to tell them."

The side of my mouth lifted. "Where do you think I'm headed?"

He took a deep breath as if bracing himself. "*All* of them."

My eyebrows bunched together, not understanding what he meant.

Hakoa swallowed. "Malina. And possibly Nikan. You need to tell them about Atara if you already haven't."

I thought he was joking, but the stone cold look on his face told me otherwise. "Why do I need to tell *them*?"

He held my stare for a moment. "Because I'm pretty sure the Roav of Morah are from Atara...all three of them."

I stilled.

That's not possible. Kya was from...

She had never told me. I had asked about it once, but she changed the subject, and I just assumed she would tell me later, after I earned her trust. But after we were mated, so much happened so fast, and I never thought about it. Until now...

"What makes you think they're from Atara?" I asked, disbelievingly.

He shrugged. "I don't know for certain. But Kya and Malina wore the feathers braided in their hair during Nailu. That's only a custom for Atarans. Didn't you notice?"

"I did, but I thought it was some kind of tribute to herself or Odarum. I never saw Malina that night though." I shook my head.

If they truly were from Atara, they would have been children when it was destroyed, not even having reached puberty when their magic emerged. So young to go through something so traumatic…

"Well, they both did. Kya was one thing, due to her wings and Odarum's, like you said. But Malina? They never talk about where they're from… I mean it makes sense. They're good at hiding, and being Roav gave them the opportunity to keep who they are a secret."

It did make sense. But what didn't make sense was why Kya never told me. Or why Eamon didn't when I took him to Atara. I guess there was only one way to find out for sure.

"I have to take care of something, then I'm going to Morah. I'll be back when I'm back."

With that, I took the book and left. Taking it where no one would expect to find it and one of the safest places I could think of.

Chapter Thirty-Five

Malina

"**S**hit."

I rummaged through my rooms, searching every nook and cranny for any coins. Though I knew there weren't any to find. I had spent the last of my money last night on a glass of something strong and a bowl of stew at The Whispering Axe.

"Shit. Shit. Shit."

Sure, I could ask some of the Scholars to help, but I wasn't one to take handouts. And I certainly wasn't going to ask Nikan. He would just think I was using it for more demid.

I needed to go on a mission. One job should get me through the next few weeks if I kept my spending minimal. Nikan would probably welcome the break, since he'd been doing all of them on his own. And I had enough demid stored up to last me a few days while I was gone.

I knew I didn't need to spend so much on alcohol, but it took the edge off and added to the effects of the demid. The combination was perfect to make me forget everything while it lasted.

With a plan in place, I quickly bathed to wash off the scent of males and taverns, then rushed down to Eamon's study.

"Oh, Malina!" someone shouted cheerily as I made it to the bottom of the stairs.

I turned to see Brixey, one of the historian Scholars, waving with one arm while holding a stack of books in the other and walking toward me eagerly. She was the youngest female to willingly go through the Raith and become a Scholar. She had thick brown hair that flowed down to the middle of her back, and it was always kept half-up with some random object holding it together. Today, it was a long stirring spoon. Her rich brown skin glowed against the beige Scholar attire, matching her sweet brown eyes. She was bright and lively, and that annoyed me at this moment.

"Hi, Brixey," I greeted with a forced smile. "I can't really talk right now. I'm on my way to see Eamon for a mission."

"Oh, that's wonderful! Are you feeling better then? Nikan said you hadn't been well," she said with a concerned look.

Good to know he didn't tell everyone what was actually going on. I'd hate to be subjected to every text in the library about the negative effects of demid being thrown in my face. Not that it wouldn't be done out of love, but I didn't have the capacity to deal with anything like that.

Her voice lowered, and her eyes softened. "Malina, how are you doing after—"

I'm not doing this right now

"I'm fine, thank you. It was nice to see you, but I need to get going," I said curtly then turned and walked away.

"He's not there."

I stopped and turned back around.

"Eamon," she clarified. "He's been away in Bhara."

"Ah. Why?" I asked.

"I don't know. No one does." She shook her head and shrugged, causing her to almost lose control of the stack in her arms.

That was odd. He always told everyone where he was going and what he was leaving for.

"Alright," I said slowly. "Do you know when he'll be back?"

"Unfortunately, I don't know that either," she said, sympathetic to my disappointment. But then she perked up. "Nikan is here though. He just got back. I think he's leaving again soon, but you could probably catch him."

I really didn't want to. I hadn't seen him in a few days since he came in to tell me about Daegel coming back. But maybe he was busy enough that he'd want me to take a job off his hands. Like the one he was about to leave on.

"Thanks, Brixey," I said with a wave and briskly left.

"Let me know if you ever want to talk or hang out..." her voice trailed off as I went back up the stairs.

I made it back to the residential level and went straight to Nikan's rooms and knocked.

"Come in," he called from the other side.

I entered to find him in his leathers and cloak, standing at the table with his bag atop it as he was packing it. He turned to face me, and his eyes reflected surprise for a moment.

"Mal. Everything okay?" he asked.

"Yeah. Uh, I went to go talk to Eamon, but he isn't here, and I heard you were back. I was wondering if I could take your mission. I know you've been busy, and I'm ready to take on a job again," I said firmly.

His eyes stared into mine for a moment before he turned back around to continue packing with a disappointed look on his face. "No."

"What?"

"I said no. You're not going on any missions." There was no room for arguing in his tone, but I didn't care.

"Why?" I demanded, crossing my arms over my chest.

"I think you know why," he said flatly.

I rolled my eyes. "I can function just fine. I did the last time."

"No, you can't and you didn't," he clipped as he spun around. He leaned back against the table with his arms braced on the edge. "Mal, the demid fucks you up way more than you think. You can't go off on an official mission while you're on it, and Gods forbid if you took it while you're there and you pass out in the wrong place."

"So, what? You're going to make me stop so I can do my fucking job?" I asked with a sneer.

"As much as I would love that Mal, I can't make you stop. You clearly have to do that all on your own. I could take you away to the end of the realm, but you would still find a way to get your fix. This isn't something anyone can do but you. And when you're ready, I'll be here. But until then, you're not going anywhere." He wasn't berating me, and his voice was gentle but firm.

"I need to work, Nik."

His lips thinned. "You need to get better. If you want to eat, you can come here, and I'll feed you. Unless…"

I refrained from rolling my eyes. "Unless what?"

"Unless you tell me who your local dealer is. I know you're getting it from someone close."

And have him kill Dax, and my only means of access to demid? Not a chance.

I didn't answer.

He shook his head with a disappointed look on his face. I hated that I was getting so used to seeing it. It was obvious this conversation was over when he turned back around, tied his pack, and left, kissing the top of my head as he walked out the door without another word.

He wasn't forcing me to do anything, yet he wasn't allowing me to do anything either. Not that I blamed him. If I did mess up, I could jeopardize the entire Roav operation that we had been working on for twenty years. I wasn't going to admit that to *him* though.

And I still had a money issue.

I went back to my rooms and sat on the upholstered chair by the wall, staring at the city below thinking about what I could do.

Then an idea came to me. One I didn't necessarily like—but one that would work.

That night, just after dark, I walked into Erryn's Lounge. It was busier than usual, which I thought was the perfect opportunity to plead for work, making it seem like I was helping Erryn more than I was helping myself. I went over to the counter and sat down, waiting for him to come over.

He was rushing around, taking food and drinks to the patrons. After several minutes, he made his way over to me.

"Back again," Erryn said with a broad smile. "Sorry about the wait. There are a lot of east-bound travelers tonight. What can I get you?"

"Employment?" I asked with a smile.

His brows raised. "You want to work here?"

I nodded eagerly. "You look like you could use the help." I pointed my thumb over my shoulder at the rowdy commotion behind me.

He looked behind me just as he was being called for by multiple tables. With a resigned sigh, he agreed. "Alright. But tonight is just a tryout. Do well, and we can talk. And I guess I don't have to call you Roav anymore. Got a name?"

Ouch.

I hadn't really thought of that. I supposed I wasn't much of a Roav anymore if I wasn't taking on jobs.

"Mal." I forced myself to perk up and beam at him. "I won't let you down," I said as I hopped off the chair and went behind the counter then began taking orders.

"*Let her go!*" *I screamed as Daegel fought to hold Kya in his grasp.*

I couldn't wield light at him, or I'd risk blinding Kya too. I couldn't throw a dagger at him either, she was too close. He was using her as a shield like a fucking coward.

I started running closer to them, away from where I had been trying to get to Nikan. He was screaming at me, telling me to stay away from him while also screaming for Daegel to let Kya go, that he better not go back on his word.

I didn't know what that meant, and I blocked him out to concentrate on getting to Kya, dodging the Glaev on the sandy beach.

"*Malina! The Kiss!*" *Kya bellowed into the night.*

No…

But I didn't hesitate. I whipped around and found her bow and a black-feathered arrow, the tip dark with the Onyx Flower's poison. I darted back toward them, my blood rushing to my head as dread pooled in my stomach.

Please let her go. Please let her go. Don't make me do this.

Once I was close enough, I stopped and aimed the arrow at them.

"*Back off! It's over!*" *Daegel roared. I saw the ire in his eyes as his hands gripped Kya tighter. He wasn't going to let her go no matter what.*

I knew it.

Kya knew it.

She began pushing back against him, both of their feet stumbling on the rocky ground beneath them.

My eyes widened, and the blood drained from my face. I understood then what she was doing…

She knew she wasn't getting away from him, and this was how she was going to stop him.

She pushed again, getting them closer to the edge of the Rip.

"Let her go! I swear to the Gods, I will kill you!" I screamed at Daegel as he continued to roar, telling me to stop.

I wasn't listening. My eyes were glued to Kya as I watched her push them back farther.

My vision blurred, my eyes filling with tears of rage and fear with the anticipation of what was about to happen.

Kya stared into my eyes, saying all she needed to for me to understand what she was about to do. What she needed me to do.

Don't make me do this!

But I had to. I knew I did.

"For them," she mouthed to me.

No…

And with a soft smile that shredded my heart she added, "For us."

I pulled back the bow string, and the tears finally broke, streaming down my face.

"Please don't make me do this," my whispered voice broke.

Kya just nodded, still smiling.

I released the arrow.

"For the love of Xar. You really do have problems." The sound of a male's voice grated on my ears.

My head was throbbing, and my body ached. I realized I was laying on something cold and hard. Again.

"Get up." A boot nudged me, and I groaned and tried to swat at it.

The male sighed and cursed under his breath. The voice was familiar, but I couldn't place it through the haze in my head.

I started falling back asleep when I felt myself being lifted and thrown over a shoulder, my head and arms dangling above the ground. I cracked my eyes open and saw the ground moving.

Or was I moving? No, I was definitely moving.

The rhythmic swaying as I was carried off was entrancing. I closed my eyes again, not caring about being hauled off like a sack of flour.

I was shocked awake as I was thrown into freezing cold water. Gasping, I flailed until I gripped the edges of stone on either side of me and pulled myself to a sitting position. I sputtered the water out of my mouth and pushed away the hair plastered over my face.

Swiping the water off my eyes, I snarled and glared up at the male who—

"Ryker?!" I screeched.

He had his arms crossed, leveling me with an expressionless stare.

"What is your problem? Wh—" I looked down to see that I was in one of the stable's drinking troughs.

Horses were standing at the other end with their ears perked up, probably wondering what I was doing in their water.

"Why am I in a horse trough?" I demanded.

"Because I have some things to discuss with you, and I need you sober," Ryker said bluntly.

"You could have been a little more gentle about it, pigeon boy," I grumbled.

I started crawling out of the trough, flopping out onto the dirt and rolling to my side. My teeth chattered, and I was shivering, curling into myself for warmth.

A wave of heat fell over me, and I looked up to see Ryker wielding warmth from his fire. Not that he looked happy doing it.

"Don't expect me to thank you, seeing as you're the cause." I pushed myself to my feet and wrapped my arms around my chest. "Now, what do you want?"

He leaned in close, and I could practically taste the fury he was holding back. From the look in his eye, he could have been asking for my life, and it was then I realized that I wanted to keep it.

"I want you to tell me where you're from."

I paused for a moment, just blinking at him. That certainly wasn't where I thought this was going. It was the last thing I expected him to ask me. Caught off guard, drunk, and still coming off the effects of the demid, I was stunned and speechless.

"Um... I... Wh—Why?"

Think, you drunk bitch. Think!

"Tell me where you're from," Ryker clipped each word with a bite.

Pompous ass.

"Tell me *why*," I pressed.

Ryker's silver eyes flared—glowing—as his shadows erupted all around us, blocking out all light. My heart raced and, instinctively, I wielded light in my fists, bright against the impenetrable cocoon of shadows.

He was fucking intimidating, I had to give him that.

"I don't have time to deal with your stubborn attitude, but I'm trying to be courteous right now. Where is Kya from?" he roared.

That's what this was all about? He wanted to know *that*, of all things?

You know what? Fuck this. No one was around to hear, and if he wanted to know where his dead mate was from so badly, what difference did it make?

"Alright," I sneered. "Do you really want to know? The same Nation she was deemed Worthy to protect. The same Nation that was plagued by the Glaev, driven from her home in the middle of the night, running for her life at six years old as she listened to the screams of her people being consumed right before her eyes. Nearly dying herself when she was trampled by those very same people, breaking her legs before her mother could grab her up and narrowly save her from death. The same Nation that was abandoned by its Goddess—who left their people to suffer on the Drift Islands." I paused, both of us breathing heavily. My lip quivered as I let out more than I realized I was holding in. "The same Nation that remained in the hearts of three children who were dumped on Morah's doorstep so we weren't forced to have our wielding suppressed like our families. Atara."

Ryker didn't say anything for a long moment, gazing into the darkness of his slowly retreating shadows, swirling against the moonlight.

"Why didn't she tell me?" he whispered more to himself than me.

I scoffed, angrily wiping the tears away from my chilled face. "What was she supposed to do? Tell the Bloodlust Lord of Oryn and risk not only her own life, but mine and Nikan's as well? You're bound by law. She was waiting to tell you until she was inducted as Lady of Oryn so she would have the power and influence to ensure we would be safe. She hoped one day, you'd find it in your cold heart to finally let our people have a home. She needed to guarantee she could fulfill her task for Kleio, *so they may return.*"

Ryker huffed. "I thought she trusted me. But between this, and her going off on her own... She didn't trust me at all."

"Maybe because you, as well as every other fucking Nation, turned our people away." I crossed my arms and stared him down. All three of us held some resentment toward each Nation because of it.

His head slowly turned to face me.

I stiffened. I had never been on the receiving end of the Lord of Oryn's lethal glare like that.

"Turned them *away?*" he said darkly. "I took them *in.*"

The world around me came to a screeching halt.

"Those who were able to escape came over the border in Oryn. We went to every corner of the continent in search of more survivors. We found out a few hid in Dusan, but those who had refused to go to the islands had been killed. We didn't get to them in time." He released a heavy breath. "The Ataran people have been living in Oryn ever since."

Chapter Thirty-Six

ZALEN

With Maera tucked against me all night, I had the best sleep of my life. I felt the connection between us becoming something more, bringing us closer together on a deeper level. Just being wrapped up in each other's arms without a looming ticking clock.

Cracking my eyes open, I nearly gasped at the warm feeling inside my chest as I watched her sleeping. Our legs were tangled together with her head on top of my arm—which was uncomfortably asleep, yet I couldn't bring myself to disturb her. I wanted just another minute to admire the remarkable woman in my bed. But I had plans for today, and I was eager to show her what I had prepared.

I kissed her forehead, and she stirred, nuzzling against my chest.

"Good morning, love. It's time to wake up," I whispered, my voice thick from sleep.

"Mmm," she grumbled with her eyebrows drawn together.

I chuckled, finding her reluctance to wake up nothing short of adorable. My finger gently traced along her jawline, lightly touching down her neck and shoulder, and kissed her cheek.

"There's something I want to show you," I said, and that had her peeling one eye open, glowering at me.

"What is it?" she mumbled.

"It's a surprise," I said with a smirk.

She turned her head and planted her face in the pillow, muffling her voice, "Can't you just tell me?"

"I could," I drawled teasingly. "But it wouldn't quite have the same effect."

Maera groaned but finally sat up. My eyes shot to her peaked nipples through the fabric of her shirt as she stretched her arms above her head. While I would have loved to push that shirt up and take her breast in my mouth, I resisted.

She noticed me staring and leveled me with a flat look. "Do you really expect me to go *anywhere* wearing this?" She gestured to herself.

"Of course not." I tossed the covers off and went to the door.

As expected, three large oak trunks, braced with brass detailing that encased the heavy wood, were waiting just outside the door. I lifted them one by one and carried them inside, pushing the heavy door closed with my bare foot. Maera leaned forward as I placed the last one on the stone floor next to the bed, unlatched it, and lifted the lid, revealing her entire wardrobe of clothes from Aedum.

Not that she'd be wearing most of these for much longer. I fully intended on giving her an entire room's worth of new Damanthus-style clothes, but I wanted her to pick out her personal favorites before I burned the rest of them.

"I told you last night that your clothes would be here by morning. Why don't you get ready, and then we can eat?" I gestured to the trunk, and she walked over and pulled out a top, skirt, and undergarments, then padded off to the bathing room.

I went over to my wardrobe and pulled out my own clothes, mindful of the attire required for the day's tasks. The timing of the servers was impeccable, arriving to deliver breakfast right after I was dressed in my dark tunic and loose pants, fastened with a belt and tucked into my boots.

By the time Maera emerged, I'd rolled in the cart filled with platters of meats and freshly picked fruits and arranged them on the table. She wanted to take her time eating, and I had to refrain from urging her to hurry. I was eager to show her what I had waiting for her.

"Should I be nervous?" she asked, pushing a slice of ham away.

I tilted my head in question.

"You stuffed your face so quickly, and you're tapping your foot," she explained. "What's the surprise? Am I going to like it?"

"You will," I said confidently, grinning. "Now finish eating so we can go."

Maera finished her plate, then I led her out of the room and through the castle, my hand resting at the small of her back. She questioned no less than four times where we were going, but I refused to even give her a hint, despite her practically begging.

We continued up to the highest level of the castle, until I brought us to a stop in front of recently crafted arched double-doors. Surrounded by a special kind of stone, the doors were embellished with continuous carvings depicting a grand tree inside an intricate bordered circle.

I spun to face her and took her hand in mine. "Close your eyes."

She rolled them, didn't even try to hide the smile creeping across her lips, before she shut them.

I hope she loves it.

I pushed open the doors and led her inside, closing them behind us so she could take in the full-effect of the room I had meticulously prepared. I had been working on it for well over a year.

"You can open your eyes now," I said quietly, keeping my attention focused solely on her, anticipating her reaction.

Maera opened her eyes and let out a soft gasp. The look on her face was exactly what I had expected, filled with shock and awe as she took in the space of the brewing room I'd made just for her.

My chest swelled with pride as her eyes roamed over the tables, cauldrons, and bottles of every shape and size imaginable. Drying herbs hung by twine next to shelves filled with books of alchemy.

With one more surprise to add, I placed my hand on the nearest wall, still watching Maera's face.

"Ljoss."

In response to the spell, the stone walls and ceiling began to transform, light streaming into the room as they turned translucent.

Maera's jaw dropped, and her eyes widened with a broad smile. "This... Is this for *me*?" she breathed.

I nodded.

"Why?" she asked with a look of astonishment.

"A witch needs a place to practice her craft. And my future Queen will have everything she needs to be the most powerful alchemist to ever walk the land." I swung out my arm, gesturing to the room. "Look around. Imagine what you'll be capable of, what you can create, once you come into your higher power."

She let out a soft laugh and squeezed my hand, enraptured by the room.

Her lips pursed in thought for a moment. "Can you take me back to the Aedum castle?"

My heart stopped, automatically assuming she was second-guessing everything and wanted to go back.

"No," I said firmly.

Her brows creased, and her eyes snapped to me. "Why not?"

"Because there is no castle in Aedum anymore. I had it burned then torn down." I shrugged.

It was a grand statement for the people more than anything, removing any symbolism of the Aedum Kingdom and making it clear Damanthus had taken over.

"But... I had things in my rooms. Notes and documents, years worth of research on potions I'd been working on. Did you not think I would want those kinds of things?" she scolded.

The side of my mouth lifted into a humorous smirk. I wasn't even the slightest bit offended she assumed I wouldn't take care of her completely.

She'll learn.

Maera's eyes narrowed into a glare. "It's not funny, Zalen. That was my life's work."

"All twenty-seven years of it?" I teased with a raised brow.

From the flare in her eyes, I guessed she had the urge to hit me.

Oh, please do. I would love nothing more than to punish you right here.

"Stop worrying," I chuckled. "*All* of your belongings have been retrieved. The entire castle was pillaged before it was destroyed. It's all being sorted through right now, but you will have everything you need."

"Oh," she said, but it still held a bite to it. "I still can't believe you destroyed it. You didn't have to be that fucking dramatic you know. However, I'm sorry I doubted you."

I lifted her chin with my finger, forcing her to look up at me, and kissed her. "Don't ever apologize, love. Not here, not to anyone. Not even me. It shows weakness, and you are anything but weak." She didn't know her strength yet. She had been raised to stifle it without giving it a chance to grow. But that would all change. "And don't thank me just yet. I haven't told you *why* I've made this room for you or what I want in return."

Her brows raised. "What is it?"

"I want you here practicing and studying. Daily. While you can brew whatever you want, I request that you focus most of your efforts on potions for offense and defense. Things you can use for protection. Like that lightning brew you threw at me the other night."

Maera had a talent for creating complex potions, and I wanted her to have the ability to enhance that talent.

"Not that I'm complaining that I get to finally explore my alchemy without restriction, but should I be worried? I'm just a witch, I'm not a fighter. Can *you* not protect me?" she asked with concern in her eyes.

"I *am* protecting you."

She tilted her head to the side questioningly.

"The greatest protection I can offer is to teach you to protect yourself." I reached up and brushed her hair behind her ear, grazing my fingertips down her neck. "And you are more than just a witch. You're the future Queen."

She leaned into my touch with a soft smile.

"The herb garden is yours to do with as you see fit. If there's something you need that isn't there, just say the word, and you'll have it."

Maera gazed around the space for a moment before looking back at me with a purposeful glint in her eyes, and reached up to pull her hair back. "Alright. Well, get out of here then. I have work to do."

Maera stayed to mess around in her brewing room, already reorganizing things to how she wanted them as I left. I told her I would leave her be until this evening while I took care of a few things. There were a lot of logistics to be dealt with when you forcibly absorbed another Kingdom—especially before even officially becoming King.

I headed down to my study to meet with Thane, who was waiting for me just inside the door.

"Thane," I greeted as I entered and made my way behind the desk in the center of the room.

He closed the door behind me then walked over to sit in the chair in front of my desk. "So, is the Samanya daughter giving you any trouble?"

"Not at all. She's quite pleased with her new accommodations." I picked up one of the reports in a pile and began skimming over it.

"Surprising. I thought she'd be much more resistant. She didn't seem like the compliant type," Thane said, leaning back in the chair. He looked tired, as if he had been up all night—which was likely.

I bit my lip to keep from smiling. She was compliant alright, but not in the way he assumed. "Maera is adjusting just fine."

"*Maera*, huh?" He eyed me suspiciously. "You know, I still don't understand how you're going to convince her to agree to be the Queen. You can't exactly threaten her with anything besides her life, seeing as you killed everyone she knew and destroyed her home."

He was clever, and I knew the moment he saw us together he'd know it wasn't what it seemed—I hadn't savagely kidnapped my enemy's heir to make her my involuntary bride. I supposed it was time he learned.

I put down the paper and leaned back, lacing my fingers and resting them in my lap as I held his pointed stare.

"Maera and I have been seeing each other in secret for years. While she didn't know what was going to happen, she wanted it all the same. I don't have to threaten her because she's happy to do this of her own volition. Had she and I not been royalty, we likely would have run off and been married already."

"So this entire plan we've been working on for the past few years has all been so you could have her for yourself?" he asked incredulously.

It seemed like a perfectly justifiable reason to me.

"For the most part, yes. But additionally, so that the Aedum Kingdom wouldn't be a thorn in my side when I come into power. And King Erix was still the most likely suspect for the murder of Makkor. I can't have some King killer out there threatening my rule. Not one with that kind of capability. But as you know, that was what drove up the timeline." I shrugged. "It worked out all the same anyway."

Thane ran a hand down his face. "Well, at least we don't have to worry about keeping her locked up or anything," he mumbled.

"Absolutely not." My voice darkened, chilling the atmosphere of the room. The thought of anyone so much as laying a hand on her—let alone locking her away—made my blood boil. "She is to be respected just as I am. And she will be going through the Drehiri ritual as well."

If I had the power, I'd have her do it now rather than wait. But the old laws ran deep within the land, and I couldn't change them. All three of us would have to wait.

"She's going to go through the ritual too?" he gaped. "Shit. She'll be the most powerful witch to have ever lived."

"I know." I smirked, enjoying the look of shock on his face at the realization that I wanted her to have as much power as possible. "We can discuss all that another time. Now," I said, leaning forward with my forearms resting on the desk. "Bring me up to speed."

Thane shook his head, clearing his mind and switching from my friend to my counselor. "We have resistance from the

Aedum magic users, but the human citizens are cooperative, as expected."

"Kill the highest ranking users who are defiant—publicly. Make sure the rest understand we will not tolerate rebellion. Reward those who cooperate," I ordered.

He nodded. "It might not be a bad idea to relocate some of the families inside the original Damanthus border, integrate them with the loyal communities. And I'd even encourage Damanthan citizens who are willing to move into the old Aedum regions as well. The more physical merging there is, the easier the transition."

"I agree. Delegate those looking for better opportunities and send them to the homes of the moved families." I pulled out a blank piece of paper to jot notes. "What's the update on Shara?"

"It's...unusual," he said.

My eyes popped up to him. "Unusual how?"

"Because their borders are closed off by order of their King. Their *new* King."

"New King? Who?" I demanded. That meant King Edmund was dead. The third King to die mysteriously in such a short time frame.

"No one knows. We're unable to access any information because we can't get inside. They have it locked down tight. If you want us to go in force, it could start a war, and without knowing who we're dealing with, I don't think that's a good idea," Thane said.

I pinched the bridge of my nose. Shara. Maera said that was where the elusive captain was from...

"Captain Lyron Vika is dead. He died weeks ago," I stated.

Thane's brows lifted. "So we can stop searching for him then."

"No. King Erix named someone else as captain to fill his place. But we don't know who. And seeing as we just killed the entire Aedum Royal Guard—" I was a fool.

"Then we have no idea who it is," he sighed. "What does it have to do with the Sharan King?"

"Apparently, he's *from* Shara." I saw the moment Thane came to the same conclusion I did.

"We already suspected the captain of being the murderer. And if he killed the Sharan King, he could have taken over Shara." He nodded in understanding.

"That's what I'm thinking." Which was a real pain in the ass if it were true.

Thane's lips pursed, and his eyes went distance in thought. "Why would he kill the other Kings if he only wanted to take over Shara? He could have tried to take over Damanthus or Innon. But instead he went back to Shara without claiming the other Kingdoms? That doesn't make sense."

I couldn't make sense of it either. It had been bothering me since Makkor's murder—why someone would go through the trouble of killing a King and not at least try to claim the Kingdom.

"Find out. Have a small unit infiltrate Shara. Have them kill a patrol and take the clothes off their corpses for all I care. We need to know who the fuck this new King is and why. And most importantly, if he poses a threat."

No. It didn't matter if he was an actual threat or not. Just the fact he *could* be a threat to me meant he was a threat to Maera. And I simply couldn't allow that.

Thane stood to leave, but I stopped him just as he was stepping through the door.

"Thane."

He turned to face me with a hard look.

"I want his head."

Chapter Thirty-Seven

KYA

I don't know if you can hear me. I don't know if you're listening. If you are, watch over Ryker. I made a mistake, and I've hurt him because of it.

Tell him I'm still here. That I'm coming back to him. That I belong to him.

Until the stars die out...

It was the same thing every single Godsdamn day.

Talum came to get Leysa and me.

Daegel took us to the island, and Leysa was given a collar.

A shield was erected over me, then Daegel would mutter some incantation with some fancy hand flourishing.

And I spent hours at a time trying to make the Glaev.

Nothing worked. No matter how hard I tried, no matter how much I willed my energy to work the way I needed it to.

"Perhaps you're not motivated enough, Diamond," Daegel sneered. He was growing impatient.

I was so fucking tired of Daegel watching my every move and barking at me to try harder. All I wanted was for him to take down the barrier so I could snap his neck.

"I told you, asshole, I'm trying. What more do you want from me? I can't do it," I clipped.

He glared at me for several moments, holding my stare.

"I thought having Leysa here, suffering, would be enough. But I guess not. How about I bring your friends here too, and put a collar on them? Nikan and—what was her name? Mal, I think you call her." His voice was cold.

I froze, not wanting to show any reaction, but my heart was racing. I wouldn't put it past him to make good on his threat.

"No? Then how about that mate of yours?" he snarled.

My blood rushed hot, and my nostrils flared.

Leysa flinched at his threat.

I snaked my Waalu down my arms, the jade energy swirling along my skin. I would peel his skin off if he so much as touched Ryker.

Daegel's expression remained neutral, but I caught the slightest twitch of a smirk on his lips. "He's been searching everywhere for you. Flying all around the continent looking for his long lost love like the little bitch that he is."

"Shut up!" I screamed, blasting out my energy all around me.

Daegel stepped up to the barrier, slapping his hands on the surface. "Maybe I'll take away *his* wings too. Would that be enough to get you to do what I fucking want?"

I roared with a rage I had never felt before, releasing everything I had in an attempt to break through this Godsdamn shield. The bond burned so fiercely I could practically smell it.

But it wasn't the bond.

Daegel's lips spread into a wide, malicious grin, staring me directly in the eyes. He glanced down to the ground.

I followed his gaze, and my eyes widened. The entire surface within the dome barrier was completely dead and desolate, the land black as night except around my feet.

The Glaev.

If I moved even the slightest bit, I'd touch it. I panicked and looked at the swirls of energy around my hands that were still a soft, jade hue. Sending out only a small bit a little ways away from it, my Waalu restored a small portion.

Breathing a sigh of relief, I created a wider space around me so I didn't accidentally step on the Glaev.

Daegel chuckled in a low, wicked tone, and I looked up. "And that's how you make a diamond really shine."

Daegel took me and Leysa back to my cell early as a reward. She had been forced to stay with me. I knew it was so we would grow closer and I would care for her more—just more incentive to do what he wanted so she didn't have to suffer as much.

I hated that it was working.

I was in a daze for the rest of the day and through the night. Leysa spoke, but I didn't register much of what she said, my murmuring responses falling from my lips without thought.

I couldn't stop thinking about Daegel, about Ryker. My body was practically vibrating with fury.

I was done. I had to get out of here. I couldn't let Daegel capture anyone else to be used against me.

Stewing with my thoughts, I lay there, staring at the ceiling trying to think of how I could possibly get out of here. I would need help. Would Leysa help me?

I wanted to believe she would, but she was so adamant for me to just submit. That was probably the easiest route, except Daegel had to have a reason for why he wanted *me* to kill that island.

"Leysa," I said in the darkness of the cell.

"Hmm?" she murmured. She had been asleep in the cramped bed next to me.

"I need you to tell me why Daegel is making me do this. What does he want? What's the purpose for everything he's been doing?" I shook my head.

Leysa let out a rough breath. "He's never actually said it, but Talum let it slip once…" she paused as if gathering herself. "He needs to take over one realm to destroy another."

I suspected as much. "Is he wanting to take over this one to destroy ours or take over ours to destroy this one?"

He was using the Glaev on Taeralia to absorb its power. It made sense if he was trying to use that power to take over Vansera. But then again, he was having me create the Glaev here, destroying the magic-rich land. So I wasn't sure what his angle was.

"I don't know," she whispered. "But Gods, I wish I did. Either way, Taeralia is in peril, and there's nothing we can do about it."

I wanted to tell her we could get out of here and stop him, but until I had a plan in place, I waited. The last thing I needed was to approach her with some half-baked idea only for her to shoot it down before it was complete. Or worse, she'd try to talk me out of it. So I would wait. And I would plan.

I closed my eyes and recalled every detail of the prison, everything I had seen and felt through my terbis on the island, everything I had learned thus far.

"So, King Zalen—"

"Don't," Leysa clipped.

"Don't what?" I asked.

"Don't even think about it, Kya. I know what you're thinking, and it won't work. He won't help us," she said sternly.

"Let's say I was thinking about it. Just humor me. Why do you say that? Maybe he'd be sympathetic—"

She threw her head back and laughed. "Ha! From what I heard, King Zalen is worse than Daegel."

I sat up and looked down at her. "Why is he so feared?"

"I'm not sure." She shrugged. "I've just heard about him being more powerful than the other Kings, or something like that, and that everyone is afraid of him."

A small flame of hope flickered somewhere in the darkness of my chest.

Perhaps he's more powerful than Daegel…

"Does Daegel fear him?" I asked.

"I wouldn't know. He's never mentioned him. I can't imagine much scares him," she said quietly. "It won't work. Trust me, I've thought about it. But even if you could get out of here—which you can't—you'd be escaping from one tyrant and running straight into the clutches of another. That doesn't solve anything."

She sighed and turned over, facing away from me.

But even tyrants wanted something.

Chapter Thirty-Eight

MALINA

"Prove it," I challenged.

I wasn't taking Ryker's word for anything. He could fool everyone about Kya since no one could confirm it wasn't true, but this was something that could easily be verified, and I was calling his bullshit. There was no chance there were Atarans living on the continent all these years, and we hadn't heard about it.

"Fine," he agreed nonchalantly.

My eyes narrowed suspiciously. He had agreed to that way too easily. I expected more pushback.

"Except..."

Called it.

"...I'm not taking you while you're all fucked up. You want proof? I'll give it to you. But you're going to be sober for it." His authoritative tone left no room for argument.

Shit.

"And," he added. I tried not to roll my eyes at what else he could possibly want. "I'll take you to your homeland."

I snorted. "So you're going to show me my people then take me to see my dead Nation? How could I possibly refuse?"

"No," Ryker stated firmly. "I will take you to Atara so you can stand on your restored Nation. The first Ataran to return."

I leaned my head back and laughed so hard my stomach cramped. But when I looked at Ryker again, his expression was unchanged, and I realized he wasn't joking.

"Wait. You're serious? How... No. It's not possi—"

Oh, Gods. Kya...

"I won't bother explaining since you wouldn't believe me anyway. But, if you want to see it for yourself and you want to see your people, you're going to stop ruining your life and the lives of everyone around you." There wasn't a shred of compassion in his eyes, and I knew if I didn't quit demid he would never take me.

At least he needs to believe I have.

"I'm not that fucking stupid, Malina. I may be using words as a courtesy, but I don't have to," he sneered.

My brows creased, not understanding what he was talking about. He leaned closer so I could see the severity in his silver eyes.

"I know your mind. I know your memories. Try as you like, but you can't lie to me."

My eyes widened as I realized Ryker wasn't moving his lips.

He's a mind wielder.

Thinking back, I remembered he had entered my mind before at the Rip. At the time, I was so consumed in my grief that I hadn't realized what happened.

"I'll be back in two weeks. If you haven't abandoned the demid by then, I will assume you never will."

"Take me there now. Let me meet them," I demanded, still shocked by the fact he could hear all of my thoughts at will.

His eyes narrowed. "They need to be protected. And you can't protect anyone the way you are now. Not your Nation, not even yourself. Get your shit together, Malina. It's not a request."

With my mouth hanging open, Ryker's wings snapped open and he thrust himself into the darkness of the night, leaving me alone.

Waking up in my bed, I had the vague recollection of slinking my way back to Morah and making it to my room just as dawn was approaching. Gasping, I sat up quickly with a cloudy memory of speaking with Ryker. So much had happened last night, and I was so delirious from the demid I wasn't sure if it was real or some kind of messed up dream. But I felt a slight dampness in my clothes, smell the faint scent of horse, and I knew it had happened.

My first thought was to take another dose and forget all about it. That would have made everything so much easier. Except Ryker's promise rested at the forefront of my mind, and I hesitated to reach for the vial beneath the mattress.

He would know.

It was outrageous. He was probably lying. I bet Hakoa or Nikan—Udon's balls, maybe even Eamon—urged him to do it. I scoffed to myself. Of course he would lie. He didn't give a shit about me.

I started to reach for the demid, aching for that euphoric numbness once again, but I stopped myself just before my fingers could wrap around the glass cylinder.

What if there really are Atarans living in Oryn? What if Atara really is being restored? Is it worth the risk of never knowing just to take another dose?

I sat on my bed and pondered. If Atara was healing, what were the chances that someone other than Ryker knew? I'd bet pretty high. It's a big-ass Nation, someone other than Ryker had to have known about it. Which meant Eamon likely knew as well. Old fucker knew everything.

Only one way to find out.

I wanted to take a dose—it was habitual at this point—but I resisted, thinking I could wait just a little longer. Hopping out of bed, I put on clean clothes and threw my messy hair into a ponytail then headed down to Eamon's study. I didn't know if he was back yet, but he had never been gone this long before, so I assumed he would be. Sure enough, I found him sitting behind his paper-covered desk, his pen scratching against parchment with his head bent down.

I cleared my throat audibly, announcing my presence. He looked up and smiled widely.

"Malina," he sighed with what looked like relief and got up to greet me with an embrace. "It's good to see you. How are you?"

"Is Atara being restored?" I didn't hesitate to jump to the point.

Eamon's lips flattened. "What?"

Mother above... "Eamon, just answer the question. Is my homeland healing?"

He remained silent.

"I have a right to know," I said firmly, standing my ground while looking up at him.

He took a deep breath. "Yes, it's true. I've seen it."

All the breath in my lungs left my body. "Why didn't you tell me? Does *Nik* know?"

I swore to the Gods... I felt so betrayed already that Eamon knew, but if Nikan knew also...

"No." He shook his head. "I've been trying to tell him, but we haven't been in the same place at the same time since I found out."

That didn't make me feel any better.

"Again, why didn't you tell *me*?" I demanded through clenched teeth.

"Malina..." he sighed.

"Eamon! There is no good reason as to why you would keep this from me—"

"There is a very good reason I kept it from you!" Eamon had never once raised his voice with me.

It startled me, and my eyes widened, hardly believing he even had the capability.

"This is important. Keeping this information contained is crucial and telling you would have been a huge risk."

I flinched at his words. He didn't trust me.

"I'm not angry with you, child," his voice softened. "But you have to accept the reality of your situation."

The demid.

I swallowed and looked away, wrapping my arms around myself.

"You know?" I whispered.

"Of course I know."

"Let me guess—Nik told you? No, wait. I bet it was *Ryker*," I spat his name.

Eamon placed his hand on my shoulder, and I glanced back at him. "No one had to tell me. I've been around for a very long time, and I know the presenting symptoms. I also know some things that can help, if you're willing to listen. Atara needs you. Kya isn't here to protect it, so it's up to us to protect it for her until she returns."

Except she won't.

"But the hard truth is right now, in your state, you're more likely to harm it."

I knew I should stop taking demid. It had gotten out of hand. I just couldn't get myself to do it. I didn't *want* to, I liked the way it made me feel. I liked how it made me forget everything and dulled the pain of my reality. While I knew it was making me hurt those around me, I also knew it would hurt *me* even more if I quit. I wasn't sure I could do it, if I had the will to overcome this desire.

But as I looked into Eamon's pleading gaze, I couldn't tell him no—I would rather lie than bear the shame of his disappointment. I already had Nikan's. I couldn't take Eamon's as well.

"Of course," I said quietly with a short, placating nod.

He breathed a sigh of relief and smiled, making me feel guilty for giving him hope I couldn't promise to keep.

"Okay. I'll write down a few titles for you to read." He turned to his desk and started making a list.

I mentally rolled my eyes and groaned. This was not going the way I planned. Somehow, it turned into being about me and not about Atara.

"What about the Atarans?" I asked.

It was one thing to keep the information about Atara from me, but to keep the knowledge of our people still living on the continent… That would be cruel.

He looked up at me with a raised brow. "What about them?"

"The ones in Oryn. Did you keep that from us too? Did you keep us away from our people?" My anger rose as I thought about it more. It would have been inconvenient for him to lose the Roav.

Would he really have deceived us like that? No. There's no way.

"I think you're confused," he said, softening his eyes. "There aren't any Atarans in Oryn. There would be records, or at the very least, rumors. And after twenty years, I would have heard about them." He offered me a tight smile and went back to scribbling titles and tips on quitting demid.

So either Ryker really is lying to me, or he has somehow been able to keep their presence in Oryn covered up so well no one else in the realm knows about them.

I would find out soon enough. But there was one thing I knew that I could confirm on my own. And I could do it right now.

Eamon turned to hand me the paper, and I took it from him, reading his list of books and instructions. I held back my scoff when I saw his suggestion to talk to someone about the 'root of the problem.'

"Thanks, Eamon," I said and quickly left the room, not even waiting for a response.

Darting back up to my rooms, I couldn't tell if I was nervous or excited. Probably both. But I also knew I was terrified. Terrified at what I would find or what I wouldn't. Either way, everything would change.

I needed to see for myself.

I packed a bag, shoving in some clothes and food I took from Nikan's rooms. I went back and forth on whether I should wait on Nikan to return to take him with me, but I needed to know now, and I could come back with him later.

Only to appease Eamon, I grabbed one of the titles he had suggested and packed it too. I debated on leaving the demid, but I just couldn't bring myself to do it. It was *just* in case.

After traveling by horse for two days, I was nearing my destination. I rode day and night, despite the cold of winter, only stopping when the gelding needed rest or food and water.

I needed to keep moving, driven by the promise I had made to myself that if Ryker and Eamon were lying—not that Eamon would have any reason to lie—and Atara wasn't being restored, then I would throw back a vial out of spite. Until then, I resisted the temptation. But just barely.

It was all I could think about.

Doing my best to keep myself distracted, I attempted to think of anything else. But most of it just brought me back to that dark place that drove me to taking the demid in the first place.

My fingers itched to reach for my pack behind me. Every clink of the glass from the horse's steps made me crave it even more.

Just one vial to hold me off until I get there. One more won't hurt. No. Don't. You can do this, Mal.

I slowed my horse to a walk and grabbed my water canteen. I tried to trick myself into thinking it was the demid or at least something much stronger. When that didn't work, I took out Eamon's list and read it over and over.

According to his instructions, I needed to recognize that I had fallen to the effects of the elixir, but I didn't feel like I had. I could stop. I had proven that already with the time I was with Nikan and again now. I just didn't want to.

But then I really thought about it. His list made it seem like it was so easy. It also made me realize how much it wasn't. The memory of my crazed desperation for it to the point I quite literally licked the demid off the floor and effectively severed any relationship I had with Hakoa.

I took a deep breath and sighed, ashamed of myself for taking this long to finally recognize it. "I've fallen to the effects of the demid."

Eamon's list also said I needed to talk to someone about the real problem, talk about what had driven me to demid in the first place.

Nope.

On and on it went about accepting what I've done, over-coming the guilt of hurting those closest to me, and a bunch of other shit.

"Oh yeah, sure. I'll overcome it just like that. If it were that fucking easy, I wouldn't have resorted to using demid in the first place," I mumbled under my breath.

Folding up the piece of paper, I put it back in the bag and pulled out the text I had brought. *Pharmacokinetics and Biochemical Factors for Substance Use.* The title made my eyes cross, but at least it would serve as a distraction. Or at least bore me to sleep.

Either way, it was effective in passing the time because the next thing I knew I was coming up to the edge of the treeline at the border of Atara as it neared dusk. Shutting the book and keeping my eyes trained in front of me, my heart pounded as I drew nearer.

I had taken this same path so many times over the years, I knew each and every tree and rock from secretly visiting my lost home. The first time was twenty years ago when my parents carried me, fleeing the Glaev with the rest of the few survivors from our decimated village.

Pulling my weary horse to a stop, I hopped off, dried leaves crunching beneath my weight. I turned to face the direction of the treeline. It was only a few more steps before I'd be able to see the other side.

For some reason, that was daunting. Unsure if it was the fear of having my hopes crushed or the anticipation of the possibility that my life would change forever. My feet wouldn't move, and my heart beat against my chest.

When I was younger, I used to wake up each morning hoping this was all some nightmare, and I would open my eyes to find myself back in my small home with my family once again—only to be disappointed each and every day, when I would see the obsidian walls of Morah surrounding me.

Closing my eyes, I took a deep breath in an attempt to prepare myself for whatever it was I would find. When I opened them, I tightened my pack over my shoulders and willed myself to move forward.

One step.

Whatever I was about to find would determine my future.

Another step.

I was either going to get rid of the demid forever...

Another step.

...or I was going to swallow my corruption.

Another step.

Then another and another.

The other side of the treeline came into view, and I nearly fell to my knees. My feet carried me across the forest floor until I was standing before an open plain of fresh, newly formed grass where there was once nothing but scarred wasteland as far as the eye could see.

"Atara..." I breathed.

...the first Ataran to return...

The memory of Ryker's words played in my head as I stared at my feet, frozen in place in front of my Nation's border.

One more step, and you're home.

The world around me stopped as I lifted my foot and placed it on the grass.

Emotion overwhelmed me as I stared at my feet. Tears fell over my smiling lips as I gasped a laugh. I couldn't believe it.

"Welcome home, sunshine."

Startling at the unexpected voice, I whipped my head around to see Hakoa walking toward me from the trees where Ryker stood with his wings tucked behind him. Nikan was standing right beside my sister's mate. I didn't know why they were here or how they knew I'd be here, and it had me on edge.

Trying to pull myself together, I straightened my shoulders and raised my chin.

Gods, I was already emotional as it was, I didn't need Hakoa here now. Not after what I had said to him. When he was near, everything was confusing. I didn't want him here, yet at the same time, I did...

I wanted him close. He made me feel wanted for who I was, not what I was capable of or what my body had to offer.

But I would just hurt him.

"Hakoa—"

He grabbed my face in his hands, and his mouth crashed into mine.

It was like a piece of my dull soul was finally filled with light at the touch of his lips.

I gasped and pulled back, hesitating.

He had to have been angry with me. I had hurt him in the worst way possible. But my breath hitched when I saw a smile tugging at his lips.

"You're here," he breathed a whisper, as if he couldn't believe it.

I nodded. "*You're* here."

My chin trembled. Tears fell down my cheeks, and he wiped them away.

"I always will be."

My heart skipped, and I knew right then what I needed to do. For him, for Nikan, for Eamon.

For them.

For me.

"I... I need help," I gasped through the tears.

The planes of his face hardened, his eyes filled with compassion and understanding I didn't deserve, but I couldn't look away.

"Okay. What do you need?"

"Take my bag," I choked out a sob. "Take it away from me. Please. Destroy it."

He nodded and kissed my forehead.

Tenderly, Hakoa removed my pack from my shoulders, releasing me from the burden it contained. The weight being lifted away from me was like a punch to the gut. My fingers contracted into claws, every fiber of my being itching to snatch it back. I thrust my hands behind me but was unable to hide the widening of my eyes—watching it as if it was my life-source.

He took a step back away from me and looked at Ryker. They were silent for a moment, then Ryker gave a single slow nod as he approached. Hakoa handed him the bag, filled with the vials I had become so reliant on, that I was so achingly desperate for.

I started gasping for air, unable to take in a full breath as the realization of what I was about to do hit me.

I wanted it. I didn't want to stop. But I *needed* to.

Ryker's lips thinned into a sad, knowing smile before he shifted his wings and swiftly took to the skies. The blood drained from my face in pure dread, and regret washed over me.

I lept for his feet in a desperate attempt to stop him, but an arm wrapped around my waist and held me firmly. I collapsed to my knees and clawed at the dirt, trying to get away, trying to get it back, as I watched Ryker fly out of sight.

"Oh, Gods…" I sobbed, cradling my face in my trembling hands.

I'm not strong enough for this. What am I going to do? What am I going to do…

Hakoa pulled me into his lap, and I buried my face in his chest as I wailed, already knowing the kind of anguish that awaited me.

"Shh," he soothed, brushing his hand down my hair. "It's okay. It's going to be okay."

This was my fault. I did this to myself. I felt like I was going to die—but I wouldn't.

Sitting in my homeland and wrapped in Hakoa's embrace, he held me as I finally let myself feel.

Chapter Thirty-Nine

ZALEN

While Thane coordinated the infiltration of Shara, I busied myself with my own plans. The biggest mistake past Kings made was not anticipating far enough ahead. With Maera here, I wouldn't allow us to be anything less than fully prepared for every possibility.

Whether it was all-out war, or traitors, or spies, or rebellion, I had a plan. But there was one thing that still needed planning, and I couldn't do it alone.

Not bothering to knock, I entered Maera's alchemy room. She had been in here all day, and from the looks of it, she had been busy. Very busy, judging by the tray of untouched food I'd had delivered.

Books were laid out over tabletops, and notes were pinned to the walls. Two small cauldrons, hanging over flames, were brewing something that smelled absolutely wretched. But it was bearable so long as I got to be in her presence.

Maera was so engrossed in what she was doing she hadn't noticed me entering. She was bent over a table littered with paper and potion bottles, swaying her luscious hips back and forth as she hummed. I came up behind her quietly and reached my hand around to grab her neck. She jumped slightly and let out a little yelp, but when I tilted her head back by her neck, she looked up at me with a relieved smile.

"Zalen," she said with a breathless grin. "You scared me."

I chuckled, stroking my thumb along her throat. Each pump of her racing pulse against my fingers went straight to my cock.

"Settling in well?" I asked as I bent my head down to kiss her jaw.

I was uncomfortably hard now, but she was so blissfully consumed in her work, I didn't want to stop her. I made myself a promise I would fuck her in this room someday—just not today.

"Oh, yes!" she said and pulled away to show me what she was working on. "I spent the morning rearranging and reviewing the texts here. Some of them are outdated, and I've replaced them with corrected versions, so I piled them over there to get rid of." She pointed to a pile of neatly stacked books by the door. "And look!" She practically bounced to another table covered in an array of tools, notebooks, and small burlap bags of herbs secured with twine.

My lips spread into a grin, pleased with how happy she was, opening up in a place of her own.

"I received my belongings from Aedum as well." She gestured to the items strewn across the table.

My grin fell. "Did they come in here?" I had given strict orders that no one was to enter this room under any circumstances.

"No. I watched a couple of men bring them over, and they put it all just outside the door then left. It's really nice being able to see out when they can't see in. I don't have to be disturbed, but I'm still aware when someone approaches."

Glancing at the translucent wall, I saw the hallway, and if someone were to walk down it, you'd be able to see their figure.

"Are you ready to call it a night? We can get some food since you didn't eat. Or would you prefer to stay a little longer?" I had a special dinner planned for us—with her as my dessert—but she was enjoying herself, so I would rather wait until she was ready.

Maera fiddled with one of the herb bags. "Do you mind if I stay a little longer? I'd like to get all of this sorted, and I have just a few more minutes until I need to add another ingredient to that brew." She pointed to one of the boiling cauldrons.

"Of course not. Would you like for me to help?" I gestured to the clutter.

Her face brightened. "I'd love that. Just arrange them into sections and organize the notebooks by date. Don't get my herb notes mixed in with saplings." Taking orders from her was definitely a turn on.

Maera returned to her brews, and I busied myself with de-cluttering the items on the table.

It was nearly dusk by the time we finished and left. With my hand at her back, I led her down to the lower level of the castle. Just as we were about to exit through the doors leading to the garden, someone called out, the voice echoing in the expansive space.

"King Zalen."

With a scowl, I spun on my heel. Not recognizing who it was, I stepped to the side to put Maera behind me.

"Don't move," I told her quietly.

A olive-skinned man with long braids was walking toward me—a human, and thus practically harmless. I noted the pin clasped at his chest, displaying the symbol of my new reign, which meant he was loyal to me. The tension in my shoulders eased, but I kept my guard up regardless with Maera around.

He was an averagely built man, just a few inches shorter than me and dressed in fur-lined clothes suited to traveling through cold weather. His species and attire indicated he was a messenger.

He stopped in front of me and stood at attention with his hands behind his back. He bowed at the waist then raised his hand in a royal greeting—touching his chest then his forehead with the tips of his fingers before gracefully lowering his hand to his side.

I nodded curtly, accepting his greeting. "What do you want?" I demanded in a much sharper tone than I had used with Maera.

"My name is Cazel, and I have a message for you from Ander." The newly appointed head of the Vord after his predecessor had become my guest in a cell. I remembered I probably should have told someone his body was still down there.

I held out my hand to Cazel. He reached into his pocket and pulled out a folded paper. I snatched it from his grasp and unfolded it, reading the message from the Vord headquarters. From the corner of my eye, I saw Maera lean to the side, trying to look around my arm to see the contents of the note. I quickly folded it back up and tucked it into my pocket.

This is a perfect opportunity for her to learn just who she's about to marry.

"You're dismissed," I said to Cazel.

Once he walked away and around the corner, I turned to face Maera who had a perplexed look on her face.

"Change of plans, love. We'll be eating in our room tonight. But I promise to make it up to you." I leaned down to kiss her and took her by the hand.

"I don't mind. What's going on?" she asked with a tone of curiosity.

We started making our way back upstairs.

"Some new information has come to my attention, and I'll need to leave immediately after dinner to take care of something—" I interrupted our conversation to address a female servant passing by. "You." The human woman froze in place with wide eyes. "Have our dinner brought up to our room," I ordered, and she scurried off in the other direction.

"Can I come?" Maera asked as we made it back to the room. Such an inquisitive little witch.

"You need your rest. You have a busy day tomorrow after all," I said and her brows raised with piqued interest.

"Is that so? I already have a schedule after being here for such a short time?" she questioned.

I shrugged and sat down at the table, pulling her into my lap with a smirk. "Of course. We do have a wedding to plan."

Maera had pressed to come with me all through dinner before I left, but I refused each time. I had hoped that she'd drop the polite requests and be more assertive toward me, as befitted the future Queen. It was important she made her decision even after my constant rejection. She needed to understand what she was about to see was her choice.

I placed a kiss on her forehead and then made my way to the Vord headquarters not far from the castle. Trekking through the darkness, I went to the compound. It was completely abandoned—with the exception of twelve men tied to wooden posts.

Standing on the frost covered ground, their clothes had been removed, and they were thrashing against the wrist bindings that secured them to the posts when I approached and lowered my hood. Their mouths were opening and closing, but no sounds came out. They had been silenced, just as I'd instructed.

The men had been taken from the Innon castle when my forces invaded, taking advantage of their weakened state. As part of the royal guard to King Belan, they would have had the most information about his death, and therefore were more valuable to me alive. For now. I wasn't going to make the same mistake I had with Aedum—killing those that still held information I could extract.

I approached the first man, and he trembled in my presence. He was pale-skinned and muscular, enough so I bet he would have been a fun opponent in a fight. I pulled out a small blade from its sheath at my waist. Grabbing his tongue, I sliced off the tip with the blade. Blood gushed from his mouth as I stepped back and moved on to the next man.

I needed them to be able to answer my questions but, seeing as they were sorcerers, I had to ensure their speech would be muddled enough they couldn't properly cast spells.

Once I had maimed each one, I moved back to the first man and dispelled his silence. He immediately started wailing, screeching into the night like a dying bird.

"Knock that shit off or I take more," I threatened.

He pressed his lips together, blood dribbling from the corners and down his chin but still whimpered.

"We'll never talk, so you might as well just kill us now," he mumbled around the wound in his mouth.

I kept my features cold and calculated. "I'll *let* you die, but you'll talk before I do."

I pulled out a glass bottle, filled with a potion I'd had brewed for me.

It didn't take more than a few minutes of the flesh-eating potion I had dripped on his hand before he began spilling all he knew about the murder of his King and Queen. He didn't know much, only that their bodies were nothing but ribbons of flesh piled on the floor of the Innon throne room.

Just like Makkor.

Convinced I had gained as much knowledge as he had to offer, I kept him alive for his screams to unnerve the others and I moved on to the next man.

Allowing only a few to live in order to keep the others in line, I gutted the rest once they had given me what I wanted, leaving their entrails hanging from their bodies, to prolong their suffering. At least, until I tired of hearing their wails and prayers—then I finally slit their throats one after another.

Whether it was the result of my sadistic father's brutal parenting, or simply that I had been born with this darkness, I quickly learned at a young age that the horrors of this world didn't disturb me at all. Screams of agony were siren songs, and blood was the paint for my masterpieces. And when I wasn't bathed in those terrors, an intolerable noise roared in my head, growing louder and louder like a beast demanding to be fed.

Only one other thing could quiet the hunger inside me.

Just as I lifted my hand to drip the flesh-eating potion on the next trembling man, I noticed movement out of the corner of my eye.

It pleased me that I knew Maera so well. She was hard-headed and stubborn, though she hardly showed it. Mix that with her undying curiosity, and her presence was expected. She had stuffed down that side of herself, but she didn't have to any longer.

I didn't stop. She needed to see me for who I was, what I was capable of—everything.

I waved my hand and muttered an incantation, eliciting wails from the man. Maera's gasp had me turning my head to find her peeking around the corner.

"Maera," I greeted.

I needed her to come to me. She had to choose this fate. She had to choose *me*.

She tentatively stepped out from behind the outer wall of the compound and stood there. Her eyes darted between me and the bleeding men. It must have been quite a sight for someone who wasn't accustomed to seeing something so grotesque.

Don't run now, curious little witch. Stay.

She stopped and stood there for a moment. Her chest rose and fell deeply, then she squared her shoulders and approached, holding my stare as she closed the distance between us. Her long fur-lined cloak brushed against the soft layer of snow covering the ground, her boots lightly crunching on the crisp frost beneath.

That's it, love.

While I had anticipated the wide array of possible reactions, a twinge of fear pinched in my gut she would resent me. Which would have been unfortunate, because she was going to be my queen no matter what.

I couldn't discern her emotions from her neutral features. But it was the glint in her eyes that calmed my soul—one of unfaltering trust. There was uncertainty and apprehension, but no anger or disappointment as I had feared.

She stopped only a breath away from me, gazing into my eyes without a single word for a few heartbeats. Then she pulled out a cylindrical bottle—a coercion potion, I noted, from the milky-white color—and handed it to me.

"It's more effective," she said quietly. "And merciful."

I stopped myself from sighing with relief at the acceptance in her eyes, knowing it was a hard truth for her to swallow. It was one thing to know I was a monster but it was another to see it so brutally. But I was still *her* monster.

"Why should I be merciful?" I asked with intrigue.

Her face remained neutral. "They lost their King and Queen, their home, and they're about to lose their lives. Why should they lose any more?"

I grazed my knuckles along her cheek, smearing blood over her delicate skin. "Because they need to be reminded that monsters are real. And one now sits on a throne."

Chapter Forty

RYKER

After I took Malina's bag from Hakoa, I flew deep into the forest and landed near a small creek winding gently between the trees. I dumped all the contents out, food, clothes, and weapons—Ayen's ass, a lot of fucking weapons—and gathered the glass vials filled with demid. I unstoppered each one and poured them into the flowing water, allowing the liquid to be washed away.

This wasn't easy for Malina, and it was about to get even worse over the next several days. I knew I was being harsh on her when I gave her the ultimatum between choosing the demid or seeing her people, but it was necessary. And effective. She needed to stop the demid, and, while no one could *make* her do it, everyone was being far too gentle. She was stubborn and hardheaded—she just needed someone to push her far enough to choose it on her own.

Not to mention, Kya would have my head if I had allowed it to continue.

I debated putting Malina's stuff back in her bag and returning it to her, but I knew users could get very creative with hiding their stash, so I decided not to risk it. Placing everything but the weapons in a pile, I flicked my wrist and set it on fire, heating the flames enough to melt even the vials, and let it burn until there was nothing left but ash and a puddle of molten glass.

Satisfied nothing was left to salvage, I grabbed her weapons and took to the skies, returning to where I had left Hakoa and Malina.

They were still holding on to each other—Malina resting in Hakoa's lap and gripping his shirt as he brushed his hand down her hair. Giving them some space, I landed back by Nikan and leaned against a nearby tree.

"Thanks for that," he said as he rested against the same tree.

I nodded, and handed him the ridiculous amount of weapons from Malina's pack. I still wanted to know more about Kya's past, I just wished she were here to tell me about it.

"How did Eamon do it? How did he keep you all secret as Roav?"

"Some knew—a few of the Scholars." He shrugged. "But honestly, no one questioned it. They just assumed we were from one of the other Nations. Either way, Eamon mostly stayed within the lines of the laws when he took us in."

"Mostly?"

That was curious. Eamon had always been adamant about the law as the High Scholar. Even for children, I had a hard time imagining him breaking the rules.

"Yeah. Technically, since we hadn't been initiated as citizens of Atara, he was allowed to take us in. But what he never did was make us become citizens of Riyah when we reached our staying age. I think most of it was due to Kya being marked for the Trial. He always had faith she'd be Worthy, and would one day become Lady of another Nation. I think he wanted her to have a full life without the restrictions of a Riyite citizen, seeing as she's the first contestant from Riyah. And I think he knew Malina and I would follow her wherever she went."

My mouth gaped. I had assumed since she was from Riyah that she was a citizen and therefore, like everyone else, she couldn't bear children. But if that wasn't the case... I swallowed, now taking in the possibility of what our future could look like. I just wanted to confirm though.

"So, none of you were forced to go through...."

Nikan chuckled, and I found it baffling how he could find any part of this situation humorous.

"Don't worry. You and Kya can have little Worthy babes running amok and terrorizing the palace. Gods help you if they're anything like her. I don't know how her parents did it."

Her parents. "Did her parents perish in the Glaev?"

Nikan shook his head. "No. Malina and Kya's parents still live on the Drift Islands as far as we're aware. They were all able to get out in time."

The way he had excluded himself had me tilting my head. "And yours?"

He stiffened and gazed out at the vast landscape before us. "They didn't make it. Tsilla didn't either—my younger sister. She was just a little younger than Kya was at the time."

It all made sense now, why he was so overbearing and protective. "Kya and Malina—"

"They're all I have, my only family. Nobody is waiting for me on the islands. I've done everything to try and make sure they're safe and taken care of."

I understood. He had always been watching out for his own.

I opened my mouth to say just that, but he pushed off the trunk and walked away, slowly stepping across the Ataran soil. I glanced over to Hakoa and Malina.

"Not to interrupt, but we need to get going. It's going to be dark soon," I said in Hakoa's mind.

"Funny. A shadow wielder afraid of the dark," he quipped. *"Just give us a few more damn minutes."*

"She needs to see Acalen. Today," I snapped.

He sighed, *"We'll be ready soon."*

"Theron," I called to the dragon.

He appeared a moment later in the newly restored plains in front of me. Nikan gave him a passing glance but didn't really react to the Spirit's presence. Theron hardly noted him and lowered his head to be level with me.

"Where have you been lately?" I asked with a snarky tone.

"Elsewhere," he clipped.

Cranky ass.

"Your mate has done well. Her task is nearly complete," he stated. I inhaled sharply at the mention of her. Theron turned his head to look at the vast land, clear of the Glaev. *"You should be proud."*

"I am."

"Yet you still hold anger toward her." A statement, not a question.

It was true. I wanted her back in my arms desperately, but the pain I felt had simmered into lividity. She had kept so much from me.

I *was* angry with her. I was angry she didn't trust me with her past. I was angry she didn't trust me enough to bring me with her to the Rip. She had made a choice. One that harmed both of us more than she anticipated. As much as I hated myself for it, I was just so Godsdamn mad at her. The bond and my soul burned fiercely for her, and I wanted her back.

I *would* get her back, but even when I did, it wouldn't be the same. How was I supposed to trust her after she left me in the way she did? She thought she was going to die and leave me in this world without her.

I snarled and glided over to Hakoa and Malina before landing with a heavy thump. "Time to go."

Theron Traveled us just outside of Acalen—a small, remote village at the south-eastern end of Oryn bordering Atara.

Nikan held his arm over his mouth in an attempt to curb his nausea. His face had turned a sickening shade of green from the sudden jolt through space. Malina gripped her stomach and bent over, trying not to heave up her last meal. Hakoa rubbed her back in soothing circles.

Pathetic as it was, seeing them together made me envious. I stopped my lip from curling and simply looked away. I instinctively reached to stroke down the bond, only to be stung by its splinters. The marriage band around my wrist felt heavy, and I wished I had Kya by my side.

"Good to know your pet is a useful form of transportation," Malina said with a grin. Hakoa snickered.

"I will eat her," Theron growled.

The side of my mouth lifted, and I chuckled. I had to admit, it was refreshing to hear some of her humor returning.

Malina stood up straight and glanced at the village. "Where are we?"

"Acalen. A village in Oryn," Hakoa answered.

"I've never heard of it," she said, shaking her head.

I shared a look with Hakoa.

"You weren't supposed to," I said, stepping toward her with my hands in my pockets. Nikan came up beside her. "Acalen has been a secret for the past twenty years. Before that, it didn't exist."

Her eyes widened. "Is… Is this where *they* are?"

I nodded. "There are ninety-six Atarans living here—"

"Ninety-seven," Hakoa added.

I looked at him curiously.

"Seraye and Itham have brought a new life into the world," he said with a small smile.

Not only were the Ataran people alive, but they were thriving, growing in numbers within their small community.

"Can we meet them?" Malina whispered, looking at Hakoa then me. She grabbed Nikan's hand.

"That's why I brought you here." I nodded.

She perked up and started pulling Nikan toward the village.

Hakoa started to follow but stopped after a couple of steps to look back at me. "You coming?"

I shook my head. "No. They need to hear the news from an Ataran."

And I didn't want to think about all the ways I had failed them as a Lord, and by not finding all of the survivors. I hated visiting. Everyone was pleasant and grateful, but it was a constant reminder of my shortcomings of not being able to get to everyone in time.

I stayed behind as the three of them left.

"Let me know when they are ready to depart again," Theron said.

"Jumping back to your realm so fast because you can't stand this one?" I jested.

"No," he clipped.

I chuckled, not knowing if he meant it wasn't because of this realm or if he wasn't going back to his.

Wait. If it wasn't his realm...

For Nox's sake! Why didn't I think of this sooner?

I internally chastised myself for being such a fucking moron and not asking Theron the right questions before now. If it wasn't for his Godsdamn restrictions on interfering, maybe he could have been more forthcoming. I spun to face him.

"Can you go to other realms besides this one and Hylithria?"

He tilted his head to the side. *"Some of them, yes."*

"Some?"

"Yes," he said, clearly annoyed.

As was I.

I ran a hand down my face roughly. *"Why can't you go to all of them?"*

"The Gods do not always create realms where Spirits are welcome," he said flatly.

Hmm. I hadn't realized that was a possibility.

"Why?" I asked.

"After we ceased all interference here on Taeralia, they were displeased and made realms of their own without Spirits."

"Can you Travel me to the other realms that you are welcome to?" I pressed.

"No," he said shortly.

"Why the fuck not?" My jaw clenched.

"Balance. You are meant to be in your realm, not another. Your presence could wreak havoc. Just like the dark wielder has done here," he said plainly. *"I can take you to Hylithria, but I cannot take you anywhere else. Only the Gods can."*

Shit.

"Alright. Then I need you to go search the other realms for Kya. At least the ones you can go to."

He blinked and blew out a hot breath. *"There are a lot of realms."*

"How many?"

He didn't respond for a few moments. *"More than the sands of Taeralia."*

I hummed as I thought for a minute. *"And you don't know what realm she's in, right?"*

"I cannot tell what realm she is in, but I have the ability to detect her through your mating bond if she is in one once I am there."

It was worth a try. Even if it took a long time, it was better than nothing.

"Search as many as you can. Find her, Theron. Please, just find her."

Chapter Forty-One

MALINA

I didn't know what I expected to happen when I walked through the village of Acalen. While I had pictured what it would be like if the Drift Islands ever returned and I could see my mother and father again, I had never considered the possibility there were other Atarans already living on the continent. At least not without me knowing about it—without *any* of us knowing about it.

With Nikan beside me, we froze in place, taking in the sight.

I thought it would have been more of a surreal moment, seeing those from Atara for the first time since its ruination, but this was just like any other village. People walked calmly along the streets, or some sat outside near gentle fires conversing. A shopkeeper was closing for the night, and a few males were walking into what looked to be a tavern. Everything looked normal.

The females didn't have feathers braided in their hair, and the wielders on the outskirts keeping a lookout didn't have their faces painted like Ataran warriors would. I didn't recognize anyone.

Nikan and I shared a wary glance. He too was skeptical that these were our people.

Hakoa placed a hand on my back, coming up to my side. "Come on. There's someone you should meet first."

I glanced back at Nikan who gave a subtle nod and a look that told me to trust the process for now but to stay alert. We followed Hakoa until we came to a home near the middle of the village. He raised his chin and straightened his spine then knocked on a stone door. Nikan stepped closer to me as he glanced around and behind us while I narrowed my eyes at the door.

A large, burly male opened it a moment later. He had long, black hair draping over shoulders nearly as wide as the doorframe. His honey-brown face was hard and unwelcoming, as were his auburn eyes that cut daggers right into me and Nikan.

Nikan inhaled sharply.

"Hakoa," the male greeted in a deep, questioning tone. "You've brought uninvited guests."

Great. He's so nice.

"Luthon, this is Malina and Nikan. Malina, Nikan, this is Luthon. May we come in?" Hakoa more commanded rather than asked.

Luthon's eyes darted between us before stepping aside, allowing us entry. I could scent the tension of everyone except Hakoa, who walked inside as we tentatively followed.

Luthon shut the door behind us, and we turned to face him. He crossed his arms and held Hakoa's stare, waiting for him to speak.

Hakoa took a deep breath, glancing at me with a brief smile before returning his gaze to Luthon. "I don't think there is a gentle way to approach this, but Malina and Nikan are Atarans."

Luthon's brows raised as his eyes snapped to us.

I stiffened, as did Nikan. This wasn't exactly something we had ever expected, and we really didn't know what to do.

"How?" Luthon asked quietly. "Lord Ryker said there were none left."

Hakoa looked at us. "This is your history to tell. You can trust him," he whispered and nodded his head to Luthon.

There was an awkward silence for a moment. We hadn't exactly talked to many people about our history, and we didn't know where to start.

Nikan cleared his throat. "We were the only survivors who weren't of age to be initiated as citizens of Atara. We were placed under the care of the High Scholar of Morah to be trained as Roav for the library."

I was surprised Nikan was so quick to be open.

"Is that even—" Luthon began, but Nikan interrupted him.

"I remember you."

My head whipped to look at Nikan, whose eyes were beginning to glisten. "What?" I whispered.

"He's from Igawa. My family visited there once when I was young, before Tsirra was born. Dego and Oya were my parents," Nikan said.

Igawa was on the northern border of Atara. It made sense they were able to escape to Oryn in time.

Luthon's eyes softened. "I remember them. And you. You were very small, you hadn't even come into your element yet. We thought you all perished in Liska…"

Liska was the capital of Atara, practically in the center of the Nation and where Nikan was born. His father, mother, and sister lived there when the Glaev attacked while Nikan was visiting Ulrik.

"And you?" Luthon asked, looking at me. "Were you from Liska as well?"

I shook my head. "No. Me and Ky— I mean, I'm from Asha. Our village was on the—"

"Western border," Luthon finished. "I've been there. It was one of the trade villages, like Igawa."

I nodded.

This was a terrible idea. Why did I think this would have been beneficial? Every memory of my family and my village were flooding into my mind, and all I could think about was how fucked up it was Kya wasn't here to meet an entire village filled with the people she would have been Lady of. She never even got the chance to learn of their existence.

My family could have been here, where they didn't have to constantly suffer. I could have been with them this entire time.

My skin crawled with guilt, and all I wanted was to stop feeling—

Hakoa grazed his knuckles down my arm, his eyes gazing into mine with concern. "Are you okay?" he whispered so only I could hear.

No.

"I'm fine," I lied.

He could see right through it. "Why don't you sit down? I'll get you some water. You've had a long day. In fact…" He looked at Luthon. "Why don't we continue this in the morning? I just wanted you all to meet. I'm sure you have a lot to catch up on."

"I'd like that," Luthon said.

"We'll be at the encampment," Hakoa stated, taking me by the hand and leading me to the door with Nikan following behind.

My ears started ringing as we left. Hakoa was talking, but I wasn't registering what he was saying. My breathing became rapid, and my heart pounded against my chest. I knew it was wrong, but I wondered if there was demid in the village. Surely someone had to have some. Or maybe there was another village nearby…

No. Stop it. You're done. You can do this. You don't want your people to see you like that.

My feet moved across the ground guided by Hakoa's gentle pull on my hand. I heard Nikan speaking with him, asking what was going on, but I was too fucked up to pay attention to the words.

I stopped in my tracks.

"Oh, Gods. I just met an Ataran, and I'm coming off demid," my voice broke. I started gasping, clutching my chest. "I'm such an idiot. Why did I come here?"

Why didn't I wait until I was recovered? It had only been three days. They were going to see what a mess I was.

Hakoa gently grabbed my shoulder as I began to hyperventilate. "You're going to be okay, Mal. Mal? Sunshine, can you hear me?"

I knew he was talking, but I could only comprehend every other word.

"Water...block...needs...alone."

No, don't leave me alone, I can't be alone. I can't get through this alone. Alone is where I'll drown back into myself.

I shook my head, trying to clear the fog in my mind. I blinked hard, and when I opened my eyes Hakoa was holding my face in his hands, brushing his thumbs over my cheeks. He wiped away something wet.

Udon's balls. I'm fucking crying again.

"It's alright. This is normal. The first few days are the hardest," he said softly over a low humming sound.

I looked up and saw he had wielded water around the two of us, like a cocoon.

"Take a few deep breaths. We're almost there, then you can sleep. That will help the most. I promise," he soothed.

"Okay," I said, releasing a shaky exhale and noting we must have been walking for a while because it was fully dark out now, and the village was in the distance.

Hakoa wielded the water away and took my hand again. Nikan walked by my side.

The next thing I knew, Nikan and I were alone in a large stone tent. I was sitting down on a pile of furs, and he was dabbing a cold, wet cloth to my forehead.

"Quit that," I mumbled, reaching up to stop him, but he just pushed my hand away.

"No. You have a fever. Your body has relied on the demid for too long, and since you stopped, you're having a bad response," he said quietly. "When was the last time you took a dose? Two, maybe three days ago?"

"Three," I whispered. I could probably tell him exactly how many hours it'd been too, if I knew what time it was.

"That's what I thought. The demid has completely left your system by now. Tonight is going to be rough. Did Eamon give you a capsule to take?" Nikan asked.

"No. He didn't give me a—anything," I stuttered, my body felt cold and hot at the same time, and I was shivering.

"It's okay. I kept one on me just in case."

"What's a capsule?" I asked.

He pulled out a small round ball from his pocket and held it in his palm. "It's a small, concentrated dose of an elixir."

"I'm trying to stop taking elixirs, Nik," I said pointedly, laying back on the furs and pulling one up to cover my chilled body.

"I know. But this one will help the symptoms you're having. It won't stop them, but it will make this process more bearable." I wasn't sure if he was telling that to me or to himself.

"Where did you get it? Is it the same one Eamon was going to give me?" The last thing I needed was something from some shady dealer on the market.

"Yes. And I got it from a healer in Dusan. I talked to over a dozen healers, trying to find the best thing to help you once you decided to stop, and I gave one to Eamon in case I wasn't around," he said quietly.

"Oh."

Tears welled in my eyes. He was an asshole, but he would go to the ends of the realm for me. He didn't deserve how I had deceived and treated him.

"I'm sorry, Nik. I'm sorry for blaming you. It wasn't your fault."

"It's okay. I just want you to get better. Swallow this. I was told it will make you sleep for a while, but I'll be here the entire time to keep an eye on you."

"Gods, you're going to watch me sleep? I'm not dying."

"No, but you could vomit, so I'm going to make sure you don't choke on your own bile in your sleep," he said.

Wouldn't it be ironic if after all the shit I'd been through in my life, I died from my own regurgitating?

The sides of my mouth lifted, and I took the capsule with a shaky hand. "Alright. But try not to kick me in your sleep this time."

He rolled his eyes and snorted a laugh. "Just swallow the damn thing already." He began dabbing my head with the damp cloth again, and it felt wonderful, chilling my fevered skin.

I put the round capsule in my mouth and swallowed it. It took only a minute before my eyelids grew heavy and darkness took me.

My eyes fluttered open. I was in the rock tent and sunlight trickled in through the cracks, dimly lighting the space. Whatever that capsule was that Nikan gave me worked because it knocked me out hard. I didn't remember a thing, and I felt a little better.

With a groan, I pushed myself to a sitting position. I was alone, and the temperature had dropped, my breath fogging in front of my face. The furs puddled at my waist, and I noticed I wasn't wearing the same shirt as before.

He changed me?

I heard people moving about outside the tent—voices and elements from many people by the sound of it. The smell of food cooking over a fire had my stomach rumbling. I was starving, and my throat was dry. I decided to get up and go find something to eat. There was a cup of water resting on the ground next to me. I quickly grabbed it and tilted it up against my lips.

"Son of a bitch," I grumbled. The water was frozen. "Damn northern weather in this freezing wasteland of a Nation…"

"Oh, stop whining. It's not that bad," Ryker's voice sounded in my mind.

"Get the fuck out of my head, pigeon boy, or I'm going to think of Hakoa's dick and let you have a good look," I snapped.

"That's…disturbing," he said.

The thick cloth flap to the tent entrance moved, and Ryker stepped inside. He had a cut above his eye and looked like he hadn't slept in days. Crossing his arms, he looked me up and down.

"You look like shit. How do you feel?"

"Speak for yourself. What are you, my nursemaid?" Since when did Ryker concern himself with my well being?

"At least until Nikan comes back," he mumbled.

I quirked a brow. "The great Lord of Oryn couldn't find someone more qualified to look after me?"

Like Hakoa. Not that I expected the Chief of the Noavo to have the time either. Or maybe he didn't want to...

"Trust me, this wasn't by choice." He pointed to the cut above his eye. "Your brother is very particular about who he allows near you."

"Nik hit you? And you let him?" I gaped.

"I'm not such a bad male," he deadpanned. "I argued about watching after you, and I may have even told him to fuck off. He swung at me, then I agreed to look after you. What did you expect me to do? Beat him because he cares about his sister?" he asked with a raised brow.

"Oh," I said quietly. He had a point. "Where is he anyway?"

"He's...dealing with something. He needed a break after watching over you for nearly three days straight."

"Dealing with what? We just got—Wait, did you just say three *days*?" No wonder I was so hungry.

"Yeah, you've missed quite a bit," he huffed.

"Such as?"

Ryker shrugged. "More than I wish I knew. At least about his personal life. I'm not getting into it." He shook his head. "Look, I was just told to check in on you and make sure to show you where the food is if you woke up. I don't have all damn day, so come on."

"You mean to tell me that you're taking orders from Nik because you're afraid of him hitting you again?" I snickered. This was a sight.

"Don't underestimate a brother's wrath," he said. "Now, let's go. I have places to be."

While I would have enjoyed taking my sweet time just to piss off Ryker, I was famished and quickly pulled on my boots and a cloak before hastily following him out of the tent.

The light was bright in comparison to the dimness of the rock enclosure, but my light wielding allowed my eyes to easily adjust. The mid-day rays of the sun's light reflected off a thick blanket of snow that covered every surface. Noavo warriors littered the encampment, and there looked to be about fifty or so of them.

"Why are there so many Noavo out here? We're in the middle of nowhere," I said, walking next to Ryker through the maze of stone tents.

He took a heavy breath and ran his hand through his dark hair. "It was set up right before I brought you here. There's a good chance the other Nations will come to claim Atara once they discover it's been restored."

"Yeah, Eamon said something about that. Are you really going to be able to defend it?" I asked.

"Yes," he said without hesitation. "But that's why I need you here too. You and Nikan. Atara needs to be protected, and you two are the only Atarans remaining that have any type of skill to do so."

"What about that burly male I met? Luthon, right?"

Ryker chuckled. "Luthon is a merchant. I doubt he's capable of killing a fly, let alone trained wielders."

"But he seemed like the leader of Acalen."

Ryker shrugged a shoulder. "More like an intermediary." He looked down at me. "This is serious, Malina. I need you to get well so you and Nikan can protect Atara until I can bring Kya back. I can't do everything myself."

Well…shit.

We turned to go around the next tent and stopped when we spotted Nikan and Mavris speaking to each other near the outskirts on the side of one of the tents.

"Nik, it's fine. You don't have anything to worry about. We can sort this out," Mavris said to Nikan. He was practically pleading.

"I have too much shit going on already. I can't deal with this right now." Nikan's hand came up and pulled at his hair as he began to pace.

Mavris stopped him, grabbing his face in his hands and pressed his lips against my brother's. He whispered something before Nikan placed his forehead on Mavris' shoulder.

I knew Nik had a thing for Mav! That lying—

"Let's give them some privacy," Ryker said quietly, walking away in the other direction.

I followed him until we came up to a large pot of boiling stew over a fire.

"Did *you* know about Mavris and Nik?" I asked.

"Not until recently. Mav usually tells me everything, but it's not my business. And right now, I don't really care about his personal life. I don't have time."

"Well, Nik is pretty private, and he can't stand you, so he probably told Mavris not to say anything. Kya and I had our suspicions though." I shrugged, grabbing a bowl and spoon. "We got a real good kick when you thought he was sleeping with her, seeing as he doesn't sleep with females at all."

His eyes grew hard and distant at the mention of Kya.

"Okay, you have your food. I'm going now." He began to walk away and shouted over his shoulder, "Don't fuck this up, Malina."

No pressure. Got it.

I poured a ladle of stew in a bowl and decided to take it back to the tent. No way was I eating out here in the cold. Just as I turned to go around a tent, I nearly bumped into Nikan.

"Mal! You're awake," Nikan said with a grin.

I slapped his shoulder.

"Eh! What was that for?"

"For lying to me," I hissed, leaning closer so no one else would hear. "I knew you hooked up with Mavris on that first night in Oryn. You told me you went to bed *alone*."

Nikan sighed and rolled his neck. "No, I said I *slept* alone." He started walking away, and I followed.

"You blatantly misled me, and you know it."

He groaned. "This is exactly what I was trying to avoid. It's done. Just leave it."

Back at the tent, he threw back the heavy cloth entrance then went over and plopped down on the furs. I sat down next to him, folding my legs beneath me.

"Was he bad in bed or something?" I huffed a laugh, elbowing him with a smirk.

His little bit of drama was just what I needed, keeping me distracted from thinking of my own problems.

"What? No…" He shook his head and looked away.

My smile quickly fell when I noticed the heartache in his eyes.

"Oh. You really like him," my voice softened. "Why did it end? Did you have a fight or something?"

"Sort of? I don't know," he sighed. "Look, we need to get going. We don't really have time to get into this right now."

We may not have had much time, but I could tell that he wanted to talk about it.

I gestured to my food. "Just explain it while I'm eating, then we can go." I started scooping up spoonfuls of stew into my mouth, eating slowly so he could see he had enough time to explain even though I would have gulped it down all at once with how hungry I was.

His shoulders relaxed slightly. "Yeah, okay. It really just started as hooking up here and there. It was more to relieve tension than anything, at first... I don't know. He started thinking it was more than that, but we had so much going on already and trying to deal with what was—or wasn't—between us would have just gotten in the way." Nikan leaned back against the tent wall, pinching the bridge of his nose. "Mav deserves someone who can give everything to him, not just a few minutes behind a locked door. So I ended it just before we left to get Vicria in Bhara. Today's the first day I've seen him since."

"Wow..." I said with a final mouthful. "You're stupid."

"Mother above," he mumbled under his breath and stood, extending a hand to me. "You're one to talk."

I wiped my hands on my pants then stood as well. "Yeah, yeah. So where exactly do we need to go?"

"To talk to the other Atarans in Acalen." He led the way out, and I stepped up to his side as we made our way out of the encampment.

"Why?"

"Well, they're antsy, wondering why we're here." He gestured to us and the Noavo Warriors. "But I wanted to wait until you were ready so we could tell them together."

"Tell them what?" I tilted my head to the side.

The side of his mouth curved up. "That we all get to go home."

Chapter Forty-Two

ZALEN

"You stay right there. Don't move," I said to Maera quietly.

She nodded her head and stayed in the Vord compound with me after she handed me the coercion potion.

Pouring a few drops down each of the remaining Innon guards throats, the effects kicked in quickly, and they answered any question I asked without hesitation. The most I learned from them before slitting their throats was that their King had left for a few days—alone—then returned one day without explanation. They found his and the Queen's remains the next morning in the Innon throne room.

It was like listening to a recount of what happened to Makkor, almost the exact same story. No trace of the murderer, no clues as to who it could be or what spell was used, no one claiming the Kingdom. *Nothing.*

Convinced I had all I could gain from the guards, I killed off the last one and left their bodies chained to the posts in the compound. Maera watched the entire time, expressionless. She hadn't even flinched.

I walked over to where she stood. Her eyes were trained on the bodies, yet she didn't run. Not from their corpses. Not from me.

"Maera," I said firmly, trying to draw her attention to me. It wasn't until I hooked a bloody finger under her chin and lifted her head that she finally looked at me. "It's done. Why don't you return to the castle? I need to write some orders for Thane, then I'll meet you there."

With distant eyes, she gave a shallow nod.

"What are you thinking about, love?" I tilted my head to the side.

She swallowed and glanced back at the bodies. "How many people have you killed?"

"Not as many as I'm going to."

Her eyes slowly dragged back to mine. "Why?" she breathed.

"Because there's someone out there that poses a threat to you. And I won't stop until I find him."

Maera returned to the castle while I met with Thane at the Vord headquarters and gave him orders to find out where the Innon King had gone just before he was killed. I didn't know if it had any correlation, but since Makkor had also just returned from being away for several days before his death, it was too similar to be a coincidence.

Thane agreed and assured me he would find out.

And my orders for Thane served a secondary purpose, allowing him to briefly study the Kingdom he was about to hold the magic for once he was able to go through his Drehiri.

Returning to our rooms, I found Maera in bed, clean and wearing a nightgown. Her deep, even breaths let me know she was asleep.

Satisfied she was sleeping, I went into the bathing room and stripped off my bloody clothes to get into the bath, washing away the stench of death.

I returned to the room after throwing on a pair of loose pants and crawled into bed next to her. I brushed back a few stray strands of hair behind her ear and found her eyes were open, staring into the darkness.

"Minn astir, are you alright?"

She didn't say anything for a few moments.

"I don't know," she whispered. "I think so." A tear fell down her cheek, and she wiped it away.

I stayed quiet, allowing her time to gather her thoughts.

"It's just… A lot has happened, and I'm not really all that upset about any of it. I don't recognize myself. I don't recognize my life. I'm not unhappy, so please don't think that. Everything is just so unfamiliar."

She needed someone she could connect with—someone other than me—that she could relate to.

"I think I'm just tired. I need sleep," she added.

I smiled down at her. "Then sleep. You're here. You're safe."

"Am I?"

"You are when you're with me," I said, kissing her softly.

I lay on my side and pulled her to me, her head nestling against my bare chest. So long as she was with me, nothing would happen to her.

Maera remained distant the next day. She went to her alchemy room and worked on her experimental potions, practicing to perfect them. A few more days, and I'd have her test them out. She needed to see them work firsthand rather than rely on theory alone. And I wanted her to have a surplus of them on hand as well.

If something were to happen and she needed to defend herself, I didn't want her scrambling for herbs or tools to use. But that was also a skill she needed to learn—how to take what you could get and make it into a weapon. I planned on taking her out west where she had never been and having her practice foraging and brewing only with what she could find and using it to her advantage.

But today was reserved for something else.

I awoke the following morning with Maera still in my arms, but her eyes were open. They were distant, deep in thought and somewhere else. I leaned my head down and placed a kiss on her hair.

She startled slightly then looked up at me. Her eyes flashed with delight upon seeing me looking at her, but that lasted for only a moment before they began to dull.

"Good morning," she said so softly I barely heard it.

"It is when I wake up next to you," I said quietly.

She gave a tight-lipped smile.

"Hey," I tilted her chin up. "I have something for you today. It'll help get your mind off things."

"More brewing?" she asked.

"Better. It has to do with lace." I bent my head down and kissed the column of her neck. "And silk," I said, kissing lower and lower.

Her breath hitched. "Zalen…" she breathed. "I'm not feeling…"

"Are you unwell?" I lifted my head and looked her over.

"No, that's not it."

I tilted my head to the side. "Are you upset?"

She leaned her head back and looked up at the ceiling. "I don't know. I don't know what to feel."

That's just unacceptable.

"You should feel good." I slowly trailed a finger down the middle of her chest. "Let me help with that."

Her skin pebbled beneath my touch as I moved lower and lower, slipping my hand beneath her undergarment and dragging my finger lightly over her slit.

"Zalen…" she said breathlessly, bucking her hips. "I don't want to do this right now."

I held her stare with hard, unrelenting eyes but didn't move. "Then tell me to stop."

Her lips pressed together firmly. She gasped when I pushed a finger inside her.

"You *don't* want this or you just *think* you shouldn't? You think it's wrong that you're wet and writhing for me even after seeing what you did—seeing who I am." I pumped my finger in and out with torturous slowness, and my little witch couldn't help but move against me. "You may think you don't want it, love, but your body sure fucking does. And I intend to worship it."

I pushed another finger in and curled them forward, watching her react to my touch. She pressed against me, letting out a breathy moan.

"You're…scary," she said through panting breaths.

I crawled over her, grabbing her wrists in one hand and pinning them above her while keeping my fingers pumping in and out of her. "Monsters are supposed to be scary."

I removed my fingers and pushed them against her lips.

"Open," I said darkly.

Maera's eyes widened, and she hesitated for a moment before tentatively parting her lips. I shoved my fingers in, pressing them to her tongue as she closed her mouth around them.

"I want you to taste your pleasure," I said, watching her through hooded eyes as she swirled her tongue around my fingers. "And now I'll have a taste for myself."

Releasing her wrists, I removed my fingers from her mouth and leaned down to kiss my way down her body. Tugging at the hem of her nightgown by her waist, I nodded for her to take it off.

She sat up, crossing her arms over her and pulled it up over her head, tossing the material to the floor. Her bare breasts were too tempting to resist.

I took one in my mouth, biting her nipple lightly before licking the sting away. Her head fell back with a soft exhale.

But this was about her, not me.

I released her breast from my mouth and pushed her down on her back before moving between her legs. Gripping the lacy fabric around her hips, I ripped it down her legs and threw it across the room.

Her perfect cunt was glistening, wet and ready. The sight had my skin trembling with desire to bury myself in her.

Tenderly, I roamed my hands up the inside of her thighs and parted her for me, seeing just how slick she was. I couldn't wait any longer.

"Stay still for me, love."

My tongue darted out, licking up from her entrance and keeping my tongue soft as I lapped at her clit. I flattened my tongue against her opening, then pushed inside her, groaning at the taste of her.

Fuck, she was the best thing that ever graced my tongue.

I wanted her to come on my mouth. I wanted to taste her pleasure and have her begging.

I nipped at her clit, causing her to flinch and catch her breath. Then I took her clit between my lips and sucked. Hard.

She let out a scream and gripped my hair, but I was relentless.

My cock twitched at the sound. I wasn't stopping until I'd had my fill.

She squirmed as if she was trying to get away but couldn't fight against the ruthlessness of my mouth.

"You can take it," I told her, my voice husky and breathless, yet still commanding.

I ravished her like a starving man, licking and sucking and fucking her relentlessly with my tongue over and over. Her breathing came quickly, and I felt her muscles tensing.

"Do I seem scary *now*?" I teased, my voice rumbling against her.

Her head shot up, piercing me with a glare. "No! Keep going!"

She pushed my head back down, smothering me against her.

I chuckled, and resumed fucking her with my tongue while watching the pleasure on her face.

There would never be a more beautiful sight than this—seeing her unravel, gasping for breath and writhing because of what *I* could do to her.

She threw her head back with a scream as she clenched around my tongue in pulsing waves of pleasure.

I nearly came in my pants from the sensation. The taste of her coming on my lips would be the end of me, and I wanted it every day.

I languidly licked her through her climax until she was too sensitive to bear it any longer. I sat back on my heels and licked the remnants of her arousal from my lips. She grabbed for me, trying to pull me down on top of her, but I stopped her.

Her brows creased. "You don't want—"

"No," I shook my head with a grin, pleased I was able to satisfy her. I would always satisfy her. "This was about you." I leaned forward and kissed her, letting her taste herself again.

"Now," I said, pulling back and helping her up to a sitting position. "Go get ready. I'll have Riva escort you to the seamstress."

"Who's Riva?" she asked.

"She's to be your handmaiden, as befits a Queen. Hurry up. We have a wedding to prepare for."

And I had a human to inform about her new status as handmaiden to the future Queen.

With a wide grin, Maera leapt out of the bed and squealed a giggle when I smacked her ass on the way to the bathing room.

I adjusted my uncomfortably hard cock, debating on stroking it but deciding I'd rather wait until later when I could put it down Maera's throat instead.

While she bathed, I put on a shirt and rushed out of the room until I found one of the servants heading toward my rooms with a tray of food.

Riva. Just who I was looking for.

She froze in place, her dark red hair swaying with her abrupt stop. I looked her up and down. She was average for a human, but I had known about her for weeks and had determined she wasn't a threat to me or Maera. Riva's past made her the perfect choice for Maera, seeing as they would be spending a lot of time together, and my hope was they make a connection.

"King Zalen," she greeted with a deep bow. "I was just bringing your breakfast to your rooms."

"I can see that, Riva," I said.

Her eyes widened at her name.

"I know everyone who walks these halls," I said flatly. I knew everyone in my home, everyone who had access to Maera. But I never spoke to any of them.

"Right. Of course." Her voice was even, and I gathered she didn't fear me like most did. I think Maera would enjoy being around someone brave.

"You may rise," I said in an authoritative tone, and she stood straight. "Why have you come to serve me?" I knew her past, but I also wanted to know her reasoning.

"Because I believe that you can be a better ruler than any King in all the Kingdoms before you," she said firmly.

"Flattery won't get you anywhere."

"I wasn't being flattering," she stated simply.

Yes, she'd be great for Maera.

"And where were you born?"

"Aedum, King Zalen. I moved here—to Kanth—when I became of age. It wasn't until after Makkor was killed that I pledged my loyalty to you and came to work here. I swear I hold no fealty to the late King Erix."

She took a risk telling me she was from my previous enemy Kingdom, but she told the truth anyway.

"Good. You won't be working in the kitchens any longer," I said.

Her eyebrows bunched in confusion.

"You're to be the personal handmaiden to the Samanya heir—soon to be the Queen of Damanthus. You will give her whatever she asks for and do anything she says. You will serve her and *only* her. Do you understand?" I tilted my head to the side, gauging her reaction.

She was speechless, her mouth opening and closing, trying to come up with words.

"Do you understand?" I clipped.

"Y—yes," she stammered.

"Alright then. After Maera and I have eaten, you will escort her to the royal seamstress and assist with any wedding planning she wishes to be part of. She also intends to work in her alchemy room, and I assume that is where she will spend most of her time. Your ultimate duty is to serve her, but you may befriend her *if* she allows it. Do not disappoint me, Riva."

She swallowed. "Yes, sir."

I took the tray from her and went back to the room, leaving Riva wide-eyed in the corridor.

My morning activities had made me late, but it was just the thing I needed to subdue my temper for later. I needed to get Maera to the seamstress quickly so I could meet with Thane. We had a lot to discuss if I was about to start a war.

Chapter Forty-Three

—◆◇◆—

RYKER

"Lord Ryker," Eraeya, one of the messengers of Oryn, came into my study just hours after I returned from the encampment outside Acalen. She rushed in, stopping just before my desk and handed me a rolled up piece of parchment. "I have a message from Bhara about your request to meet with the other Worthy."

From the look on her face, it wasn't good.

I grabbed the paper from her hand and unrolled it, reading it aloud, "Lord Ryker, your request to meet with the Worthy has been denied. Lord Jymar of Gaol, Lord Dainos of Torx, and Lord Voron of Ulrik have declined your proposition to gather at the temple in Bhara for a collaboration..." I trailed off.

Shit. I needed them. I needed them to work with me to ambush Daegel.

"Is this all?" I asked Eraeya without looking up, rereading the rejection letter.

"No. The other Lords, I... Well, I was told by one of the representatives... Actually, I think it was a Vaavi who told—"

"Out with it Eraeya," I snapped, looking back at her.

She took a deep breath and ran a hand through her short, cropped hair. "Two of the Nations have pulled all active members of their forces together. They're about to mobilize their armies."

Gods, they know already.

I remained calm and expressionless, not wanting to worry Eraeya just yet. "Which Nations?"

"Gaol and Ulrik," she stated.

I nodded slowly, my mind reeling.

"Thank you, Eraeya," I said with a polite smile. "I will look into this. You're dismissed."

She left, and I stood, walking to the window and blankly staring at the snow-covered mountains with my hands behind my back. Once I heard the click of the door behind her, I reached out to Arra.

"Where are you?" I asked in her mind.

"Gah!" she startled. *"Ryker, I told you I don't like this mind invasion. Stop it."*

"I need you to tell me why I'm just now hearing Gaol and Ulrik have concentrated their forces, and I had to hear it from a messenger and not the leader of the Vaavi," I growled, not caring I violated her request.

She was silent for a moment. *"I'm on my way. We may have bigger problems than I realized."*

Several minutes later, Arra stormed through the door. She looked frazzled—her usually kempt red hair was fraying out of its braid as if she had run her hand across it over and over. There were dark circles beneath her eyes like she hadn't slept for days.

"I told you to silence those rumors, Arra. You failed, and now Gaol and Ulrik are about to march across the continent to take over Atara. Why have I not heard about this from *you?*"

Arra squared her shoulders and shook her head. "Because I didn't know—"

"But you *should* have known. You fucked up," I snapped.

She flinched but didn't cower. "The Vaavi that were sent out haven't returned, and they've missed their check-ins. There are only two reasons they would have disappeared."

I closed my eyes and sighed. "Either they were compromised and captured, or killed."

"Yes," she bit out. "I've been searching for them, but this is a recent development. I was planning on going out and finding them on my own, but if the other Nations know about Atara, then they're likely dead."

"How many?" I asked.

"Five," she whispered.

Five incredibly talented wielders lost. We couldn't stand to lose more.

"Pull everyone out of Gaol and Ulrik. Everyone, not just the Vaavi. They've denied my request to meet, which means they have no interest in diplomacy. They know."

Except for Dusan.

I raised my head. Lady Asmen wasn't mentioned in the letter. If she didn't deny my request, maybe she didn't know. Or if she did, perhaps I could sway her to help me before Jymar and Voron had the chance.

"What about Torx and Dusan?" Arra asked.

"Torx denied the meet, but I haven't heard about their forces. Nor Dusan. Find out what you can, I need to speak with them."

Asmen was a new Worthy, she hadn't had much time to make enemies or allies yet. She was the best option and easier to mold. Dainos on the other hand... I'd worry about him next.

I sat down and wrote out a note—an order for Hakoa. Arra watched as my pen scratched the parchment then I folded it and handed it to her.

"Get this to Hakoa. Immediately," I commanded as I began to leave.

Arra followed. "Where are you going?"

"Dusan. Now go," I barked.

She didn't hesitate and ran around me, bolting down the staircase to the Noavo station.

I felt useless. I wasn't any closer to finding Kya, and now her Nation was under threat of being lost to the other Worthy.

I took a moment and stepped into a spare room mainly used for storage. Slamming the door behind me, I walked to the center of the room. I needed to release all this pent up rage. And since I couldn't fuck my mate or kill anyone at this moment, this room would have to do.

With a roar, I threw my hands out, blasting my flames in a ball of fire that exploded around me. It incinerated anything it touched and heated the cold glass windows so quickly they shattered in a singular piercing snap as the shards flew out into the winter air.

But it wasn't enough.

My shadows erupted from me, mingling with the flames and consuming their brightness until all that was left was scorching heat and darkness.

Damnit! I'm sick of this! I'm tired of taking one step closer to figuring out how to get Kya back only to be pushed three steps backward. Enough of this! I want my mate back, and I want her now!

I pummeled every burning item in the room until it was smashed into nothing but ash.

How am I supposed to get to her? How am I going to find her and bring her back when every Godsdamn thing keeps getting in my way?

My fist slammed into crates and shelves over and over with the thought of every obstacle.

The Rip.

The Worthy coming for Atara.

My duty as Lord.

Daegel.

A knock sounded. "Ryker, are you alright?"

"Leave!" My voice boomed so loudly the walls shook.

The door opening sounded over the crackling of the flames, and my father walked in.

Shit.

Pulling back my shadows and extinguishing the fire, I slumped to the floor and rested my head in my hands, smoke billowing all around me. I hadn't even realized, in my tantrum, I had shifted my wings and my scales.

Losing Kya was awakening a beast within me, and I didn't like who I was becoming.

Cadoc carefully walked over to me and bent down, placing a comforting hand on my shoulder.

I wanted Kya in my arms. I wanted to hear her voice, her laugh. I wanted her beside me, knowing she was safe.

"I just want Kya back..."

"I know, son. I'm here to help you."

I raised my head. He looked...different. I was hesitant to think he looked better, but he certainly seemed more put together than he had in the last fifty years. His hair had been trimmed, and his clothes were clean. Standing tall, I had almost forgotten he was the same height as me and Mavris. His eyes seemed brighter, clearer—unlike the lifeless glaze he'd had for so many years following the disappearance of my mother.

I noticed the dark book in his arms. "I told you to keep that away from here."

"I know you did. But..." He looked down to the book in his hand. "You were right. With this, we can find our mates. Together."

I blew out a breath, thankful to have more assistance. "There's something I need to take care of first."

Chapter Forty-Four

KYA

P *lease. Ease his pain. He shouldn't have to suffer because of the choice I made.*
Tell him I love him beyond the bond.
I never got to say it back…

It was a strange feeling to know something was coming, but not when or exactly what. I knew this wasn't what was left for me, this wasn't my fate. I was tired of waiting. Something big was coming…

Over and over, we did the same fucking thing. The same walk to the sacred stepstone. The same incantations and shields. The same exhaustion from using my Waalu to create the Glaev.

The only difference was that so long as I did what I was supposed to, Leysa didn't have to wear the collar anymore. It certainly kept me motivated. It tore me apart when I had to listen to her cries of anguish, being punished for something she had no control over, so I did as I was told to spare her the torture.

By this point, I had nearly finished—the once lush, thriving land was now ruined with the same black death that had plagued Taeralia. The more I destroyed, the more impatient and irritable Daegel became. He had stopped putting a shield around Leysa several days ago, forcing her to move along with us. While she and I had to stay on a very narrow trail across the island to move from the stepstone to the other end of the island, Daegel had the ability to touch the Glaev.

The only good thing about doing something so repetitive was I didn't have to think about it anymore. Going through the motions, it allowed me to focus my mind elsewhere. I had never had the time to do it before, so I took the opportunity to finally learn about myself—about the magic bestowed upon me.

The orbs closer to the surface were easier to access, like my invisibility and aligist magic from Kleio and the energy from Odarum. But there was more, buried deeper within the recesses of my soul I had never tunneled down to.

Until now.

Keeping the Waalu flowing from my fingertips, I fell into myself to explore what was shrouded in darkness. It was more difficult, since I had to keep my eyes open, constantly distracted by my vision. But after days of trying, I was finally able to separate my mind from reality.

It was like traveling through a dense fog with no sense of direction. But I pushed through the seemingly endless haze until I saw a soft glow. There, tucked away in the darkness, was another orb, another gift from the Silent Goddess.

It looked like glass with blue streams rippling across the surface. I tried to reach for it, but it was as if there was resistance.

I didn't know what it would do if I pushed it, and it was a risk attempting this in front of Daegel. But I did it anyway, forcing myself through the wave of resistance and latched myself around it.

It felt unnatural and wrong, giving me a sense of unease and putting a knot in my stomach. I came back to my conscious vision and subtly looked around, glancing at myself to see if there were any visible changes.

Nothing.

Great. Another orb I didn't know how to use or what it did.

I continued to hold on to it, which only exhausted me faster, but I wanted to see what it could do before I was forced to wear the collar again.

The sun was setting over the curve of the vast ocean before me. I couldn't do any more today.

In addition to my exhaustion, Daegel was in a particularly foul mood, only aggravating me further.

"More," he bellowed over and over all Godsdamn day.

Fuck him.

"I'm done," I snapped as I spun on my heel to face him just outside the magical dome barrier with nothing but a pearlescent sheen between us.

His eyes narrowed into slits. "What do you mean you're done?"

"I'm finished," I clarified, throwing my hand out to gesture to the Glaev I had created today.

He tilted his head to the side, clearly not understanding.

I smirked. "What? You've never heard a female tell you they've finished before? I'm not surprised."

His face twisted into a sneer. "I've warned you, Diamond."

He lifted his hand and waved it. The collar lifted and wrapped around my throat. Gods, I didn't want it back on. No matter how many times he kept forcing me to endure its magical suppression, I would never get used to it, and it was the one thing I resented most.

I closed my eyes and lowered my head, waiting for his stupid incantation that would bring me nothing but pain and suffering until we returned again.

"Lauss," I muttered under my breath, just like I did every time.

The collar fell to the ground.

Chapter Forty-Five

KYA

I stilled, my eyes snapping open to see the metal band lying in the grass in front of me. I didn't move, didn't breathe. *Did… Did I do that?*

It had never worked before. Nothing was different except… *The orb.*

Before I could even open my mouth, the collar was back around my neck, and he had uttered the incantation to seal it. Those orbs inside me turned as lifeless as the land around us.

Forcing myself to stay standing, I glanced up. Daegel eyed me suspiciously. I didn't react, acting like nothing out of the ordinary happened.

"I ought to rip out your throat for that mouth of yours." With a wave of his hand, the shield came down, and he came at me.

There wasn't anything I could do. I couldn't run, seeing as I was surrounded by the Glaev, and I couldn't use my magic. And with all this pain, there was no way I could fight him.

I braced myself.

But before he could reach me, Leysa lunged in front of him.

"No! You'll kill her!" she screamed, frantically—attacking him with what little strength she had.

Daegel grabbed her by the throat and spun, throwing her down the narrow trail of clear land. Her body slammed to the ground with a sickening thud. She lay there, gasping for air, and Daegel stalked forward. He bent over her and hissed something in a whisper too quiet for me to hear then began beating her.

I rushed at him, kicking and pounding on his back. "Leave her be! What is your problem? You can't do this!" I screamed.

Daegel whipped around and grabbed me by the throat just above the collar, getting in my face.

"I can, and I will! I will do whatever it takes! Look around you. You may have done all this to *one* island, but I will do it to your *entire* world."

"You…can't just…destroy an entire—" I struggled to speak through his unrelenting grip around my throat, cutting off my air.

"It's my world or yours. You think I wouldn't rip apart everything for her?" he said with a vicious lethality. "I may be the villain in your story, but I'm the hero in hers…and I can live with that."

What?!

Daegel released me then pushed me back. I started coughing and began to crawl toward Leysa.

"Want me to hurt her more?" Daegel snapped, and I froze. "No? Then don't fucking move," he growled.

Grabbing Leysa by her shirt, he lifted her from the ground and placed her on her feet. He said something to her then shoved her forward until she started walking back toward the stepstone.

"Let's go," he barked as he turned to look back at me.

With a sneer on my face, I followed. But I couldn't help the small, malicious smile that crossed my lips. I had finally learned something about Daegel. And it had to do with *her*.

***

After Leysa and I returned, we ate the little food they gave us and lay together in the dark. Thankfully, her cuts and bruises healed quickly. She wasn't permitted to wash me or herself tonight—a small addition to our punishment.

But I couldn't stop thinking about what Daegel had said.

"Who was Daegel talking about?" I asked Leysa.

She shook her head. "I wish I knew. That's the first time I've ever heard him mention that."

Well, that's not helpful.

What did destroying my world have to do with someone else? Why would killing land result in him being a hero to anyone?

If there was someone he cared for, she could be used against him. Just like he was using Leysa against me.

"Thank you for what you did earlier," I whispered.

"You don't have to thank me. I thought he was going to kill you," she said quietly.

"Are you okay?" I asked.

"No. Are you?"

I took a deep breath. "Not until we get out of here."

My mind was riddled with questions—some about who Daegel was talking about but mostly about the new magic I discovered.

What did the orb do exactly? Was that really what happened, or was I delusional from the exhaustion? What if it really did happen and I could use their magic? How would it work?

I'd need to pay attention to everything they said and try to understand what everything meant. I could use this. Now, I just had to learn it without Daegel figuring it out which would be difficult seeing as the only time I could was when the collar was off, and he was watching me the entire time.

Maybe I could somehow find a way to put the collar on him long enough to get away, then go find King Zalen...

I'm trying, Ryker. I'll come home soon. I promise, I said uselessly down the fractured bond, mostly trying to reassure myself.

"So," Leysa began, "When is this little escape attempt happening?"

"Hmm?" I hummed, acting ignorant.

"If I've learned anything about you so far, it's that your mind doesn't stop running. I know you're coming up with a plan over there," she said in that motherly tone of hers.

I rolled my eyes. "I'll know it when I see it. Why, do you have something better to do?"

"No. I just want to make sure I'm far away when it happens," she stated flatly.

I leaned up on my elbows. "Leysa... Don't you want to come with me? Don't you want to finally get out of here? To go home?"

She swallowed. "Of course I do. I just..." she said timidly.

She was scared.

"How many times have you tried?" I asked after a few moments.

She sighed heavily then sat up, moving her legs over the side of the bed and facing away from me. She reached around her midsection and lifted her shirt up.

"What are you—"

The words died on my tongue as she revealed her back—a canvas of horrendous scars. Then she rolled up her sleeve and her pant leg, showing more of the same.

Gods, what had they done to her?

"I stopped counting..." Leysa whispered. She tenderly ran her fingers up her arm, over the scars, then pulled her sleeve and the rest of her shirt down. "Does this look like I don't want to get out of here?"

I'm such a bitch. How can I be so heartless to assume she doesn't want to leave as much as I do? If each scar was for every time she tried to escape…

She turned back around to face me with tears welling in her silver eyes.

"I've tried, Kya. I've tried *everything* to get back to Cadoc. Do you really think the bond would allow me to do any different? I know what you're feeling. I know that desire. It hasn't stopped, and it never will. But I'm begging you to just finish your task. Do what Daegel wants. Please. Don't make this more complicated than it needs to be."

Chapter Forty-Six

MALINA

"**A**re you insane?"

I didn't blame the wariness of the Atarans gathered in the village as Nikan and I told them Atara was nearly restored. Luthon had remained quiet until now, but he clearly didn't believe us.

"We've seen it with our own eyes," Nikan said, gesturing to me.

I hated being here in front of all of them with their mixed looks of hope and disbelief.

"It's true. Just before we came here, we stood on Ataran land. The Glaev is disappearing quickly, and it won't be long before you can walk to the border and see it for yourself."

"We're not lying," Nikan defended, stepping forward. "Additionally, Lord Ryker has seen it. He's the one who told us about it in the first place and who brought us here."

"Why hasn't Lord Ryker come to tell us?" a female with a fiery look demanded with her arms crossed over her chest.

"Because Lord Ryker is otherwise engaged in preventing *your* Nation from being taken by another," a low, commanding voice said behind me that had me whipping my head around.

Hakoa approached, giving me a brief glance before looking over the group of people before us with the hard expression of the Chief of the Noavo.

"And you don't need to hear it from him because he has sent you two Atarans to tell you. Additionally, *I* am telling you. Malina and Nikan deserve nothing but your trust," his voice carried over the small crowd.

The respect they had for him was evident as they nodded at his words.

I, on the other hand, wanted to crawl into a hole and never come out. But Hakoa subtly brushed his fingers against mine, comforting me.

"Is that why there are so many Noavo stationed just outside the village? Because another Nation is coming?" Luthon asked.

"From the information we've gathered, the other Nations are now aware of Atara, and they have assembled their forces. Without a Worthy or a people, they see Atara as open land up for grabs," Hakoa stated.

"But it does have people," the fiery female said, gesturing to the Atarans.

"Yes, but no one knows that, Niabi. They all think we're either dead or on the Drift Islands. Hence why we've been confined to this village for the past twenty years," one of the males a few paces away from her said. "Or did you think we just wanted to keep our existence a secret for fun?"

They looked so similar, like they could be related. Both had white hair and dark skin, but their eyes were different. While his were a dark brown, hers were a light caramel.

"Shut up, Lucar. I know that. I'm not stupid," Niabi seethed.

"I beg to differ," Lucar quipped.

Niabi growled and lifted her hand, giving him a crude gesture.

Definitely siblings.

"What I mean is we *are* here. Can't we just go in and reclaim it for ourselves, and they'll back off?" Niabi clarified, speaking to Hakoa while glaring at Lucar.

"That's the plan, but it's likely to result in them killing all of you and taking it by force anyway. That's why we're here—to defend it," Hakoa said, gesturing to us and the Noavo encampment.

"And how do you plan to do that?" Luthon asked earnestly.

Nikan shared a glance with me before looking back at Luthon. "We're working on it."

***

"We're working on it?" I asked Nikan once we made it back to the encampment. He wielded two rocks from the ground into chairs for us to sit inside the tent.

He plopped down on one and ran a hand through his hair. "Sort of."

"Well, do you have a plan? Because I sure don't," I huffed, crossing my arms.

"Not entirely, but what I do have mostly involves you teaching them how to defend themselves and keeping them safe until Kya returns," he said nonchalantly.

I blinked. "Me?"

"That's what I *just* said."

"Why not you or Ryker? Or literally *anyone else*." They clearly didn't trust me.

"Ryker already has a Nation, he can't lead another one. Not to mention, he's preoccupied looking for Kya while simultaneously trying to prevent a war from ensuing. And I'm going with him," he said.

"What?! You can't just leave," I said incredulously.

He leveled me with a serious look. "You need time to recover. Additionally, I have diplomatic experience. I've dealt with the Scholars and the Sages for years as well as the Worthy. If I can do anything to help prevent a coming war I have to try."

"So you and Ryker are going on some buddy trip together? You two hate each other. You just punched him in the face the other day." I crossed my arms over my chest.

"I think we're actually understanding each other a little more now, and despite me hitting him, we're not as hostile toward one another. I don't know." He shrugged. "He's not so bad."

"He's still an ass…" I grumbled.

Nikan chuckled, "I didn't say he wasn't. But regardless, I'm going with him, and someone needs to guide the other Atarans"

I pursed my lips. "I still don't understand why it should be me."

"They've been isolated for the last two decades, and none of them seem to have the skills or knowledge on how this needs to be done."

I scoffed, "And I do?"

Nikan held my stare for a moment. "You grew up in Morah. You've studied our realm and our Nation's history. And you know Kya. You know how she would handle things. How she *will* handle things. We just need to protect Atara until she comes back."

I tried not to roll my eyes. I wasn't about to get into another argument with him about this. I still didn't believe she was alive, but I could at least do this for Nikan, for my people. I wouldn't do this with the hopes Kya was coming back but with the expectation she wasn't. We could hold off until things were settled with the other Nations, hold a vote and—

Ayen's ass… Am I actually considering doing this?

"Nik," I sighed. "They don't trust me."

"Then make them. You're off the demid. You'll always struggle with it, but show them who you are, and they'll see." He placed a hand on my shoulder. "I won't be gone forever, and when I'm able, I'll be right beside you. Then we'll have Kya by our side too."

"Yeah, how is that going to work exactly?" I asked, leaning back.

"What do you mean?"

"What is your grand plan to bring Kya back?" I clarified.

"For starters, I'm going to be the lure for Daegel. The dark book is the bait. If we can subdue Daegel, Ryker thinks we can convince him to trade the book for Kya."

"The book we don't want him to have? We don't even know what he wants with it or what would happen if he got his evil little hands on it," I said.

This whole situation was just fucked up.

"Can't you just kill him?" I asked.

"Trust me. I would love to. But I'm not sure I can. Not to mention, we certainly can't until we get Kya back from him."

"This is a shit plan," I mumbled under my breath.

We sat in silence for a few minutes, listening to the peaceful bustle of the warriors outside getting ready to settle down for the evening.

I heard Hakoa in the distance, and I wanted to be near him. I could still feel the electric shock from when he grazed his knuckles across the back of my hand from before. And I wanted to thank him for stepping in and standing up for me.

"When do you leave?" I said, breaking the comfortable silence.

"Before dawn. So, I better go get some sleep." Nikan stood, pulling me to stand and embracing me, then placed a kiss on top of my hair.

As he left, I caught a glimpse of Hakoa walking between the tents a few rows down. I rushed out, waving to Nikan as I followed where Hakoa was headed until I caught up to him.

He entered his tent, the cloth flap closing just as I approached.

I didn't know where we were together. I had been horrible to him back in Morah, but then we shared that moment after I asked him to take the demid from me. We hadn't actually spoken since then unless it was in Acalen about the Atarans.

I didn't deserve his forgiveness nor his kindness. After all I had done to him, he had been there for me. He could have just been there in Atara because Ryker made him. But he touched my hand earlier...

"Uh, Hakoa," I called quietly. "It's Malina."

My heart raced, and my stomach knotted when no answer came.

"I just wanted to talk to you for a minute. But if you don't want to—"

A hand popped out from inside the tent and grabbed my wrist, yanking me inside through the opening. My body slammed into Hakoa's, and I looked up just before his lips pressed against mine.

I wasn't going to question it. Just like back in Atara, the feeling of his lips against mine was like coming up for air. We needed to talk, but right now all I could think about was his hand reaching up to cup my face, tilting my head back to deepen the kiss. There was a desperation to it but it wasn't rushed.

His tongue swiped across the seam of my lips, and I parted them for him. The moment I felt his tongue against mine, everything else fell away. I didn't feel the pain and shame I had been carrying for so long. I didn't remember anything, living only in the comfort of the moment. All the noise in my head finally quieted, and I was at peace.

This was better than any poisonous drop that had ever touched my lips.

I met each languid stroke of his tongue with my own. Each movement made my stomach flutter, and every place he touched me was scorching like fire against my skin. It was too much yet not enough at the same time.

My hands wrapped around the back of his neck, running my fingers through his short hair.

The kiss was slow and controlled, as if he were savoring every moment just as much as I was. There wasn't anywhere I had to be. No one to keep it hidden from. Nothing to get in the way.

I wasn't going to push him away again.

Hakoa pulled back with a small smile on his face and rested his forehead against mine. "Sorry. I had to. I couldn't stop myself any longer," he whispered.

"It's okay. I'm glad you did," I breathed.

It certainly helped to clear things up on how he felt.

He took half a step back but reached down to take my hand in his. "How are you?"

"Right now? Fantastic."

His smile widened, showcasing his teeth. "Good. Because I can't promise I won't do that again."

Yes, please do.

He pulled me over to a set of small chairs, and we sat down next to each other, with my hand still in his. "What did you want to talk about?"

My mind blanked. I had completely forgotten everything, too distracted by his lips from moments before.

"I...um. Oh, I wanted to thank you," I said, finally remembering.

He tilted his head to the side slightly. His thumb stroked the back of my hand.

"For kissing you?"

"No. I mean, yes. Thank you for that too," I stumbled on my words.

For Nox's sake, Mal. Get it together.

"I wanted to thank you, for earlier. When you backed me up in front of the Atarans. And for the other day with...you know," I said sheepishly.

Hakoa's face softened. "I didn't do anything, Malina. You did. It was all you. It was your decision. And as for earlier, you're welcome, but I meant what I said. You are deserving of their trust."

I gave a tight-lipped smile. I didn't feel like I deserved it.

"I, um, also wanted to say how sorry I am for what I said to you back in Morah." I looked down at my lap, not wanting to look in his eyes. "I was trying to hurt you—to get you to leave. I was so obsessed with taking another dose, and I didn't want you to see who I had become."

He tensed, squeezing my hand and staying silent for several moments.

Shame washed over me. I still wanted demid. I wanted it every second, but I knew how far I had fallen, and I never wanted to be like that again.

"It's ironic, really," he said finally. He hooked a finger under my chin and lifted my head to look at him. I was surprised to find a grin on his lips. "Because now you understand the same obsession I have with you. And how damn hard it was for me to walk away."

"But...what I said to you... You deserve someone better."

"I deserve you. We're meant to be together. I know it," he said with certainty.

"If we were truly meant to be together then the Gods would have willed it with a bond." I had never really cared about the bond, but the words left my lips before I realized.

"Then they made a mistake. I refuse to believe it was an accident we were created to exist in the same lifetime and not be made to be together."

My heart leapt. "But I've messed everything up."

He stroked his thumb over my lip. "I don't care what you've done or who you've fucked before *this* moment, so long as after it, you're with *me*." His eyes were hard and unyielding.

My lip trembled and tears welled, blurring my vision. I closed my eyes, and the tears fell down my cheeks. His thumb pulled at my lower lip, brushing against it before he kissed me softly.

"I'm not mad at you, sunshine. Yes, it hurt. I won't lie about that. But you walked away from that overwhelming fixation on your own, and trust me, I know how difficult it is. Even *I* wasn't strong enough to do it. Not from you. I am so fucking proud of you," he said against my mouth and kissed me again. "Now, come here."

Hakoa pulled me onto his lap and held me, kissing me through the tears falling down my face.

I didn't deserve this. I didn't deserve him. But I was grateful, and I promised myself right then I would never hurt him like that again.

After I was done crying like some emotional idiot and pulled myself together, it was time to start making up for the mistakes I had made.

"I won't let you down. I promise never to take demid again. I won't even drink," I swore.

"You can probably still drink—"

"No," I said firmly. "I don't trust myself not to spiral. And I want to prove to my people I can be trusted like you assured them."

He nodded slowly. "Alright."

"And I want to show them Atara. They need to see it. I won't let them think you vouched for me falsely."

The side of his mouth lifted. "I agree. When do you want to show them?"

"Right now."

Chapter Forty-Seven

RYKER

I met Theron on the roof several hours later after he returned from another realm.

"Anything?" I asked the dragon, desperate for good news.

He shook his large head. *"No. I checked several realms, and she was not in any."*

I released a heavy breath. *"Alright. I need to go to Pliyya then I want you to keep searching. But first, we need to get Nikan along the way."*

He growled slightly but Traveled me away when I placed a hand on his scaly leg. After getting Nikan at the Noavo encampment outside Acalen, Theron took us to Pliyya.

We appeared just outside the capital of Dusan behind a patch of trees barely large enough to hide Theron's massive body.

"I'll let you know when I need you," I said as Nikan and I began to walk away, but we stopped short when a wolf as large as a small horse, materialized in front of us.

The creature—the Spirit—had white fur that glowed in the sunlight streaming through the trees. It bared its teeth and released a low, threatening growl. Theron lowered his head next to me, snapping at the wolf with smoke rippling through his fangs.

They stared at each other for a few moments in some silent conversation.

"Daciana has concerns you are here to harm her Worthy and insists you are not welcome in this Nation," Theron said, relaying the words of Asmen's Fylgjur.

"I'm not a threat to Asmen. I only wish to speak with her," I said to the wolf.

Nikan stiffened. He couldn't hear Theron's thoughts and was wary of Asmen's Guardian.

She looked at me for a moment before returning her gaze to Theron as they conversed again, completely ignoring the Roav next to me.

"You are permitted to speak with Udon's Worthy, but she will remain in your presence for the duration of your stay," Theron said after a minute. *"I do not recommend stepping out of line near Daciana. She is a temperamental bitch who will attack you if she feels her Worthy is in danger. Behave so I do not have to eat her,"* Theron huffed then disappeared into thin air.

I looked at Daciana who had her eyes narrowed at me. "Lead the way, Guardian."

It had been nearly two hundred years since I stepped foot in the capital of my birth Nation and while so much had changed since then, it was shocking how much hadn't. New homes had been erected, but the larger buildings had stayed the same. I didn't need the Spirit wolf to guide me through the city, with its straight roads going north to south and east to west, it was the easiest city in the Nation to navigate. Not to mention the Pliyya palace was a beacon on the southern tip of the city where you could see the ocean on the horizon when you stood on the roof.

The atmosphere here was different. People walked calmly along the streets with a sense of refinement that mirrored their clean-cut appearance of light-colored attire and skin devoid of tattoo markings. It was astonishing how different I had become, with my body covered in black clothing, and my skin riddled with ink over my arms and torso.

It wasn't surprising so many heads turned as we walked beside the wolf toward the Pliyya palace, not just because we looked so out of place amongst the citizens but because I was the Lord of another Nation. Very rarely, and generally not for good reasons, did Worthy enter other Nations. If uninvited, it was typically considered an act of war, but with Asmen's Spirit beside me, the concerned looks eased a bit.

Winding our way through the city, we finally came to the Pliyya palace—a large rectangular building towered into the sky, made of cerulean-colored stone with a pyramidal roof. Skorn warriors of Dusan stood guard at the palace door, but upon seeing Daciana, they allowed us to pass. We were led through the foyer into a small sitting room where the wolf growled at us then left.

I assumed she went to retrieve Asmen, so I took the opportunity to glance at our surroundings. Colorful art decorated the walls above fashionable furniture, making the palace feel homey and engaging—

I stopped dead in my tracks when a voice I didn't recognize sounded in my mind.

"The Lord of Oryn. How interesting."

I spun on my heel to find Asmen, the new Worthy of Dusan standing in the doorway with a polite close-lipped grin. I remembered seeing her in the Temple of Odes during the Trial, but she looked different now.

Her rich, dark skin was swathed in a white dress that matched her Spirit wolf standing next to her. Her once half-shaven head of curly, black hair now extended down to her shoulder on one side and down to her waist on the other. The glint in her bright brown eyes reflected curiosity and intrigue.

My jaw nearly dropped when she spoke into my mind again.

"Welcome to Dusan, Lord Ryker. We have much to discuss." Her eyes snapped to Nikan before returning to me. *"In private."*

"Nikan, wait for me in the foyer. I'll let you know when you can return." I nodded toward the doorway.

Nikan and I had discussed him joining me. I tended to get a little hostile with these kinds of encounters, and he had political experience, regularly dealing with discrepancies between parties. Asking him to leave defeated the purpose of him being here, but this wasn't my palace or my Nation so the respectful thing was to accommodate Lady Asmen's wishes.

Nikan nodded then left the room, closing the door behind him.

"Lady Asmen," I verbally replied to her intrusion. "You're a mind wielder."

Not only was being a mind wielder forbidden, but it was extremely rare. So rare, in fact, I had only ever encountered one other naturally-born mind wielder. I heard a few weeks later after meeting him he had been discovered by the Sages and was killed by the Nex. It took me by surprise, finding another person with mind abilities. Not to mention if she told anyone about mine…

"I'm not actually," she said. "I'm a born air wielder, but my gift from Udon is imitation."

I tilted my head to the side. I had never heard of a magical ability like that. The God of Mischief certainly gave her a unique gift.

Asmen sighed. "It's more of a proximity thing. When I'm near someone, I can imitate their abilities, elemental or otherwise, but only to a certain degree. For example…"

She reached out her hand toward one of the fire-lit sconces and wielded it toward her, holding a small flame above her palm as it pulsed like a gentle heartbeat.

"I can manipulate fire when I'm near a fire wielder such as yourself, but I can't create it, and it can still burn me. I can move water and wield terbis, but I can't shape it or morph it. And with mind," she paused, then spoke directly in my head, *"I can hear your thoughts and speak in your mind, but I can't do much else. Which means you can do so much more. Tell me, Lord Ryker, do you see memories? Do you erase them? Can you change my thoughts or even fill my mind with ones that were never there?"*

I kept my mind focused on anything else than the answers, actively thinking of only her words over and over so she was hearing herself rather than the truth.

I cleared my throat. "That's impressive. It's a gifted ability I've never seen, and one that could be very beneficial."

Imitating Jymar's elemental negation came to mind specifically.

"And how would Lord Jymar's negation be beneficial to me?" she asked, clearly having listened to my thoughts.

I leveled her with a hard stare. "It's impolite to mind wield without permission," I seethed.

Asmen shrugged. "I don't really know how to stop it."

In an instant, I penetrated her mind. I found as many memories as I could and grasped them, bringing them to the forefront and flooding her mind with them. She shook her head and blinked rapidly, trying to clear the thoughts. With her mind so overwhelmed, she was unable to hear *my* thoughts. Her hands came up to her head, grabbing it tightly, and she began whimpering.

"Learn how to stop it, or I will force you to," I demanded.

Her wide eyes met mine with a look of pure horror.

I pulled back, releasing my hold on her memories and putting them back where they belonged. I heard her throwing around vulgar thoughts about me before I left her mind entirely.

"I'm just one Worthy. Imagine facing several coming for you. Which is exactly what will happen if you and I don't work together. That's why I'm here," I said, bringing us to the reason I came to speak with her in the first place.

"And why do you believe they would come for me?"

"Because you're alone. You're new. You've never had to defend your Nation before, and the other Worthy will take advantage of that." I crossed my arms over my chest.

"I'm listening," she said with a twinge of fear.

"First, I have a question. Do you know why the other Worthy denied a meeting with me?"

"Yes," she said without hesitation.

"Care to share?" I asked.

"They're plotting to march on Atara and claim it once it's fully restored. And at the rate the Glaev is disappearing, I'd say it's going to happen soon," she stated.

I stilled and narrowed my eyes. "How do you know about their plans? Are you in an alliance with them?"

"They certainly wanted me to be, but no. After the panel regarding your mating, Jymar and Dainos offered a handsome proposition. One that would result in sharing the land and resources of Atara, and giving Dusan a larger portion."

"Why would they do that?" I asked through gritted teeth.

"Because they wanted to use Dusan as the point of entry. Mainly to stay away from you. They can't exactly march through Oryn, and you could meet them on the field in Riyah," she said.

"And you denied their proposal?" I asked suspiciously. "Why?"

"I have morals. I think it's wrong to capitalize on a dead Worthy's land. Not to mention, I don't want anyone from Ulrik in my Nation. It's bad enough I have Gaol on one side of Dusan, I don't want their filth on the other side too."

"Since you refused to work with them, does that mean you would be open to working with me? To protect Atara." It was helpful enough that she wasn't allowing Gaol and Ulrik to use Dusan as a strategic point of access to Atara, but if I could get her on my side, it could increase the chances of actually holding them off.

"You want me to send my people to fight for Atara, an empty Nation with no Worthy, not just once, but forever? I may be new to leading a Nation, but even I know that's unrealistic," she scoffed.

What's the harm in telling her the truth?

"What if I told you Atara's Worthy *isn't* dead and she's coming back? You wouldn't have to help me protect it forever, just for a little while."

Asmen bit her cheek as she contemplated this new information. After a moment, she nodded. "I'm intrigued. Why don't we discuss it?" She gestured for us to sit.

"I'd like to bring Nikan back in if you don't mind. He's the brother to Worthy Kya."

Asmen nodded.

I walked over and poked my head out the door and told Nikan to come in with us. I took the chair across from her while he sat in the chair beside mine.

"Start with where your mate is coming back from." Asmen crossed her legs and leaned forward, listening intently.

I summarized what happened. That Kya fell into the Rip, sacrificing herself to rid the realm of the dark wielder, but that our bond hadn't broken and I knew she was alive as well as Daegel. I explained that Daegel's appearance after his fall was proof he was able to somehow travel between realms and that meant I could find some way of getting Kya back to ours.

Nikan stayed silent during the interaction, allowing me to lead until I needed his interference as previously discussed.

"So," Asmen started after my explanation. "What would this cooperation between our three Nations entail?"

"Well, for starters, I want to ensure it will be mutually beneficial for all parties involved." No matter what we agreed on, I would make certain Kya didn't suffer simply because she wasn't here. "That leaves our first order of business: what do you want out of this alliance?"

She raised her chin. "I want open trade between the three Nations, with permitted travel across the borders for merchants. I don't want Dusan to rely on doing business solely with the other Nations if we're going to war with them."

Seemed reasonable. I nodded and opened my mouth to agree but stopped when Nikan spoke.

"With the agreement of single checkpoints for the inspection of goods. No prohibited merchandise should be allowed to pass any of the borders," he said firmly.

Like demid.

"Agreed," I said with a nod.

"Agreed," Asmen replied. "And what is it that you want for Oryn and Atara?"

"Dusan fights alongside Oryn to protect Atara. This will also extend to Dusan if you were ever under the threat of attack. We would join forces in all instances of assault against our Nations." It felt wrong setting terms and agreements on Kya's behalf without her consent, but if I hadn't, then there was a chance she wouldn't have a Nation to come back to.

Asmen contemplated for a moment. "For how long?"

"Whether it's for the next five years or five hundred—as long as you, Kya, and I live—the guidelines of our alliance will be upheld by all parties," I offered. "Additionally, we should also be open and forthcoming with any and all information about the other Nations with one another."

"I can agree to these terms." She nodded and leaned back in her seat.

"And that we keep each other's gifted abilities a secret," I said into her mind.

"I have no qualms with that whatsoever. It wouldn't do either of us any good if our abilities were discovered, and we were killed. Having magic giving me forbidden abilities wasn't what I anticipated." She grinned.

It wasn't a perfect agreement, but it was a start.

"Thank you, Lady Asmen," I said as I stood to leave now that we had an agreement between our Nations. Nikan stood as well, bowing his head.

"What about Torx?" she asked, stopping me mid-step. "He hadn't agreed with Jymar and Voron, but he didn't flat-out deny them either."

I sighed.

Fucking Dainos…

"We'll be going there now. I'll keep you informed." I nodded, then we left.

Chapter Forty-Eight

Ryker

Theron Traveled us just outside of Narh, the capital of Torx. The last time I was here, Kya and I had our first encounter in an alleyway that didn't exactly go as planned. I tried not to think back on that memory and kept my mind focused on the task at hand—going to the palace and meeting with Dainos to convince him to work with me to defend Atara.

Theron disappeared, returning to his search, as Nikan and I made our way into the city. The streets were eerily quiet. While Narh was typically bustling with people during the day, it seemed more barren than I had seen in the past. And there was an unusual amount of people from other Nations.

Torx people were generally distinguished by their dreadlock hair and muscular bodies, but I noted several people from Gaol and Ulrik—with their pierced faces and half-shaven heads. I eyed them warily and kept my hood up as we wound our way through the city.

"So," Nikan drawled. "When the war starts, Mavris will be joining us in Atara, right? He'll be there?"

"Why?"

"I just figured you'd want your brother there. I'm sure he's a powerful wielder. What was his element again?" he asked.

I refrained from audibly groaning, but I couldn't stop my eyes from rolling. "Nope. We're not doing this."

"Doing what?" he feigned ignorance.

"I'm not getting into your relationship with my brother." I shook my head.

I didn't care who Mavris slept with but I really didn't want to get involved in their drama. I had enough shit on my mind I didn't need to add whatever it was they had going on to my mental load.

"I don't know what you're talking about." He shrugged.

"Uh huh. I swear, the two of you..." I shook my head. Mavris kept doing the same thing—subtly asking about Nikan whenever he could. "Look, whatever issues you two are having, I don't want to be in the middle of it. If you want to know about Mavris, you'll need to talk to him." I hoped that would be enough to make this stop.

"I was just asking if he's going to be fighting with us or not," he clipped.

"Well, that depends. Are you two going to be able to be in the same place without sneaking off behind tents? Or do I need to keep you separated?"

His jaw fell as he gawked at me.

"For someone who doesn't want people to know your business—and a Roav at that—I'd think you'd attempt to be a little more discreet." I smirked.

I didn't have to look at him to feel his glare boring into me.

"Yeah, well, at least I didn't follow my mate around the continent because I was too scared to talk to her," he snipped and shrugged his shoulders.

I chuckled. "I guess we both have communication issues."

Nikan huffed, but he didn't argue. We remained quiet until we made it to the palace.

The Narh palace was smaller in size but grandeur in design. The exterior stone was carved in an artistry of elaborate detail of landscapes and people, creating a masterpiece of Torx history through time. It was a monument I had a great appreciation for, but now wasn't the time to marvel.

The last time I had come to the palace to meet with Dainos, his Watch guarded the entire perimeter. This time, there were only four of them stationed at the doors. We approached slowly, walking up the steps to the entrance. The Watch barely glanced at me and let me pass through the doors without so much as a word. It seemed they were expecting us.

Upon entering the palace, Coen—Dainos' advisor—was waiting for us just inside. Dainos had been the Lord of Torx since the last Trial over one hundred years ago, and I had met Coen on multiple occasions. His dark, dreadlocked hair was longer than the last time I had seen him, and he somehow looked more broad than before.

"Lord Ryker," Coen greeted, bowing his head.

"Coen," I said, keeping my head held high. "This is Nikan."

Coen nodded to Nikan.

"Why do I get the feeling you knew we were coming?" I asked.

"I don't know what you mean, Lord Ryker," he said.

I narrowed my eyes. "Don't feed me that shit. You know damn well what I mean. Why are the streets practically empty, and why were you waiting for us?"

His shoulders slumped and he sighed. "Lord Dainos had a feeling you would be coming. A lot has happened recently, and he didn't want mayhem to ensue if the people saw you storming through the city. Not to mention, he *heard* you."

Ah.

Dainos was gifted the ability to manipulate sound by Cethar, the God of Nature. He could hear from great distances, amplifying the smallest emissions for only himself or for anyone he chose. And I heard he could even silence an entire city no matter how loud it was. It was a unique gift, and one that had proven to be useful, both on and off the battlefield.

During the last battle he'd had with Gaol, he would silence his forces movements or enhance sounds in the ears of the enemy to distract them and blow their eardrums. He would listen to the opposition's strategies to learn where they would strike next and plan accordingly. Dainos made sure his gift was used to his advantage, but he still couldn't hear thoughts.

I raised a brow. "I'm here peacefully. I just need to speak with Dainos."

"He's in his study," he said, gesturing for us to follow.

Coen led us to the northern wing of the palace and stopped outside a set of double doors, pushing them open to Dainos' study.

The Lord of Torx was sitting at his desk with his hands clasped in front of him.

"Dainos," I greeted with a nod.

"Ryker." He nodded in return, ignoring Nikan entirely. "You are excused, Coen."

Coen bowed at the waist then left, closing the doors behind him.

"It's a bit unorthodox to show up unannounced in another Worthy's Nation, you know," Dainos said, leaning back in his chair, the wood creaking with the shifting weight.

I sat across from him as Nikan remained standing near the door behind me. Torx and Oryn hadn't been in a major skirmish in decades, and we had remained somewhat civil with one another in past years.

"I'm aware. But from the looks of things, you don't seem all that concerned."

He remained quiet for a moment. "I know why you're here, Ryker, and I can't do it," he said, almost apologetically.

"I don't need you to fight for me. I just need you to stay out of it," I implored.

He pursed his lips. "I'm afraid it's too late for that. I've accepted Jymar and Voron's offer. Torx has joined forces with Gaol and Ulrik."

My blood instantly ran hot.

"Why would you do that? You can't stand Jymar," I said in a low, lethal voice. My shadows snaked across the floor as my temper rose, and I stood with my fists clenched.

Dainos leaned his head back to look up at me with an unconcerned expression. Nascha, Dainos' Fylgjur, appeared on the desk between us.

The Spirit owl's wings were splayed in threat. Even with the curled horns coming from the top of her head and the deep ebony eyes that looked like they drank souls, the Spirit owl had a gentle, almost kind look about her. From the top of her head down to her tail feathers and wings, she was the color of sand on a beach, and her underside was pure white. While she didn't seem threatening at this size, I knew better than to mess with her. One wrong move and she could shift until she encompassed the size of a building and spear those that threatened her Worthy with her talons.

A second later, the building rumbled with the weight of a dragon landing on top of it.

"Just in case?" I asked Theron.

"Nascha is more unpredictable than Daciana," he said.

I leaned to the side, looking past her and glared at Dainos with a snarl.

"I didn't have much of a choice," he said.

"You had the choice to not cooperate with them and agree to launch an attack on Atara. It's on the other side of the continent for God's sake. What could you possibly want from it you're willing to lose wielders for?" my voice raised.

Dainos slapped his hands on the desk and stood leaning over it and glaring at me. "I *didn't* have a choice! It was either I risk losing a couple of trained wielders in a war against an empty Nation or guarantee wielders and citizens would die at the hands of Gaol and Ulrik forces when they turned their attention to Torx after Atara. I had to think of what was best for my people. *That's* my duty." He sighed, then continued, "If I piss off both Gaol and Ulrik, Torx would have enemies on both ends of the Nation's border. In case you haven't noticed, we're surrounded by them. They've already formed an alliance, and if I went up against them, they'd see Torx as another obstacle. I can't risk fighting alone against two Nations rather than marching on a defenseless one."

"It's not defenseless. And it's not empty. It's not even without a Worthy," Nikan interjected coldly.

"And there is no evidence of that." Dainos' eyes flicked to him. "Even if there were, it doesn't change the fact it would be neglectful on my part as Lord to oppose two powerful, bordering Nations and endanger my citizens."

Gods, I wanted to rip his head from his shoulders. Him and Jymar *and* Voron. These arrogant, greedy—

"But there is another option. One I think could prevent any loss of life," Dainos said, sitting and waving for his Spirit to leave, but she only flapped her wings and glided to perch on the window sill.

"I doubt I'd be interested," I seethed.

"Look, Jymar wants Atara for its land. He wants to capitalize on the resources and have the space to expand his people. I tried to talk him out of it, but he's extremely adamant. Voron is just following him and trying to make his mark as a new Worthy to prove himself. However, I'm willing to talk to them again on your behalf. I'm betting something could be worked out, and Jymar would be open to negotiations on splitting the land with Oryn to avoid a full-out war," Dainos appealed.

He didn't want this fight, but he knew it was coming.

I backed away and recalled my shadows before walking toward the doors with my answer.

"Ryker," Dainos called out just before I yanked the doors open.

I gleaned at him over my shoulder.

"As a courtesy, expect to see all three Nations in a fortnight. You don't have much time."

My blood boiled. Courtesy or not, he was planning to join the attack on my mate's land, forcing my hand to defend it. My eyes flashed with the promise of death.

"The next time you see me, I'll be painting the ground with your blood."

Once we left the palace, I swiftly made my way through the city, Nikan remaining silent as I simmered in my rage, until we came to the open plain outside Narh. Theron appeared a moment later.

"Agitating multiple Spirits in one day. That is impressive even for you, Worthy," he said flatly.

I smacked my hand against his shoulder. *"Just take me back to Oryn,"* I growled. *"I have a war to win."*

Chapter Forty-Nine

ZALEN

M aera was headed off to the seamstress with Riva, something to keep her content and occupied. I, on the other hand, had to deal with the complexities of absorbing two additional kingdoms while also working out what was going on in Shara—the latter being the more pressing but with the least bit of information.

Upon entering my study, there was a tala thread waiting for me, hovering over the desk. I walked to the other side of the desk and sat down before running my finger down the thread.

"I'm headed to the Shara border," Thane's voice sounded. *"Several of the scouts were compromised and killed on sight, but a few should be making it back soon. They're going to meet me to debrief, then keep their cover and return to Shara..."*

"They should remain until told otherwise or killed," I mumbled to myself as I flipped through the pages of the latest transportation reports in Aedum.

"...and I will inform them to hold their position until further notice with daily debriefing, or until they are compromised and killed."

This was why I appointed him as the King's advisor. Our similar thought processes are what made us work together so well. The light-blue thread disappeared, ending his message.

I didn't like this. I hated not knowing what was going on and who the fuck was killing the Kings. Three Kings killed by someone in the same way, by the same person. The pressing question was, did the new Sharan King hide behind his borders in fear, or was he waiting for something?

The simplest way to find out was for me to barge through the Shara border and cut out any possible threat by just killing him myself. But if he was capable of murdering the most powerful sorcerers in the Kingdoms without having absorbed magic like I had, he would have been a force to reckon with.

Since I had now absorbed the magic of two Kings, I was powerful for someone who hadn't gone through the Drehiri ritual and come into my royal magic, but I wasn't ignorant enough to think this man would be as easy as Erix.

In order for me to officially become King, I had to go through the Drehiri. The old laws of the Elders required for me to be married before I did so. Then I could take the ritual. It was one of the reasons I pushed for Maera and me to wed so quickly.

Women didn't have as many conditions. Only that they had to be married before they could become Queen. It was the best way to ensure whoever held the throne would have an heir, which was needed to keep the royal bloodline intact. The Drehiri was still a ways away so, for now, I needed Maera to work on improving her alchemy skills.

In the meantime, I still had other matters to take care of. After sorting through reports on the progress of integrating Aedum and Innon as part of the Damanthus Kingdom and eradicating any lines or borders between them, and sorting out the logistics of Thane becoming the magic holder for Innon, it was time to meet with Ander.

I got up from the desk, scooting the chair across the stone floor, and made my way from the castle to the Vord headquarters.

The Vord's numbers were significantly reduced after Makkor's funeral. Once the execution of Osar had been carried out, any of the remaining Vord who were loyal to him followed him to the grave. I wanted a clean slate of humans and magic users, and I wouldn't allow any Vord to be a disruption under Ander's new leadership.

Ander was in his study, writing at his desk, when I entered. He immediately stood and bowed low at the waist. "King Zalen," he greeted.

"Ander." I walked over to one of the chairs by a shelf of maps and sat down. "I just read a report stating the resistance in Aedum has calmed, but I haven't heard much from Innon. Tell me about the defiance there."

"There's nothing to tell. There's no hostility in Innon." He shrugged. "You ordered any opposition to your rule was to be snuffed out."

My brows raised with intrigue.

"I know you went a little easier on Aedum—I'm assuming because of the future Queen—but you gave explicit orders not to tolerate any rebellion. So I haven't. Anyone who has shown any refusal to comply has been made an example of. After the first few, everyone else fell in line, and it's been a relatively smooth process since," he said firmly. "I believe it's also partially due to their weakened magic."

I had to hand it to him, he wasn't disappointing me.

"Are there any other matters I need to be aware of?" I asked.

He shook his head. "Not particularly. However…" he was hesitant to continue. "We did find something that may be of interest to you."

Ander walked over to the door leading into a storage room and ducked his head inside. He returned holding a notebook and a stack of old-looking pages.

"Is that Maera's notebook?" I asked, recognizing her handwriting as he flipped through the pages after taking the seat next to me.

"It is. We found it amongst her things and discovered something as we were analyzing the contents of the Aedum castle."

"And what is it that you found so significant in a witch's notes?" I questioned, taking the notebook from him.

"Well, I think she found something that has been lost for a long time. Something ancient." He pulled out one of the sheets of paper and leaned over to show me some of the text. "This is from the vaults of the Aedum castle. It used to be bound, but the binding practically disintegrated when it was touched. Do you remember the old stories about Odes walking the land and being among the people?"

I cocked a brow. "The one where he threw an entire village of people in a lake of his piss, and they crawled out as magic users?"

Ander's eyes widened with an appalled look. "I'm pretty certain it was a lake of his *blood*."

I shrugged. "It's weird either way."

He shook his head. "That's not important. Anyway, the lore says that where he stepped created stones with special properties. Specifically, allowing sorcerers to travel between them."

"Oh?"

"Well…I think the Samanya heir found one," he said, staring pointedly at the notebook.

Maera had drawn some kind of design, but it honestly looked more like doodling than anything. I took the pages from Ander. There was a passage about these stones—Horgor—with a faded illustration next to it.

I sighed heavily and pinched the bridge of my nose. "Am I missing something? Why do you feel a few random mythical rocks are important right now? And what does Maera's sketch have to do with it?"

Sure, it was a fun bit of information, but it was the least of my concerns.

"Because according to legend, there are at least two of those stones in each of the Kingdoms," he said with a ghost of a smile.

My lips curled with a snarl. "I'm getting tired of you trying to have me guess what you want me to know. Just fucking say it already."

"Fine. If these stones aren't just a myth, then in theory, we could figure out a way to use them to travel directly into Shara. And look, there are landmarks near her sketch. If she knows where it is…"

"We can find it and get into Shara," I finished for him, realization dawning.

"Exactly. Then we won't have to worry about breaching the border," he said while nodding.

My lips pursed as I thought it through, inhaling sharply as I came to an understanding.

"That's how he was able to travel so quickly," I whispered under my breath.

"Who?" Ander tilted his head to the side.

I looked up at him. "The killer of the Kings." I stood abruptly. "Lock down the borders. No one in or out until I say otherwise."

Without another word, I bolted from my seat and left Ander's study, making my way back to the castle with Maera's notebook in hand. Throwing the doors open to the side entrance, I stormed through the empty halls. My boots thudded against the stone floor, echoing off the walls lined with portraits of past Kings until I came to the northern side of the castle where Maera was meeting with the seamstress.

Riva was waiting outside, leaning against the wall with her arms crossed and her head tipped back to rest against it. She looked bored, like she was about to fall asleep, until she saw me approaching and pushed off, standing with a straight spine. I flicked my hand at her, shooing her away. She didn't hesitate and darted off down the corridor.

I stopped in front of the room and peered through the crack between the doors.

Maera was standing on a pedestal in the center of the room, with the pinch-faced seamstress circling her and occasionally touching random pins threaded through the fabric draped over Maera. I watched in fascination as Maera took charge of the encounter.

"Arnesia, this side needs to be let out more, and the embroidery needs to be more even down the front. No, not there. Here, yes. See?" Maera said with her hands on her hips. I loved watching her be authoritative.

"Okay. I'll take it back and make the adjustments." Arnesia helped Maera out of the fabric that would soon be a dress, leaving her in nothing but a band around her breasts and a lacy undergarment. Arnesia then folded the fabric around her arm and left through the other door.

Maera stepped off the platform and walked over to a table with swatches of different fabrics and colors, picking them up and inspecting them one by one.

My lips lifted into a mischievous smile, and I slipped through the doorway. Slowly and silently, I approached her from behind, unable to take my eyes off her ass. All I could think about was digging my fingers into the soft flesh while she bounced up and down on top of me. Every thought I'd had before walking in here completely left my mind.

Our talk would have to wait.

She still hadn't noticed my presence, and I made a mental note to have her work on being more aware of her surroundings. Once I was directly behind her, I placed a hand on the middle of her back and pushed her face down on the table. Her body tensed, her arms shooting out to the sides to try to catch herself. She shrieked, whipping her head to the side to look at me with horror filled eyes before relaxing upon seeing me.

"What are you—" she began, but I pressed a finger against her lips.

"Taking you," I said roughly.

She tried to move, but I wouldn't let her, pushing down on her harder.

I unbuckled my belt and loosened the fastenings to my pants. Seeing her in this vulnerable position and anticipating having her around my cock in mere moments had me hard. I pulled down my pants, wrapping my hand around my length and stroking it once.

Maera gasped when I pressed against her ass.

My fingers trailed down her spine, causing her skin to pebble, until I reached the top of her undergarments and pushed them down her legs.

I kicked her feet apart, widening her stance, and guided my cock to rub along her slit back and forth, back and forth.

Her breath hitched, and her arousal soaked me. She liked it when I scared her—when I took her when she wasn't expecting it.

I gave her a short warning, aligning myself with her before I slammed into her hard.

Maera let out a sound—something between a scream and a moan—and gripped the edges of the table.

I groaned at the feeling of her cunt stretching around me as I pushed in deeper and deeper, and I only gave her a moment before I started pounding into her relentlessly. I held her firmly against the table and grabbed her hip in my other hand.

Fuck, I was close already, having had the built up tension from this morning stewing all day.

I leaned forward, letting go of her hip and reaching around her. My fingers brushed against her clit, and I could feel myself fucking her with my fingertips.

Maera let out a breathy moan as I began to swirl my fingers in a circle between her legs. Her breaths became rapid and erratic, matching mine, as I stroked and fucked harder and faster.

My balls tightened, and I couldn't hold it back any longer, craving to fall over the edge of euphoria.

I slammed into her with a deep moan as I began spilling into her, and the feeling of pure bliss flooded through every vein in my body.

I didn't stop fucking her, pushing through the oversensitivity to feel her come around my cock which felt nearly just as good as my own release.

Maera started moaning loudly, sounding animalistic as she began to tense. She let out a throaty sound when her head shot up, and she screamed with her climax, squeezing and pulsing around me.

I pumped in and out of her slowly as we both came down from the high.

She relaxed and slumped against the tabletop. I pulled out of her and grabbed one of the ugly swatches to clean her up as best as I could before pulling up her undergarment and refastening my pants.

I pulled Maera up and took her in my arms. "Hi."

She giggled, "That certainly was a wonderful hello." She lifted to the tips of her toes and kissed me.

"I came here for a different reason, but when I saw you, I couldn't stop myself," I said with a shrug.

She smiled and stepped back, giving my hand a squeeze before going to her clothes. "Don't ever stop yourself from greeting me that way."

"Anything for you, love."

She got herself dressed before walking back over to me. "So, what's the other reason you came to see me?"

I held up the notebook I'd tucked into my pocket and displayed the sketch of the stone in front of her. "We're going on a little trip."

Chapter Fifty

MALINA

"So you want us to all pack up and *leave*?" Luthon asked skeptically.

I was honestly surprised it was such a struggle to convince the Atarans to go back to Atara. I thought they'd be more receptive to the idea of finally being able to return home.

The entire population of the village had gathered to discuss this matter as I stood before them.

"Don't you want to go back?" I asked incredulously.

"Back to what?" Nyla, one of the females asked. "There's nothing there."

"Not yet. But there will be when we rebuild it," I pressed.

"Additionally, when Worthy Kya returns her people should be there," Hakoa added.

Except she won't.

I didn't argue with him, but I also wasn't going to use that as a false motivation for them to go back.

"Ryker is the only Worthy we've ever known, and he's pretty much stayed out of our way and let us live in peace here. We're grateful to him, and we really don't have a need to return to an empty Nation," Nyla stated.

...restore the balance so they may return...

That was the entire point of Kya sacrificing herself, to fulfill her task for Kleio and bring the Atarans back to their homeland. And possibly not just the ones here…

"There is a reason," I said. "Kya was given a task by Kleio, as all Worthy are. Her task was to restore the balance so we may return to Atara. She did just that." I gestured south, in the direction of Atara. "Before Kya…*fell*," I chose my words carefully, "she exhausted her reserves to clear the Glaev with her magic. She did all of this for *you*. And she didn't even *know* you."

For them. The last words she said to me.

"The very least we can do for her sacrifice is protect what she restored so it wasn't all for nothing." I hadn't realized my voice grew louder until I saw their raised brows.

But I meant it.

"Thank you, Malina," Luthon said earnestly, nodding. "We didn't know any of that."

"I'm not finished," I said, raising my chin. "Kya thought her task meant more than just restoring Atara. She thinks it may reference our people on the Drift Islands returning. Now that Atara is being healed, the Spirits could bring them back. And I fully intend on being in our Nation when they do. I'm going to protect Atara with the Noavo so our people trapped on the islands have a home to return to." I took a step back. "I hope I won't be alone."

Everyone was silent for a moment, taking in my words.

"I think we should go—to fight to protect our Nation. At least some of us. It shouldn't just be left to Oryn to protect what is ours," Niabi said as she stepped forward.

"I agree." Luthon nodded.

"Have any of you actually fought before? Even if you have, no one has in over twenty years," Nyla stated. She wasn't being difficult. Just realistic, and I respected that.

"Then like Niabi said, just some of you—who are willing and able—come. I can teach you to fight, or at the very least defend yourselves," I offered.

"I think that's reasonable. Then we can talk about settling when Worthy Kya returns or the threat of the other Nations has ended," Luthon announced loudly so everyone could hear.

It wasn't exactly what I had in mind, but it was a start.

It takes a while for nearly half a village to gather all of their belongings in preparation to leave. I helped as much as I could, packing and loading carts that would carry the Atarans' things to our Nation.

Almost every Noavo from the encampment outside Acalen joined in our travels. They acted more as an escort in the event we encountered one of the other Nations. Everyone was provided a horse, and several pulled carts filled with belongings.

Hakoa and I rode side-by-side in the lead as we guided the group around the Ataran border where it was clear at the crosspoint with Riyah and Oryn.

With a practiced motion, he wielded the snow in front of us, clearing a path so we wouldn't have to trudge through the deep powder that would otherwise come up to our knees.

Hakoa and I talked during the day-long ride, and it was the most we had spoken to each other since we met. Just hours and hours of me telling him about being a Roav, the missions I'd gone on and places I'd seen. Being so much older, his own life was filled with stories of the past from decades and centuries before I even came into existence. It made me realize I had barely even lived in comparison, and I had so much ahead of myself.

Keeping a smile on my face, I felt shameful inside. He had lived hundreds of years, gone through horrendous wars, watched people die, and it took only twenty-seven years for me to nearly destroy my life from demid because I lost my sister. I felt like a failure. But I also knew I had overcome it. And now, I had my whole life ahead of me—in my homeland.

Walking alongside the Ataran border, there was nothing but black on the other side—not even the snow touched the decimated land. I could hear the whispers behind me: still disbelieving Atara was healing and they had left Acalen for nothing.

Soon. Soon, they would understand.

"How far are we from the Noavo base?" I asked quietly.

"Not far. A couple more hours." He steered his horse closer so he could put a hand on my thigh. "Don't worry about them," he whispered and nodded his head back toward the group behind us. "They'll see for themselves. Not much longer now."

He was right. While we were still a bit away from the base, the Glaev had cleared farther up than our destination. After going around a tree-covered hillside, we stopped in our tracks and gasps sounded all around.

I would never tire of seeing this.

Where there was once nothing but desolation that promised death, there was now the newly formed life of Atara.

We all dismounted and stepped up to the border, standing side-by-side.

The imaginary lines our ancestors drew between the Nations had never been more evident. The tips of our boots were resting on the clear divide—our feet standing on a layer of snow in Oryn that met the beginnings of vegetation regrowth in Atara.

The vast, empty landscape sang to us all, calling us home.

Everyone seemed hesitant, so I took the first step into Atara to show them it was safe. I looked at each and every one of them. Tears flowed down their cheeks and mouths gaped in awe. I turned to face Luthon who was next to me.

"It's… It's real," he breathed a whisper of disbelief.

"It is. It's what we'll be fighting for." I smiled broadly, honored to be here for this moment.

I took his hands in mine, and he looked at me, his auburn eyes glistening. I took a step back, pulling him forward so he too could stand on our land for the first time in twenty years after being driven out by the dark magic.

"Welcome home," I said, voice breaking.

We may not have known each other, but we shared the same loss, and now we got to share getting it back.

The moment his foot stepped onto the grass, his eyes closed, and tears streamed down his cheeks.

I stepped away, leaving him to have this surreal moment.

One by one, I went to each and every Ataran, taking their hands and leading them forward to stand on their land once again.

Hakoa watched the entire time with a proud grin. I walked over and stood in front of him. He was still standing on the snow-covered land of Oryn.

It was more representative than anything, but I wanted him to know that I wanted him here with me too. That he was welcome. I grabbed his hands and held his tender gaze, tugging him as I remained in place. He stepped forward until our bodies pressed against each other, and I had to tilt my head back to look up at him.

His eyes were like fire, burning into me with a passion that made my breath hitch. His hand came up and brushed my hair behind my ear.

I leaned into his touch, and he lowered his head toward me, his eyes locked on my lips. My own parted as he neared—

"Alright, you two," Niabi interrupted.

Hakoa stopped and rolled his eyes.

I huffed a laugh and smiled, turning my head to look at her.

"You can have your moment later. Let's get going," she said and went back to the cart she was riding in.

Hakoa chuckled and leaned down to kiss my forehead then gave my hand a squeeze. "Later it is then." He winked.

My stomach fluttered. "Only if you think you're up for it," I said with a playful grin, and walked back to my horse, putting a little extra sway in my hips because I knew he was watching.

I heard him sigh before he got back on his horse next to me. Then we all headed back down the path.

As we came around the ridge a few hours later, we arrived at one of the bases on the border of Atara to Riyah. From the looks of it, they were in the late stages of setting up and were nearly ready to face what would come.

I hadn't realized how many Noavo there actually were. Only having seen the command station outside Voara, the base was filled with more warriors than I thought they had in their entirety. But this was just one base, and Hakoa had informed me there were dozens along the border.

After dismounting our horses, terbis wielders began erecting tents and settling in for the evening. Hakoa took me by the hand and led me to the center of the base where there was a recently erected larger stone structure, the dirt still clinging to the rock walls from where it was wielded from the ground. It didn't have a cloth covering for the doorway as the tents did and was left open.

Upon entering, I noticed a familiar figure with a head of red hair.

"...yeah, well, when your Chief arrives he can tell you himself. But in the meantime—"

"Arra," Hakoa greeted with a warning. "What have I told you about being nice to the warriors?"

Arra spun on her heel, her boots crunching the frost-covered grass beneath her. "It's about time you showed up!" She placed her hands firmly on her hips. "And I *am* being nice to them. They're just overly sensitive little brutes."

"It's called wanting to be respected," Hakoa argued with a raised brow.

"I'm *respecting* the fact that they need more discipline rather than having someone who placates their feelings." She crossed her arms over her chest.

The warrior male started to leave and raised a hand to her, displaying a crude gesture.

Arra bared her teeth and flicked her hand. A gust of wind whipped through the air, smacking the warrior in the back of the head on the way out.

Hakoa sighed and pinched the bridge of his nose. "Arra, it's getting late, and I'm tired. We've been traveling all day. Just give me the reports, and I'll... I'll let you yell orders at the warriors during the formation exercises tomorrow."

Arra pursed her lips in contemplation. "Fine," she said with a sweet smile—well, about as sweet as a raw radish dipped in pepper oil. "But I get the morning *and* afternoon runs."

I bit my cheek to keep from smiling. I forgot how much I liked her.

She grabbed a stack of papers from the table and handed it to him then started to leave with a pleased grin. "Good to see you, Mal. Wanna grab a drink? I could use someone who can hold down their liquor."

Yes.

After such a long day, winding down and throwing back a few sounded like a great way to end the evening. My gut twisted.

"Uh, no. Thank you though. I think I'll just head to my tent and rest up for the night. I have another long day ahead of me training the Atarans," I said.

She tilted her head to the side and looked at Hakoa. "*You're not training them?*"

"We're kind of preparing for a war," Hakoa said flatly.

"That's kind of the point of having generals—to take some of these burdens from you," she said pointedly. "Besides, isn't the purpose of all this to protect Atara *and* its people? Someone needs to train them in basic defense at the very least."

"That's the plan for Malina." Hakoa nodded.

She rolled her eyes before meeting my stare. "Malina, how many people have you trained for combat?"

Damn. Okay, then.

"None," I said quietly.

Arra nodded. "My point exactly. And Hakoa here has trained thousands. Not to mention, who better to protect them than the greatest water wielder in Oryn?"

I felt a hit to my pride. "I can protect them too, you know."

She leveled me with a flat stare. "Against a few others? Sure. I have no doubt. I've seen you spar. You're extremely talented. But against a mass of very powerful and trained wielders? Be real. Your light wielding is cute and all, but it's not going to stop them from slaughtering your people. No offense."

Now I remember why I didn't like her at first.

But she was right. Light wielding wasn't as effective as a physical element that could actually kill. And other than training *with* Kya and Nikan, I had never actually taught someone before.

"Then I'll help train them too, and at the same time, show Malina how to train anyone in the future," Hakoa offered with a nod. "Does that sound good?"

Someone shouted Arra's name from outside and she glanced toward the voice and nodded, holding up a finger to them before looking back at us. "Yeah. Sounds good. Malina, are you sure you don't want a drink? We should catch up."

It sounded like fun, and I really didn't want to miss out on the opportunity. I didn't want to turn her down, and for a split second, I thought maybe just one drink wouldn't hurt. But I knew it would. And I knew it would lead to much worse.

"I'm sure," I said with a forced smile, hiding my disappointment. "I'll catch up with you later."

"Alright then. See you on the line in the morning, Hakoa." She waved as she left.

Hakoa ran a hand down his face. "She's exhausting, but she means well," he sighed. "Come on. We're done for the day."

"Thank the Gods." My legs were killing me from riding.

He led me to what I assumed was my tent near the middle of the base. He gestured for me to go inside, pulling back the thick cloth of the entrance. I entered, and he followed.

From the clothes in the corner, to the maps laid on top of a table, I realized this was actually *his* tent.

"Where—" I was cut off when Hakoa spun me around and pressed his lips to mine. It was soft and gentle yet desperate and hungry.

Melting into him, I parted my lips, meeting his tongue for each languid stroke.

"I want to do more than kiss you, but I need to know if you want that too," he said against my lips.

My eyes fluttered open, flicking up to meet his searching gaze. I bit my lip. Holding his gaze, I grabbed the hem of my shirt and pulled it up over my head, discarding it on the floor. I took him by the wrist and brought his hand to my breast over the binding.

"Does that answer your question? Because I want to do more than kiss you too," I whispered.

I missed him. I missed his touch, the feel of his body against mine with nothing between us.

His lips curved up. "Then tell me exactly what you want."

A warm feeling pooled in my lower belly. He was giving me control, despite his own usual preference for dominance.

"Undress me."

Without hesitation, he slid to his knees and unlaced my boots, pulling them off and placing them to the side. I watched as he unfastened my pants and began to pull them down, kissing up my thigh slowly. He lifted each foot from the cold ground, removing my pants one leg at a time until I was left in nothing but my undergarments.

When he stood, his eyes trailed down my body, drinking me in with a pleased purr. I saw the outline of his hard cock straining against the fastenings of his pants.

I knew he wanted me to be in control, but I needed him to do the work. I needed him to bring me pleasure. I needed to feel as if I was more than a tool for release—more than just payment. *That* was the control I needed.

"Keep going," I breathed.

With a hungry glint in his eyes, Hakoa slowly removed the band around my breasts. His breath hitched, and his tongue swiped across his lower lip before he bent down and flicked each nipple with his tongue after grazing his teeth over them.

I wanted those teeth to bite hard enough to leave an impression like they had before, but I resisted the roughness for now, allowing this to be a much more gentle experience.

He slowly slid down my panties, and I stepped out of them. He inhaled deeply, scenting the arousal pooling between my legs. He took a step back, and I wasn't sure he was breathing when he took in my bare form completely exposed.

Flashes of my shameful actions seeped to the forefront of my mind, and I felt self-conscious all of a sudden—thinking of how all of those males had only cared for what my body had to offer.

"Tell me what you want, Malina," he demanded gently, rising and stroking a gentle finger across my jaw.

I backed away and went over to the pile of warm furs to lay down on my back, spreading my legs in invitation. No one had been on top of me since him, as I had been the one to service others.

I swallowed and breathed a whisper. "I want to forget."

The side of his lips twitched up into a smirk as he came to kneel at my feet. "With pleasure."

He gracefully flourished his hand, wielding a small stream of water. It was surprisingly warm as it wound its way up my calf, my thigh, until it reached my core.

The sensation of the water flowing over my clit was unlike anything I had ever experienced, the rush thrumming against me and making my eyes roll to the back of my head.

I gasped a loud moan.

"Shh," Hakoa shushed. "Those cries are only for me now. No one else will ever hear them again."

I suddenly became fully aware of the sounds of people just outside the tent which only excited me more. I bit down on my tongue, forcing myself to keep quiet through the waves of pleasure rushing up from between my legs.

"Tell me what you want," he said in a husky voice.

I opened my eyes to find his heavy, lust-filled eyes trained on my face.

"More," I rasped as the pressure of the stream increased.

With the water still humming across my clit, Hakoa pressed a finger to my entrance, pushing it in. Then he added a second finger, stretching me blissfully. He pumped his fingers slowly, curling them forward to hit the point that made my vision spotty.

My fingers dug into the furs, gripping them in my palms, needing to hold onto something.

He leaned forward so he was over me, his mouth hovering above mine and allowing his fingers to go deeper. He worked me thoroughly and with such attentiveness—watching every facial expression. It was as if he was challenging himself, seeing how much pleasure he could bring to the surface before tampering down and dragging it out tortuously.

But it was the look in his eyes that took my breath away.

"Ha—Hakoa," I moaned, louder than I should have, but I couldn't help it.

"Do you remember now?" he asked, keeping his eyes on me.

"It's not just forgetting. I don't want to feel anything either," I said, but beginning to realize perhaps I was wrong.

"It's not about not feeling anything. It's about feeling the right things. Does this feel right to you?"

"Gods, yes."

It wasn't just what he was doing to my pussy. It was something else... I wanted more of it.

I reached for his pants and slid my hand inside.

He groaned as I wrapped my fingers around him. The fading sun's light glowing from behind the cloth created deep shadows over the contours of his tense features.

I gave a long stroke up and down his shaft, from the base to the tip—where there was a bead of moisture. I rubbed my thumb over it, spreading it around as I imagined it was my tongue lapping up his arousal.

"Unfasten your pants," I commanded breathlessly, my body tensing as my release neared. I had to admit, giving an order to the Chief of the Noavo felt good—powerful—and it only turned me on more. He had always been the one to tell me what to do, to stay still, to take it. But he was giving me that power for the first time so I could be in control here.

Hakoa sat up on his knees, removed his fingers from me, and licked them, groaning at the taste. He did as I said and tugged at the seam until it was loose enough for me to pull his cock free.

I didn't hesitate to take what I wanted, and I leaned up to wrap my mouth around him.

"Oh fuck, Malina," his voiced strained in a whisper.

The water reverberated against me more intensely, keeping speed with my enthusiastic licking and sucking. I was so, so close. It was almost too much yet not enough. This sensation was like nothing I had ever felt before.

"Tell me what you want," Hakoa said, almost pleading.

I drew him in deep to the back of my throat before I pulled myself off him. Pure, craving desire was etched across his face as I gazed up at him.

"I want *you.*"

His pupils dilated, and there was a pause for just a heartbeat. He threw his hand out to the side, wielding the water away from me, leaving me feeling cold as it splashed against the stone wall of the tent.

His mouth was on mine in the next moment, teeth and tongues clashing in a frenzy of desperation for more of each other.

I grappled at his shirt, pulling it off him at the same time he practically tore his pants off. I opened my legs a little wider as he settled between them, wrapping my arms around his shoulders. He leaned his hips forward, pressing the tip to my core.

He paused and looked down at me with his arms caging me in. "There's something you need to know."

He pushed forward until the head of his cock pressed inside me. "You're strong."

My breath caught, and he pushed in a little farther. "You're beautiful."

Gods—his words and the feeling of him slowly filling me was about to send me toppling over the edge.

"You're fierce, passionate, and capable." He leaned down to kiss me with something more than just physical adoration. He pushed all the way into the hilt, stretching me around every glorious inch even as I was practically dripping around him.

"You're deserving."

He rested against me, bringing a hand up to cup my cheek, and held my gaze.

"You're everything I want and more."

He didn't wait for me to respond before he began fucking me, stealing any words from my throat and replacing them with uncontrollable moans.

He took my mouth, swallowing the sound.

I gripped his broad shoulders and met him for every pounding thrust. He reached behind one of my knees and bent it up to my chest, allowing him to go even deeper.

My core tightened, and every nerve in my body jolted, electrified as my release rushed through me.

He immediately followed, tensing and jerking with a muffled groan into my mouth.

I pulsed around him, drawing him in and draining him of every last drop as he spilled himself into me.

Breathing heavily, my mind was completely blank, free of the haunting memories I had desperately wished to forget. I realized I didn't need demid. I didn't need anything, not when I was with Hakoa.

Even after how much I had hurt him, he was still there for me, waiting patiently. And it wasn't out of obligation or convenience...

He wasn't just what I needed—he was who I wanted.

"I love you," I choked, struggling to get the words out.

He smiled widely and placed a soft kiss on my lips. "It's about damn time."

Chapter Fifty-One

------◆◇◆------

RYKER

Once Nikan and I were back in Oryn, I went down to talk to Mavris, ordering Nikan to stay put in the hall for the time being. I needed to update Mavris on my conversations with Asmen and Dainos, and I needed him to focus.

I had hoped to gain Dainos as an ally in this upcoming war, but I understood strategically why he couldn't. At least I was able to gain Asmen. Having Oryn on one side of Atara and Dusan on the other side, it at least reduced the perimeter that would have to be guarded. Only the edge bordering Riyah and the coast would require warriors to be posted.

Mavris had returned to Voara directly after his conversation with Nikan and had been running things in my absence.

Not wasting another minute, I entered Mavris' study, finding him finishing up a conversation with several Noavo.

"…and make sure there are enough supplies on hand to accommodate the influx of citizens. That'll be all," he dismissed them, and they passed by me with a bow as they left.

I approached, and Mavris stood, running a hand through his long hair and greeted me, "Ryk. Thank the Gods you're back. How did it go?"

"Not as well as we hoped, but better than it could have. Dusan has agreed to work with us. Torx has sided with Gaol and Ulrik," I grumbled.

"I don't understand Voron. He's new. He still has a lot to learn about running a Nation, and one of the first things he does is sign up Ulrik to fight in a war? Is he from Gaol? Does he still hold some loyalty to Jymar or something?" Mavris asked incredulously.

"He's from Oryn, actually. Arra said his family kept him well-hidden until the Trial, fearing he'd be killed. Maybe he holds a grudge for it. I don't know. Either way, we're about to go up against three Nations. Dainos was *considerate* enough to warn me they'll be at the Ataran border in two weeks," I stated bitterly.

"Shit…" he whispered. "At the very least, it allows us to prepare." Mavris shrugged.

"It does. And I plan to slow them down as much as I can. I'll have the Vaavi infiltrate their forces in Riyah and do what they can from the inside."

"Can we get Riyah to stop them? Deny them passage?" he asked.

I wish.

I shook my head. "They won't, and it wouldn't matter anyway. Riyah doesn't exactly have a defense system."

He tilted his head to the side. "But they have a few blood wielders in Bhara. Three, last I heard. That's as good a defense system as any," he said with a smirk.

Like the one I saw at my mating trial.

He was right. Blood wielders were the most powerful of the elements, but they were locked up until they were needed. I was grateful Mavris would be with us. Having a blood wielder on the field with us was a significant advantage.

"Speaking of blood wielders…" Mavris gave me a knowing look.

"Absolutely not," I snapped, shaking my head.

"You would be stupid not to have him with us," he scolded.

"It would be a cold day in Odes' grave before I—"

The sound of a bang and a shout from a familiar voice stopped me short. My eyes narrowed.

"Don't give me that look. This is war. He's a strong wielder. He's the one who taught me how to hide my ability and the only reason I'm still alive. That's strength you can't find in a regular warrior. We need him," he said as heavy footsteps approached.

"I know we do, but he can't handle it, Mav," I hissed through my teeth.

Mavris crossed his arms. "Things have changed."

I rolled my eyes just as the door swung open, and my father stormed in. I had noticed he was different earlier, during my outburst. But I worried it was just a one-time thing.

"Kleio's tits, Ryker. It's about time you showed up. I was beginning to think this wasn't your palace seeing as you're never here," Cadoc said, coming over and slapping a hand on my shoulder.

"Father," I greeted warily. "How are you?"

"I'm alright. Your brother has been keeping me company since he got here. And I've been reading over the translation notes in the book. Most of it doesn't make sense, but from what I can tell, it appears to be some alternate magic system unknown to us. If that book belongs to the dark wielder, and he's from another realm, it could be a kind of magic that our realm has never seen before. It's like a guidebook." He spoke so articulately I hardly recognized him. I wouldn't have believed it if I hadn't seen him with my own eyes.

My eyes darted to Mavris, and he shrugged with a grin.

"Care to explain?" I asked in Mavris's mind.

"I really can't. He was already here when I came back from the encampment, and he was like this." Mavris jutted his head to Cadoc.

"I'm glad you looked over the notes. Did you find anything useful?" I spoke out loud to my father.

"It depends on what you define as 'useful'. There's a lot of confusing information in there, but you said that Daegel wanted the book, right? That's what I've been looking for specifically—whatever it is that he could be so desperate for. There's a lot of dark stuff in there that's scary as shit. I haven't gone through all of it just yet, but I'll continue if you like," he offered.

I raised a brow. My father hadn't offered to do anything other than obsess over my mother in the fifty years since her disappearance. Not that I blamed him, especially now that I understood the ache in his soul. But I supposed if this information got us closer to Daegel, then it got us closer to my mother as well. Kya too.

Cadoc took a deep breath. "I told you Ryker...something changed. I can't explain it, but ever since you told me what happened to your mate—ever since you finally listened and believed me—I'm...hopeful. So, I want to help. Whatever I can do to get our mates back."

"I'm working on it, but I still don't know how to find them," I sighed and glanced at Mavris. He gave a nod for me to continue. "Additionally, we have the concern of a war coming to Atara—my mate's Nation."

"Which is where you could be of the most help, Father," Mavris interjected, giving our father a knowing look.

Cadoc sucked in a breath. "And this would help you concentrate more of your efforts on finding Leysa and Kya?"

"It's not quite that simple, but yes. It would help," I said.

"Your wielding could make a huge difference in the outcome of the war," Mavris added.

"That's a big risk. For both of us," he directed toward Mavris. Then he smiled, something I hadn't seen in decades. "Let's go to Atara. I can continue to read over the book there and find out whatever I can. If we can find out what this dark wielder is looking for, we can use it against him."

"Agreed. Which reminds me…" I paused.

"You can come in now."

A moment later, Nikan walked into the room. Mavris' silver eyes widened slightly, meeting Nikan's.

"Nikan, I'm going to answer your earlier question. Mavris will be joining us in Atara." I turned my head to look at my brother. *"You* could also make a significant difference in the outcome as well."

I didn't outright say it, not wanting to reveal Mavris' life-threatening secret.

Mavris had a good point earlier. Having a blood wielder on the battlefield was a smart tactical advantage. And having two blood wielders was even greater. It would have been foolish for us not to utilize the best assets available to us.

Mavris nodded, agreeing with me, but he didn't take his eyes off Nikan. "Let's go to Atara, then."

We had to wait for Theron to return before he could Travel us to Atara. Since this wasn't urgent, I wanted him to finish his thorough search before coming back. We were standing on the rooftop waiting.

Before we came out here, I had assembled the diplomats, instructing them to take care of matters of the Nation while I was away. They would be working with the Noavo to evacuate the citizens near the Riyah and Ulrik border and move them inland. The last thing I wanted was for the other Nations to turn to Oryn while we were stationed in Atara, leaving those near the border vulnerable. They would also coordinate with the Vaavi to have several of them infiltrate the other Nation's forces and do what they could to slow them down by cutting off their supply lines.

Theron finally returned, and no matter how hard I tried not to, I hoped and prayed he would return with good news. But that hope was crushed with a small shake of his head, and I internally cursed. My hands balled into fists, and I took a deep breath to calm myself.

Soon.

"I forgot how big he is," Cadoc said quietly, marveling at Theron as he placed a hand on his scaly leg. Nikan and Mavris followed.

I did the same. *"We need to go to Atara,"* I said to the Spirit, then in a blink of an eye, we appeared in a field.

In the distance, I heard the faint sound of voices—the Atarans, back on Ataran soil.

"Keep looking," I growled, commanding Theron.

He snarled in response, but vanished once more.

Nikan grabbed Mavris's hand and pulled him away, walking around the hill for privacy. My father gave me a questioning look.

"Lover's quarrel or something." I shrugged.

He flashed a grin so slight I almost missed it. "Best leave them to sort it out then."

Cadoc and I began walking toward the sound of bustling until a large group came into view. We watched as they were setting up a base along the border, hundreds of warriors readying themselves for war to defend another Nation. It had been many years since they'd been mobilized, and it was an incredible sight to see. This was only one group out of dozens of others, creating an army of thousands of warriors along the border.

"I'm sorry, Ryker," my father said, bringing my attention back to him. He continued to stare out at the brave wielders.

"What for?" I looked at him from the side of my eye.

"For not telling you what a great Lord you are. Not only do you care deeply for your people and protect them at all costs, but you care just as much for your mate's land and people that you have made it just as much a priority as finding Kya—something I never would have been strong enough to do. I know what you're suffering right now. I know it all too well. And you've managed to do so much more despite it." He took a deep breath.

My duty to Oryn and to Kya had warred with each other since the moment she fell. I didn't know if I was making the right choices, but I was doing the best I could.

I didn't really know what to say to that, but I gave a short nod of gratitude before leading him into the base, winding our way until we found the operations tent.

Hakoa leaned against the table with his arms crossed, his back facing us as he addressed one of his generals and four warriors.

"For the love of Xar, she's just a little rash and…yes, hothead-ed at times. You are supposed to be strong, fearsome warriors," Hakoa hissed, lowering his voice as he leaned forward. "You can handle a little scolding from someone *half* your size."

I bit back a smile, guessing who he was talking about. "I think we all know that size doesn't matter," I said, announcing my presence.

Hakoa pushed off the table and turned to face me with a flat stare. "You're not helping."

I chuckled. "Arra giving the Noavo a hard time?"

"The Chief gave her permission to take over the formation runs this morning, and she's berating every single one of the Noavo for mundane things and making them more worried about her than actually doing what they're supposed to be doing," Enzo, one of Hakoa's generals, complained.

"I didn't give her permission to take over. I told her she could bark orders to blow off some steam. And if everyone was doing what they were supposed to, she wouldn't have said anything." Hakoa rubbed his temples. "Lord Ryker, care to step in."

"Nope. I'm good."

Hakoa sighed. "You're dismissed."

The general and four warriors bowed then left.

"Ryk. Have a nice trip?" Hakoa asked.

"Hardly," I grumbled.

"Figures. Cadoc." He nodded to my father standing next to me. "It's nice to see you, although… Well, I don't really know how to say this, but what are you doing here?" He looked at me pointedly.

"My father is here to help. He's a—"

Cadoc interrupted with the loud clearing his throat and raised his brows at me.

"Yes?" I said into his mind.

"I haven't kept my ability a secret for centuries just for you to go and expose it to the world," he snapped.

"Such little faith, Father."

"He's a powerful wielder and can provide assistance on the front," I continued.

The only ones who knew of my father's blood wielding ability were me, Mavris, and my mother. He had spent centuries working diligently to keep it hidden so he didn't become a target of Bhara and taught Mavris to do the same. Hakoa knew about my brother's ability, it was his decision to tell him.

"Do you need to train? I haven't seen you wield in decades. Not since…" he stopped himself. "Not in a long time."

Hakoa was under the belief Cadoc was a water wielder. Having met when they were young, my parents had ensured they were always together. My father practiced the motions of water wielding while my mother honed her training so she could wield with only the smallest, indiscernible hand movements. It was the biggest contribution as to how he was able to hide his true wielding element.

"No," Cadoc stated firmly. "I'll be fine. I can assure you."

"Just put him to use helping around the base for now, Hakoa. At least until the fighting starts. We can use anyone we can get."

My father and I joined the warriors and helped set up, preparing for what was to come.

The terbis wielders began creating a wall along the perimeter of Atara. Taller than any tree and as wide as ten males, the warriors caused rock to erupt from the land, making the ground tremble beneath our feet.

I didn't have to convince them to defend Atara. They took their orders and carried them out, creating a fortress around the healing Nation we were desperate to protect.

I spent the day overseeing the front lines alongside Cadoc until Hakoa joined us. Nearly the entire Noavo force was along the border to Riyah, and with everything ready, it was time to meet up with Malina.

I found her near the outskirts of the base with a small group of Atarans in a field dusted with snow, running them through basic defense forms. Nikan obviously had no issues finding her, as he was standing next to her while she gave instruction.

Watching for only a minute or two, I was impressed by how she was mindful of each of the different elements, teaching them how to use their abilities in more combative ways. It was more natural for someone to teach within their own element or use maneuvers that were broad enough for all of them.

But she wasn't paying attention to their exhaustion. She had likely grown up with grueling training and hadn't yet dealt with those who needed to build their stamina.

"Malina," I called, summoning her with an authoritative tone.

My voice interrupted the Atarans' concentration as they struggled to hold up their individual elements around their bodies, encasing them. Water splashed to the cold ground, and rocks tumbled. The air wielders lost their hold, releasing gusts of wind while the fire wielders nearly burned those around them.

"What?" Malina snapped her head to me with a glare of ill intention.

"They need a break," I commanded more than suggested, approaching her. "And I'd like to speak with you privately."

She looked back at the group and opened her mouth to speak but then closed it, not knowing what to say.

"Dismiss them," I said quietly so only she could hear.

She nodded. "Be back in an hour," she barked harshly, and they all rushed off, giving her wary glances as they passed.

"Thank the Gods." Nikan blew out a breath. "I couldn't watch that for much longer. I'm going to make sure you haven't chased them out of the Nation after that debacle."

I snorted a laugh.

Malina playfully punched him in the shoulder before he jogged off to catch up with the rest of the Atarans.

"Remind me not to let you and Arra work together," I mumbled under my breath. "You do know those are *your* people, right? That they've never done this? Try not to break them on their first day."

Malina crossed her arms and shrugged. "I don't exactly have time to go easy on them. They have a lot to learn."

I nodded my head to the side, gesturing toward the hills away from the base. "Take a walk with me."

"Why?" She looked at me questioningly but kept pace as I began to walk away.

"Because I need to talk to you about some things you won't want anyone overhearing."

She sighed deeply. "Such as?"

"Like how you're doing. You've been through the toughest part of coming off demid, but it doesn't mean you don't still crave it. And it certainly doesn't fix the issue that led you to the elixir in the first place," I said, keeping my eyes on the gently rolling hills before us.

"And you're just concerned about my well-being?" her voice dripped with sarcasm.

I turned my head to look her straight in the eyes. "No. I need to make sure you're not going to fuck everything up when things get ugly. Because they will. And soon."

"I struggle. I'm not going to lie about that. And I think about it constantly. But I'm *not* going back to it," she said defensively. I could practically feel the anxious waves of defiance and determination flowing through her.

Good. I needed her to want to fight this. Even if it was just out of spite—to prove me wrong.

"Additionally," I continued. "I want an assessment on the Atarans."

"It's *only* been a day," she retorted.

"And I need to know now if they have potential or if they're going to be a liability."

She reared her head back. "Liability?"

"Yes," I said sternly. "If they don't have what it takes to defend themselves or help in protecting Atara, then they need to get out of the way. I commend them for wanting to fight for their home, but the fact of the matter is, they can just as easily become part of the problem."

It's the hard truth. It wasn't worth having another body on the front lines if it wasn't useful.

"I mean…I don't know. A few of them are grasping it faster than the others," she said plainly.

I opened my mouth to respond but stopped when Theron's voice roared in my head.

"Ryker!" Theron appeared behind me, shielding me with his body.

I spun on my heel just in time to find Daegel emerging over the hillside.

Chapter Fifty-Two

KYA

I'm not asking to be saved. I got myself into this.

I'm only asking for a little grace. Break your silence and allow me to return to him. Allow me the chance to end his torment.

That's all I ask...

Something felt off the moment I woke up. Nothing looked different, not that I could tell at least, but it was like the atmosphere had changed. Leysa and I woke up, we were retrieved by Talum, then led into the forest to the stepstone to go to Kitall for the day.

Except something *was* different. For the first time, Daegel wasn't waiting for us at the ancient stone. Instead, Talum stepped up holding out his hand for us to follow.

Leysa and I exchanged a confused look. Talum had never come to the island with us, and Daegel was always here.

He leveled us with a flat stare, as if he knew exactly what we were thinking. "The same conditions apply. You'll still be placed in the barrier and you'll do as you've been told."

"Did Daegel die?" I asked with a hopeful grin.

Talum rolled his eyes and sighed. "No."

"Damn," I muttered under my breath.

"Did he go back to..." Leysa started.

From the knowing look Talum gave her, she knew—Daegel was in Taeralia. Leysa's features twisted into a sneer as she looked away and stepped onto the Horgor.

I pursed my lips. "Why do we still have to do this if Daegel isn't here?"

"Because your work isn't finished yet," he said.

"Then why did—"

"Just step on the stone, Diamond," he snapped.

Both Leysa and I raised our brows. Talum had always been the calm one, and his short temper was just another indicator something was wrong. Maybe it was the Gods, or perhaps the tension in the air, but whatever it was had the hair on the back of my neck tingling. I obeyed, staying on edge and watching everything with a wary eye.

Once all three of us were on the circle stone, Talum waved his hand in a practiced motion.

"Fara," he said roughly.

We were on Kitall Island a moment later. I instantly felt the rush of magic flooding into me, but I remained standing, trying not to whimper as it filled me beyond my natural capacity and demanded to be released. Even with the majority of the island destroyed by the Glaev, the remaining parts still held so much magic it overloaded my reserve.

Talum's temper didn't lessen as he pushed Leysa and me off the stone. He ungracefully slapped a collar around Leysa and left her groaning in pain on the ground.

"Hey! I'm doing what I'm told! Take that off her!" I went to reach for her, but Talum held me back.

"I'm not taking chances. Do as you're told, *then* I'll take it off," he snapped.

"It's okay, Kya," Leysa grunted out. "Just get it done. It's not your fault."

Talum shoved me down the path through the Glaev-stricken land I had spent weeks on until we came to the area I stopped at last time, leaving Leysa behind near the stepstone.

His harsh demeanor had my pulse racing with worry, having become used to his normally care-free behavior.

Talum went through the same motions and uttered the same incantations Daegel had and threw up the pearlescent shield over me.

"Lauss," he said and released the collar. Then with a clipped tone, "Fjold." Which I had assumed by now was the command for me to begin. "Get going. Daegel wants this finished by nightfall," he said.

"Nightfall?" I gaped and looked around at how much of the island was left untouched by the Glaev. "I can't do it by then."

It would take me at least two—maybe three—days until I could realistically wield that much to finish.

"If you don't, I've been instructed to leave Leysa here until you do. No matter how long it takes." He crossed his arms with a cold expression.

That would mean she would be stuck here for days with the stupid collar on, suppressing her magic and enduring excruciating pain.

I'd been holding back, drawing out the process to give myself more time for a chance to get out of here—to come up with a plan. But I couldn't live with myself if all I was doing was making Leysa suffer more.

With a huff, I did as I was told, wielding my energy and contorting it into the decimation, plaguing the land until it was nothing but ash.

I wanted to be done with this. I wanted to go back, run into Ryker's arms and finally stop this unbearable burning inside me. I just had to do as Daegel said long enough until I could finally break free. Yet I feared what he would do with me when he didn't need me anymore...

As I went through the motions of creating the Glaev, a realization hit me, and my lips lifted into a wicked grin.

Daegel isn't here.

I knew what needed to be done.

After several hours of killing the land and searching for the perfect spot, I had finally found it. There, just ahead of me, was a crack in the rocky cliff next to the edge of the island I had been working along. It wasn't very big—just barely large enough for me to fit my body into if I tried to squeeze in it, but I hoped it *looked* big enough.

Talum certainly wasn't as observant as Daegel, and while he did watch me, it wasn't as obsessive. In fact, he looked exceptionally distracted, his eyes darting all around, never focusing on one thing. He seemed...anxious. I didn't know why, but I was going to use it to my advantage. It was the best opportunity I would have, and I had to take it while I had the chance. Everything had to be perfect, or it would all be for nothing.

Make my escape, get Leysa and myself off the island, and find King Zalen. I'd even be willing to make a deal with him, if it meant I could get back to Taeralia.

I had a plan.

I kept moving forward, subtly glancing over my shoulder to keep an eye on Talum for when he wasn't looking directly at me. Thankfully, something drew his attention away, and he turned his head to the side.

Now or never.

I took a step toward the crack and stopped the Glaev from leaving the tips of my fingers, redirecting the energy to what was natural to me—the soft jade hue. I lifted to my toes just as I reached the edge of the crack.

Please let this work.

All at once, I slammed my feet to the ground as hard as I could, causing the ground to shift and rumble as it lowered—the only amount of physical wielding I could do, just like I used to back at Morah—while simultaneously blasting my energy inside of the crack, causing dirt and rock to fly up all around me.

I screamed, making sure it was loud enough for Talum to hear, and fell to my face. The moment I hit the ground, I wrapped around that translucent orb, enabling my invisibility.

Then I waited.

Talum's eyes went wide, and his mouth fell open when he looked in my direction. He couldn't see me.

"Diamond!" he shouted.

I rose to a crouch, careful not to shift any rocks beneath me.

He came right up to the shield, pressing against it to look closer.

"Shit…" he seethed and lowered the barrier. He rushed down the path and came right up to the crack, waving his hand to clear the dust through the air.

I slowly rose to a stand, carefully balancing myself on my toes.

From Talum's perspective, it looked as if the Glaev had caused a rupture in the ground, and I fell through. Which was exactly what I needed him to think—at least long enough for me to get away.

My stomach twisted with anticipation, adrenaline, and a twinge of fear. But I had to go *now*.

Just as he reached the crack, I slammed my heels down and dropped the ground again. Talum toppled forward. As if time had slowed, I watched as he fell into the crack.

That was all I allowed myself to see.

I bolted down the path with my hand behind me, throwing out the Glaev on the remnants of undisturbed land. It was a risk, not knowing if Talum had the ability to walk on it like Daegel did, but one I was willing to take. I stayed light on my feet, flying down the path as fast as I could go.

"Diamond!" Talum bellowed.

I didn't look back to see if he was following, and I couldn't feel vibrations past the Glaev. I kept running, pushing myself faster and faster until I could hardly see through the wind hitting my eyes, causing them to tear. Or maybe it was the trepidation of not knowing if he was right behind me. Or perhaps it was the taste of freedom, the hope each desperate step across the rough terrain was bringing me closer to Ryker.

I was quickly approaching Leysa, who was rocking back and forth with her head in her hands near the stepstone where Talum left her.

"Leysa," I whisper-shouted.

We could do it—we could finally get out of here. She could finally get back to her mate after fifty long, torturous years.

Her head lifted, and she looked around for the sound of my voice.

Once I was directly in front of her, I remembered my invisibility and released my hold on that orb, appearing before her.

She flinched, surprised and confused at my sudden appearance.

"Leysa, we have to go. Now's our chance," I said hurriedly. *Gods, please let this work.*

I wrapped myself around that glassy, rippling orb buried deep within me. I wished I had more time to explore it, to practice with it. Though, if this worked, I supposed that was the real test. I needed her to be able to wield in case we had to fight back, in case Talum caught up, in case we were discovered and chased.

I waved my hand at Leysa like I had seen Daegel do day after day and repeated the same word I'd heard so many times, "Lauss."

My lips lifted into a triumphant smile as the collar fell from her neck, freeing her from its magical suppression.

"Kya. What are you—" she breathed. She looked to the path, then back to me with wide eyes. "Oh Gods… No." She shook her head, the fear emanating from her was palpable. "No, Kya. No! What are you doing? How did you—"

"I'll explain later. We don't have time." I grabbed her arm and began pulling her toward the stepstone.

She yanked her arm from my grasp and took a step back away from me.

Talum shouted, the sound of his voice growing closer.

"Leysa, we have to go *now*," I clipped.

"No! I can't—We can't, he'll catch us." Her wide, fear-filled eyes enraged me.

What the fuck is wrong with her?! I want to get back to my mate, and I want to go now!

"I'm not asking," I snarled. "Let's go."

I looked over my shoulder, searching for that blond head of hair coming around the bend, terrified he would any second now. I didn't know if Leysa and I could take him on, even with the additional magic flowing into us. I wished I had my bow. I reached for her arm again, but it was slapped away with a stream of water, the sensation stung more than just my skin.

"Kya, stop!" she said with a low tone that made a shiver run down my spine.

"Why?" I demanded.

"I... I can't tell you. I'm sorry."

My lips parted, confused and baffled. I couldn't understand what she was doing. Talum was going to come around the bend any moment now, and she was wasting time.

"I can't let you do this. You're almost done!" She lifted her arms and wielded a massive wave of water from the sea beside us, and slammed it down on me.

The force threw me to the ground with a sickening thud, and pain shot up my side.

"Leysa—" I tried to speak but it was cut off by another wave of water.

Fear took over as I tried to get away. Every hit brought back a memory—the nagasai in the river, the assassin in the Voara palace, the heill after I had come here. The memories flashed in my mind, threatening to make me buckle from the sheer terror I felt.

No. I can take it. I can take it.

She pushed me down, over and over and over.

"All you had to do was finish your task!" she roared, finally letting up on her attacks. Her body trembled with rage.

I couldn't respond, too busy coughing up the water.

"You're so close, Kya! Why can't you just finish?" she practically screamed at me, and I could see tears falling down her distraught face.

"Why do you want me to finish so badly? We can go now! If you don't want to come with me, then just fucking stay here!"

I rolled out of the way as she whipped another stream of water at me, the tip of it slapping the ground where I had just been hard enough it cracked the rock.

If I finished, Daegel would have what he wanted. I didn't know what the purpose was, but I knew in my gut it would somehow hurt my world, those I loved and cared about. I just *knew* I couldn't finish, even if I didn't know why.

"All you have to do is finish your task, and I *will* leave," she snarled.

"What?" I breathed heavily as I paused, taking in her words.

She roughly pulled down the collar of her shirt to reveal a black splotch in the center of her chest. The same one I had seen before. The same one that took her friend's life as she had broken her bargain.

Fuck!

"No... Leysa," I whispered. "You made a deal with him..."

Her chin trembled. "I just have to get you to complete your task, and Daegel will let me go back to Cadoc," her voice cracked.

My eyes narrowed as tears of anger and hurt welled in them, and I began to slowly crawl backward away from my mate's mother.

"And what about me? Will he send me back too?"

She held my stare for a moment—a moment we didn't have to spare.

"No." More tears fell down her cheeks as she took a step back, stumbling over the uneven land. "I made the deal before Daegel brought me to meet you... I didn't know—I didn't know *you* were the Diamond. But I can't leave yet. You *have* to finish. Otherwise..."

I nodded slowly. I understood. Her mating bond was driving her to do anything necessary to get back to Cadoc. But she wasn't the only one with a bond. We were both consumed by it, forced to do whatever it took to get back to our mates.

It was either her or me.

I met her eyes, glistening with heartbreaking tears as they now streamed down her face. They were never going to let me return home, no matter what I did. I was never going back. She had the only chance she had and took it. And I didn't blame her. It's what I would do too. What I was about to do...

"Diamond!"

I turned my head to see Talum coming around the bend with a deadly purpose.

I was out of time.

I turned to run toward the stepstone, willing to leave Leysa behind. A wet band of water wrapped around my legs, pulling my feet out from under me and slamming me face down to the ground, my mouth instantly filling with the taste of blood. I quickly flipped over to my back with a snarl, trying to scramble to my feet.

"I can't let you go, Kya. This is my only true chance of finally getting out of here. I won't let you take that away from me," she said darkly, raising her arms and wielding what looked like the entirety of the ocean above her.

My heart stilled, and I stopped breathing. I couldn't let her do this. She wasn't going to stop me. Not when I was so close. I wouldn't get an opportunity like this again. She would *not* stop me.

"You're going to try to kill me, Leysa?" I asked, a pang of betrayal stabbing into my heart. I stared up at the mass of seawater and let my energy flow down my arms. "All for trying to get back to my mate—your *son?*"

She didn't even blink. "I'm not going to kill you, because I still need you to finish. I just need to subdue you."

She slapped her arms together, twisting them, then pushed them out toward me, throwing the water up from the sea in a harsh, swirling, massive vortex. It sucked me into its grasp, spinning me head over foot as it pushed me back, and it didn't stop. She continued to draw from the sea, tossing me across the ground past the stepstone, as I struggled against the force.

I couldn't breathe. Even as I released my energy all around me, siphoning from the magic-imbued land, it wasn't enough to stop her torrential waves.

My lungs ached. I was craving air to the point of desperation. It was all I could think about. I lost my hold on the Waalu as my vision turned spotty, and I caught glimpses of Talum approaching.

Time slowed.

Talum was lifting his hand, holding the collar. His lips moved, and the collar levitated for a moment before it started coming for me.

My eyes widened. I had to get to the stone. I had to get away from here. I had to get back to Ryker. No matter what...

It all happened in the blink of an eye.

As the collar came toward me, threatening to take away my chance to finally escape this Godsforsaken place, I summoned the strength to lift my hand and wield my energy into the dark, merciless Glaev.

I threw my power all around me, blasting it into the rushing water until it was consumed by darkness. Digging my fingers into the soil, I quickly clawed my way to the stepstone and watched as the Glaev ate its way through the flood of water with an otherworldly roar.

My dark energy consumed all in its path, the collar turning into ash before it could reach me, but I needed to stop the source of the water.

With a throat-tearing scream, I pushed it out harder, putting everything I had into it.

My throat tightened as I raised my other hand to Ryker's mother, my Waalu snaking down my arm.

She couldn't stop it. The bargain she made wouldn't allow it. And neither would her bond.

Her eyes widened, and her lips parted just before I struck her in the chest with my energy, and in a flash, the dark spot crawling across her chest disappeared, her deal erased just as the Glaev had been.

Regret hit me instantly as I realized what I had done—what I didn't realize I could have done sooner. But it was too late…

The energy was too much for her body, and her pale skin glowed with a jade hue.

Talum's eyes were horrified as we both watched Leysa take her last breath just before she imploded into nothing, the water she had been wielding splashing down on the land around her.

Talum snapped his head toward me and rushed for me as he began to say something with his hand outstretched.

Magic is energy.

Smacking my hand onto the Horgor, I redirected my Waalu onto the stone, the symbols flowing with the jade energy. I lifted my other arm and twisted it in a flourish like I had seen before—the blue of Talum's magic coming at me through the air. I quickly uttered the proper incantation while holding onto the orb of otherworldly magic, "Fara."

In a flash of light, I was back in the forest and—for the first time since I was brought here—without a collar.

I didn't wait to run, jumping to my feet and sprinting deep into the trees to hide until I could figure out what I was going to do. I didn't have time to think about what I had just done.

I had made my choice. I just hoped it was the right one.

Chapter Fifty-Three

RYKER

My stomach dropped at the sight of Daegel. Instinctively, I shifted my wings and scales. My shadows burst forth, infused with the singing heat of my fire, blasting into the skies to create a wall of burning darkness and concealing the base.

"Ryker, what—" Malina said from behind me, startled.

"It's Daegel. Run, Malina! Get the warriors!" I bellowed in her mind.

She didn't hesitate and bolted back to the settlement.

Maybe if there were enough of us...

"Hakoa, he's here!" I warned.

"We're on our way!" he assured.

Daegel stopped at the top of the hill and stared down at me. He glanced to the shadows.

"I'm not here for them. I only want one thing," he announced, his voice grating against my very bones.

My body vibrated with ire and pure malice. I barely heard his words over the roaring in my head. This was exactly what I wanted—what I was hoping for. I wanted him to follow where Nikan was since he had approached him multiple times before. I just thought I'd have a little more time. I had honestly hoped he would have shown up when we were with one of the other

Worthy, but he came right where I had my forces concentrated, and that would have to be good enough.

Subdue him. Don't kill him yet. He has my mate...

"Give me Kya," my voice thundered with the wrath of a Worthy.

"Give me the *book*," he remarked in a low lethal tone.

Theron growled and splayed out his wings. *"Do not give him what he desires. He will destroy the realm and everyone in it. Your mate will have nothing and no one if you do."*

I pierced the dark wielder's mind, penetrating as deep as I could go before he had the chance to shut me out like he did during our last encounter. Within the span of a heartbeat, I tore through his memories voraciously, seeing his world through his eyes until I found her. *Kya.*

My heart stopped. He was holding her by her throat with her feet dangling above the ground and—

I was thrust out of Daegel's mind as he shut me out, blocking my access. Unable to control it, my flames ignited all around me as the image of his hand around her neck with the look of terror in her eyes was embedded into the forefront of my mind.

Daegel's hands opened at his sides with the blue wisps of his dark magic. "I'm tired of these games. Give me the fucking book before I send this land back to the dark hole your mate pulled it out of," he demanded. "And maybe I'll make you go with it."

Theron roared so loud it shook the land beneath our feet—the air distorted from the heat emanating from his maw. He didn't wait for Daegel to make a move and ejected a stream of fire toward him.

Daegel's own magic flared from his hands, blocking the flames from searing his body with a grunt.

I ran toward him, snaking my shadows along the ground ahead of me. Daegel threw his arm up in an attack, casting the dark magic of the Glaev at me.

I leapt in the air just in time to avoid it.

"Ahhh!" I heard the crippling sound of a scream from the base behind me. "No! No, no, no!"

I didn't know who it was and I didn't have time to think about it.

Theron continued to blast fire at Daegel, steadily walking closer, forcing him to keep his magic concentrated on the dragon while my shadows gripped his leg. I slammed back down to the ground and wrapped my shadows around him, but they were cut off with a slash of his blue magic. Theron's fire had finally reached him, and he roared from the pain.

"Fine!" Daegel shouted, rage dripping from his voice.

Theron and I hesitated for a moment.

"I will give her to you," Daegel said with a curled lip. "*If* you give me the book."

The one that could destroy everything.

"No," Theron growled.

"This is *your* choice. You have ten days," he warned.

In an explosion of blue, Daegel disappeared.

"Damnit!"

I could still hear wailing coming from the base, and I turned. Hakoa and the warriors had just breached my shadow wall with the help of one of the fire wielders, but they were too late. That whole encounter was too short. I thought he'd put up a greater fight, but perhaps our numbers had intimidated him. As the screams continued, I ran toward the sound, shifting my scales away.

The pained cries grew louder and louder as I neared. It was so unnatural and raw, it grinded my heart. I followed to where several people were gathered, bent over a figure.

Malina looked up at me as I approached with horror in her eyes. She moved to the side, revealing my father.

He was grabbing at his chest, clawing at his skin grotesquely as his nails drew streaks of blood.

"No! No! No!" His screaming pleas shook me, paralyzing me momentarily.

I bent down and pulled his wrists away, stopping him from harming himself.

"What happened? Are you hurt?" I asked, glancing over his body.

"The bond. The *bond*! No, please. Leysa!" he mourned.

I felt the blood drain from my face. My mother had died.

Oh no.

Father gasped, struggling to breathe as the bond faded into nothingness.

"Take me with you. Take me with you," he whispered.

I reached for the bond to Kya, needing the reassurance it was still there no matter how fractured. It was terrifying that this could happen to me at any moment—that I could truly lose her, and there was nothing I could do about it.

I stood abruptly and flared out my wings, thrusting myself up and soaring through the air toward where Daegel had stood in front of Theron. There was no trace of him. Nothing to follow, nothing at all.

"Fuck!" I threw my head back and roared to the skies, cursing the Gods.

The Gods…

…only the Gods can…

Turning slowly to face my guardian, I shifted my wings away. He had told me more than once that *he* didn't know where she was, that *he* couldn't take me to other realms. Maybe I didn't need *him* to take me to Kya. I needed a God.

But the Gods didn't answer our calls, they didn't interfere in our realm. With the exception of when I was chosen, I had never spoken to any of them.

I couldn't speak to a God *here*. But I knew where I could.

"I'm coming, little gem," I said down the bond, holding onto it tightly.

Then I placed my hand on Theron's snout. *"Take me to Hylithria."*

It had been three hundred years since I had been in the Spirit realm. The only time I had been here was when Xareus had brought me after he deemed me Worthy following my Trial. It was then I trekked up the mountain to Galadynia where I was judged. During the Test of Fate, the mirror reflected my past, present, and future. Then Theron chose me.

Hylithria was exactly as I remembered. The field of tall grass swaying gently in the wind with sparse, large and ancient trees. The mountains towered in the distance.

A sense of peace washed over me. It was tranquil and enchanting, yet not enough to smother my troubles and distress—the bond still burning.

"How do I find Xareus?" I asked Theron beside me.

"He is your God. Call upon him."

A twinge of worry pinched inside me that he wouldn't answer. He never had before. Though that was in a realm he was forbidden from interacting with.

I nodded then took a deep breath as I stepped forward. Lifting my head, I released my bellowing call to the glowing sky.

"Xareus, God of Chaos and Father of Oryn. Your Worthy summons you."

My voice boomed through the air and across the vast land. I didn't know if he would grace me with his presence, but this was the only way I could think of to talk with him and plead for him to help me. So I waited, unmoving and alert.

After several moments, Xareus appeared before me.

More than a head taller than me, his body glowed with divine light, and his long raven hair wisped behind him in the breeze. With the upper half of his body left bare, a cloth wrapped around his waist and hung down to the top of his feet which hovered just above the ground.

"Thank you for answering my call." I bowed deeply at the waist for the first time in centuries before rising to meet the emotionless gaze of his black eyes. My initial instinct was to cower in his presence, but I refused to back down—even from my God.

Theron dipped his head, and Xareus returned the gesture—a mutual respect for one another.

"Worthy Ryker, what is it you seek?" Xareus's voice demanded of me but was just as expressionless as his features.

"My mate, Kya of Atara and chosen Worthy of Kleio, has been taken to another realm. I wish for you to bring her to me," I requested with my head held high.

"This cannot be done. I know of your mate, I chose her for you. I watched her Trial as she was chosen by Kleio, having guided the Goddess to her. But your request is not something I am able to grant."

My gut twisted.

"You're a *God*. You're able to do anything you desire," I seethed, trying to tamper down my frustration.

"If that were true, do you believe the realms would be as they are?" he asked.

I didn't know what to think of that.

"Gods have limits, just as Spirits do," he added.

"I...I don't know what that means. I just want to get to Kya and bring her back. If you can't do it, can you at least tell me where she is so Theron can take me there? Do you know where she is?" I asked desperately.

His eyes flicked to Theron briefly. "The Spirits cannot go there. They are forbidden."

I bit back a snarl.

"Unless," he continued. "They are completing their duty."

This time, I didn't hold back my snarl. "Then you know where she is. If you won't go there and if Theron can't, just send me. I just need to find her!"

He didn't respond, remaining still enough he could have been a statue.

"What about Kleio? She's *her* Worthy. She can't just stand idly by while Kya's in another realm where she's not meant to be. She has to get her. Or let me speak to her. She's your mate. Call for her. I'll ask her myself," I clipped.

Xareus's face darkened. "You dare to command me? Kleio is a Goddess. It is her will, and I will not obstruct it."

These fucking Gods...

"In three hundred years, not once have I asked you for anything. I've fought against the ones you chose to challenge me. I've protected the land and people of Oryn in battle and blood—against any threat. I've entrusted my life to you and dedicated myself to fulfilling your task. *You* bound me to Kya. *You* wove the bond between us. I am trying to do my duty as her mate to protect her. So please, just fucking let me, and tell me where she is!" I roared in his face.

It certainly wasn't the smartest decision to raise my voice to a God. But at this point, I didn't care. I wanted her in my arms, for reasons far beyond the bond. Even if I had to call and plead with every single one of the Gods, I would.

"Yes. I wove the bond between you. I made you her mate. But I did not make you love her." To my surprise, Xareus looked pleased—proud even. The edges of his mouth spread, peeling his lips apart to display the first expression I had ever seen from him.

"Your loyalty has not faltered, and it seems Theron's fire now flows within your blood." He tilted his head, studying me for a moment with that same blank expression. "She prays for you. Your mate."

I inhaled sharply. My throat tightened, and I swallowed down the lump forming there. "She does?"

"Every day."

I wondered what she prayed about, what her worries were. Was it out of fear or sorrow? Was it for my well-being or for the shared burning we felt?

Xareus took a deep breath and glanced away, contemplating. After a moment, he returned his gaze back to me. "Your mate was taken to Vansera, a realm born from Odes before his fall. I will take you there so you may fulfill your duty to her. But do not forget your duty to *me*, and what I have asked of you, Worthy Ryker."

...*reveal the darkness*...

My pulse raced with anticipation and impatience. Finally. I would finally have her back.

Xareus started to lift his hand to touch my forehead.

"I will not forget. Thank—"

Xareus's hand stopped mid-air, and his eyes flicked above me as he looked at something.

The feeling of hot air burst against my back and had me whipping around, finding a dark pair of eyes that made every drop of blood in my body still.

"Odarum…"

The winged Spirit Guardian of Kya lowered his head with his ears pinned back. The sound of his deep, demanding voice rumbled in my mind, dripping with the wrath of a Fylgjur.

"Where is my Worthy?"

Chapter Fifty-Four

KYA

*W*hat have I done...

I didn't have a choice. Leysa was going to keep me there—force me to finish Daegel's task, and I wouldn't have been able to leave at all. And who knows what he would have done with me once he had gotten what he wanted.

I didn't know I could have tried to break her curse. I wasn't sure I would have even had the time to try.

I didn't blame Leysa for making a deal against my life in exchange for her return. I probably would have done the same after so long.

Oh Gods... What am I going to tell Ryker? What will he think when he finds out I killed his mother to get back to him and I had the chance to save her?

I slumped against the trunk of the tree as I straddled a branch high up in the canopy of the forest and wished things had been different. I wouldn't have been alone right now if I hadn't taken her life. A gaping pit of grief and guilt opened in my chest. But it was mixed with confusion and frustration.

Was anything Leysa and I had real? Did she actually care about me because I was her son's mate, or was it all because I was the key to her finally going back to hers?

My head fell back, resting on the coarse bark behind me, and I closed my eyes. The constant whirling in my mind was tearing me apart.

Thunder rumbled in the distance, and a light sprinkling of rain began to drop, falling on my closed lids. The cool droplets on my heated skin was a welcome sensation, and I inhaled deeply through my nose, scenting the storm as it fell on the forest around me.

Ryker hadn't even known his mother was alive, and now his wife had killed her. And Cadoc...

I couldn't even imagine what he was going through right now. If the fracture of a bond was this bad, I never wanted to know what it was like to lose it entirely—to have half of your soul ripped away and tossed out into the empty void of the After.

The sound of voices had my eyes popping open, and I sighed quietly.

These bastards are relentless.

I leaned over to look down at the base of the tree. Standing there, eyes searching the dense canopy, were five blond males—sorcerers. Even this deep into the forest, hours away from civilization, they still scoured every bush and tree searching for the escaped prisoner. *Me.*

While staying up in the trees allowed me to have the advantage in the situation, I missed being on the ground where I could feel vibrations. Although I had spent so much time unable to use my terbis it hadn't bothered me as much.

I had been silent for the past two days, moving only when I knew no one was near. Staying hidden in the trees was something I had mastered in my years as a Roav, and it came naturally to me. But I also wanted to take extra precautions. With my invisibility, I was practically undetectable. But it also meant I was constantly depleting my reserves, leaving me weaker and more drained than I was used to when in hiding.

The males searched high and low through the foliage, day and night, but had failed to find a single trace of me. They prowled along the forest floor, speaking with one another when their efforts were unsuccessful.

"Talum's going to have our heads," one of the males—*men*—grumbled, running a worried hand through his hair.

"Talum has himself to worry about. He's the one who lost her. It's Daegel who concerns me. He's been on a rampage since he found out she escaped after killing that pointy-eared pet of his." The other one paced back and forth, shaking his head with a look of frustration.

"What if she crossed over the—"

"Then we'd have even bigger problems," the second one snapped. "If she did, we'd all be as good as dead."

I perked up at that. What were they concerned about me crossing? Whatever way back into my own realm? The border to find King Zalen? It made the prospect of finding him even more enticing if they were so worried about it, and I couldn't stop the edges of my lips from lifting at the thought.

"Come on. Let's just find the bitch so we can keep our heads," the first one said as they continued their search.

So I waited, clinging to the safety of the shadows.

The rain began to pick up, battering the leaves around me in a soothing symphony. Once the sorcerers were far enough away, I lifted to my feet. The bark shifted under my weight, letting out a soft groan that was muffled by the downpour. Using the moon's glow behind the clouds as a guide, like a beacon, I continued on my journey, moving from limb to limb—careful not to slip on the slickening wood.

I didn't know where I was going, but all of the sorcerers came from the same direction so I went opposite of that, pushing forward in the hope I would find another Kingdom.

Just as I climbed to another limb, a jolt rushed through me nearly bringing me to my knees.

I gripped the trunk of the tree, bracing myself through the waves of intensity as I gasped through the crushing sensation. A rush of emotions came over me. Fear and anger—a soul crushing desperation. And hope...

Tears pricked my eyes before they fell down my cheeks, mixing with the rain coating my skin as I felt every splinter, every crack and fracture of the bond, mold back together.

Soothing swirls of shadows curled around the once shattered tether. I latched onto it as if my life depended on it—which it did—knowing without a doubt. I howled down the bond.

"Ryker!"

My shadow had come for me.

Chapter Fifty-Five

RYKER

"*R* *yker!*"

My knees buckled as the bond painfully—and blissfully—mended back together. I gripped it, wrapping myself around it as if I could hold onto it tight enough to keep it from shattering ever again.

It's her. She's here.

The long-lost sound of my mate's voice rang in my head—a shimmer of life down the tether connecting our souls together. The longing with which my name was spoken tore the icy layer around my heart, making it feel as if it would burst out of my chest, and my breath caught.

"*Kya!*" my voice broke. "*I'm coming, Kya!*"

Not wasting a single moment, I shifted my wings. Something was wrong. I felt weaker, heavier, as if I was being slowly crushed by an invisible weight. I pushed past it and strenuously propelled myself into the air, flying away from the glowing stone arch I had just passed through and trusting the bond to lead me to my mate as it had done so many times before.

I could hear Kya softly sobbing and grunting, as if she was struggling.

The worst images came to mind. Was she trapped? Was she bound? Was she locked away?

"Talk to me, little gem. Tell me where you are." I needed to hear her voice. I never wanted to lose that precious sound again. Not now that I had finally gotten it back.

"I'm—hrmph," she grunted, and it sounded like something had punched her in the stomach, making me anxious. *"I'm running. I don't know where I am. I'm in a forest, in the trees."*

"Just follow the bond. It'll lead you to me," I pleaded.

Rising higher in the air, I glanced around, squinting to see through the downpour. There were dense patches of trees in every direction, but only one the bond was pulling me toward—straight ahead, toward the awe-inspiring moon that encompassed the sky. But it was a long distance.

I needed to get to her *now*.

I pumped my wings harder, soaring through the air so fast the rain stung against my skin. It took more effort than it should have, and my muscles screamed in protest.

"Ryker, I'm so sor—"

"Don't," I rasped in a strained voice. *"I don't care about that right now. I just want you back in my arms."*

I just needed to get her back, to have her with me. We could sort out everything else later.

Her soft cries made my heart clench, and it wasn't just the rain that blurred my vision. My throat tightened, and I swallowed past it, forcing myself to focus.

"Are you hurt? Are you safe?" I couldn't feel anything from her beyond the flood of overwhelming emotions.

"No," she said through a broken voice. *"No, I'm not. I have to get out of here right now."*

"Okay, okay. Shift your wings and fly toward me," I tried to keep my voice level, though I couldn't prevent the worry slipping through.

"*I can't—Shit! They heard me running, they found me!*" she screamed, pure terror rushing down the bond.

"*Keep going, Kya! Don't stop! Just get to me, and we'll get out of here.*" I had no idea who they were, but I didn't want them getting anywhere near her. I just had to get to her, then I could fly us back to the arch.

"*I won't,*" she said between her panting breaths.

I could barely see the treeline in the far off distance through the penetrating rain. I pushed myself even harder, faster.

"*I'm coming. I'm coming. I'm coming,*" I promised over and over without even thinking.

"*I know,*" she whispered breathlessly. "*Ahh!*"

My stomach dropped at the sound of her blood-curdling scream. "*What? What's happening?*"

"*They're attacking,*" she grunted. "*I can't hold my invisibility and attack them back at the same time. There are too many of them. I don't know where they all came from.*"

I could faintly see flashes of blue and green coming from within the trees.

"*Don't fight, Kya. Try to keep up your invisibility so they don't know exactly where to hit. Just run. Do you hear me?*" I said in a demanding tone. "*Run!*"

I didn't care who those fuckers were, I would burn them where they stood for attacking her.

"*I'm here! I'm in the field!*"

In the far distance, I saw a small, dark figure emerging from the trees, sprinting toward me as I fought to get to her. *My mate.*

The bond purred with relief after finally laying eyes on her after so long. But that feeling was tarnished when a horde of people breached the treeline behind her. They were gaining on her.

Every heartbeat that passed felt like an eternity.

I pushed myself faster as I watched her fleeing for her life away from the mass of wielders throwing their magic at her, ducking under their blasts of magic and stumbling but never falling. She would deflect with her jade energy then disappear before reappearing farther to one side—zigzagging so they wouldn't know where to aim.

"Keep running! Don't stop! Don't look back!" I roared.

I released my shadows on the land below, racing them across the plain toward the onslaught chasing Kya. My wings pumped harder and harder.

Faster, faster, faster!

Flashes of color chased her, some materializing into chains and ropes, striking the ground and narrowly missing Kya as her feet slapped against the mud. She sprinted faster and faster, pushing her body's limits as she attempted to defend herself and counterattack with her Waalu.

My shadows reached her, parting around her to seek her pursuers. I bellowed with rage as I guided them to as many people as I could, forcing the darkness within every orifice of their bodies—suffocating them and tearing them apart. Yet still, more came. Too many for the both of us to fight against.

"Ryker!" Kya cried across the landscape. I was close enough to hear her and see the paralyzing fear in her features. "He's here!"

My gaze lifted to see the unmistakable form of Daegel emerging from the forest, running at full-speed.

We were out of time.

I dove at an angle, aiming straight for Kya. In the blink of an eye, one of the flashes of color transformed into chains and hurdled through the air toward her.

It wrapped around her legs, binding them together, while the other end attached to the ground and the entire thing became taut. She struck the ground so hard I heard something crack. My blood boiled.

"Ryker!"

Without thinking, my flames burst into superheated spheres that flew through the air so fast they went straight through the bodies approaching her. Except for Daegel, who had managed to evade the scorching projectiles.

I slammed to the ground harder than I intended, and the land shook beneath me with the force. My wings splayed out, eliciting gasps from the approaching enemies. My eyes locked with Daegel's just as he lifted his hands with a malicious grin, and roared an incantation that rippled through the pouring rain.

I barely had time to react. Out of instinct, I threw myself over her body to shield her from Daegel's magic, cocooning us with my wings. I curled myself around Kya's trembling body, holding her down as she tried to scramble up to get to me.

She whimpered, and I tightened my hold on her as we waited for the dark magic to hit.

But it never did.

The land trembled around us just before a guttural roar ripped through the air with a primal ferocity, loud enough to rattle my very bones. The hair stood on the back of my neck as the sound made a shiver run down my spine despite the overwhelming sensation of scorching heat.

I had never heard something so horrendous and formidable.

Daring to look, I lifted my head to find my Spirit dragon—with maw wide open—spewing fire so powerful it was consuming Daegel's magic and incinerating those that stood within the path of his flame. Theron bellowed in outrage as he did his duty to guard his Worthy, the depth of his rumbling power morphing into a high-pitched screech as he stood over us, caging us in and shielding us with his head lowered in front of us—protecting us.

I turned Kya over and gathered her into my arms, her wet, tangled hair splattered across her thin face. She held onto me tightly with a sob, kicking her legs frantically.

"Get them off! Get them off!"

The chains were still attached to her legs, and I threw my hand out, burning the ends of the metal attached to the ground with my fire—heating them so intensely they melted, separating the links.

She kicked them off of her as tears flowed down her cheeks, mixing with rain pattering her skin.

Theron took a step forward, swinging his head side to side to extend his flames down the mass of wielders.

"Time to go, Worthy!" he commanded with distress in his booming voice.

"Hold on to me!" I said, looking down at the precious body in my arms.

Kya gripped my shirt, clinging to me with desperation as I pulled her against my chest. I slapped a hand on the dragon's leg, and we vanished from this Godsforsaken realm.

Chapter Fifty-Six

KYA

Clinging to Ryker with my hands fisted in his rain-soaked shirt and my face buried against his chest, Theron Traveled us away from Vansera, away from Daegel, away from the realm that had been my prison for so long.

It took a lifetime for us to finally return home.

Then suddenly, a weight lifted off me. Everything was bright, and I felt the cold bite of the wind.

I inhaled a shaky breath, taking in the intoxicating smell of cedar and bergamot—of Ryker—and the familiar scent of the mountainous air in Oryn. My feet rested on frozen stone, and I felt the vibrations of the Voara palace beneath us, the city in the valley below, and the people there—alive.

Ryker grabbed my face, tilting it up to look at him—those silver eyes filled with longing. He slammed his lips onto mine, and a breathtaking shock jolted through my body.

Every emotion was in that one kiss. Undying love, anger, passion, pain, relief. It was in the desperation between our lips—the intensity flowing through the bond.

"Why did you do that, little gem?" he asked against my lips as his tears ran along the edges of my mouth.

The pain in his voice cracked my heart, and I choked on a sob, "I—I'm sorry. I'm so, so sorry."

He ran his nose along mine. "I can't tell you that I forgive you. I don't."

My chest tightened. I didn't forgive myself either. I never would.

"What you did, what you put us through... You were willing to *die*," his voice broke. "And I love you too fucking much to be okay with that."

He kissed me again with the ferocity of the fight he'd battled across the realms to get to me. Our tears merged, falling onto our laps as we were once again together as we always should be. My head fell against his chest, and he held me tightly as I wrapped my arms around his warm body and cried.

I was finally home, right where I belonged.

I didn't want to move. Never again did I want to leave the embrace of my mate, my husband. I never wanted to leave his side, feel his warmth leave me, or have any distance between us again.

Our bond thrummed with contentment as we stayed in each other's grasp.

We didn't move for several moments despite the freezing air. This moment of reunification was everything and nothing else existed as we remained in this world of our own, absorbing every ounce of emotion flowing between us, every sound of our breaths, every heartbeat thumping and throbbing with the passion and pain we shared.

Ryker kept me in his arms, holding me tightly as if afraid I'd disappear.

For the first time since I went into the Rip, I was able to stroke a soothing caress down the bond.

He exhaled a deep sigh, pulling me even closer and met my caress with affection and relief.

I didn't know if it was from the emotions threatening to burst from me or the cold, but my body shivered. Heat flooded from Ryker, warming me. I'd missed his warmth.

"Let's go inside," he whispered softly against my hair.

I didn't want to let go. I wanted to stay in this moment while it lasted.

I nodded and released my grip on his shirt, pulling away from him to stand, but he tightened his hold on me, not letting me go. I looked up at him, gazing into the silver eyes I dreamed of every night, and a lump formed in my throat.

"Please. Let me keep you in my arms just a little longer," he begged and stood, lifting me with him.

I sighed with relief, thankful to remain in his embrace.

I wrapped my arms around his neck and glanced over his shoulder to see Theron.

"Thank you," I mouthed silently.

He dipped his head in acknowledgment, holding my gaze with a tenderness in his daunting eyes I had never seen, then disappeared.

Ryker shifted his wings away and carried me inside, down long corridors and to the bedchamber where he took me into the bathing room. He gently placed me on the edge of the tub.

I gripped the lip of the porcelain to steady myself and winced when I adjusted my legs down to the floor. The chains from earlier had whipped around me so forcefully, I was sure the bones had cracked.

I glanced up at Ryker.

His eyes traveled along my body with an expression on his face I couldn't read. Between all of the emotions within him and me, I couldn't tell what he was feeling.

I wanted to speak, but I didn't know what to say. I had imagined this moment so many times, but now that it was here, every word that crawled up from my heart died in my throat.

He didn't know what to say either. With his mind or his voice, I desperately wished for him to say something. Anything.

My heart sank when he turned and began to walk away. I opened my mouth to protest him leaving the room, but I stopped myself. I had no right to ask him not to leave, not after I had even when he begged and pleaded for me not to, but I still couldn't help but think it over and over.

Don't leave me. I'm sorry. Please, don't leave me. Please, my shadow.

"I'm not going anywhere," he said quietly, having heard my thoughts, and turned around after grabbing a cloth from the shelf by the door. "I'm not letting you out of my sight again."

His promise was cold and angry.

I didn't blame him. I didn't want to leave his sight again. Never again. I learned my lesson and suffered the consequences for it—we both had.

I swallowed past the dryness in my throat. "I don't want you to," I said hoarsely.

He walked back over to me, holding my stare the entire time. "Let's get you out of these clothes, then we can bathe you." He reached for my shirt.

My eyes widened when I remembered my wings. I didn't want him to see. Not yet. And the thought of water…

"No." I raised a hand, and my breaths came faster.

He lowered his hand to his side and gave a single nod. "We…have a lot to discuss."

Leysa…

"Yeah. We do," I agreed sadly.

"What happened while you were there?" he asked softly.

"I don't want to talk about it right now…"

Gods, I didn't want our first interaction back together to be me telling him I killed his mother whom he had thought dead all this time.

His eyes briefly flicked to my forehead.

"Don't," I said quickly before he had the chance to see my memories.

He flinched slightly, almost imperceptibly, and looked...hurt. "I wouldn't do that to you."

"I'll tell you," I whispered, tears falling down the chilled skin of my cheeks. "I should be the one to tell you. I don't want you to see it. Right now, I just want to be with you," my voice broke. "I'll tell you everything tomorrow, I swear. I just want to get out of that place for right now. Please. Just for a little while before I'm dragged back there through my memories."

His heartbroken gaze held mine. "Alright, little gem."

Chapter Fifty-Seven

RYKER

"Shalna, get to my bedchamber right away," I shouted from the doorway before rushing back and leading Kya from the bathing room toward the wardrobe after she had cleaned herself with a cloth, refusing to get in the tub.

I opened the wardrobe to grab some clothes, holding on to her hand, then handed them to her.

"Thank you," she whispered and took a step back, deliberately facing me as she began to remove the filthy tattered fabric she had been wearing.

I didn't know if she just wanted to keep her eyes on me or if it was something else.

My soul was settled having her back in my presence, but my heart ached when I looked at her. It took everything in me not to go right back to that realm and tear Daegel limb from limb for what he had done to her.

My calm demeanor was temporary, and I knew it wouldn't last for long. I had to keep my mouth from gaping as she removed her clothes.

When I saw Kya running toward me in that field, I hardly recognized her. But seeing her now, it was as if she was in a different body altogether—nothing more than a husk of what she used to be.

I didn't even know how to react, too shocked at the sight of her. So frail, so unlike the healthy, strong female that had walked through these halls before.

Her hair was a tangled mess of mud and twigs. Her skin... It clung to her like wet paper, revealing every bone in her sickeningly thin body. She was utterly emaciated. Dark shadows circled her sunken, bloodshot eyes.

They did this to her. They kept her on the brink of death.

I swallowed back my anger and heartache.

For now.

I leaned against the bed as the healer looked over Kya, stepping around the chair she was sitting in to inspect every inch of her body. The healer examined her arms and legs, her eyes, throat, and abdomen. She asked Kya questions about food and liquids she'd consumed, anything she was exposed to and what her environment was like—being as thorough as possible. All she knew was Kya had been taken to a foreign place and held captive.

"You're weak due to malnourishment, dehydration, muscle atrophy, and sleep deprivation. Now, I need to ask you another question, but I need to know if you would prefer to discuss it in private," Shalna asked Kya gently.

Kya's brows pinched. "You can ask whatever you need to in front of Ryker."

Shalna glanced at me from the corner of her eye before taking a deep breath. "Alright. Were you sexually assaulted during your captivity?"

I froze. Unblinking, unmoving, unbreathing, and I was sure my heart stopped as I waited for the answer.

The slight widening of Kya's eyes formed a pit in my stomach.

"I only need to know so I can check you for injuries or pregnancy, if needed," Shalna whispered softly, comfortingly.

Kya swallowed and raised her chin. "I have no injuries and I'm not pregnant."

She turned to look at me and spoke into my mind. *"I was touched. Once. I stopped him before he could do anything. I'm sor—"*

"You will not apologize for what was done to you. It was not your fault, and you are not to blame," I said firmly, trying and failing to keep my voice calm and level.

My blood boiled, and I couldn't control my shadows from darkening the room. I wanted to find who touched her—who had laid a hand on my wife. I wanted to tear his skin off and make him pay for touching what is mine—what belongs to me. It didn't matter that he was stopped. The thought of anyone doing *anything* to Kya sent me into a blinding rage.

Shalna gasped.

"Ryker…" Kya said warily, her hand reaching for me.

"I'm not upset with *you*. I want to kill—"

"He's already dead. He suffered for it. I promise. It's done now, and there's nothing that can change it," she bit out.

The tension in the air was thick—not for each other but for what had happened.

I nodded and withdrew my shadows.

Shalna cleared her throat. "The last thing I need to check is your back. Can you lift your shirt please?"

Kya stiffened and hesitated. Her eyes began to glisten, and her lower lip trembled. But she nodded and stood, turning to face away from us. She pulled at the collar of her shirt behind her neck until her back was exposed.

"Gods…" I whispered under my breath.

Two large gruesome scars marred the skin where her wings once were. They were pitted and disfigured, creating horrendous images in my mind of what could have possibly happened.

She had endured so much.

All my anger towards her withered away. She didn't deserve the suffering of my frustration for leaving me on top of everything else she had already been subjected to.

Shalna didn't make a sound and began tenderly pressing a finger around the areas. Kya's skin twitched and shivered at the lightest touch.

"Are you in pain? Do they feel tender?"

Kya sniffled. "They feel wrong."

"Hmm," Shalna hummed. "Can you tell me what happened so I can better understand what I'm looking at here?"

Kya took a shaky breath.

I stepped around them until I was in front of her and took her hand in mine, leaning forward to kiss her softly.

"It's okay," I whispered down the bond.

"I know. It's better they took my wings than my life," she said quietly then wiped at her cheek and cleared her throat.

"They carved out my wings with a knife while I was kept immobile. I think they were trying to be quick about it, but it still felt like a lifetime."

She was awake…

"Then one of them came back and cleaned the wounds with some kind of healing liquid of theirs." Her voice broke, "Is there any way you can fix it?"

Shalna pulled down the shirt, and Kya turned around to face her, leaning against me with my arm wrapped around her thin waist.

"I'm sorry. I don't know anything about shifting. I think it would be a question best directed to the Spirits since that's whom it stems from originally." Her lips pulled into a tight line.

Odarum...

Kya needed to know. I wanted to tell her immediately, but it wasn't the right time—not that there really was one. So much had already happened in the last few hours, I didn't want to overwhelm her.

Shalna walked over to her bag and pulled out a few vials, setting them down on the table next to us. "Take one of these each day for the next ten days. It will help replenish the nutrients your body has been deprived of. Drink plenty of water and eat well, but not so much you make yourself sick. I'll have food and water brought up for you. And you need to rest. If you have issues with sleeping, I have something that can help."

Kya turned to the table and grabbed one of the vials. Shalna gave me a knowing look and nodded toward the door. I followed behind her, and she stopped as she placed her palm on the handle.

"It's not just her body that's broken, Lord Ryker," she whispered so only I could hear.

I nodded slowly.

"I know what's going on at the border, and I know she needs to be involved, but your mate needs to heal. Her body will do that in a few days' time, but everything else... That will take longer."

After we ate, Kya and I sat on the bed, her hand resting in mine as she stared down at it.

"I need to tell you some things that happened while I was there, what I learned," she said, glancing up at me.

I missed gazing into those pine-green eyes. Even through everything, they were still filled with promise—the smallest embers of that once blazing fire within them.

I smiled, and those embers grew with the lifting of my lips. "Not tonight, little gem. We just need to rest tonight."

She relaxed against me and looked at the pillows longingly with exhaustion in her gaze.

I guided her to bed and crawled in after her, not even bothering to undress.

"I missed you so much," she whispered as I pulled her into me. "I love you, beyond the bond."

My heart swelled, and I kissed her on the forehead. "Beyond the bond."

It took mere seconds before her breaths were long and even. I closed my eyes, caressing the bond connecting us, content for the first time since she disappeared. Just as I was about to fall asleep with my mate back in my arms, Theron's voice sounded in my head.

"Odarum wishes to see his Worthy."

Chapter Fifty-Eight

ZALEN

I had shown Maera the sketch of the stone in her notebook, and she remembered right where it was. The next morning, I had a horse brought up to take us into the forest near the northeastern side of what used to be Aedum. I sat her in front of me as we rode across Damanthus, weaving our way through the trees during the journey that would take us half a day.

"So this stone," I started, struggling to focus as her ass swayed in the saddle, rubbing against me. "How did you find it?"

She shrugged. "I just stumbled upon it. I was foraging for some herbs I didn't have access to, and I was curious about what it was. I knew it wasn't natural, and most of it was buried under dirt and grass and moss with just a small section exposed. So one day I spent a couple of hours uncovering it, then I drew a rough sketch."

"Have you been to it since then?" I asked, resting my hands on her thighs as she held the reins.

"Yes. Only after I figured out what it was." She turned her head to the side to look at me.

My mouth spread into a grin. Of course, she couldn't let some new discovery go forgotten. She was such a curious little witch.

"Then you know what it does," I stated.

She nodded.

"And did you tell anyone?" It was important for me to know who was aware of its location.

"No," she said quickly. "I didn't want anyone else to know about it. Not after I knew what it could be used for. Could you imagine what my father would have done if he found out?"

Likely not much different from what I was going to do.

"Hmm," I hummed. "Unfortunately, I think it's already been discovered."

She twisted her body in the saddle to face me. "Why do you think that?"

"Because I believe that's how the King killer has been traveling around so quickly from Kingdom to Kingdom," I stated.

Her face fell. "Oh," she said quietly. "So he's still out there?"

I sighed. "It's possible the captain you were betrothed to killed not only Makkor and the King of Innon but also the King of Shara. There's reason to suspect he's now taken over the Shara Kingdom."

Her eyes widened, and her spine stiffened.

I offered a reassuring smile. "Don't worry. We're taking care of it. But I need to find that stepstone."

It wasn't long before Maera led us to an area in the old Aedum forest that was tucked within a dense patch of vegetation. She pulled the horse to a stop in front of a mass of thicket.

I dismounted then grabbed her by the waist and lifted her from the saddle, setting her on the ground.

"It's in here?" I asked, approaching the blockage of vines covered in thorns. I pricked my finger on the sharp nettle.

"Wait. This is a flaki from one of my potions. And a strong one at that. You *won't* get through," she warned. Her hair fell around her face as she began rummaging through the small satchel at her side, the glass jars and vials clinking against each other.

"I won't, huh?" I asked as if it were a challenge.

"Nope," she said with a pop of her lips. "You're welcome to try, but you'll just come out of it looking like a bloody pincushion."

She was probably right. Using a flaki potion was clever. It was an exceedingly difficult compound to create and, therefore, a rare encounter. The brew was designed to create an impenetrable barrier of a seemingly endless tangle of shrubbery. Swords and spells couldn't tear through it, only a counter potion to stop the continual regrowth and force the plants to wither back into the ground.

Maera pulled out a palm-sized jar of the retraction potion with a pleased grin. She unstoppered it and poured the liquid in a line the width of our bodies. The thorny barrier slithered apart, creating a passage.

I loved watching her work.

I gave her a proud smile and took her by the hand, leading through the foliage. On the other side, there was an open area surrounding a patch of rich-green grass. The round stepstone of Odes was in the center.

It was large with a wide enough diameter that I could lay in the center and my head and feet wouldn't meet the edges. I stepped closer, letting go of Maera's hand and bending down to inspect the sacred footprint—lined with the symbols of God. I felt the magical thrum in my blood as I carefully placed the palm of my hand on the stone.

"It's called Horgor," Maera offered. "Which means—"

"Sanctuary step," I finished. "Do you know how it works?" I looked up at Maera. It wouldn't be useful if we didn't know *how* to use it.

"I…" she stopped herself with a guilty look and fiddled nervously with the fabric of her blue skirt.

I stood and gave her a knowing look with a raised brow. I knew she wouldn't lie, but she was holding back.

She sighed deeply. "There's a human… A friend of mine. Or she was, until she died a few years back. Long ago, one of her ancestors knew the spell to unlock the use of the stepstone. Humans hated magic users, you know that. So they passed down the information from generation to generation, holding this secret for hundreds of years. But Lara… she didn't have anyone to pass it down to. She was the last in the line of her family, having been born barren. When she saw me researching the stepstone, she told me, and I wrote it down so it wouldn't be lost forever. She died four months later…" Her bright eyes held mine from beneath her lashes. "You want to use it, don't you? To kill others?"

I didn't bother responding. She knew my answer even if she didn't like it.

She nodded, not arguing, and I saw the acceptance cross over her eyes. She hated violence, but she was learning who I truly was—who she was in love with.

She had been so damn good, accepting me and my depravity. I took her face in my hands before pressing my lips against hers.

"You're *extraordinary*."

Her cheeks flushed, and her eyes brightened at the praise. It's amazing how something as small as a few heartfelt words can make such a positive impact on someone.

"Come on. Let's head back, and I can let Thane know where the stepstone is. You wouldn't happen to recall the spell in that brilliant mind of yours would you?"

Her cheeks reddened even further, lifting with her smile. "Fara."

Our ride back to Kanth was an experience unlike any Maera and I had shared. We took our time, keeping the horse at a steady walk while we talked for hours. I don't think we had ever talked this much in one sitting. And not one word about the worries of the future.

She asked me questions about my past we'd never had time for before. She knew the overall story of my life but not specific details and memories. I asked her questions about certain times in her past as well, but her life had been much lonelier than mine.

We were deepening our understanding of each other.

"You should have seen the look on my mother's face." I huffed a laugh as I told her of the time I got into a mess of trouble with a group of children, vandalizing the castle portraits with obscure drawings. My father was furious, but of course, that was the point and only the beginning of my unruly behavior during my childhood.

Maera giggled. "Is that how you and Thane met?"

"No. His father was Makkor's advisor, so we had known each other for years at that point, though we didn't grow close until much later."

"Well, don't leave out the exciting part." She nudged me with her elbow. "What happened?"

I chuckled. "Do you really want to know?"

"Obviously," she said pointedly.

At least she couldn't say I didn't warn her. "Thane was very small as a child, and it wasn't until his late teenage years that he grew into his size. Add that to being the royal advisor's son, he had few friends. Anyway, one day I was coming back from a hunt and saw him being dragged into the forest by a group of teenagers, stripping him naked and beating the shit out of him. I really didn't care about Thane at the time—I actually hated him because of who his father was. Normally I would have just kept going, but I was still riding the adrenaline high from my kill."

"And you stopped them?" she asked.

"Permanently."

She turned her head to face me, and I held back a chuckle at her expression. "You *killed* them?"

"With my bare hands."

She opened her mouth to speak but stopped at the sound of a distant snarl over the crunching of the horse's hooves on the snow-covered path.

I gently tugged on the reins I was holding around Maera's waist, bringing the horse to a stop so we could listen more easily.

Another snarl. It sounded weak but that could have been from the distance.

"What is that?" Maera asked quietly.

"I have no idea." I shook my head. But my interest was piqued.

I led the horse off the path, following the melancholic sound.

"Zalen," Maera hissed in a whisper. "What are you doing? You don't know what it is."

"Not yet." I shrugged.

"Well," she scoffed. "Aren't you afraid it's something danger-ous?"

Oh, my little witch. You still don't understand.

I leaned in close, my lips brushing behind her ear. "I have nothing to be afraid of when I'm the most dangerous thing here."

477

She shivered. "So, what—you don't have any fears?"

I reached around and gripped her chin, turning her head and gazing into her eyes. "Just one."

One so paralyzing I would do *anything* to avoid ever encountering it.

After several minutes of winding through the trees, we came upon a grotesque scene, and Maera gasped. Even my eyes widened at the sight.

A large snow leopard lay on the forest floor, nearly dead and snarling at the pain of a gaping hole in its chest. I had never seen one, only heard of their kind being up in the northern mountains of Innon. They were extremely rare. There were wounds from bites and claw marks all over its body, and it was unable to continue, having created a wide trail of blood from where it had crawled and fallen here. *She* was bleeding out.

A young cub, maybe only a few weeks or months old, raised its head from behind her.

"Oh, the poor thing," Maera said and slowly got off the horse.

I quickly hopped down, holding my arm out in front of her to stop her from approaching the animals. "Let me take care of the mother first."

"Take care of her?"

"Give her a merciful death."

"You're not going to try to save her?" she asked sternly.

I softened my voice. "She's beyond saving. It would only prolong her suffering."

"Oh."

"I'll make it quick. Stay here," I said firmly.

I slowly crept forward, so as not to startle the cub, and crouched down in front of its mother. Her eyes were open, glazed with a milky-white sheen as she waited for death. I gathered the large head into my hands, careful to keep the mouth facing away from me. Her skull was as large as my lap. The white fur was soft beneath my fingers as I orientated my hands on either side of her head. With a sudden jerk, I twisted, snapping her neck. She released a final breath, then her chest was still.

I glanced back at Maera, who was tense with worry, and I nodded my head. Her shoulders dropped, and she stepped forward, walking around the carcass. She tenderly collected the cub in her arms.

"She's so thin," Maera said, looking over the orphaned animal.

I rose to a stand. "It won't survive without its mother," I said and extended my hand toward her.

Maera looked at my hand as if it was offensive and leaned back away from me. "What are you going to do with her?"

"Kill it so it doesn't suffer by starving to death or getting mauled by another creature. It's more merciful this way. It will be painless. I promise," I offered softly.

She gazed down at the cub, stroking its head and holding it closer to the warmth of her chest.

Don't pet the beast or you'll want to keep it.

She looked back to me, raising her chin stubbornly. "I'm keeping her," she said sternly, leaving no room for argument.

I rolled my eyes, knowing I shouldn't have let her touch the damn thing.

Maera raised her brows. "Are you going to deny me saving a life? I think it's only fair after so many you've taken."

I sighed heavily and dropped my arm, but I couldn't help the side of my mouth from lifting. "No. I'll deny you nothing."

"Good. Because I was going to keep her anyway. It's what you get for killing my parents," she quipped with a grin.

I chuckled and gestured for her to return to the horse. I picked her up and set her on the saddle while she held the cub, then climbed up behind her. Reaching around to grab the reins, the cub snapped its sharp little teeth at me, and I glared at it.

"Am I going to have to get you a new pet for everyone I kill?" I drawled playfully, leading us out of the forest and back to Kanth, leaving the dead mother behind for nature to consume.

"Is that a problem?" she asked in a sweet tone, nuzzling the leopard with her nose.

"No. I just don't think the castle is big enough. We might have to expand."

She stiffened for a moment, realizing what I meant, but then relaxed at the touch of my lips on her cheek. "I suppose I can live with that."

Chapter Fifty-Nine

―◦―

ZALEN

"How large?" I asked Thane.

He had just returned from Shara with his report from the infiltrators. This new King—still a complete mystery despite our best efforts—had ordered an assembly of his masses, building an army of any able-bodied magic user or human.

"We don't have an exact number, but if they really are forcing every man and woman over the age of sixteen, then it will be in the tens of thousands. The humans alone triple their numbers." He sat across from me in my study, alert and at the ready regardless of how exhausted he must have been.

"And with the additional witches and sorcerers from Aedum and Innon we've absorbed, that still rivals our numbers." I leaned forward and started jotting down the numbers, comparing them.

"Unless," Thane said slowly. "We increase our numbers too."

I glanced up, meeting his knowing look at what he was insinuating.

"No," I stated plainly.

"It's a tactical advantage to at least get more boots on the ground," he argued.

"I said no."

He took a deep breath. "Can I ask *why*?"

"I don't care if they live or die, but the humans would be nothing more than dead bodies getting in my way. One magic user is worth thirty humans in a moment of battle. We don't need to outnumber them. We need to outmaneuver them—and better yet, overpower them. With me holding the power of two Kingdoms, the people also have increased power."

"Alright. What's your plan?" He crossed his arms over his chest.

"For starters, we're going to get into Shara undetected and slaughter as many of those fuckers as we can."

His brows creased. "How are we going to get in undetected?"

I spun the book in front of me so it was facing him, already open to the page Ander had shown me about the Horgor.

"At the same time, I want to line the border with every magic user we have, creating a blockade to keep anyone from escaping Shara," I said.

"*Escaping* Shara?" he asked, looking up from the book. "Isn't the concern about us getting in, not them getting out?"

"The biggest threat to Damanthus' rule lies within those borders. I want to contain it, then destroy it from the inside."

"What about everyone inside?"

"Let them burn." I shrugged.

"Hmm. But other than those who are already there, how are the rest of us going to get in? With these God-touched footprints?" he asked skeptically.

I pulled out a map and laid it across the desk, trailing my hand across the parchment until it reached the area of the woods where Maera had shown me the stepstone.

"Here is the Horgor. We can use it to get into Shara." I glanced up to Thane who was deep in thought, waiting for his response.

"How do you know it leads to one in Shara? Is that the next step or is there one closer?" he asked after a moment.

I blinked. "What do you mean?"

He nodded to the book I had just shown him. "They're stepstones that travel you from one to the other right?"

"Yes," I said dryly.

"Well, do they go in order? Can each one only take you to the next one, or can you go to any you choose?"

I hated to admit it—I really did—but I had no idea. It wasn't something that had crossed my mind. But since it was his thought in the first place...

"I guess you'll find out." I shrugged with a sly grin.

He rolled his eyes. "Fine. But—Ah!" Thane nearly jumped across the room when he looked down. "What is *that* doing in here?"

I quickly stood and looked over the desk at his feet. I groaned internally when I saw a white and gray mass of fur pawing at Thane's boot. The sounds of footsteps approaching had me raising my head to see Maera pushing open the ajar door to my study with a confused look.

She looked up from her search, and her eyes met mine, wide with embarrassment. "Oh, I'm sorry. I was just looking for—Anera! There you are."

"You named it?" I said with an amused smile.

"*Her*," she corrected sternly. "And of course I did."

Maera crossed the room and gathered the beast in her arms. Anera pinned her ears back when she saw me, and I bared my teeth in return. Maera rolled her eyes, watching the interaction.

"You two will get used to each other soon enough. Just be nice to her, Zalen." She leveled me with an adorable, stern look in her eyes.

"I let her live. That seems pretty nice to me." I shrugged.

"You have a cat? I hate cats…" Thane grumbled under his breath but not low enough Maera couldn't hear.

She glared at him.

"She's a leopard, not some mangy alley cat. You'll deal with it," I ordered Thane, and Maera raised her head proudly. "Thane, you can leave now. I want a few minutes with Maera."

Thane bowed his head in my direction then to Maera and left, softly closing the door behind him.

I stepped around the desk and came up to Maera, gripping her throat and pulling her lips to mine. I kissed her deeply until she was out of breath.

"You're going to have to find somewhere Anera can be locked up tomorrow night," I said as I pulled away and let go.

"Why?" she asked through a pant, smiling.

"We can't have her running around the castle unattended during the wedding." I smirked.

"The wedding? *Tomorrow*? I thought we still had another week!" she exclaimed.

I chuckled. "It seems the days have passed you by with everything going on."

"No. I know exactly how long it's been. You killed my father only a week ago."

"Yes, but my father was killed a week before that. And according to the old laws, a fortnight is the allocated amount of time." Perhaps I should have been more communicative with her about this from the perplexed look on her face.

"I'm an idiot. I had it in my head that since you took my father's power, you'd have to wait two weeks after *his* death," she said, shaking her head.

"Only if I were going through the Drehiri on Aedum land, but I'm not. Both of us will do it here in Damanthus. After we wed. It will be done privately and discreetly."

"When did you decide this? That I'd be going through it too." She was getting worked up.

"A while ago."

Her smile faltered. "Why?"

I guided her to sit down in the seat, running my hand through my unkempt hair as I sat next to her.

"Now that I know of the stepstones, I'm guessing the murderer is using them to get from Kingdom to Kingdom. I don't trust anything or anyone right now so I want us to go through the Drehiri as soon as possible—especially you."

"Why does that matter? I'm a witch. Not a sorcerer." She shrugged as if it was pointless. "I can't make fancy shit happen with the muttering of a word and a flick of my wrist. I don't really see the point in me going through it."

She didn't understand my deep-seated fear that something would happen, and she wouldn't be able to protect herself like she could after going through the Drehiri. If the murderer was going after royals, then both of us were targets. I refused to allow either one of us to be caught fighting against someone while we weren't as powerful as we could be.

"You know the lightning potion you used back in Aedum to hold me off while you tried to run away?" I asked.

She nodded.

"When you go through the Drehiri, you'll gain royal power, and the next time you brew a lightning potion, it'll be strong enough to destroy this entire building rather than just a single room."

"Oh." Her eyes glanced around the room as if she were mentally measuring it. "What about the coronation?"

I smiled and took her hand in mine, bringing her wrist up to my lips and kissing her imperceptible scar. "By this time tomorrow, you will be Queen of Damanthus."

"You seem nervous," I said as Maera and I approached the throne room.

Her arm rested on mine, but she was tense and fidgeting with her ceremonial gown—which I couldn't wait to rip off later.

"A little," she said with a shaky breath but reassured me with a smile.

Arnesia had worked through the night to get her gown completed, and I had to admit, she did very well.

A cream dress and a hooded robe, perfectly fitted to Maera's form, draped to the floor, cascading behind her as it softly brushed the stone floor with her movements in the dark hall. The shoulders of the robe were covered with white fur. The low-cut dress exposed the top of her breasts and was stitched with golden lace. Staying with tradition, her head would remain hooded until the coronation, when she would be crowned immediately following the wedding ceremony.

I wore a long, blue tunic—so dark it appeared black—also covered by a hooded robe and paired with my dark pants and boots. Though we differed in many ways, we were the perfect accompaniment for each other.

She was the beacon of light within my darkness.

We stopped in front of the large double doors. "Are you ready, minn astir?" I asked, looking down at her.

She gazed up at me with her bright blue eyes from beneath her hood. "I'm ready."

Oveus—the only Elder I trusted—presided over the ceremony. He stood in front of us on the dais and recited the prayers for the heavens to bless our union. I didn't need a lost God's blessing. We would be together no matter what—no God nor Kingdom would stop this union. But I remained silent and allowed the traditional words to be spoken.

"Join your hands and state your words of honor." Oveus gestured between Maera and I.

We turned to face each other. I took her hands in mine and brought our heads together, our lips nearly brushing against each other. No magic would be used.

Joined in breath and body, we spoke our oath in unison.

"I give you my promise, my eternal dedication, and my unwavering devotion to you and you alone, surpassing beyond this mortal life."

Maera's face brightened, elation glistening in her eyes. I had never seen her so happy before. That look on her face would be etched in my memory forever.

"Zalen," Oveus began. "Please kneel."

I winked at Maera, making her blush, then turned to face the Elder with my head held high, kneeling in front of the throne right where my father's body had lain. I stared at the throne. This was the moment I had planned for years. Everything was falling into place.

"Zalen Drolvega. As the only living royal of the Drolvega line, you are tasked with the honor and responsibility of the Kingdom of Damanthus." Oveus stepped out of my line of sight and returned a moment later holding the crown I'd had crafted.

The crowns of Damanthus, Innon, and Aedum had been melted and reformed as one. A trophy, a symbol of my triumph and power over what was once three separate Kingdoms and forged into one. And I intended to add a fourth, erasing any lines of separation that divided the lands.

One crown, one Kingdom—one King and Queen.

Slowly, I removed my hood, letting it fall behind me as Oveus raised the crown.

"Do you, Zalen Drolvega, swear to uphold your duty to the Kingdom, reining over it until your last breath?" he asked.

"On my honor."

He nodded and placed the metal on my head. I stood, and Oveus bowed low at the waist.

"King Zalen Drolvega."

I turned to face Maera who began to lower in a bow, and my nostrils flared.

"You do not bow. Not to me. Not to anyone."

Her spine straightened, and she gave a shallow but firm nod.

The side of my mouth lifted, and I sat down on the throne behind me. "Siyna," I uttered with a wave of my hand next to me, breaking the concealing spell.

Maera's lips parted in a gasp as another throne appeared next to mine. Two thrones made of three, just like the crowns. She would be the first Queen to have a throne.

It was her turn to be crowned. I watched her kneel before her throne, and Oveus stepped in front of her.

"Maera Drolvega…"

I inhaled sharply. Fuck, that had a nice ring to it, and it sang to my ears. Just hearing her name paired with mine had my chest swelling with pride.

"…formerly Samanya. As the joined royal of the Drolvega line, you are tasked with the honor and responsibility of the Kingdom of Damanthus."

He grabbed another crown and placed it upon her head.

Everything else seemed to disappear, and all I could see was Maera as she swore to uphold her duties to *our* Kingdom. I stood and held the honor of announcing her reign.

"Queen Maera Drolvega," the words felt so good as they crossed my lips.

She smiled widely, displaying that sweet mouth of hers, and I stepped toward her. I waved Oveus away, and he quickly exited the throne room, leaving the new sovereigns alone.

In the darkness of the midnight hour, with nothing but the glow of the moon streaming through the windows for light, I took her face in my hands and kissed my wife—my *Queen.* My hand wrapped around to the back of her head, brushing against the cool metal of her crown, and deepened the kiss.

She pulled back, a blush running up her neck.

"What now?" she whispered, gazing around the room in awe.

I glanced at the throne behind her, then slowly trailed my eyes back to her with a look of unmistakable intent. Her breath caught, and her knowing eyes widened with thrill.

"I told you I was going to fuck you on every throne in the realm." I grinned, wrapping my arm around her waist and pulling her against me. "Now, I keep my promise."

Chapter Sixty

RYKER

I hadn't slept all night. I couldn't. No matter how hard I tried.

Every time I closed my eyes, I was terrified I'd open them to find her gone again—to find that she'd left me again. So I stayed awake, holding her all night and listening to the soft sounds of her sleep. She twitched and jerked all through the night, and each time I would hold her a little tighter, grazing down the bond to soothe whatever was tormenting her slumber.

I was tempted to enter her mind, to see what horrors haunted her dreams. I wanted to aid in her rest and chase away her nightmares, but I resisted. Losing her had turned me into something I never wanted to be, and I refused to be that beast now that she was back. She didn't need that kind of invasion, and if I was being honest with myself, it was better I didn't see. I had to trust she would tell me in time.

Even if the trust between us was brittle.

Just as the winter clouds began to flush soft shades of pink with the morning's light, I decided to wake my slumbering wife.

"Kya." I brushed her hair away from her face, pushing it off her neck and behind her shoulder.

She didn't stir, stuck in a deep sleep. I hated to wake her, but Odarum was only going to wait so long before he came barging in here demanding to see his Worthy, and I didn't want that to be the way she found out.

"Kya," I said out loud this time, softly rubbing my hand up and down her arm.

She still didn't move aside from her eyes darting back and forth beneath her lids.

I leaned my head forward and placed a kiss on her dry, cracked lips. "Little gem."

Her eyes snapped open with a gasp, looking around frantically and breathing heavily.

"Easy. It's okay. You're safe. You're home," I soothed.

Her face relaxed, and a ghost of a smile splayed across her features. "I thought..." She swallowed. "I was afraid it was all a dream. But you're really here." She nuzzled into me, sighing.

"It's real. I'm here. *You're* here." I kissed the top of her head.

"He insists he see her. He knows she has rested," Theron said from wherever he was.

"Tell him we'll be there shortly," I clipped.

"Thank you," she whispered.

"You don't have to thank me. I would have done anything to get you back. But I do want to prepare you, today is going to be an...emotional day," I said quietly

She looked up at me with concern, and I could hear her worried thoughts.

"It's nothing bad. But it will be a lot to take in," I reassured her.

"What is it?" She sat up, and I noticed the dark circles under her eyes were lighter.

I took a deep breath. "I'll tell you, but I want you to remain calm." Even though I knew she wouldn't be.

She grinned. "I'll be fine."

I smiled in return. "I went to Hylithria to talk to Xareus, demanding he send me to you."

"You made demands of your God for me?" she breathed.

I flicked the tip of her nose playfully. "Little gem, when are you going to learn I would do so much more than that?"

Her cheeks blushed.

"While I was there…" I squeezed her hand. "I saw Odarum. He's alive, and he's here. To see you."

Kya's entire body froze, and I thought she didn't hear me for a moment, but then she leapt out of the bed and stumbled her way to the wardrobe.

I threw the sheets off me and walked over to her just as she was taking out some warmer clothes.

"Kya, wait. You said you'd remain calm." I grabbed her shoulder and turned her around to face me.

She looked more confused than anything, and she stared blankly in the distance for a moment. "Why can't I speak to him? The bond is—"

"I don't know. But you don't need to rush this. He'll still be there when you're ready. He's not going anywhere."

"Odarum wishes to see her now," Theron growled.

"Just give her a fucking minute!" I barked.

"Get dressed and eat something, then we can go see him." I soothed down the bond again, trying to keep her calm and needing her to take care of herself first.

She shook her head. "I can eat after. I need to see him."

"No, you will eat before," I said firmly. "It's not a request. I know you're eager to see him, but a few more minutes and a belly full of food won't hurt anything."

She sighed and nodded then began to change. "Alright. But I want to hurry."

Dressed and fed, we briskly walked down the corridor to the balcony. Once we rounded the corner and saw the doors leading outside, she stopped—frozen in place. The palace was silent and everything was still.

I reached out to touch her, to see if she was alright.

Then she ran, bolting through the doors and darting toward the roof as I chased after her, her loose hair flying behind her.

She gasped a sob at the sight of her Spirit Guardian standing in the center of the building with Theron behind him.

Odarum raised his head with his ears turned forward, his black wings shimmering in the morning light peeking over the mountain tops.

She didn't stop, dashing across the cold stone roof and threw herself against Odarum, wrapping her arms around his thick neck. His head curled around her back as a low, soothing rumble sounded from his chest.

I slowed to a walk, placing my hands in my pockets, and went over to stand next to Theron so Kya and Odarum could have their reunion.

"What are you doing here?" I asked the dragon.

"I brought Odarum," he said as if it was obvious.

I glanced at him from the corner of my eye. *"You* brought *him? Why?"*

Theron lowered his head. *"Because he can no longer Travel in the ways of the Spirits."*

"How come? Is he still injured?" I asked with a pinched brow.

I glanced to Odarum with Kya rubbing a hand over his mane, still holding him. He didn't look injured.

Theron was silent for a moment, watching the interaction between Odarum and Kya. *"Odarum made a sacrifice. He is bound to guard your mate until her last breath. He made that choice when he chose to be her Fylgjur. In order for him to survive so he could continue to protect her, he chose to sacrifice his immortality."*

My head whipped to him. *"What?! What does that mean?"*

Theron's fire-filled eyes met mine. *"It means that Odarum is no longer a Spirit. He still holds the bond to her—now reformed with their reunion—as well as his magic, but he can no longer Travel. He is no longer welcome in Hylithria. He is mortal."*

He gave up his immortality. He did that for her.

Odarum looked at me then and held my gaze. He lowered his head toward me—a gesture of gratitude.

The side of my mouth lifted, and I nodded in return.

Kya took a step back and ran a hand down her Guardian's face with a tear-streaked smile. She shivered, and I could tell she was cold, so I released heat far enough to reach her while she continued to stand there for a long while.

I assumed they were talking to each other, and I waited beside Theron for well over an hour while they reconnected, giving her time with her Fylgjur.

"Odarum and I aren't bonded. We don't have a connection. So how was he able to talk to me in Hylithria?" I asked Theron. I figured since we were sitting here, I might as well get some answers to my endless questions.

"What we are able to do on Hylithria is different from here. At least it is now," he said.

"Care to elaborate?" One of these days, this cranky-ass would actually offer up information freely and not make me pull it out of him.

"Not particularly, but I will. Spirits used to be able to communicate with all life here in Taeralia. But ever since the accord to no longer interfere with your realm was created, we no longer have that capability. Except with our Worthy."

"Oh. It seems that 'no interference' bullshit has caused a lot of problems for everyone," I huffed.

"Not as many as there were before," he said seriously.

That was unsettling. I struggled imagining it being worse then than it is now, our realm plagued by a dark wielder and on the brink of a continental war.

My mind wandered. This was only the beginning of what had changed while Kya was away. She still didn't know about Atara or the Atarans. And I wasn't looking forward to telling her she had her Nation and her people back, only for me to tell her about the impending threat of war with the Worthy.

"We have our bond back," Kya said, bringing me out of my thoughts to see her walking toward me with a soft smile that melted my worries away.

I had missed that smile. I missed everything about her. I reached for her hand, needing to touch her again.

"That's good." I pulled her closer to me and kissed her forehead.

"He said he gave up his immortality so he could stay with me…" Her head fell.

I brought my other hand up and lifted her chin until she looked at me. "I know. But it was his choice. It wasn't your fault."

"I know." She nodded. "You both made such great sacrifices, and I…" She blew out a breath and closed her eyes. "I have to tell you something."

I rubbed my thumb across the back of her hand. "What is it?"

Her eyes opened, holding an anguish that had a chill running down my spine. "It's about your mother."

Chapter Sixty-One

KYA

I took Ryker by the hand and led him inside, letting Odarum know I'd be back soon. This was a conversation that deserved privacy.

"You saw her?" Ryker asked quietly just as we entered the bedchamber.

"Yeah. We were…imprisoned together."

I didn't really know how to say that her life was being used against me. I also didn't know if it was her choice or Daegel's to grow closer to me, to build a relationship with me so I would be more inclined to do what he wanted in order to spare her.

"Your father had been right the whole time. She was alive—"

"How did she die?" he asked with a stone expression.

For a split second, I was confused on how he could know she died. But then I understood.

Cadoc.

My eyes lowered to the ground. I couldn't look Ryker in the eye. I wasn't sure what he would think of me, of what I'd done—the choices I'd made.

Please don't hate me…

"I never will," he said through our bond, hearing my thoughts.

I toed the floor, unsure of where to start.

"Leysa…" I released a shaky breath. "Daegel wanted me to complete a task for him, and I kept refusing. Your mother was being used as an incentive, so I would do what he wanted. He kept us together constantly, which was nice because I got to know her." I swallowed.

"A couple of days before you came for me, Daegel was gone, and I saw an opportunity to escape, so I took it. I tried to get Leysa to come with me but…she had made a deal with Daegel. She was cursed. She had to get me to complete his task, then she could go home. She made the deal before she knew who I was, but it didn't change the terms. If I didn't finish his task, if I didn't do what he wanted, she wouldn't have been able to uphold her end of the deal. When I was trying to escape, she tried to stop me." My lower lip trembled as I whispered, "I wouldn't let her."

Ryker remained still for a minute, and I continued to stare at the floor. I waited for his reaction, assuming he would be repulsed and furious with me, but it never came.

He lifted my chin with a finger, dragging my eyes up to meet his mournful gaze. "I'm sorry you had to do that."

"Wha—Why are *you* sorry? *I* killed your mother."

"But you killed your *friend* and the only person you had there. And I don't believe you killed her. Her deal with Daegel did." His lips pulled into a tight line.

"I thought you'd be more upset about her death."

He sighed heavily. "I am. But I've gone through the past fifty years thinking she was dead already. I have already grieved and accepted her death long ago. And it was my fault for assuming she was dead and not believing my father. It wasn't until you fell that I realized my father was right. I feel guilty about it. I mourned her while she was fighting to survive, to get back. Like you."

"Did… Did Cadoc tell you?"

497

He frowned and nodded. "I was there when their bond was broken. Mav was too."

Oh, Gods. Cadoc and Mavris… Would they be as understanding when they learn I was Leysa's murderer? It doesn't matter. They have a right to know.

I swallowed my nerves. "I should tell them."

He bent his head down and kissed me softly. This really wasn't how I was expecting this to go. I had spent days in those woods anticipating his reaction, and this wasn't how I imagined it.

"We'll tell them together. But now there's something *you* should know before we go. Something…important."

The tense look in his eyes made my stomach twist, making me think whatever he was about to say would break my heart even more.

The last two days were already filled with so much emotion I wasn't sure I could handle anything else. All I wanted was to stay here in this room with Ryker for a while and forget everything else outside of it. I just wanted a chance to breathe for a moment. I wanted to be able to be in his presence without the weight of so much on our shoulders. Just once.

But I knew the reality of the world, and problems didn't disappear just because I had returned.

"What is it?"

He led me to the bed and sat, pulling me down next to him while he trailed his fingers up and down my mating mark and wedding band.

"I'm sorry to give you so much all at once, but this isn't something that can wait. When you cleared a path for you and Malina to get to Daegel at the Rip, your Waalu continued to spread."

I held my breath, anticipating what he was about to say and praying to the Gods I was right.

"In the months you've been gone, Atara has nearly healed completely."

My jaw fell.

"And," he continued. "There are Atarans there waiting for you."

I gasped with a smile. "The Drift Islands returned?"

Did I do it? Did I complete my task for Kleio and restore the balance so my people could return? My family—

"No," he said softly, seeing the disappointment on my face mixed with confusion. "The ones who have been living in Oryn for the past twenty years."

My eyes widened. "What?! Who are they? How many? Why didn't you tell me about them?" I stood and spun to face him with my hands on my hips.

Ryker stood slowly, standing to his full height and towering over me. "Because I didn't know *you* were from Atara."

Oh shit.

"You know?" I whispered.

"Yes. And I didn't find out from my *mate*. I didn't tell you about the ninety-seven Atarans who have been living here in secret for the past twenty years because, even though you were the Worthy of Atara, you were going to be Lady of Oryn, and they live *here*. I've considered them my people all this time, and I still do. I've ensured they've been protected and had everything they needed. Just like I do with everyone else in Oryn. Had I known you were from Atara, I would have told you, but I didn't think it would matter since I didn't know you had any connection to them. Not to mention, they still couldn't go back. Atara was gone with no indication it would be restored. So regardless, you were going to be Lady over them."

Oh...

"You're right. I should have told you I was from Atara, but I was afraid for Nik and Mal. They aren't Worthy and had no protection from a Nation. And," I paused to take a breath, "I wanted to wait until I was inducted as Lady of Oryn so I could provide a safe place for my people on the Drift Islands to return."

"Because you didn't trust me," he said plainly. He wasn't being demeaning, just stating the truth.

I blinked back my tears. I should have trusted him long ago, but my trust had been clouded by the warnings of others, going against my better judgment.

"I was scared. I admit that. But…"

Gods, I'd made so many mistakes.

"I trust you, Ryker. Fully."

He held my stare for several moments. "I've seen little evidence of that, Kya. You haven't shown me you trust me. But I need you to. I *really* do. Because Atara is under threat from the other Nations, and if we want to defend it, we need to trust each other."

"Why are the other Nations a threat to Atara?" I asked.

"When it was noticed Atara was healing, three of the Worthy decided to take the opportunity to expand their Nations and use Atara for land and resources. And since it was uninhabited and everyone thought you were dead—"

"I wasn't here to protect it," I interjected. For the love of Nox. I hadn't even had the chance to see Atara, and I already had to worry about it being taken away.

So many mistakes…

Ryker slumped to the bed and ran a hand through his messy hair. "The Noavo, a few of the Atarans, as well as Malina and Nikan, are stationed at the border waiting."

"Well, let's go!" I couldn't just sit here and not be there to protect Atara with them.

I turned to rush out the door, but Ryker gripped my arm and pulled me back.

"Stop, stop, stop," he said gently. "You've only just returned, and you still need to rest. The other Nations won't be there for a while. We can go tomorrow."

"I can rest while we're there."

"Little gem," he whispered, his eyes pleading. "I need one day where I don't have to worry about you. Please. I swear, I'll take you tomorrow."

I couldn't help the slight smile despite my resigned sigh. "Alright."

I spent the next several hours with Odarum. Ryker stayed nearby, but he kept distance between us so Odarum and I could have our time together. Odarum flew down to meet me on the front lawn which was covered in a thick blanket of snow.

We walked alongside one another talking about his few weeks in Hylithria while he healed and my months in the realm of Vansera. We aimlessly strode through the Voara palace grounds until my toes nearly froze, but I welcomed the biting temperature against my skin. It made me feel alive.

"And there's nothing I can do to get them back?" I asked, resting a hand on his shoulder while we walked.

"Your shifting is not magic. It is a part of your physical form just as your arms and legs are. I am sorry, but the loss of your wings is permanent," Odarum's voice was gentle as he reiterated again that nothing could be done to get my wings back.

I had already accepted they were gone forever, having made multiple attempts to try to shift while I was hiding from Daegel.

I just held onto the hope something could have been done to restore them.

I blew out a breath, deciding to leave that topic alone and move on to my other questions.

"How did you survive? And why didn't you come for me when I was in Vansera? Ryker said Spirits couldn't go there, but Theron did."

"I wanted to. But it took a long time for my soul to heal from the dark magic used against me. I was able to make a sacrifice to fate, giving up my immortality in order to continue living alongside you so I may continue to do my duty and guard you. By the time I healed, I was mortal, and I could not Travel to you. Then your mate came to Hylithria.

"As far as Vansera, it is a realm created by Odes before his fall. It, along with several other realms, is blocked from Spirits. He wanted a world where he was the only higher power. Those people are not connected to the land as you are since they—and their world—have no Spirits. Theron was able to go to Vansera because the bond between a Fylgjur and their Worthy surpasses any restrictions a God places on their world. When Ryker's life was in true danger, Theron was able to go to him, and therefore, you."

We came around the bend of the mountain, having reached the open area where Voara was visible before us.

We stood there and gazed at the restored city. It was where I thought Odarum had been killed by Daegel. Yet he stood next to me now.

"Thank you, Odarum." I swallowed past the tightness in my throat. *"Thank you for coming back."*

He turned his head to look at me, his dark eyes boring into mine. *"I am grateful you have returned as well."*

As dusk quickly approached, I went back inside as Odarum flew away, promising to return in the morning. I was tired from the flood of emotions of the day, but I wouldn't have it any other way.

I was back with Ryker. Odarum was alive. And in the morning, I'd finally return to my homeland.

Ryker ensured an excessively large meal was prepared and waiting for me when I returned to the room.

I ate everything, then took the nutritional elixir and drank so much water I thought I would burst.

"Did you get enough to eat?" Ryker asked, but it sounded more like he was encouraging me to eat more rather than asking my opinion.

"I did. If I take another bite, I might vomit," I huffed a laugh.

He made a disgruntled sound but nodded. "Alright. Well now, I want to show you something."

My shoulders slumped. "I don't think I can handle much more today."

He chuckled, "It's nothing like that. I promise. Come on."

He stood from the small table and offered his hand. I took it, lacing my fingers with his, and he led me to the bathing room. Over in the corner of the room, it looked as if some kind of work had been done recently, and there was a strange hole at the top of the wall near the ceiling in the shape of a narrow rectangle.

"What is that?" I asked as I squinted my eyes at the holes.

"It's a bath—but one you don't have to be submerged in. I wanted you to be able to bathe without any fear of the water. And I know how much you enjoy waterfalls." He winked at me, and my stomach fluttered.

He turned a knob and water began flowing from the rectangular hole, rushing down and gently splashing against the floor before draining through the small holes in the stone below.

My jaw fell. It looked just like a smaller version of a waterfall. No intimidating depths for my irrationality to imagine creatures or the need to submerge that would make me think of the assassin who nearly drowned me.

"Ryker," I breathed in astonishment. "When did you do this?"

"When the palace was being rebuilt. I wanted to do it after I realized you were okay with the waterfall in the cave." He shrugged as if this wasn't a big deal.

Gods, I couldn't deal with any more emotion today, but it didn't stop the warmth spreading through my chest.

"Thank you."

I was so ready to feel clean again. I took a step forward and removed my clothes.

With my back to him, I heard Ryker suck in a breath as my last article of clothing fell to the floor. I pulled my shoulder blades together, swallowing back the insecurities about the scars on my back. I hadn't even seen them. I didn't think I could stomach it.

I glanced over my shoulder, expecting Ryker to be staring at them only to find his eyes intently staring into mine. All the worries of the world melted away when I looked into those silver irises.

I turned around and reached for his hand, pulling him closer to me while holding his gaze. "Will you bathe with me?"

He didn't speak, only removed his clothes in answer, and followed me underneath the warm, falling water.

My stomach flipped with nerves as we stood bare together once again.

His arm grazed against me as he reached around, grabbing the soap and a cloth before he began to gently stroke my body clean. He was delicate with the scars on my back, lingering there only long enough to clean the area before moving on.

We didn't utter a single word, allowing the comfortable silence between us to fill the space as we alternated cleansing each other's bodies. The intimacy of washing one another soothed more than just the scars on my skin.

And bless this wonderful male for getting soaps and shampoos that smelled of lavender and eucalyptus that he lathered me with, scrubbing away any remnants of that nightmarish realm and washing it down the drain forever.

I kept my mind from it. I had been prisoner there long enough, I refused to let it continue to hold me there in any capacity. Instead, I occupied my thoughts with what was to come. Spending time with Odarum, going back to Atara for the first time, being with Ryker.

His fingers moved to my hair, massaging the suds into the strands.

"Lean your head back," he coaxed in a whisper.

I tilted my head, allowing him to guide my hair under the stream. I closed my eyes, relishing in the feel of hands kneading across my scalp. The closeness of our bodies felt so fundamentally right. I didn't want this moment to end.

My heart fluttered when I felt his lips press against my collarbone. I leaned up slightly and opened my eyes.

The look of pure adoration on his face had my lips pulling up. I wanted to kiss him. The love between us flooding down the bond made me wish to be with him, to once again fuse our bodies as one.

I lifted to my toes, aching to feel his body against mine, but stopped when he turned off the water and took a step back.

"I'll leave you to get dressed," he said with a soft smile before handing me a towel, wrapping one around his waist and striding out of the room.

A pang of hurt struck my chest. Maybe he didn't want that. Maybe it was the scars, or the fact I was touched by another that tarnished his desire.

I shook the thoughts away, choosing instead to relish in the moment we had just shared.

I dressed and went back into the bedchamber. Ryker was sitting on the edge of the bed waiting for me, and he looked up at the sound of my approaching footsteps.

A wide grin spread across his lips. "You're smiling."

"I'm happy." I hadn't even realized I was smiling.

He stood and walked over to me. I raised my head to gaze into those silver eyes that called to my soul. He trailed a finger down my jaw to my chin, gripping it gently.

"So am I." He pressed his lips against mine in a soft kiss.

I had missed this so much. I pressed against his mouth a little harder, and his hand came to my waist, snaking his arm around me and pulling me closer. I parted my lips, and my body tingled all the way down to my curling toes when his tongue met mine.

How I missed the taste of him.

It didn't matter that we only just dressed. There was nothing holding me back. I missed him desperately, and all I wanted was to feel him inside me—for us to join our bodies again.

I wrapped my arms around his neck, tangling my fingers through his hair and gently tugging on the strands.

He tilted my head up higher, giving him better access to my mouth and deepening the kiss with a low, pleased growl. His hands moved to my shirt and began to unbutton it.

Each brush of his fingertips against my skin felt like a blazing flame I wanted to burn in. I pulled at his bottom lip with my teeth as my patience started to wear thin.

With the last button finally undone, the fabric fell open, baring my breasts to the chill of the air. I lowered my arms and shrugged the shirt off the rest of the way, letting it fall to the floor before reaching for Ryker's and pulling it over his head.

My peaked nipples brushed against his abdomen—every touch sending a jolt through my body and straight to my core—as I slammed my mouth against his. I felt insatiable with a different kind of hunger as my fingers fumbled with the fastening of his pants. It only took a moment before I was tugging at the hem, and his beautiful cock blessedly sprung free.

My mouth watered at the sight. Instantly, my arousal pooled between my legs, and I rubbed my thighs together.

It nearly took my breath away, not having realized how much I craved it, how much I'd missed it. I wrapped my hand around his length, relishing the feel of it in my palm again, and Ryker rumbled a groan.

He pulled himself away from me, making me whine with displeasure. He bent down to pull my pants and panties down all at once, never allowing his gaze to leave mine.

I yelped when he lifted me by my ass, his hands molding to my cheeks, and my legs naturally wrapped around him.

He smiled against my lips as he carried me to the bed and placed me down gently on my back, resting between my legs.

He didn't wait, and thank the Gods because I didn't want him to. His cock pressed against my core and pushed in just past the tip.

"Little gem," he groaned, and his head fell to my shoulder. He kissed up the column of my neck, leaving a trail of heat, and whispered against my skin, "Don't ever try to leave again. Because I won't let you. You belong to me."

He pushed all the way in, and I let out a long, breathy moan, unable to contain it with the glorious feeling of him inside of me again. The bond purred as we were once again joined.

"Never," I breathed. "Never again."

He pulled out slowly and pushed back in, and he somehow felt deeper. "Promise me."

He thrust again, harder this time.

"I... I promise," I struggled to get the words out when he lifted my leg over his shoulder and thrust himself even deeper.

"Fuck," he grunted. "You feel so good."

"Then don't stop."

His pupils dilated as he watched my face, and he thrust in slowly, over and over, savoring it. Each thrust sent tingles of pleasure down my spine. It was slow and torturous in all the right ways that had me squirming beneath him.

His eyes traveled down to where our bodies were joined.

I raised up to my elbows so I could see. I wanted to watch as his cock slowly slid in and out of me, coated and glistening with my arousal. My eyes glazed with lust, with pleasure, as the sight drove me closer to the brink. But when I looked back up to Ryker, I found him staring at my face, watching the sensual expression across my features.

My lower belly tensed as my release built. I wanted to chase it, and at the same time, I never wanted this feeling to stop. I wanted to stay like this forever, keeping us both sealed in this room, this moment never ending in a world of our own.

"Don't stop. Don't stop," I begged.

He didn't stop, but he kept his movements slow and sensual, drawing this out as long as possible.

I could feel his pleasure heightening, flowing through the bond and mixing with mine, and knew he wasn't going to be able to drag this out much longer.

I smiled as he bent down and bit my lower lip, sucking it into his mouth.

He twisted his hips slightly, making his cock hit at just the right angle, and that was all it took to send me over the edge with blinding pleasure.

I screamed his name as spots of black clouded my vision. The waves of ecstasy crashed down the bond.

Ryker roared as his release tore through him. He thrust and poured himself into me, each pulse of his eruption only adding to the intensity of my climax.

It was the only pleasure I'd had after months of nothing but constant pain. The contrast made my climax hammer through my veins, debilitating me to a state of intoxication.

When I could finally see clearly again, Ryker was staring into my eyes with undying admiration, as if I was his most treasured possession. And I *was* his. He would have me beyond the end of time. But he was also mine.

"I love you," I whispered down the bond, running my fingers up his neck until I held his face in my hands.

"And I love you, little gem." He nuzzled against the crook of my neck. "Beyond the bond, beyond anything fate could put between us, I will never stop loving you."

Chapter Sixty-Two

MALINA

"They're all going to die," I grumbled under my breath, visibly cringing while looking over the Atarans as they practiced.

Hakoa rolled his eyes at my remark. "They'll be fine. They won't be at the front, but at the very least, you've taught them basic defense and offense maneuvers. That's more than they knew before and gives them a better chance."

I gave him a flat stare and pointed to one of the females. "That one just slipped on her own ice."

Hakoa pursed his lips. "Maybe we keep them very far back from the front then."

This was just great. I was going to get the Atarans killed all because I had the delusional thought they could learn to fight in such a short amount of time. I definitely wasn't cut out for being a trainer. Nikan was here. He should have been the one to do this, but he was busy doing Gods-know-what every damn day, constantly disappearing.

Hakoa reached for my hand. "Hey. They'll be fine. In fact, the best case scenario is if they don't even have to fight. If they do, it means the border has been breached, and we're all fucked anyway."

"How comforting. Let's hope it doesn't come to that."

I glanced back at the massive wall behind me, casting a large shadow over us as the sun faded. I hoped it was big enough. The purpose wasn't for it to be unbreakable—a few dozen strong terbis wielders could take it down—but for it to delay them long enough for us to take out the terbis wielders, eliminating at least one of the elements to fight against.

If it could stand and we kept the battle on the other side, we could keep Atara protected.

"Alright, everyone. We'll end for the night. Be back here at dawn," I barked at the panting Atarans.

Hakoa smirked and put his arm around my shoulders and led me back to the base with the Atarans following behind.

"What are you smiling about?" I grumbled.

There wasn't exactly a lot to be happy about right now. Not with the impending war and his Lord having mysteriously disappeared after fighting with Daegel. First Kya, now Ryker. No Worthy to help protect Atara. The stress was getting to me, and I itched for a vial of demid.

"I just really enjoy your authoritative side. It suits you." He shrugged.

I forced myself to let his praise erase my previous thoughts.

"I bet you do." I winked.

His brows raised. "Maybe we should *skip* dinner tonight."

I snorted. "Not a chance. I haven't eaten all day."

He chuckled.

As we came around the corner, Nikan was walking toward us with Mavris. My brother glared at Hakoa. Hakoa's features turned stone cold—that of the Chief of the Noavo—and his arm around my shoulder tightened.

I rolled my eyes. I doubted any male could ever get Nikan's full approval.

"Hey, Mal," Nikan greeted as we approached, then he grumbled his acknowledgement to Hakoa. "Chief."

It was getting dark, so I flicked my hand and wielded balls of soft light above us, illuminating each of our faces.

"Sunshine," Hakoa chuckled under his breath so only I could hear.

"Shut up, brute," I grumbled and elbowed him.

"Any news on Ryker?" Mavris asked Hakoa.

"Nothing. And no sign of Theron either." Hakoa shook his head.

"Is that normal for him to just disappear like that?" I asked.

"It's not *not* normal, but he usually isn't gone for this long. At least not without informing at least one of us," Mavris said.

"Hakoa, have you...*heard* from Ryker?" Nikan asked with a weird look.

Hakoa glanced at me from the side of his eye. "It's fine, Nikan. She knows about his ability."

My mouth fell open, and I glared at Nikan. "He told you about his ability before *me*? He can't stand you," I scoffed.

Nikan rolled his eyes. "Ayen's ass, Mal. It's not like he chatted with me about it. He...*talked* to me when I was being held by Daegel back in Voara. Not to mention, we've spent some time together recently, and it was needed."

I noticed Mavris grow pale and a worried look in his eyes. "Mavris, are you okay?"

He shook his head. "I'm just on edge. Daegel shows up and disappears, then Ryker disappears too without saying a word. No mental warning or anything."

"I saw him leave willingly with Theron though. He wouldn't let anything bad happen to his Worthy," Hakoa said reassuringly.

"Except if something did happen, we would never know." Mavris shrugged.

That would fuck everything up so much more. Not only would Oryn be without a Worthy, but with him gone, Asmen likely wouldn't join in against the other Nations coming for Atara. We couldn't defend it without Ryker and Dusan.

I pinched the bridge of my nose. "Mavris is right. It's very concerning. If the other Nations show up—"

"Malina," Hakoa interrupted.

Mavris perked up and smiled.

I glanced at Hakoa, and his eyes were distant for a moment before he looked down at me, and his lips spread into a wide grin.

"Udon's balls... Why are you smiling so much today?"

He gasped a quiet laugh and grabbed me by the hands, pulling me back.

"What are you—"

"Come on! Nikan, you too. Let's go," he said quickly.

I glanced at Nikan, who was looking between Mavris and Hakoa with a raised brow like they were the strangest things he'd ever seen then looked at me questioningly. I shrugged.

"Hurry up!" he said with surprising excitement and pulled me farther along as Mavris darted ahead of us.

"Okay, okay." Nikan rushed up next to me.

"Hakoa, what has gotten into you?" I asked as he dragged me through the tents with Nikan right behind me while we followed Mavris.

He didn't respond and continued to lead us toward the plains. And just a couple of minutes later, I saw the form of a dragon in the quickly passing spaces between the tents.

I moved faster, hopeful to see Ryker and get some answers as to where the fuck he'd been the past few days. But as we came around a corner with the field in full view in front of us, I stopped, frozen in place.

Blood rushed to my head, and there was a buzzing in my ears, blocking everything else out. I faintly registered Nikan sprinting past me, but still, I couldn't move—I couldn't *breathe*. I just...stared, disbelievingly.

My vision blurred, and all of a sudden my feet moved, slowly bringing me closer and closer toward the phantom of my torment. My heart beat heavily in my chest—every thump bringing with it a different emotion.

Doubt.

Guilt.

Shame.

Relief.

Anger...

Figures parted before me as I approached the almost unrecognizable yet unmistakable form that had caused me so much pain and anguish, driving me to my self-destruction. And when I was close enough to gaze into the pine green eyes of my lost sister, my reality shattered.

Words were lost on my tongue, but my hand wasted no time in cutting through the air toward her face. The sharp sound registered before I felt the stinging sensation on my palm. Tears poured from my unbelieving eyes as I lowered my hand.

Chapter Sixty-Three

ZALEN

There's something to be said about power. It wasn't something as simple as strength at a man's fingertips or even the control it offers. It rested in the hungry eyes of the forbidden woman I fucked on fallen Kingdoms. The eyes of my Queen.

Power was the domination of fate—the ability to take something out of your control and force it to yield.

And I wanted more. I wanted it all. For myself and for my Queen.

Exhausted and utterly spent, Maera and I slept well into the afternoon hours the day following our wedding and coronation. Once we were rested, we went our separate ways as if it were just another day. With the battle we anticipated coming our way, she needed to continue her work on honing her brewing as much as possible while I went to my study to continue to monitor the invasion efforts.

It didn't sit right with me that witches were forced to rely on external sources for their strength, while sorcerers held their strength on their tongues and fingertips. It was simply a fact witches were inherently weaker. But I refused to accept that fate for my wife. I would find a way to make her stronger than any man that walked this Godforsaken land.

While Maera spent her time enhancing her abilities as best as she could, I scoured every text I could find on the Drehiri with the help of Thane.

"So there's nothing at all about witches? No one's ever tried?" I asked Thane as he sat on the other side of the table with multiple open books before him.

"Not that I can tell." He leaned back in his chair and rubbed his eyes. "Only Kings have the authority to decide who goes through the magical ritual. And from the looks of it, not a single one permitted another besides themselves—man or woman."

The concern wasn't *if* Maera could go through it, it was how it would *affect* her. It was an intense and painful process on the mind, body, and soul—changing the very fabric of their being and lacing their veins with more magic than anyone else. Since she would be the first witch, there was no telling what would happen, how greatly she'd be enhanced or how harshly she would suffer.

The transition into the higher power was permanent, only to be released with death.

But she could do it. She was strong-willed, and if her past proved anything, she had the tolerance to withstand it.

"What's the update with Shara?" I asked, giving myself time to think.

"The report that came in this morning showed even more masses being assembled, and they're moving closer to the border."

"We're going to need to act soon then," I sighed.

"If you are wanting to stick with the infiltration strategy, then yes. But..."

I raised a brow. "But what?"

He bit his cheek in thought for a moment. "Have you considered having a contingency plan? What if they breach the blockade line and come into Damanthus while half our forces are inside? The Kingdom would be vulnerable, and Kanth would be their target. At the very least, you should have a plan in place to relocate the Queen up north to a secure location."

That was why we were here. The plan wasn't to relocate Maera but to give her the strength to overpower anyone who dared threaten her. But if all went according to plan, that would never happen.

"That won't be necessary. Maera will be going through the Drehiri. Tomorrow. I will do it right after her," I stated.

"After? Why not before?" He tilted his head to the side.

"Because both of us will be vulnerable during, as well as immediately after, and I want to make sure she's alright before I go through mine. I don't want to be completely compromised while she's going through hers. She needs to have her new power while I go through my ritual. I'll be confined within the Drehiri, so if anything happens, she needs to be able to defend herself during that time until the ritual is complete."

"The recuperation period takes hours though."

"Which is why she will be doing it at dawn, and I will take it at dusk."

The Drehiri was a process of transition and, as such, coincided with the transition of the sun from light to dark. It was more fitting as well for her to complete the Drehiri at dawn, emerging in light while I emerged darkness. It was unclear if it actually made a difference, but I enjoyed the symbolism regardless.

"And after you come into your power, we'll infiltrate Shara," Thane said with an approving nod.

"Two more things need to happen. You'll be taking the following Drehiri window for the Innon Kingdom. Which means you have to get married," I said firmly.

"I—"

"What? You thought you wouldn't have to? It's not some personal request, it's law."

"Yeah, I get that. I just… I didn't even think of that. It's not like I've known this was coming my entire life." He shook his head. "Who will I marry?"

"Doesn't matter to me." I shrugged. "So long as she's devoutly loyal."

"You don't want to pick her?" He tilted his head to the side.

"I will if you don't."

Thane ran his hand through his hair and blew out a sharp breath. "We'll be allied sorcerers in their higher power. This will be a first."

"Exactly. No one will suspect it." I rose. "And two sorcerers in their higher power are greater than one."

With a plan in place, it was time to fill in Maera.

"Get everything ready to head into Shara. I'll see you at the House of Elders at dawn. And find a wife before I find one for you. You'll marry after my ritual," I commanded then left in search of Maera.

I didn't have to go far to find her because she found me. Or more like barreled into me as we came around a corner in the tower at the same time. I caught her just as she nearly fell from the impact, fumbling and dropping papers and vials in a frenzy.

Her hair was in a disarray, and her skirt had traces of herbs where she had rubbed her hands.

Maybe I should remove it, so she wasn't so filthy. Or just lift it and press her against the wall again as I—

No. Stop. Talk first, then fuck.

"Oh God, Zalen. You scared me," she said, catching her breath. Her eyes fluttered, meeting mine.

Shit, I have problems if her eyes alone make me hard.

"Didn't mean to scare you, love. But I was coming to find you," I said, releasing my arm from her waist and bending down to pick up the scattered pages.

Anera came out from behind her and playfully pounced on the pages. I shooed her away, and she growled at me.

Mangy beast...

"Me too!" Maera exclaimed. "I wanted to tell you what I did!"

Anera mewled, pawing at Maera, likely wanting to be fed.

"What is it?" I asked as we stood, and I took the rest of her belongings from her hands.

She looked so giddy with her wide grin and bright sparkling eyes. "Use the silencing spell on Anera." She nodded down to the annoying cub.

Gladly.

"Kyrr," I hissed with a vengeful smirk, twisting my hand and closing it in a fist to cast the spell.

But nothing happened. The damn cat still whined at Maera.

The spell didn't work. My eyes widened and snapped to Marea, who was beaming up at me. "What did you do?"

"I made a potion that makes someone immune to spells. And the best part?" she squealed. "They're *not* immune to other potions! So if someone took this one," she pointed to one of the bottles in my arms, "and we wanted to counteract it, all we'd have to do is get some of this other one on their skin. They don't even have to drink it!"

All I could do was stare at her in awe. I had never heard of anything like this being possible.

"I tried it on Riva—don't worry, she was happy to be part of my experiment. Then she went to one of the guards, and he tried a confusion spell on her, but it didn't work! I tried it too, and again, the same result. And same thing with the sorcerer who was guarding the entrance. I guess Riva knows

him well, and he was a willing participant when she asked."
She shrugged.

I couldn't believe it.

"Maera," I breathed. "This changes everything."

If we could get this recreated and distributed to the Vord,
we'd be unstoppable in Shara. The threat of the new King was
as good as extinguished.

I dropped everything in my arms and grabbed this incredible
woman around her waist and hoisted her up, her legs wrapping
around me. Fuck it, I couldn't contain myself. Her cleverness
deserved a reward.

"You bright, brilliant witch." I crashed my mouth onto hers,
pressing my tongue between her perfect lips and claiming her.

She giggled gleefully against me and looped her arms around
my neck. I spun and pushed her up against the wall. With her
holding herself up, my hands came down to her thighs and
gathered her skirt to push it up to her hips.

"Minn astir," she said breathlessly. "Not right now. I need to
get back to my alchemy room."

"Yes, right now. I want my face between your legs." I lifted
her leg to put it over my shoulder as I began to get down on
my knees.

"Thistle," Maera whispered.

I halted, instantly stopping at the sacred word. Without
hesitation, I placed her feet back on the floor and lowered her
skirt then took a step back.

"Thank you," she said with a soft smile.

I leaned forward and placed a kiss on her forehead. "You
don't have to thank me for that. That's why we agreed on it
in the first place."

While Maera was a gentle soul, I was hard and rough and
ruthless. It was important for her to have a single word that
could stop anything that went too far.

"I promise I'll make it worth your while later." She rested her head back against the wall, running her fingers down my arm and grabbing my hand.

"That's not how this works," I said gently.

She had only ever used the word once before, and I wanted to make sure she didn't feel guilty for it.

She shrugged. "But I think you should get rewarded for it."

My brows raised. "Oh?"

She leaned forward to whisper in my ear, "I'll let you fill my mouth for your patience."

Tempting little witch.

A low growl rumbled in my chest at the thought of her promise, the image of her head bobbing up and down in my lap. I was more than happy to wait.

"You better run along back to the alchemy room and finish up what you need to do. Because tonight, I'm going to stuff my cock in your mouth until I'm spilling down your throat," I promised with a wicked tone.

She sucked in a sharp breath, and her cheeks reddened. She cleared her throat. "So what was it that you wanted to talk to me about?"

My mind was temporarily blank. I had become distracted by the thought of her lips eagerly wrapped around me. I blinked the thought away, clearing my head and forcing myself to remember the importance of what was about to come.

"With what's developing in Shara, I want to take extra precautions and ensure your protection. And you remember what I said was the best way for me to protect you right?"

She nodded with a concerned look.

"Good. Because I want you to go through the Drehiri tomorrow. At dawn."

She didn't move apart from her eyes darting between mine. I was waiting for her to push back a bit, but to my surprise, she acted as if it was the obvious thing to do.

"Alright," she said with a shaky breath and swallowed her nerves. "I'm the Queen, and I'm the only one who has ever had this opportunity. I won't pass it up. What do I have to do?"

"Nothing. The Elders will talk you through it. There's not much you can do while the ritual occurs. You're essentially immobile during the process. It's not pleasant, as I'm sure you've heard, but you'll survive. And just think about what kind of potions you'll be able to brew once you've come into your higher power," I said with a light tone, hoping she would think of the additional benefits of this rather than concentrate on the negative effects. "And," I continued and brought her hand to my lips. "I'll be there the entire time. It doesn't take but a few minutes, but I won't let anything happen to you."

She nodded and gave a half-smile. "Okay. But what about yours?"

"I'll be doing mine tomorrow evening. And you'll be there too. Then Thane the following morning after he marries tomorrow night."

She relaxed a bit and pondered for a moment. "Can I bring Anera?"

I sighed and closed my eyes, trying not to roll them. "Yes. You can bring Anera."

She beamed and lifted to her toes, kissing me quickly. "Good. Then I'll see you tonight." She winked then gathered her things, skipping down the hall with the cub trailing behind her.

Chapter Sixty-Four

RYKER

That was not what I had expected.

Kya's head snapped to the side with the impact of Malina's hand. No one moved for a moment, too shocked at Malina's unforeseen reaction.

Pure, blinding rage struck down the bond. Something dark crossed Kya's face as her eyes slowly trailed back to her sister before Kya's fist met Malina's stomach with a speed I had never seen from her.

It was as if something possessed her. Kya lunged for Malina, tackling her to the ground. The two of them kicking and thrashing against each other.

I moved on instinct, driven to protect Kya, but Nikan stepped in front of me and locked my feet in place with his terbis, the rock from the ground coming up over my ankles. I snarled.

"Stay out of it," he demanded with no room for argument. "This is between the two of them."

My lip curled in a sneer, but I didn't advance any farther. Satisfied I wasn't going to interfere, Nikan released my feet. I was less worried about Kya's well-being when I noticed

Odarum looking relaxed, but I still wasn't happy about it. So I watched Kya and Malina work out their issues with their fists.

They grunted and rolled, hitting and blocking each other as the frosted ground crunched beneath their bodies. Kya was faster, but Malina was stronger.

"What's going on?" Mavris asked beside me, staring in abject horror at the skirmish of the two females.

I worried how distressed he would be when Kya and I told him about our mother. But, like me, he had also grieved her long ago so I held hope it wouldn't hurt him as badly.

"I have no idea." I shook my head.

"You *bitch!*" Malina screamed in Kya's face, rolling on top of her and throwing a punch.

Kya blocked Malina with her arm. "What the fuck is wrong with you?!"

"You!" Malina rammed her head into Kya's, and I flinched but remained still. "*You're* what's wrong with me."

Kya elbowed her in the nose, making Malina's head recoil back and giving Kya the opportunity to flip over her.

"I didn't do shit to you!"

"You died!" Malina screamed, and Kya paused with her fist raised in the air. "You *made* me kill you. Did you think that wouldn't fuck me up? Make me drown myself in alcohol and demid? Make me wish I had died instead?"

"I saved your life," Kya said, clipping each word. "I saved both of your lives." She jutted her chin toward Nikan. "And I thought I was saving *everyone.*"

Kya shoved herself off of Malina and rose to stand. Malina jumped up to her feet.

"Well, you didn't," Malina spat. "Daegel is still alive."

"I'm aware," Kya said darkly. "I fucked up, Mal. I know that. You think I don't? I did what I thought was best at the time. It was either me or all of us. Now, I've suffered enough. I'm not taking the blame for your choices just like I don't expect anyone to take the blame for mine. You made the decisions that led you there. That's not on me."

Kya shoved Malina, who looked struck by her words, then Kya spun around and glared at each one of us individually, going down the line of males watching. From Hakoa, to Mavris, to Nikan, then me.

"You let her get on demid?" she asked us collectively.

"Kya, you know what demid does to someone," Nikan said calmly. "We didn't even know about it at first. What did you expect us to do?"

"Tie her up? Beat some sense into her?" she suggested pointedly as if it were obvious.

Nikan took a step forward. "We tried to stop her on more than one occasion. She had to make the decision to stop on her own. You know that."

I couldn't stand to see the hurt in her eyes. I ran a soothing caress down the bond, and she visibly relaxed then turned to look at me, unshed tears coating her eyes.

"You were right, little gem. Her actions do not fall on you. It was her choice. That's not your fault."

"I know. But it feels like it is." Kya closed her eyes and took a few deep breaths then slowly turned to face Malina.

"I'm glad you didn't kill yourself," Kya said, a truce offering of sorts.

Malina roughly swiped a tear off her cheek then crossed her arms. "I'm glad I didn't kill *you*."

Kya huffed a laugh. "It was a good shot. With your archery skills, I half expected you to hit me in the stomach," she jested.

The side of Malina's mouth lifted. "Well, I *was* aiming for your face."

We all snickered at that, relieved that the tension between them lessened.

"Mother above…is this normal for them?" Mavris asked under his breath.

"Unfortunately," Nikan grumbled.

I couldn't help but notice Mavris stiffen slightly, and my eyes flicked down to see Nikan brush the back of his hand against Mavris'. I returned my attention to Kya and Malina who hugged.

"Oh," Malina started. "Uh, welcome to Atara, by the way."

"Definitely wasn't the welcome I anticipated." Kya nudged Malina playfully.

"We have a lot to catch up on," Malina said with a smile and put her arm around Kya's shoulders. Nikan came up next to them. "Come on. There are some people I want you to meet, and you can tell me what you've been up to for the last few months."

Kya whipped her head around to look for me, but I was already following, and she smiled when she saw me right behind her.

"Don't worry. I'm not letting you out of my sight." I winked.

"Good."

Odarum stepped up beside me while Theron stayed behind. It seemed Odarum wasn't letting Kya out of his sight either.

We followed the Roav to the base, heading to where the Atarans were gathered. Just as we were passing through the tents, Kya stopped dead in her tracks, her eyes fixed on the approaching male as dread flooded down the bond.

Oh no.

I jumped up to Kya's side, the hair on the back of my neck standing, unsure how my father was going to react. My eyes snapped over to Mavris who was already rushing forward to stand with me. I took a subtle step in front of Kya. But she moved around me and met my father with her shoulders squared.

"Mav, I'm sorry. We were going to talk to you about this privately later," I said to him but I had a feeling he already knew what it was going to be about.

"Cadoc—" Kya started to say but cut herself off when my father's hands came up to cradle her face.

I stiffened, worried about his reaction at seeing my mate having returned while his mate died.

Everyone else walked away, leaving me, Mavris, and Odarum watching the interaction between Kya and Cadoc.

He didn't say anything for a moment, only gazing deep into her eyes. Kya trembled slightly, and I wanted to reach for her.

"Did you get to meet her? Leysa?" my father asked with a heartbreaking softness.

Kya nodded. "I did."

Cadoc sucked in a sharp breath. "Were you there when..."

I came up next to Kya and wrapped an arm around her waist.

"Yes." A tear streamed down her face, and she swallowed. "I was there."

"How did it happen? Did she suffer?" my father's voice broke.

Mavris came up behind me and tapped my back. I listened to his mind.

"He's tapped into her blood, reading her pulse. I've got a hold around her heart, but be careful. Remain calm."

A wave of fear washed through me, but I didn't move, keeping my features and breathing under control.

"Don't say anything, Kya," I said firmly. She didn't listen.

"No. No, I promise she didn't suffer," Kya whispered. "It was quick."

"He deserves to know," she responded. *"I would want to know. You would want to know."*

"She cannot lie. He'll be able to tell," Mavris warned.

Cadoc relaxed a little. "How did it happen?"

527

Kya opened her mouth, but I spoke before she could. "She was cursed," I said quickly.

Cadoc didn't take his eyes off Kya. "Cursed how?"

"She made a deal with a dark wielder—Daegel. She was trying to get back to you. I'm sorry, Cadoc. I'm so sorry," Kya's broken voice strained.

My father nodded slowly, taking in the information as his eyes went distant. He took a deep, shaky breath.

"You cared about her." He removed his hands from her face.

"I did. We spent a lot of time together and grew close," Kya confirmed.

"At least she had you there before she went into the After." My father gave a brief, sad smile. "At least she wasn't alone," he whispered so quietly I almost didn't hear.

"He let go," Mavris said, and I instantly felt relieved.

"Thank you for being there for her, Kya," Cadoc added with fresh tears.

He pushed past us and walked out into the field over the hills.

Mavris let out the breath he had been holding. "That could have gone a lot worse."

"I'm sorry you had to hear about it this way." My lips pulled tight. I glanced back at Odarum who looked bored. "I'm surprised you didn't step in, Guardian."

His tail swished gently.

"He said he wasn't worried about him, that he held no ill-intent and wasn't a threat to me," Kya's quiet voice had me looking back at her. Her red eyes reflected the exhaustion she felt.

"Are you okay?" I rubbed the back of my knuckles down the sleeve of her coat.

"I'm fine. I just… That was hard."

"I know."

Kya leaned against me, and I wrapped my other arm around her, resting my head on top of hers. Mavris walked away while we stayed there for a moment, allowing Kya to gather herself.

"Do you want to rest somewhere? Or go back to Voara? We can come back tomorrow," I offered.

I didn't know what she needed, but I needed her to be okay. We both needed to be okay, and a lot had happened in the past few days. Months, really.

"No. I've been gone for too long. I want to be here. I want to meet my people." She stood straight and took a deep breath.

She grabbed my hand and looked up at me with those eyes I would cross the realms for.

"Then let's go meet your people, Worthy Kya."

Chapter Sixty-Five

—◆○◆—

KYA

R yker led me to an area on the other side of the Noavo base. With dusk having fallen, I could see light from a large fire flickering off the stone walls of the tents as we approached. I felt dozens of people surrounding it through my terbis, moving about from person to person.

"Are you nervous?" Ryker asked.

I glanced up at him with creased brows. "No. Why?" I swallowed the truth.

"Because you're squeezing my hand awfully hard for someone who claims she's not." He gestured to our joined hands with a smirk.

"Oh." I hadn't even realized it, but my knuckles were white. I loosened my grip. "Sorry."

"You have nothing to be nervous about. They're all pretty nice," he reassured. "Well, Niabi is a bit rough, but she comes around quickly."

I huffed a laugh, appreciative of his attempt to ease my anxiousness. I knew I was just working myself up, but this was what I had been working so damn hard for.

Glancing down at my thin, emaciated body, I deflated internally.

This wasn't what I imagined it would be like when I met my people again. I wanted to make a good impression, to show them I was worthy enough to protect them and make our Nation grow and thrive. Right now, I barely looked alive, let alone able to command the respect of a Nation.

No. You're going to get your shit together. You didn't do all of this to be beaten down. Because then, Daegel wins—all your enemies do. You're going to show them who you are, not what you were reduced to. You're a Worthy.

"Yes, *you fucking are,*" Ryker said, clearly having heard my thoughts. The prideful glint in his silver eyes had me holding my head a little higher.

I was glad we were connected in every way again, able to know what the other was thinking at all times. I wouldn't keep anything from him anymore. Never again.

I shoved those insecurities down, deep beneath the surface. I may not have been proud of how I looked but I wasn't about to meet them looking weak and acting timid. I would show them why I was deemed Worthy by Kleio, and why I was also worthy of them.

We emerged from the tent line where a large pile of timber burned, illuminating the night and the dozens of people standing around it.

They all stopped as Ryker and I approached hand in hand. I continued to hold my head high despite their scrutinizing stares.

Nikan broke from the group and came to meet us with a wide smile on his face. He grabbed for my hand, and Ryker let go of my other one as Nikan led me forward. They all gathered closer—Malina as well—and Nikan stopped us in front of them.

"Everyone," he began. "This is Kya. Ataran by birth, born from Otoka and Kaiyana of Asha, Roav of Morah, mate to the Lord of Oryn," his voice boomed over the silent crowd with only the sound of the crackling fire between his words. "Deemed the *first* Worthy of Kleio, Lady of Atara."

I didn't move, but I met each and every one of their stares, memorizing every face.

Malina stepped in front of everyone and approached until she stood directly before me. She reached around the back of my head and unwound my braid so my hair fell loose. Then she reached beneath her own and pulled a feather from a braid behind her ear. Her hands came up to the top of my head as she wove the feather into my hair, displayed on the side.

"You have earned this honor, Kya," she whispered with a shine in her eyes. She stepped to the side revealing the Atarans lined up behind her.

One by one, I greeted them. I listened to each of their names and learned their faces, attaching them to my memory. I would not forget a single one of them. Each of them came up and pulled a feather from their hair and braided it into mine around the crown of my head and down the length of the strands.

Having a single feather braided into the hair was an honor reserved only for those who were initiated as citizens of Atara. The only ones who had ever had a flowing crown of feathers were those chosen to be Lord or Lady of Atara. And I was the first Worthy to have that honor. This was their symbol of acceptance, an extension of their welcome in the highest accord.

Ryker stood off to the side with Hakoa, watching the ceremonial tradition take place with a soft smile on his lips.

Nikan approached me, and I closed my eyes, taking a deep breath as he braided the final feather in my hair. "Eamon was right, you know."

I opened my eyes. "About what?"

He smiled broadly and leaned in close to whisper so only I could hear, "Your title describes you."

I huffed a laugh as tears welled in my eyes. "When did you get so sentimental?"

He kissed my forehead. "When you became the master of your own fate, overcoming it against all odds."

I shrugged. "Or it's because you're getting old."

He sighed dramatically. "Yeah, it could be that too."

"One last thing," Malina said as she walked up with a male I remembered was called Luthon.

He held a small bowl of black paint in his hands. "Welcome to Atara, Lady Kya."

He lifted his paint covered fingers to my face, and my breath caught as I closed my eyes. His hand spread the paint in a straight line across my eyes from temple to temple. When he was finished, and I felt him step back, I lifted my lids and my breath caught.

All of the Atarans were bowing before me.

I glanced over to Ryker. He and Hakoa also bowed at the waist.

"Come here, my shadow," I called down the bond.

He didn't hesitate and walked over to me. I smiled up at him and took his hand.

"You are my mate. We do this together," I said resolutely. *"We're here for them. They deserve the same respect they offer us."*

He nodded with a proud grin.

And for the first time in history, the people were given the same respect as Ryker and I—two mated Worthy, Lord and Lady—bowed to the people of Atara.

It was a powerful moment, one I would never forget as my bent body represented my life and loyalty to my people.

But the moment was short-lived.

I felt one of the Noavo warriors rushing toward the group. "Chief Hakoa," he called.

Ryker and I rose, glancing over to the male as he leaned in to speak quietly with Hakoa. Hakoa listened for a moment before his eyes widened and snapped over to Ryker.

Ryker stiffened a moment later.

"What is it?" I asked, seeing the concern on their faces.

Ryker slowly turned to face me with a grave look in his eyes. "The other Nations are almost here."

My heart stopped as I waited for him to say the dreaded words.

"The War of the Worthy is about to begin."

Chapter Sixty-Six

―――◄○►―――

ZALEN

"What do I need to wear?" Maera called from the bathing room an hour before dawn.

We had only just gotten out of the bed, but neither of us slept well. Maera tossed and turned through the night, the worry of her Drehiri ritual this morning eating at her sleep.

I had been up dealing with new developments in Shara. A large portion of their forces were seen on the move, and we feared they were going to force our timeline up. I ordered nearly all of the Vord we had to the border. We'd worry about the infiltration later. It was important there were no disturbances for the next day while Maera and I went through the Drehiri.

After that, everything would change.

"You don't need to wear anything specific. Even what you're currently wearing is fine if you want," I said, pulling on a pair of pants.

She popped her head in the doorway. "I'm in a *nightgown*, Zalen," she said flatly.

"It really doesn't matter what you wear. You're going to be naked anyway." I shrugged.

"I'm *what*?!" she asked incredulously, coming out of the bathing room with wide eyes.

Oh. Maybe she didn't know about that part.

"You'll be naked for the duration of the Drehiri."

"Why?" She eyed me warily, crossing her arms.

I walked over to her, unable to resist touching her in some way when she was in the same room. I brushed her hair behind her shoulder.

"Because, love, the Drehiri is a transformation, rebirthing you in the deep magic that lies within Vansera. Your body must be pure." Not that I particularly enjoyed the thought of my wife and Queen being bared before others, but it was something that had to be done.

"Oh. Well, okay then. That makes sense, I suppose." She rested her head against my chest. "And you'll be there the whole time?" she whispered.

"The whole time," I assured her with a nod.

She released a deep sigh then lifted her head. "I guess I'll just throw something on really quick, then we can go."

After a couple of minutes, I led her out of the bedchamber while she held Anera in her arms. I really didn't want her to bring the little beast, but if it made her feel better then I'd deal with it. However, she definitely wasn't going to mine.

The city of Kanth was still and quiet in the early morning hours, the crisp air held a refreshing bite that woke me up. Maera shivered, and I draped her robe over her shoulders more, wrapping my arm around her as we crossed the city.

The House of the Elders rested in a valley between the gentle rolling hills just outside Kanth, only a few minutes walk from the castle. The Drehiri was a private affair with only those necessary in attendance.

All of the Elders had to be present, as the joining of every single one of them at the same time was required—even just one missing would mean the ritual couldn't be performed. Collectively, they cast a series of spells, conjuring the magic capable of transitioning the sorcerer into their higher power. Other than me, they would be the only ones present for Maera's Drehiri.

We approached the House of the Elders. On the outside, it looked small, no bigger than the throne room of the castle, but that was just the entrance. The House extended deep beneath the surface, spiraling down into a cavernous space that held the pool where the Drehiri would take place.

Maera shivered as I led her inside, not from the chill but from nervousness.

"Deep breath, love," I said quietly.

She inhaled and released a shaky breath as I guided her down the wide, spiraling staircase down into the cavern where the Elders were already waiting. They all bowed as we stepped off the last stair and approached the center of the space where they stood.

"Queen Maera Drolvega," Ekatla, the oldest woman to become an Elder, greeted. She had long silver hair that was loose with several braids and beads woven into them. Her soft blue eyes were welcoming and reflected the wisdom of her ancient years. "It's almost time to begin the Drehiri. Please, follow me."

Maera glanced up to me, and I nodded, taking the sleeping cub from her arms and staying right behind her as she followed the Elders down to an opening on the other end of the cavern. It led to a small cavity, lit with the flame of torches lining the walls, making them seem to glisten and shimmer from the collected moisture.

There, nestled in the side of the rock, was the stone basin filled with magical silver liquid.

Heill was a rare but natural substance that came from beneath the ground. The House of Elders and the basin before us were built around a naturally occuring pool of the thick fluid.

The Elders gathered around the basin, parting for Maera so she could approach it.

"Queen Maera," Ekatla began. "Please remove all worldly possessions and enter the heill in the way in which you were born."

Maera audibly swallowed, the sound echoing in the space.

"Breathe," I reminded her in a low whisper.

She took a deep breath. She could do this. I knew she could.

She began to remove all of her clothes, from her robe to her undergarments, until she was completely naked, and her skin pebbled from the cold air. Then she removed each band of her braids one by one. Once she was finished, she stepped forward.

No one could be part of the ritual, not even to courteously hold her hand as she entered the stone basin of the fluid. She had to do everything on her own.

She turned around to face me, and I couldn't help the proud smile as she held onto every shred of bravery she had.

Ekatla stepped in front of her, her robes swishing quietly against the damp floor. "You will immerse yourself in the heill. *Completely*. Accept it into your lungs and allow the Drehiri to breathe your power into you. It will not kill you, no matter how much you think it will. Keep your eyes open. The Drehiri wants you to see your transition. Once you submerge yourself, the Elders will begin."

"And it only takes a few minutes?" Maera asked. She knew the answer, having asked me a dozen times already.

"Yes. You will know when it is completed. Your magic will sing your new name to you." Ekatla stepped back to her place. "When you are ready, Queen."

Maera's eyes met mine. All of her fear vanished as I smiled at her. She held my stare as she lowered herself into the silvery liquid, laying back until her head went under the surface and I could no longer see her. I placed Anera on the ground.

The Elders began their incantations, entering a trance of sorts that wouldn't break until the ritual was over, and I stepped up to the magical spring, gazing down into the eyes of the witch who held my heart and soul, barely visible through the heill.

"Hold on, minn astir. You can do this. It'll be over soon." I doubted she could hear me.

She jerked a bit, struggling to hold her breath.

Don't fight it. Just breathe. It'll be over soon, love.

It wasn't but a few moments before her mouth gaped open, her lungs desperate for air.

It was then I realized I may have been mistaken, perhaps past Kings did love their Queens and it wasn't that they didn't want them to have great power like them, but that they didn't want to have to watch their beloved endure so much pain.

Maera's eyes bulged, and she thrashed, flailing her arms and legs the moment the heill seeped down her throat.

My heart stopped, and I wanted to rip her out of there, but I forced myself to remain still and instead held her gaze so she could see me the entire time. It felt like an eternity, watching her body fight the transition as the cavernous space was filled with the deep magical words of the chanting Elders.

You could see the moment it happened, when power flooded into Maera, and the Drehiri was complete, even before the Elders stopped their incantations. Her body relaxed, and her eyes turned hard. But it was her lips that made my heart start again as they lifted into a triumphant grin.

That's my fucking Queen, right there.

Without breaking my stare, Maera lifted herself from the basin, the silvery heill dripping down her bare, glorious form.

She took my offered hand as I helped her step down on the ground.

The moment she was completely out, the Elders stopped.

"Look at you," I praised Maera. "You did so fucking good. How do you feel?"

Her movements were slow and calm. "Different," she breathed. "And…weak." She swayed on her feet a bit.

"That's normal. But you should feel fine in a few hours. You just need rest." I bent down and grabbed her robe, wrapping it around her and gathering her wet hair to drape over her shoulder then pulled her to me, kissing her on her head.

Maera turned in my arms, wobbling so much I had to catch her from falling as she faced the Elders when they gathered closer together.

"Reborn in the magic of Vansera, you are the first witch to come into a higher power. State—"

Ekatla was cut off when Maera collapsed. If I hadn't had my arms around her, she would have fallen to the ground. I held her up, cradling her to my chest.

"Thank you, Elders. We're done here." I began to leave, not caring about her discarded clothes on the floor, only concerned with getting her into a bed and watching over her while she recuperated. I stopped when I heard a soft whine, echoing off the walls.

I sighed. "Come on, beast," I said to the leopard cub.

Anera trotted up to my side and walked with me as we left the cavern of the House of Elders.

I would return tonight, and Maera and I would become the most powerful magic users to ever rule.

Chapter Sixty-Seven

RYKER

The worst part of war was the wait, the anticipation of the coming onslaught of bloodshed. The suspense of it was paralyzing.

But only temporarily.

"Let's go, little gem." I shifted, the leather of my wings tearing through the thick fabric of my clothes, and swept Kya into my arms as I thrust us into the air—up and up until we reached the top of the immense wall erected along the entirety of the border between Riyah and Atara.

Odarum followed, landing next to Kya and me, his large hooves clicking against the stone.

Nikan wielded a rock from the ground, elevating himself along with Mavris, Malina and Hakoa up the colossal wall all the way to the top until they stepped off the wielded platform and came to stand next to us.

"Everyone stay still," Kya said.

She stepped toward the edge of the wall and bent down, slapping her hands on the outside of the wall and remained there for several moments.

"What is she doing?" Hakoa asked.

"Shh," Malina hissed.

"She's feeling the vibrations, trying to assess their numbers and their proximity," Nikan offered in a low whisper.

"Wow," Hakoa said under his breath.

We patiently waited for Kya for another few moments before she started shaking her head.

"There's a lot. Thousands. Too many for me to get an exact number." She stood then turned around to face Malina and nodded at her.

Malina stepped forward. She threw out her arm and countless dots of light sprung forth from her hand, swiftly flying across the Riyah landscape in the skies.

Everyone nearly gasped in unison as Malina's balls of light illuminated a mass near the horizon, showcasing the assembled rival Nations that had stopped for the night. You could see a clear gap between the three Nations of Gaol, Torx, and Ulrik all gathered together to create the largest opposing force in history.

They'd be here by nightfall tomorrow.

"Well," Malina started. "We're fucked."

She's not wrong.

"Hakoa," I addressed the Chief of my forces. He stood straight with his arms behind his back. "I want the night watch on high alert. Do we have any burrowers at this post?"

"Yes."

"Send them to scout the perimeter. I want reports by sunrise. What's the status of the Vaavi?"

"Arra left a couple of days ago for the checkpoint. She should be back soon. Do you want me to send someone for her?" Hakoa asked.

"No. Let her do her job. Fortify the wall and don't let anyone slip through during the night." I ordered. "Everyone is required to get sleep tonight." I looked at Kya pointedly.

Kya spun to face me. "Ryker, I don't think—"

"*Everyone* is getting sleep tonight. The last thing we need is to be sleep deprived once they get here. And you need it most of all. You're still not recovered."

"I need to be down there."

"No." There was no room for argument. If she thought I would agree to her going out in the middle of three enemy Nations, she was dead wrong.

"They think I'm dead right? Isn't that why they're doing this? They think there isn't a Worthy to protect Atara. If I go show them I'm alive, maybe they'll back off." She put her hands on her hips and gave me a stern look.

Gods, I loved her fire.

"I wish it were that simple. If it were, I'd take you down there myself. But they already know you're alive. They don't care. Atara is easy for them to take since it's practically unoccupied." I shrugged.

Kya narrowed her eyes. "They just want the *land?*" she questioned, glancing at each of us.

We all nodded.

Kya looked skeptical and only hummed a response, pursing her lips in thought.

"*...it doesn't make sense...there has to be something more...*" I heard her frustrated thoughts.

"*You can't rationalize the actions of those that crave power,*" I responded, trying to ease her chaotic mind. "*And land offers more than you might think. The more land they have, the more resources they have. And therefore, more power.*"

Her eyes flicked up to mine—the ferocity in them shook me. "*They can't have Atara, Ryker. They will not step foot in this land. They will not take a single life.*"

I nodded slowly, and warily. "*They won't. But we can't stop them on our own.*"

I hooked my finger under her chin and lifted her head, leaning close so she could see the seriousness in my eyes. "No running off and trying to take things into your own hands."

"I won't. Never again," she promised.

"Good." I pressed a soft kiss to her lips.

Hakoa cleared his throat. "We need to make contact with Dusan."

"Agreed. We'll go first thing in the morning." I nodded to the stone platform at the edge of the wall, and we stepped on as Nikan lowered us down the stone barricade.

"What's going on with Dusan?" Kya asked.

"We've allied with Lady Asmen. She will be fighting alongside us against the other Nations," I explained. "Nikan was there for the negotiations. We have it all worked out."

"Why?" she asked skeptically.

"Because we need them," Nikan stated.

"No, I mean why would they be willing to fight with us?"

"Maybe she's just a cranky, vengeful bitch and wants bloodshed," Malina said with a too chipper voice for her choice of words.

Everyone looked at her warily.

"What?" She shrugged.

"She *is* from Ulrik. I'd want vengeance on them too if it were me," Nikan added.

"Or it's because she couldn't stand against the other Nations on her own and wants this alliance just as much as we do," I said pointedly.

Nikan wielded the stone platform back into the ground, and we all stepped away from the wall.

"She has something we want, and we have something she wants. We need her forces, and she needs us to stand with her in the event of any retaliation from the other Worthy. We'll also have open borders and trade between the three Nations," I said to Kya. "We had to negotiate on your behalf, but we didn't do anything that would be harmful to Atara. I promise."

"I wasn't exactly here to do it myself." She shrugged.

"But you are now. And you'll come with me to Dusan at first light. From here on out, you'll be part of everything." I glanced over to Hakoa and nodded. "Get those scouts out."

"Right." He turned and began barking orders. "Bavel, Preya, Aleksi."

Two males and a female jogged up to him and stood at attention.

"Take the river channel to the coast. I want a report on naval activity in the sea. Be back before daybreak," he commanded.

They bowed, and we watched as they darted toward the river bend. They wielded a sheet of ice on the surface of the water and leapt on, wielding themselves quickly down the river, waves crashing against the icy bank in their wake.

Hakoa continued to order more scouts to the rest of the border checkpoints he'd set up. He had a handle on things, and I left him to it.

I grabbed Kya by the hand, bridging it up to my mouth to kiss the back of her palm. "Come on. You need rest. We're going to have a very long day tomorrow."

I rolled over on the furs, warmed by the heat of the smoldering coals in the dark hour of the morning, and sighed when I felt Kya's body tucked up next to me. I had barely slept, too worried I would wake up to the nightmare of her absence—just as I had each night since she'd returned. Pure exhaustion was the only thing that allowed me to drift off to sleep.

Every time I even thought of closing my eyes, the panic of waking to her having left me again set in. Except she was still here—safe and asleep beside me—and all my worries melted away against the feel of her skin as I curled myself around her.

But as I began to wake, I remembered why we were on a pile of furs in a tent at the border of Atara, and those worries of her safety seeped back in like venom violently coursing through my blood and straight to my heart.

We needed to get up. We needed to leave for Dusan to meet with Asmen, and prepare for the approaching Nations.

But at this moment, I couldn't move. I didn't *want* to move. I just needed to hold my mate for a little longer where she was safe and warm and protected.

A few more minutes. I just need a few more minutes of peace.

One day, this would all be over, and we could live our lives side by side without the worries of the realms on our shoulders. We'd be free from burdens and tasks and just be in a world of our own.

Gods, I wanted that more than anything.

I wanted to thrash and snarl and burn every threat that stood outside these walls. I wanted to shield her from the coming dangers approaching and the horrors that would follow when they neared. I wanted to take her away and hide from anything that could threaten her.

"Easy, my shadow," Kya's soft voice whispered down the bond. *"We can't run away from this."*

I realized then I was holding her tightly. I relaxed my arm, and she rolled to face me.

"I'm right here. No one will take me from you ever again. Not even me," she soothed, rubbing her hand down my side.

My fingers trailed up and down her arm. "It's just... Kya, if something happens to you—"

"I will be okay. We both will." She smiled up at me. "We haven't endured what we have for it to be in vain. I'm not done with you yet."

I relaxed at that, trailing my fingers up her arm and over her shoulder then up to hold her face with my hand. But when my fingers brushed her neck, she flinched and sucked in a sharp breath with wide eyes.

"Are you okay?" Did I hurt her?

She cleared her throat. "Oh, uh," she huffed a laugh. "I'm fine. It's nothing."

"What—"

"We should get going. We need to head to Dusan. It's almost dawn," she cut me off and pressed her lips to mine, taking away all other thoughts besides the feel of her mouth.

She tried to pull away after too brief a moment, but my hand came to the back of her head and held her still. I needed just a little bit longer. She opened her mouth for me, and I deepened the kiss, savoring every languid stroke of our tongues.

I knew we didn't have time for more than this, but I took what I could get, indulging in this precious, peaceful moment with my mate. But it was only a moment.

I forced myself to pull away, hating the increasing amount of space between us. But seeing the smile on Kya's face was worth it.

"I love you," I said softly.

"And I love you."

"Come on." I sat up, not missing the desire on Kya's face as her eyes trailed down my exposed chest and stomach. If only we had the time. "First, you need to eat. Then, we'll go win a war."

I held Kya against my chest as we flew to Dusan. She could have ridden Odarum who flew next to us, but I wanted her with me. It reminded me of the first time we flew to Dusan together, except this time was very different.

I was all too aware of how much lighter she felt in my arms, of the looming threat that awaited us back from where we left. Yet I was also aware of how much stronger we were together, how the bond thrummed between us, and how we had a fighting chance.

It didn't take but a couple of hours flying across Atara before we were in Dusan. We continued until we saw the blessed sight of a great mass of wielders gathered and on the move toward the border. We weren't far from the edge of the Rip, so I made sure to steer clear of the chasm. We descended and landed ahead of the Dusan force, keeping a bit of distance between us.

"You certainly enjoy making a dramatic entrance, flying in here holding the lost Worthy like she's the savior of us all," Asmen said in my mind.

It irritated me to no end that she had this capability.

"It is her Nation we're fighting for," I replied, searching for her in the halting crowd of prestigious warriors.

I knew she was here. She had to be to imitate my wielding.

Sure enough, after a few moments, Asmen stepped out from the mass of people with several of her Skorn flanking her and Daciana, her Spirit wolf, by her side. She wore brown fighting leathers that nearly matched her skin tone, and her long hair was done in a bunch of small braids that were pulled back and tied behind her head.

"Lady Asmen," Kya greeted. "It's good to see you again."

"Good to see you're alive, Lady Kya. I trust Lord Ryker has informed you of our agreement?" she asked as she and Daciana stopped in front of us, her warriors staying back a few steps.

I noted Daciana and Odarum stepping off to the side.

"Yes, he has, and I'm willing to uphold Atara's end," Kya said with a nod.

"Good. Because we're about to go to war with my neighboring Nation, and I'll expect you both to return the favor of defending Dusan if and when they retaliate."

"We will," I assured her. "How many wielders do you have?"

"Five thousand trained wielders stand behind me. I have another two thousand along the borders and stationed in larger cities," she stated.

"Five thousand?" That was considerably more than I had anticipated, though I wasn't complaining.

Asmen shrugged. "I can't take credit for the numbers. It was all the late Lady Zana's doing." The Worthy who forfeited her life in the last Trial so Asmen could take her place. "My people are eager, and I don't want to tire them by delaying their arrival to Atara. Do you mind if we continue on?"

"Of course. We're not far from the border. We're going to head back and see you when you get there." I said, flaring my wings out and reaching for Kya. I pulled her to me.

All of our heads whipped to the Spirits when Daciana snarled then disappeared. Odarum suddenly flared out his wings and took to the air, flying deeper into Dusan.

"What's going on?" I asked Kya, wanting her to reach Odarum.

She remained quiet for a moment, her eyes glazing over as she spoke to her Guardian. She blinked a moment later. "I don't know. He just said he'll be back shortly."

I looked at Asmen who was also staring off, likely speaking to the wolf.

She looked at the both of us and shrugged. "Daciana said she has to check something but isn't saying anything else."

"Should we wait for Odarum?" I asked Kya.

She was quiet for a second then shook her head. "No. He said we should get back to Atara. and he'll meet us there."

Spirits… At least I wasn't the only one whose Spirit was less than forthcoming.

"Let's go then." I grabbed Kya's waist and lifted her with one arm behind her and the other under her knees as she wrapped her arms around my neck. "We'll see you soon," I said to Asmen, then took to the skies.

It was only a couple of minutes before we could see the clear boundary of Atara below us, the northern forest of Dusan meeting the vast open plain of the once decimated Nation. It would be nice to see trees here once again. I knew Kya loved the forests, and I hoped they would grow soon.

"Ryker, look. Down there!" Kya shouted over the wind roaring past us.

I glanced down to see two figures below running across the landscape, wielding the ground beneath them to carry them faster across the land. They were frantically waving their hands above their heads with their faces tilted up, calling for us. I recognized them as Noavo and immediately began my rapid descent, Kya gripping me tighter with the steep fall.

We landed, and I placed her on her feet as the two male warriors rushed up to us. They looked disheveled and exhausted, as if they had been traveling all night.

"Kieran. Tarek," I greeted, straightening my back and wrapping an arm around Kya's waist to pull her against my side.

They bowed quickly.

"Lord Ryker. Lady Kya," Tarek panted, catching his breath. He looked directly at Kya with disbelieving eyes.

Kya raised her chin.

My arm tightened protectively around her. "What is it, Tarek?" I tried to direct his attention to me, unsure of what was going on.

He continued to look at Kya for a moment, and I felt her tense until the side of his mouth lifted.

"Lady Kya," he said softly. "We were on border patrol along the coast. And…"

He took a breath and glanced at Kieran who nodded eagerly for him to continue. I was half a second away from losing my patience and forcibly getting the information from his mind before he looked at Kya again.

Tarek swallowed and put his shoulders back with his arms behind him. "The Drift Islands are approaching the coast. The banished people of Atara are returning."

Her family…

I could practically feel the chill run down Kya's spine as she grew still.

"Shit," she whispered as her pace paled, coming to the same realization I had.

This was terrible timing. We were about to go to war, and her family was on those islands. Maybe that's why Odarum and Daciana left so abruptly.

"Um, thank you, Tarek. I…think," she stumbled on her words.

"How many islands are there, and how long do you estimate until they reach the shore?" I asked for her, giving her time to process.

"Seven islands," Keiran offered. "From the rate at which they're approaching, we think they'll arrive within four—maybe five—days."

"Four to five days…" Her breathing became rapid and her eyes were wide.

I stepped in front of her, blocking the Noavo from her sight, and took her face in my hands. Her anxiety reverberated down the bond.

"Look at me, little gem," I coaxed gently. Her deep green eyes met mine. I expected to find tears in them but all I saw was dread.

"They're coming back to a war." She shook her head. "They don't deserve that. I—"

"We will figure it out. We'll usher them to Oryn if we have to. We'll take care of them, I swear." I brushed my thumb across her cheek. "We still have a few days to sort it out. Right now, all we can do is go back to the wall and do everything we can to make sure no other Nations get into these lands. Alright?"

She nodded and took a deep breath. "Yeah. Okay. We need to get back."

"One thing at a time." I huffed a breath. Except we had so many things all at once.

"Right," she scoffed.

I turned around to face the warriors. "Go back to the coast. Keep an eye on the islands and report with updates on their approach. We'll be at the northern post. Don't let them out of your sight and make sure to let the naval patrol know not to get too close to the islands. Their spiritual nullification extends slightly beyond their perimeter, and we don't need anyone else having their abilities suppressed."

They bowed and left, wielding the land to move beneath them as they headed east toward the Ataran coast.

"Do you need a minute?" I asked Kya, glancing down at her and brushing a stray hair behind her ear.

She shook her head. "No. I don't want to dwell on it right now. I need to keep my head straight. Like you said, there's nothing we can do right now so let's just go back."

My mouth twitched up, and I scooped her up into my arms. "Hold on tight. We're late." I winked and just as I was about to thrust us into the air I heard the faint sound of screaming, and stopped.

We both whipped our heads toward the sound, coming from behind where we had just left. We were momentarily frozen in place as we listened to the Dusanians' screams. We needed to get to the border, but we needed to go find out what was happening.

I heard the sound of wings beating, and looked up at the canopy of the treeline just before Odarum flew into view and swept down, landing with a heavy thud in front of us.

Kya jumped down from my arms and stared at him intently.

I didn't have time to ask what was going on before he turned to the side, lifting Kya into the air with his head and throwing her on his back.

"Hey! What—"

"Let's go!" Kya shouted, gripping onto the black hair of his mane as Odarum spread his wings and quickly propelled into the air.

Damnit!

I followed, thrusting my wings hard to catch up next to them.

"What's going on?" I asked her, shouting over the roaring of the bitter, cold wind.

"He said Asmen needs help," she replied.

We saw smoke and dust kicked up into the air ahead of us near the Rip and we aimed for that, going faster, driven by the blood curdling screams of the Dusan army under attack. All I could think was that we made a mistake and Gaol had come through Dusan, or the other Nations came from the southern sea and the armies camped in Riyah on the other side of the wall were just a distraction.

Except it was much worse.

The bloodbath beneath us wasn't from war. It was caused by something even more horrific.

Like a swarm, a sea of blond-haired males stepped from the treeline.

"Oh Gods," Kya gasped. "Daegel."

The name alone ignited fury in my gut, fueling my wrath for the dark wielder. Those same beings from Daegel's realm poured in from the forest, an army of magic wielders we didn't know how to defend against.

I didn't see Daegel himself, which worried me more than anything. If he was here, I wanted my eyes on him at all times.

"Ryker, we have to help them! They're getting slaughtered," Kya shouted.

I nodded as Odarum dove and I followed. My shadows burst from me, rushing across the landscape, and it was like I was reliving Kya's rescue all over again as I steered them around the Dusanians and toward the mass of invaders.

But before my shadows could reach them, Odarum roared, the warning making my blood tremble. He dove faster toward the ground littered with warriors and otherworldly beings, throwing his wing around me to force me down with him to an open area in the trees. Kya's scream made my heart stop.

We crashed.

I rolled, sticks and rocks snapping and crunching beneath my body until I came to a stop. Adrenaline coursed through me as all I could think about was getting to Kya.

I scrambled to my feet and ran over to where she was pulling herself up. I wrapped my arms and wings around her, the leathery material dripping with blood from the tears.

Thank the Gods she seemed okay, Odarum having taken the brunt of the fall with feathers torn from his wings along the cold ground. He leapt to his feet and immediately looked to the skies despite the approaching magic wielders.

Perhaps I shouldn't have thanked the Gods.

Kya and I followed his gaze toward the darkening sky, shadowed by omnipotence above us. The breath left our lungs, and I held her tighter. All we could do was stare.

Our Gods had come.

Falling like meteors from the sky, a thundering clap of force burst from where they landed. With only a split second to react to the oncoming wall of celestial power, I threw Kya and myself down to the ground, landing on top of her and shielding her as best as I could.

Bodies were flung across the landscape and tall, ancient trees were snapped in half, sending them crashing to the forest floor on the other side of the clearing with splinters of bark blasting outward.

Kya trembled beneath me, and I grunted as I dug the claws of my wings into the dirt, trying to keep us from sliding farther across the ground. We closed our eyes against the stinging spray of dirt and rocks flying through the air.

As the pressure receded, I opened my eyes, blinking away the dust. I quickly lifted off Kya and pulled her to her feet, checking her over, but I was admittedly distracted by the sight before us. Our mouths dropped in awe. Every one of those vile beings were being thrown over the edge of the Rip or their corpses scattered like leaves, the dirt soaking up their blood.

But it wasn't the expulsion of the magic wielders that took the words from our throats. It was the two Gods standing before us like megalithic beings.

Odarum stepped up beside Kya and me, extending a leg and bowing deeply to the almighty Fathers. Kya got down on her knees, following Odarum's lead. But I didn't move. All I could do was stare into Xareus's eyes as he stood next to Udon.

"What are you doing here?"

His cold stare had me rooted in place, but I refused to back down. His deep, bone-chilling voice filled the air around us.

"Saving the realms from peril."

Chapter Sixty-Eight

------◆◇◆------

ZALEN

"A re you sure you're feeling okay?" I asked Maera.

She had slept for most of the day and only just woke up a couple of hours ago. I made sure she had plenty to eat and drink and insisted she try to sleep a bit longer since there wasn't much time before my Drehiri.

"I'm fine. I promise," she assured me. "Honestly, Zalen, I feel better than I've ever felt. I feel so alive right now." Her lips spread into a wide smile.

I breathed a little easier. "Good. Because it's time for us to go."

"Not that I don't want to, but why do I need to be there?" she asked as I began to usher her out of the room.

"Because it's not safe for you when I'm not around, and I'm going to be in a vulnerable state for a bit. You'll need to be protected."

"I don't know if you know this but I'm a pretty powerful Queen of the greatest Kingdom that has ever existed," she said with a playful smirk.

"You are. But you also don't know how to use this new power of yours, love."

"Yeah, there's that," she grumbled as we made our way out of the castle. "When we get back, and you're recovered from your transition, we can work on our new magic together. I'll make it my goal to create a potion that can beat your spells."

Such a fiery little witch.

I chuckled and placed my hand around her waist, pulling her closer to me as we walked along the road before dusk.

"See to it that you do," I challenged.

Something pounced on my leg, and I nearly kicked it out of instinct but stopped myself when I saw it was that fucking cat.

"Oh, Anera. How did you get out?" Maera gathered the cub in her arms and began walking again.

"No. That mangy beast is not coming to my Drehiri," I stated firmly.

"Oh, she'll be fine."

I rolled my eyes. "If she so much as tries to disturb my Drehiri—"

"You'll eat her. I know," she rolled her eyes with a grin.

Damn right I will.

I released a sigh, and we continued on to the House of the Elders.

Thane waited for us just inside the entrance. He was there purely for Maera's protection. As were the hidden Vord all around the city and House of Elders. While we had kept everything quiet about it, there was the possibility that word of our temporary vulnerability got out and was exploited.

It's what I would have done. And that was why I wanted every King dead before I went through my ritual.

"Thane," I greeted shortly and continued walking toward the stairs. I wanted to get this done as soon as possible.

He nodded in acknowledgment and followed. His orders were to keep his eyes on Maera until the end of my recuperation. But there were so many Vord outside these walls it was practically impenetrable.

"Did you find what you were looking for?" I asked him.

"I did."

"And?"

"Riva."

My brows raised. Interesting choice, a human for a wife.

I nodded, respecting his decision and leaving the rest of the conversation for later.

We made our way down the winding staircase, and I kept Maera by my side as we were once again greeted by the Elders.

I was pleased to see Oveus step forward to preside over my Drehiri.

"King Zalen Drolvega," he began. "It's time to complete your Drehiri. Please, follow me."

For tradition's sake, I went along with it despite having heard it only this morning. We approached the heill basin, and I stopped before it, Maera at my side. Thane waited by the entrance to the alcove to guard.

Oveus turned around to face me. "Please remove all worldly possessions and enter the heill in the way in which you were born."

I nodded and began removing my robe, shirt and pants. I had kept my attire simple. I stood bare before everyone, ready to finally do this.

"Breathe," Maera whispered behind me, giving me the same order I had given her.

I turned my head and winked at her, then returned my attention to Oveus.

He raised his chin. "You will immerse yourself in the heill. *Completely.* Accept it into your lungs and allow the Drehiri to breathe your power into you. Keep your eyes open. The Drehiri wants you to see your transition. Once you submerge yourself, the Elders will begin. Your magic will sing your new name to you once the ritual is complete and you have come into your higher power."

I took a step back and turned, grabbing Maera by the nape of her neck and pressing my lips to hers, invading her mouth with my tongue. It was quick, but it gave me the jolt of excitement I needed. I'd be thinking about that mouth the entire time, ready for more once this was done and over with.

I released her, leaving her breathless and blushing as I went into the stone basin of silvery heill, submerging myself immediately.

I could feel the change in the liquid the moment the Elders began to chant their incantations, beginning the Drehiri. The heill felt as if it solidified above me. Even if I had tried to get out, I couldn't, and I understood then how Maera was able to thrash without disturbing the liquid. I didn't blame her for being unsettled by it. It was a daunting sensation.

I kept my eyes on the surface, waiting to see her face appear above to give me something to concentrate on when I breathed in the burning liquid into my lungs. But after a minute, I began to worry. Especially when I saw faint flashes of light.

Another minute.

I wouldn't be able to hold my breath much longer, and I needed to breathe it in to begin.

That worry was washed away as I saw a figure come into view. But as it leaned closer, becoming clearer through the thick substance, all the breath finally left my lungs.

A woman with hair the color of fire and the eyes to match leaned over to look at me, her skin so pale she seemed to glow. I forced myself to resist taking in the liquid as she spoke.

"The great King Zalen, conqueror of Kingdoms. But can you truly be called a conqueror when I did most of the work for you?"

My eyes widened. Her ethereal voice was clear, as if there wasn't a thick fluid pooling in my ears.

She *killed the Kings? Killed Makkor?*

Time seemed to stop when she pulled Maera up over the basin by her hair. Her face was bloodied and her shirt torn. I couldn't see much else.

Where the fuck is Thane?!

I opened my mouth to scream for Maera to get away, and my lungs filled with the heill. It felt like fire and ice all at once, burning and freezing every bone, every drop of blood in my body. But I hardly registered the pain, too concentrated on Maera being held by this wretched witch as she clawed and struggled against the woman's hold.

"Witch? Ha! I'm a Goddess, you *mortal*," she spat the word like it was rancid on her tongue. "You think a witch or a sorcerer or a realm full of them could stop me? You Kings are arrogant fools, the lot of you."

She yanked Maera's head back, making my wife grunt in pain, and ran her long, sharp fingernail across her delicate throat, drawing precious blood even as Maera tried to push against her arm while she screamed. It wasn't deep, but I understood the threat.

I thrashed, trying to free myself from the heill to no avail.

"Here's the thing, King Zalen," the Goddess started. "You want your little witch to live, and I want someone to die. So I have a task for you, one all of the past Kings failed to accomplish. But perhaps someone as powerful as you can finally complete what needs to be done, and I won't have to kill you, too. Maybe you mortals just needed more incentive."

I thrashed even more, muttering every spell I could, but magic didn't work during the ritual. Not for the one enduring it.

"Let her go!" I roared, my voice swallowed by the heill.

"I will. But only if you give me the power I need."

I stilled.

She wants me to give a Goddess power? She's fucking deranged.

"Oh you don't need to worry. I will be gracious and give you the tools suitable to complete my task. Your heart is black and so shall be your blood, imbued with the power of two, to wield the dark magic required." Her hand flourished and a large book materialized, floating by Maera.

Dark magic?

"Fuck you! Let Maera go now!" my words were garbled, but she clearly understood them.

"I could kill her where she stands if you prefer." Her lips curled into a sneer.

I stopped thrashing. I didn't know what to do. I couldn't fucking do anything but watch her threaten my wife.

"No? Then behave like a good little King. I'll keep your pretty witch until you get me the power I need."

I stared into Maera's eyes, telling her I would get her out of this no matter what with a single look. I knew she understood. She tapped the imperceptible mark on her wrist and nodded subtly.

"I'll keep her safe, far away from here. She won't be harmed unless you fail," she promised darkly.

She raised up, dragging Maera with her, and I heard her cry out, the sound of her feet kicking against the stone reverberated even through the thick liquid.

The Goddess's lips drew back with sinister delight, exposing the glossy whites of her teeth. "I'll be back once you've made your choice."

And then they vanished, gone like they had never been there to begin with.

I began screaming, thrashing, and fighting to get out and go after her. All I could see was the fear on Maera's face over and over again, the pleading in her eyes as she realized I had broken my promise to protect her and keep her safe.

A voice sang in my soul, but I barely heard it over my own screams of rage.

Then, the Drehiri was complete, and I was able to lift myself out of the basin of heill.

The Elders were still in their magical trance, and I saw Thane lying on the floor, barely breathing in a puddle of blood on the damp stone.

I crawled out of the silver liquid and stepped onto the cavern floor covered in shattered glass of potion bottles where Maera had to have fought back.

The Elders stopped their chanting.

I couldn't hold myself up, and I fell to my knees, slicing my skin on the jagged shards.

The Elders gathered around me with horrified looks, aware of what occurred but were unable to do anything about it during their chanting, having been held inside the ritual just as I was.

"King Zalen..." Oveus breathed in disbelief, assessing my magical transformation. "Your power..."

"Complete the ritual." I said in a cold, lethal tone. I glanced over to see a familiar leather-bound book on one of the steps.

No one moved. They remained in stunned silence, our collective breaths the only sound in the quiet space.

"COMPLETE THE RITUAL!" I roared.

They all trembled as my wrath boomed off the walls, shaking the stone beneath us. I breathed heavily, wishing I wasn't so fucking weak right now so I could burn the realms down to find Maera.

Oveus swallowed nervously. "Reborn in the magic of Vansera you are the first... *Dark* sorcerer. State your title."

I inhaled deeply, my reborn name searing itself into my soul as I stood. Black blood dripped from the wounds the glass had opened in my flesh, and I spoke the word that changed everything.

"Daegel."

Epilogue

he flames that burn in her heart rage like a storm, pushing and pulsing in a way that will not be contained—she will not be contained.

This has gone on long enough and entirely too far. I can't hold her back any longer. I did what I had to do and I have no regrets—I never will.

Her silent wrath thickens the air, its tensions threatening her arrival.

It's too late. My once granted pleas have been cast aside.

My eyes cut to the skies as I wait, anticipation stirring for the consequences to come—for my decision, my choice.

It wouldn't be long now.

The ire in her eyes pierces my soul. But I also sense fear buried deep within them. I brace myself as I know I will do whatever it takes to prevent her fall.

If I let the Nightmare blanket us in darkness, the Silence will perish. It's time to end this once and for all.

Acknowledgements

They say it takes a village to raise a child, but it takes a community to publish a novel, and that's exactly what I have. I couldn't have published—not just one but—TWO books in a single year without the support from so many incredible people.

To my husband, you are everything I've ever wanted and more than I deserve. There's no journey I'd ever want to take without you by my side. You didn't ask me to do this, and I know it's been a huge task—impacting our lives in a way we never imagined—but you have been by my side through all of this, no matter what. You took on so much, waking me up in the mornings after I stayed up all night typing away, taking care of our family, and giving me the opportunity to do this guilt-free. You took care of me and kept me sane while I locked myself away so I could get this book written. You have made more sacrifices than anyone, and I can't thank you enough. I love you more than anything, handsome.

A huge thank you to my family and friends! I love you all so much, and I can't begin to tell you how grateful I am for your unending support. You lived without me for days and weeks at a time, and you never gave me anything less than your support. You constantly listened to me talk about books and publishing nonstop for months. My love and gratitude are endless.

Brit, you have been my rock through everything. You came in like a storm and helped me take my author journey to a level

I never could have reached on my own. You pushed me, held me up, and took on anything and everything thrown your way. From the late-night calls to the early morning messages (several likely made you question your decision on working with me, haha) to running so much of this operation we've created together, not once have you faltered or given me anything less than 100%. You've never just been a PA to me—you've become one of my closest friends. And your friendship is one of the greatest gifts. This book, this story, and my author journey has you to thank. You are the lomf. See? I can learn ;) Muah!

To Colleen, I am so grateful you had no idea how Google Docs worked! If it weren't for that, this story wouldn't be where it is today. You always give me the unhinged thoughts, and that has made this book better than I ever thought it could be. (He will never "coo" again, I swear!) You're there to listen to any and all of my wild ideas and help me solve plot holes no matter how crazy they are. Your dedication is one to be admired. Our evening calls keep me going, and I hold dear to my heart every moment we share.

To Mallory, no matter where we are in our crazy-busy lives, you're always there and willing to pick up the phone or read something random at the drop of a hat. Your insights and help in everything have been invaluable, and I am so happy to call you my friend! Thank you for always being there for me.

To my beta team: Allie, Courtney, Doug, Elyse, Hannah, and Sara. You guys were amazing, and you pushed through reading the chapter sets under such short time constraints. Your comments and love for this book drove me to do better with each word on the page. These characters wouldn't be where they are today without you!

To Noah, thank you for working with me and taking on this story! You helped me get this story where it needed to be, and you have taught me so much, helping me improve my skills as a writer. Your encouragement and guidance have been so valuable in getting this book where it is now.

To Jen, thank you so much for catching the smallest of details! This story reads so much smoother because of you. And I will notice all of the unnecessary "that's" in everything I read now haha.

To El, you have been amazing, and I'm so happy that you started with me on this journey from the beginning! You've made such a difference not only as my beta but also as a proofreader and wonderful supporter! Thank you so much, and I hope to come down your way someday!

To the wonderful authors who have been there to answer my unrelenting questions, your advice has helped me navigate this crazy author world we live in. Mallory Benjamin, Melissa K. Roehrich, Courtney Whims, Cortney Winn, Kate King, Renna Ashley, Miranda Lynn, R. Lynn Hanks, Laura Elizabeth, and all of the other amazing authors, from the bottom of my heart, thank you, and I hope to meet you all one day!

To my Roavs of Chaos: Allie, Amber, Annalisa, Cara, Christina, Emilie, Emma, Hannah, Heather, Jessica, Kacey, Katie, Kirsten, Leanne, Lex, Mariesa, Paige, Rita, Sarah, and Tiffany. You all have made such an impact in getting this book in front of readers! You have been an amazing support system, and this is hands down the best street team! Because of you, this story has reached so many others, and you keep me motivated to keep going every day.

Finally, to my readers, you have been the driving force in making this story the best it could be. Your love and hype kept me going late at night, sitting in my car when I had a spare five minutes and even when I wanted to give it all up. Thank you. And thank you for your continued support and love for this story. I can't wait for you to see where it goes next!

About the author

A.N. is a dark fantasy romance author. She loves spending time with her husband and kids. She's a homebody who enjoys escaping into other worlds, either through reading or writing.
Website: www.ancaudle.com
TikTok: tiktok.com/@ancaudleauthor
Instagram: instagram.com/ancaudleauthor
Discord Reader Group: https://discord.gg/NBPgtRapg5

Made in United States
Troutdale, OR
12/22/2024

27149314R00354